D0028324

OFF
THE
PAGE

OFF
THE
PAGE

Jodi Picoult
&
Samantha van Leer

EMBER

Text copyright © 2015 by Jodi Picoult and Samantha van Leer
Interior illustrations copyright © 2015 by Scott M. Fischer

All rights reserved. Published in the United States by Ember, an imprint of
Random House Children's Books, a division of Penguin Random House LLC, New York.
Originally published in hardcover with additional artwork in the United States by
Delacorte Press, an imprint of Random House Children's Books, New York, in 2015.

Ember and the E colophon are registered trademarks of Penguin Random House LLC.
Visit us on the Web! randomhouseteens.com

Educators and librarians, for a variety of teaching tools, visit us at RHTeachersLibrarians.com

Library of Congress Cataloging-in-Publication Data is available upon request.
ISBN 978-0-553-53559-4 (tr. pbk.) — ISBN 978-0-553-53558-7 (ebook)

Printed in the United States of America
10 9 8 7 6 5 4 3 2 1
First Ember Edition 2016

TO KYLE AND JAKE:

Mom says I'm her favorite. You're okay.
Love, Sammy

TO KYLE AND JAKE:

Sammy's lying. You're ALL my favorites.
Love, Mom

PART ONE

Just because you've picked up this book, you know, doesn't mean it belongs to you.

Quite a lot went on before you even arrived. There was a spark of an idea one day, which ignited into a fire of imagination. Each lick of flame burned a line of text, spreading from chapter to chapter.

And where were you? Probably in some other book, not even aware that this was happening someplace in the universe.

From this blaze came smoke, and from that smoke came silhouettes, marching across the pages, each with a voice to be heard. As they spoke, their edges grew sharper and more defined. Their features rose to the surface. And soon they were characters in their own right.

They picked up the lines that had been laid across the page and carried them on their shoulders, wrapped them around their waists, tugged and twisted, and became the story.

And still you weren't here.

Then one day you reached onto a shelf, and out of all the books in the world, you chose this one.

Now, don't get me wrong. It's not as if you're not important. For the moment you opened this tale, your mind awakened the characters. If a tree falls in the forest and no one is there to hear it, does it really fall? If a character sits in a book and no one reads it, is he truly alive? As your eyes moved across the pages, as you heard the story in your head, the characters moved for you, spoke for you, felt for you.

So you see, it's quite difficult to know who owns a story. Is it the writer, who crafted it? The characters, who carry the plot forward? Or you, the reader, who breathes life into them?

Or perhaps none of the three can exist without the other.

Perhaps without this magical combination, a story would be nothing more than words on a page.

DELILAH

I've been waiting my whole life for Oliver, so you'd think another fifteen minutes wouldn't matter. But it's fifteen minutes that Oliver is alone on a bus, unmonitored, for the first time, with the most ruthless, malicious, soul-sucking creatures on earth: high school students.

Going to high school is a little like being told you have to get up each morning and run headlong at sixty miles an hour into the same brick wall. Every day, you're forced to watch Darwin's principle of survival of the fittest play out: evolutionary advantages, like perfect white teeth and gravity-defying boobs, or a football team jacket keep you from falling prey to the demons that grow to three times their size when they feed on the fear of a hapless freshman and bully him to a pulp. After years of public school, I've gotten pretty good at being invisible. That way, you're less likely to become a target.

But Oliver knows none of this. He has *always* been the center of attention. He's even more undeveloped socially than the boy who enrolled last year after nine years of being homeschooled in a yurt. Which is why I'm actually breaking a sweat, imagining everything Oliver could be doing wrong.

At this point, he's probably ten minutes into a story about the first dragon he ever encountered—and while he might think it's a great icebreaker, the rest of the bus will either peg him as the new druggie in town, who puts 'shrooms in his breakfast omelet, or as one of those kids who run around speaking Elvish, wearing homemade cloaks, with foam swords tucked into their belts. Either way, that kind of first impression is one that sticks for the rest of your life.

Believe me, I know.

I've spent my entire school career as *that* girl. The one who wrote *VD Rocks!* on all her second-grade valentines and who literally walked into a wall once while reading a book. The one who recently reaffirmed her subterranean spot on the social-status totem pole by accidentally punching out the most popular girl in school during swim practice.

Oliver and I make a *fabulous* couple.

Speaking of which . . . I kind of still can't believe we *are* one. It's one thing to have a boyfriend, but to have someone who looks like he just stepped out of a romantic comedy—well, it doesn't happen to people like me. Girls spend their lives dreaming of that perfect guy but always wind up settling when they realize he doesn't exist. I found mine—but he was trapped inside a fairy tale. Since that's the only world he's ever lived in, acclimating to this one has been a bit of a challenge. How he came to be real—and mine—is a long story . . . but it's been the biggest adventure of my life.

So far, anyway.

"Delilah!" I hear, and I turn around to see my best friend, Jules, barreling toward me. We hug like magnets. We haven't seen each other all summer—she was exiled to her aunt's house in the Midwest, and I was totally preoccupied with Oliver's arrival. Her Mohawk has grown out into an Egyptian bob, which she's dyed midnight blue, and she's wearing her usual thick black eyeliner, combat boots, and a T-shirt with the name of her favorite band du jour: Khaleesi and the Dragons. "So where is he?" she asks, looking around.

"Not here yet," I tell her. "What if he called the bus his trusty steed again?"

Jules laughs. "Delilah, you've been practicing with him the whole summer. I think he can handle a fifteen-minute bus ride without you." Suddenly she grimaces. "Oh crap, don't tell me you guys are going to be Gorilla-glued together, like BrAngelo," Jules says, jerking her head toward Brianna and Angelo, the school's power couple, who seem to have an uncanny ability to be making out on my locker at the exact moment I need to get inside. "I think it's great that you have a hot new boyfriend, but you better not ditch me."

"Are you kidding?" I say. "I'm going to need your help. Being around Oliver is like when you're babysitting a toddler and you realize the entire house is a potential danger zone."

"Perfect timing," murmurs Jules as Oliver's bus pulls up to the front of the school.

You know how there are some moments in your life when time just slows down? When you remember every minute detail: how the wind feels against your face, how the freshly cut grass smells, how snippets of conversation become a dull background buzz, and how in that instant, there's only the beat of your heart and the breath that you draw and the person whose eyes lock with yours?

Oliver is the last one to step off the bus. His black hair is ruffled by the breeze. He's wearing the white shirt and jeans I picked out for him, and an unzipped hoodie. A leather satchel is strung across his chest, and his green eyes search the crowd.

When he sees me, a huge smile breaks across his face.

He walks toward me as if there aren't three hundred people staring at him—the new kid—as if it doesn't matter in the least that the popular girls are tossing their hair and batting their lashes like they're at a photo shoot, or that the jocks are all sizing him up as competition. He walks as if the only thing he can see is me.

Oliver wraps his arms around me and swings me in a circle, like I weigh nothing at all. He sets me down, then gently holds my face in his hands, looking at me as if he has found treasure. "Hello," he says, and he kisses me.

I can feel everyone's eyes on me, their mouths gaping.

Not gonna lie: I could get used to this.

★ ★ ★

I met Oliver inside a book. Last year, I got obsessed with a kids' fairy tale that I found in the stacks of the school library—in particular, with the prince who was illustrated throughout the pages. Now, lots of readers crush on fictional characters, but mine turned out to be not so fictional. Oliver wanted out of his book, where every day was the same, and into a life that didn't have such a rigid plotline.

We had a bunch of failed attempts—including one involving a magic easel that reproduced him in the real world but flat as a pancake, and a brief period of time where I got sucked into the book and found myself swimming with mermaids and fending off a deranged princess who fancied herself in love with Oliver. Our last-ditch attempt to get him written out of the story included a covert trip to Cape Cod to find the author of the book, Jessamyn Jacobs, who had written the story for her son, Edgar, after his dad died. As it turned out, Edgar was a dead ringer for Oliver, and just the replacement we needed in the book for Oliver. For the past three months, Edgar's been living in the fairy tale, and Oliver's been living on Cape Cod, impersonating him—American accent, teenage moods, twenty-first-century clothing, and all. After weeks of persuasion, Oliver finally convinced Jessamyn to move here, to New Hampshire, so he could be with me.

Oliver and I walk down the hall, where girls bunch together, jockeying into position to take a Snapchat selfie; bros try to jam a shipping container's worth of sports gear into a locker the size of a carry-on suitcase; cheerleaders gaze at themselves in their locker mirrors, putting on lip gloss in slow motion, as if they're starring in their own Sephora commercial. Suddenly two nerds zoom down the hallway, clutching stacks of books to their chests, careening off bystanders like human pinballs.

Oliver nearly gets mowed down in the process. "Is there a fire?" he asks.

"No, we only have fifteen minutes till class starts. To a nerd, that means you're already a half hour late." I glance down the hallway. "They run *everywhere. All the time.*"

I can feel everyone's eyes on my back as Oliver and I pass. As we move through the crowds, I purposely bump into him every so often. I do this so I can make sure he's really here. You have to understand—I'm just not a lucky person. I never win a raffle; every penny I come across is tails-up; my last fortune cookie said *Good luck with that.* This is literally a dream come true.

Suddenly I realize that Oliver is doing the queen's wave as we head down the science wing. I grab his hand and pull it down. "These are not your subjects," I whisper, but when he threads his fingers through mine, I completely forget to be frustrated.

Before I realize what he's doing, he's pulling me around a corner, into the narrow hallway that leads to the photography lab. In a delicate choreography, he spins me so that my back is against the wall and his hands are bracketing me. His hair is falling across his eyes as he leans forward, lifts my chin, and kisses me.

"What was that for?" I ask, dizzy.

He grins. "Just because I can."

I can't help smiling back. Three months ago, I never imagined that I could even reach out and touch Oliver's hand, much less sneak away during school for a secret kiss.

The terrible thing about falling in love is that real life always gets in the way. I sigh, taking his hand. "As much as I'd like to stay here, we have to get you to class."

"So," Oliver says. "What's my first task?"

"Well," I reply, taking the printed schedule out of his hand. EDGAR JACOBS, it reads, startling me. It's hard for me to remember that Oliver is masquerading as someone else; how difficult must it be for *him*? "Your first *class* is chemistry."

"Alchemy?"

"Um, not quite. More like potions."

Oliver looks impressed. "Wow. Everyone here hopes to be a wizard?"

"Only the ones with a death wish," I murmur. I stop in front of a bank of lockers, matching the number to the one on his schedule. "This is yours."

He tugs on the lock, frowning at the numerical puzzle of the combination. Then suddenly he brightens and, out of nowhere, pulls out a dagger and hacks it against the metal.

"Oh my *God*!" I shout, grabbing the knife and stuffing it into my backpack before anyone else can see. "Do you want to get arrested?"

"I'm really not that tired," Oliver says.

I sigh. "No knives. *Ever*. Understand?"

His eyes flicker with remorse. "There's just so much here that's . . . different," he says.

"I know," I empathize. "That's why you've got me." I take off the numeric lock, using the code on the back of Oliver's schedule, and replace it with a padlock whose combination is five letters. "Watch," I say, using my thumb to roll the wheels until they spell *E-D-A-H-E*. "Everyone deserves a happy ending."

"I think I can remember that." He grins and backs me against the lockers. "You know what else I remember?"

His eyes are as green as a summer field, and as easy to get lost in.

"I remember the first time I saw you," Oliver says. "You were wearing that shirt."

When he looks at me like that, I can't even remember my name, much less what I'm wearing today. "I was?"

"And I remember the first time I did this," he adds, and he leans in and kisses me.

Suddenly I hear a voice over my shoulder. "Um," a boy says. "You guys are kind of draped across my locker?"

Oh God. I've become BrAngelo.

Immediately I shove Oliver away and tuck my hair behind my ears. "Sorry," I mutter. "Won't happen again." I clear my throat. "I'm Delilah, by the way."

The kid jerks the metal door open and looks at me. "Chris," he says.

Oliver extends his hand. "I'm Oli—"

"Edgar," I interrupt. "His name is Edgar."

"Yes. Right," Oliver says. "That is my name."

"I feel like I haven't seen you before," I say to Chris.

"I'm new. Just moved here from Detroit."

"I just moved here too," Oliver replies.

"Oh yeah? Where from?"

"The kingdom of—"

"Cape Cod," I blurt out.

Chris snorts. "She doesn't let you talk much, man. Where are you guys headed?"

"Edgar's got chemistry with Mr. Zhang," I say.

"Cool, me too. I'll see you there?" Chris shuts his locker and, with a wave, walks down the hall.

Oliver watches him. "How come *he's* allowed to wave?"

I roll my eyes. It's 8:15 a.m. and I'm already exhausted. "I'll explain later," I say.

I have enough time to drop Oliver off at his chemistry classroom before I have to head to French. As we turn the corner, Jules slips up behind us and links her arm through mine. "Guess who broke up," she says.

Oliver smiles. "This must be the famous Jules."

"Reports of my awesomeness are usually underrated," Jules answers. She gives Oliver a once-over and then nods and turns to me. "Well done."

"I'm kind of in a rush—I'm trying to get him to Zhang's room before the bell rings," I explain.

"Trust me, you want to hear this. . . . Allie McAndrews and Ryan Douglas?"

Oliver looks at me, questioning.

"Prom queen and king," I explain quickly.

He looks impressed. "Royalty."

"They *think* they are," Jules agrees. "Anyway, they broke up. Apparently being faithful comes as easily to Ryan as Shakespeare."

Having been in Ryan's English class last year, I know that's saying a lot.

"Speak of the devil," says Jules.

As if we're watching a soap opera, Allie turns the corner, flanked by her posse. From the opposite direction, simultaneously,

Ryan swaggers down the hall. We bystanders freeze, holding our breath, waiting for the inevitable train wreck.

"Oh, look! What a rare sighting," Allie says loudly. "A man-slut in the wild!" Her girls giggle in response.

Ryan looks her up and down. "Did you eat *all* your feelings, Allie?"

At that, Allie propels herself at him, claws out. Just in time, a kid steps between them—James, the president of the LGBT Alliance, who has his own bow tie business and runs conflict-resolution training for student mentors. "Walk it off, girlfriend," James says to Ryan, who shoves him into the wall.

"Back off, fairy," Ryan growls.

Before I realize what's happening, Oliver is no longer standing next to me. He's heading straight for Ryan.

"Oh crap," Jules says. "You had to date a hero?"

But Oliver rushes past Ryan, moving toward James, who's now sprawled on the ground. He extends a hand and helps James up. "Are you all right?"

"Yeah, thanks," James replies, brushing himself off.

This is good, this is really good. Oliver has created the best reputation possible. Everyone is looking at him as if he is a champion.

Including Allie McAndrews.

Oliver puts a hand on James's shoulder. "Fairies here are *much* bigger than I expected," he says, delighted.

For a moment, time stops. Something flickers across James's face—disappointment. Resignation. Pain.

What happens next is so fast I can barely see it: James pulls back his arm and socks Oliver hard so that he falls backward, knocked out cold.

Oh yeah. This is gonna be a *great* year.

I fly to Oliver's side, crouching down. By now the crowd has scattered, afraid of repercussions. I help him sit up; he winces as he leans against the wall.

"Let me guess," Oliver mutters. "*Fairy* means something different here?"

But I can't answer, because when I look at him I see it: the trickle of black from his nose, the stains on his white shirt.

"Oliver," I whisper. "You're *inking.*"

OLIVER

It's been five whole minutes and my face still looks like I've been clobbered by a giant. I push aside Delilah, who's holding a wet tissue to my nose. "The correct term," she says, "is *gay.*"

"I didn't mean to insult him," I mutter. "I just didn't know."

"Don't be so hard on yourself. This is all new to you."

But the guilt aches more than my bruises. I resolve to find James later and offer him a gentleman's apology. "If two people wish to be together, why is it anyone else's business?" I ask. "Bloody hell, my best friend was a basset hound, and he was in love with a princess, and no one ever batted an eye."

Speaking of eyes, I wonder if mine will be black soon. I lean closer to the mirror. "I don't understand this," I say. I've literally jumped into the fiery mouth of a dragon and leaped off fifty-foot cliffs into the ocean and nearly drowned, yet I recovered faster than I have from this measly blow.

Plus, it *hurts.*

Suddenly it all makes sense. "Delilah," I say, swallowing, "I fear I'm dying."

"You're not dying. You got sucker punched."

"I should have healed already."

"Only inside your book," Delilah says. "In the real world, you can't just turn a page and feel better."

I gingerly touch the bridge of my nose and wince. "Pity," I say.

I must admit, this is not quite the start I was expecting. I've been rather excited about the idea of going to school, in spite of all that Delilah has told me about it. She makes it sound like being chained in a dungeon, but to me, it's anything *but* that. I've been chained in a dungeon before. Over and over and over again, in fact. Even getting walloped by a stranger is new and exciting and unexpected and *different* from the same sixty pages I've repeated my whole life.

"You have to get to class," Delilah says. "You're already late. Just say you got lost—no one will question a new student on the first day. You remember what we talked about?"

I begin ticking off the points on my fingers. "Don't bow when I meet someone. Don't refer to myself as royalty. Take notes in class as if I am interested, even when I am not. The teacher's the king of the classroom, and I am not allowed to get up and leave unless granted permission. Oh, and no knives, ever, in school."

Delilah smiles. "Good. And one more . . ." She points to my face. "Don't say or do anything that might make *that* happen again."

She pokes her head out the door—we have ensconced

ourselves in a privy that is only meant for the teachers to use. When Delilah sees that the hall is empty, she pulls me out beside her and pushes me in the direction of my potions class.

"Remember," she says. "Just follow your schedule and I'll meet you at lunch."

I nod and turn but am called back by the sound of her voice.

"Oliver," she says. "You can do this."

I watch her walk away. When Delilah talks like that, it's easy to remember why I gave up everything I knew in order to be with her. She believes in me, and if someone believes in you wholeheartedly, you start to believe in yourself as well.

I take a deep breath and forge ahead into the great unknown.

I've been performing all my life; this is just another role.

I have a sudden flash of Frump, my best friend in the fairy tale, his tail wagging as he yelled at all of us to take our places as a new Reader cracked open the spine of the book. I wonder if Frump is rounding up the cast even now.

I wonder if they miss me.

But. I have my own work to do, here.

Whatever butterflies are swarming in my stomach are not the result of fear. Just excitement.

I push open the door of the classroom and offer my most charming smile to the tutor standing in front of the seated pupils. "So sorry I'm late. My deepest apologies, Your Majesty."

The students snicker. "Mr. Zhang will do," the teacher says flatly. "Take a seat, Mr. . . ."

"Jacobs. Edgar Jacobs. Formerly of Wellfleet."

"Fantastic," Mr. Zhang intones.

There is only one open seat, and to my delight, it's next to someone I know: Chris, whose locker is adjacent to mine. He looks up and cringes. "What happened to *you?*"

"A miscommunication," I say.

"Okay," Mr. Zhang announces. "I'm going to hand out a little pop quiz to see how much you guys already know. Don't panic, it's not going to count toward your final grade." He moves through the aisles, giving each of us a sheet of paper.

Chris hunkers down over the quiz, his pencil scratching vigorously. I glance at the page and frown.

"I beg your pardon," I say, getting Mr. Zhang's attention. "I think mine is written in the wrong tongue."

"English isn't your first language?"

Indeed it is. The Queen's English, to be precise. But this writing is full of strange dashes and arrows and chains of *C*s and *O*s that look like insects.

The teacher sighs. "Then just tell me three things you know about chemistry."

I take a pencil from the leather satchel I've carried to school.

1. Eye of newt and dragon's breath, combined in equal volume, can cure the common cold.
2. The juice of forget-me-nots, distilled, will restore a lost memory.
3. One should never lick the spoon.

By the time we pass in the quiz, I'm quite pleased with myself, and awfully grateful for the time I spent in the wizard Orville's cabin, watching him craft his concoctions.

I manage to sit through class, nodding along and taking

notes as Delilah instructed, although I really have no idea what the point of a table is if it's periodic rather than constant. As the teacher speaks, I let my attention drift, marveling as I look around the classroom. With the exception of Chris, I don't recognize *anyone*. It's as if this world keeps reproducing new people, as if they are coming out of the woodwork. Having grown up with the same cast of thirty, I marvel at features and clothing and faces I've never seen before. One girl, sitting in the front of the room, has a ring through the side of her nose, like the oxen in the fields behind our castle. A boy carries a wheeled board strapped to his satchel, as if he must be ready to zip away at any instant. I glance at the girl to my left; in place of notes, her tablet is filled with swirling images that stretch from corner to corner—she must be an artist of sorts.

The bell rings, startling me. It seems to serve as a cue; everyone stands up and starts packing away their books.

Chris glances at me as he zips up his satchel. "So what made your family move here?"

I don't really have the answer to that. After I realized that Edgar was in the book and I was really, truly out of it, my first step toward becoming real was to masquerade as the boy whose life I stole. That meant getting Jessamyn Jacobs, the author of the fairy tale and Edgar's mother, to believe that I was her son—and I do not think there is anything more challenging than trying to fool the one person who knows a child best, namely, the mother, who's been there from the very first moment of his life. There were many near disasters when Jessamyn seemed on the verge of discovering that I was not Edgar. She would stare at me for long moments, a curious expression on her face. I caught her once going through the drawers of the furniture in Edgar's chamber. Each night at dinner, she'd ask me if I was feeling all right, because I didn't seem quite like myself. That was troubling enough, but even more devastating was the fact that this foreign world was so much bigger than the sixty pages to which I was accustomed: the girl I'd traded everything for lived four hours away. I had to get Jessamyn to believe that it was necessary for us to move to Delilah's hometown—and I had to do it in a way that Edgar might have. After weeks of shooting down my creative excuses (Less air pollution! Struck by Cupid's arrow! Better school district!), Jessamyn suddenly announced one afternoon that moving to New Hampshire would indeed be a good idea. I still don't know what changed her mind. I'm just incredibly relieved that it changed.

"My mom's, um, a freelance editor. She was ready for a fresh start, and she can work anywhere." I look at Chris. "How about you?"

"My dad got a job here, and my mom liked the idea of raising her kids in fresh air," Chris says. "Detroit's kind of the anti–New Hampshire. In lots of ways. I've never seen so many white people in my life." He grins at me. "So how long have you and Delilah been together?"

"Technically, three months," I reply.

"Ooh, serious, huh?"

"Well, I'm trying *not* to be. She wasn't too thrilled when I proposed. She wants to do something called *dating*."

Chris looks at me. "Where are you from, again?"

"Wellfleet," I say. "Have you found true love?"

"It's only second period," Chris laughs. "You're the closest relationship I have in this school so far."

I follow him into the hallway, and we both turn toward the staircase. "I've got trig with Baird," Chris says. "Apparently she only wears black and keeps rocks in her desk drawer. I hear she's a total witch."

"Really?" I say. "Then how come she isn't the one teaching potions?"

Chris smiles. "Dude, you're weird, but you're entertaining. See you later."

He heads downstairs and I turn to the staircase, nearly colliding with just the person I hoped to find. "James," I say as his eyes slide away from mine and he starts up the steps. "Wait."

"Honestly, I think you've said enough for today."

"But I said the wrong things." I wait for him to stop moving and face me. "I never meant to offend you. Where I come from, that word means something different."

"And where is that? Never Land?"

"Something like that." The sea of students parts around us, as if we are stones in a river. I think about how I would have done anything to be with Delilah, how there was no point being in any world unless she was with me. "The very reason I *moved* here is because I believe that everyone should have the right to be with the person they love."

James stares at me for a long moment, as if he is trying to gauge my sincerity. Finally he nods. "You should think about joining the LGBT Alliance," he says. "We could use more allies like you." He fiddles with a pin on the strap of his pack and affixes it to my chest like a knight's medal.

I glance down and see the rainbow fastened on my shirt.

James glances over his shoulder as he walks off. "Sorry I messed up your face." He grins. "It was pretty."

★ ★ ★

Inside room 322, a woman with frizzy gray hair stands facing the whiteboard, scrawling *Ms. Pingree* in perfect cursive. She turns around as the bell rings again and surveys the class, her eyes lighting on each of our faces. "'What's in a name?'" she asks. "'That which we call a rose / By any other name would smell as sweet; / so Romeo would, were he not Romeo call'd / Retain that dear perfection which he owes / Without that title. . . .'"

The other pupils in the class are fidgeting and yawning, ignoring this impromptu performance. But I recognize a great actress when I see one . . . and I even know the script from which she is quoting. It was one of the books on Rapscullio's shelves that Queen Maureen read over and over—the most classic of classic love stories.

Ms. Pingree finishes her recitation and I jump to my feet, strolling up the central aisle until I stand only a few feet away from her. I fall to one knee, professing my undying love. "'I take thee at thy word,'" I say, letting loose the reins on my British accent. "'Call me but love, and I'll be new baptiz'd; / Henceforth I never will be Romeo.'"

Her jaw drops; two bright spots of color appear on her cheeks. For a moment, she's speechless, no doubt swooning at my excellent thespian chops. "Well, well," she says, recovering. "I see the gods have granted my wishes and finally given me a student worth teaching. Are you a fan of Shakespeare?"

"Am I a fan of Shakespeare?" I repeat. "Is Hamlet indecisive? Is Lady Macbeth mad? Is Falstaff . . . portly?" I realize, midsentence, that I am still speaking in my British accent, and clear my throat. "I'm Edgar," I say, mimicking the flat American sounds of everyone else's speech. "New kid in town."

"And one I hope to see in the drama club this year. Thank you, Edgar, for joining me in a rousing performance from our first reading assignment this semester: *Romeo and Juliet*. Mark, Helen, Allie, come help me pass out books."

I take my seat again, feeling awfully chuffed. Wait until Delilah hears about this. And *she* thought I wouldn't fit in. I have a sense that English is going to be my strong suit. Perhaps I will even advance a grade level, or be asked to proctor a course. . . .

Suddenly a book is slipped onto my desk, pushed closer by a slender hand with red polish. I look up to find the very girl who precipitated the fight that led to my morning beating. Delilah's nemesis, Allie McAndrews, stands before me. Her sleek blond hair is shoulder length, and she has so much makeup on her eyes that when she flutters her lashes, all I can think of are spiders. Her lips turn up in a half smile, as if she knows a secret and I don't.

"Maybe for once," she says, "English will be interesting."

★ ★ ★

At midday, when I enter the cafeteria, I see that Delilah is pacing. "You made it," she says, grabbing my arm, as if she needs to convince herself I'm still really here. I understand; I feel the same way about her. "I thought maybe you'd end up in the principal's office." She scrutinizes my face. "You don't have a black eye." In truth, I've forgotten about the fight—so much has happened.

"Delilah, this place is spectacular!" I say, beaming.

She looks up at me, quizzical. "Maybe you got hit harder than I thought."

"No, truly—there must be hundreds of students in this school, and each one is a mystery! And in chemistry, I get to *choose* who my scene partner is, instead of being told with whom I have to work—"

"*Lab* partner?"

"Yes, right, that's what it's called. And the best part is that nothing about my day has anything to do with saving a princess."

"Congratulations," Delilah says. "But trust me, the novelty wears off."

She pulls me into a line and hands me a lime-green tray. Behind a plastic shield, what appears to be a troll in a hairnet is glumping slop onto a plate. "What is that?" I ask Delilah.

"Lunch."

"But it's . . . alive."

"It's not quite a royal banquet, but it meets the federal nutrition standards, apparently."

Reluctantly I take the plate as it is offered to me. "I'll go get us water," Delilah says. I wander toward students clustered in small groups at tables. This, according to my schedule, is Lunch

Period. The freedom is almost unbearable: imagine a half hour every day when you are able to do whatever you want, without worrying that someone is going to open the book and force you back into place on page one. I take stock of the scene, marveling at how lucky I am to live this charmed life.

Then I notice someone waving. It's Allie, from my English class, seated with her ladies-in-waiting, who all look unnervingly similar.

"Edgar," she says as I walk over with my tray. "You can sit with us."

I glance over my shoulder to see Delilah standing on the periphery, looking for me. "I'm so sorry, I already have plans for Lunch Period."

Allie's gaze follows mine to light on Delilah. Her hand touches my arm. "Just so you know," she says coolly, "I'm kind of a big deal at this school. So when you're done geeking out with the village loser, text me." She pulls out a sparkly pink pen and writes a series of numbers on my forearm, punctuating it with a fat heart.

I walk back to Delilah and tap her on her shoulder. "Looking for me?"

She grins. "Always." Delilah leads me to a table where Jules sits, trying to sculpt her mound of food with her utensils.

"Nice artwork," I say.

"Does it look like those Easter Island heads to you? 'Cause that's what I'm going for," Jules says.

I try to pull Delilah's chair out for her, because that's what princes do, but the chair is oddly attached to the table and doesn't budge. "It was a nice gesture, Oliver," she murmurs, putting her hand on my arm—and then her fingers slide down to my wrist, pulling my hand up so she can read what's written on my skin. "What's this?"

"Allie requested a text from me," I say. "I'm thinking she might enjoy *Beowulf*."

Jules spits her chocolate milk across the table as Delilah's eyes fly to mine. "Why do you even *know* her?"

"She's in my English class. Which, by the way, I *stoned*."

"You mean *rocked*?" Jules corrects me.

"Were you flirting with her?" Delilah says.

"It was nothing more than a conversation," I explain. "Why would I be interested in Allie McAndrews?" I wait for her to meet my gaze. "I've got you."

Jules puts down her fork. "I'm barfing rainbows."

"Do you know Snow White?" Delilah asks.

"Not personally . . ."

"Well, that apple might look pretty on the outside, but just remember, she's poison at the core."

"Mind if I sit down?" a voice says, and I turn to find Chris standing behind us.

"Please do! You already know Delilah. And this is Jules. Jules, Chris. He just moved here from Detroit."

"Welcome to hell," Jules says. "I hope you got your complimentary brimstone cocktail when you checked in."

"And my free hundred dollars in chips," Chris replies smoothly. "Or is the casino on the fourth floor just a prank they play on the new kids?"

"There's no casino," Jules laughs. "But don't miss the Olympic-sized pool up there."

I nudge Delilah's shoulder. "There's no fourth floor," I whisper.

"It's a joke," she answers.

I reach for her hand, and as I do, I notice the numbers crawling up my forearm. Twisting it so that they can't be seen, I thread my fingers through Delilah's. I've held her hand enough times now that it shouldn't feel like electricity running up and down my skin, but just touching her, there are still sparks. "So," I say quietly. "You and I . . . are we okay?"

She looks away. "Sure," she says, but her smile doesn't quite light up her eyes.

I smile back. Or try to, anyway. Because if there's anything I know, it's when someone's acting.

★ ★ ★

When I get home from my first day of high school, the woman who is not my mother—yet who created me—is waiting. "How did it go?" Jessamyn asks. "Scale of one to ten?"

"Five hundred," I reply. "It was spectacular."

She seems surprised. "Is it that much better than school on Cape Cod?"

"Infinitely."

She folds her arms. "You've never been such a big fan of school before."

"I never had a girlfriend there before." As the words escape, I hope they're true.

Jessamyn purses her lips. Delilah didn't make the strongest of first impressions on her. In fact, she came off as a little insane—a crazed sycophant who'd run away from home and traveled four hours to beg a reclusive ex-author to change the ending of her book. When Mrs. McPhee arrived to pick Delilah up, she was not amused. It took weeks of apologies before her mother even let her out of the house. Luckily, in the brief hours between our realization that I was really, truly, wholly free from the book and her mother's arrival to drag her home, Delilah created a magical portal for us, so that we could communicate even from afar.

She calls it *Skype*.

Those first few weeks were terrifying. Not only was I missing Delilah, but I had to impersonate a boy I had only just met, and do such a cracking job that his own mother would be fooled. It was exhausting being someone other than myself.

I wasn't expecting to be released from a book in which I spent every moment pretending to be a person I'm not only to wind up doing it all over again.

In my favor, Edgar had been somewhat less than chatty. He spent a great deal of time in his room with his video games, which gave me time for Delilah's daily lessons on how to act like a teenager. For example, in this world, an adolescent is supposed to do the opposite of what his parents ask him to do. Grunting is an appropriate form of communication before noon, and eye-rolling is acceptable at all times. Also, thinking before acting is a sure way to be sussed out as an imposter.

It was the little things, though, that were the hardest—a lifetime of moments Edgar had with Jessamyn Jacobs that I did not. Until she mentioned it, I did not remember the vacation she and Edgar took to Belize, where they both got so sunburned that they had to sleep sitting up; I didn't know that Edgar used to roam the beach with her, looking for coral shaped like the first letters of their names. I didn't know Edgar's favorite color or food or book. I had to re-create a life I'd never lived.

"And how *is* Delilah?" Jessamyn asks.

"She was the perfect welcoming committee," I say diplomatically.

Jessamyn laughs. "Oh, to be young and in love."

I grimace and turn away. Even when I was a prince, I didn't want to hear about my faux parents' love affair.

"I didn't just create you out of thin air, you know."

"Go figure," I murmur.

She follows me into the kitchen. One thing I've noticed is that in this world, I seem to want to be either sleeping or eating all the time. I take a box of cereal out of the cabinet and stick my hand inside, pulling out a fistful of small yellow puffs. I stare at the insane cartoon on the box. Cap'n Crunch. Honestly, it's as if whoever drew this has never met a real pirate.

"So," Jessamyn says, sitting on a stool at the counter. "What are your classes like? Who's your favorite teacher so far?"

Every time we have a conversation, I get flustered. I feel as if I'm being interrogated. As if there are right and wrong answers and I am bound to fail. I take a deep breath and paste a smile on my face. "I was gobsmacked by my English teacher," I tell her, pulling a carton of milk from the refrigerator and nearly drinking from the spout before remembering that seems to be one of Jessamyn's pet peeves. "She was brilliant."

"Gobsmacked," she repeats. "Brilliant. You know, you've

been picking up a lot of slang lately that seems a little out of
character for you."

You have no idea, I think. "I've been reading Dickens. . . ."

"How interesting, since I couldn't even get you to read Shel
Silverstein."

"Delilah gave it to me," I say quickly.

"Of course. Delilah." Jessamyn nods. "I suppose she's responsible for your new look as well."

I glance down at my jeans and sweatshirt, which—yes—
Delilah chose for me so that I would better fit in on my first
day. "People reinvent themselves all the time," I say. "Look at
that picture of you and Dad on the mantel. Your hair was a different color and the size of a hot-air balloon . . . and you were
wearing leather pants. Clearly you've improved."

Jessamyn laughs. "What happened in the nineties stays in the
nineties," she says, and then she grows more sober. "It might be
fun to change it up, Edgar, but don't forget who you are."

I think of what Delilah told me—how to respond to your
parents when they start giving you life lessons. "Relax, Mom," I
say, unzipping my sweatshirt and tossing it over a chair. "I just
got better-fitting jeans. It's not the end of the world."

An odd expression ghosts across her face. "Of course not,"
Jessamyn says. Then her eyes widen. "Edgar! What did you get
all over your shirt?"

I look down. Until now I've actually put this morning's de-
bacle out of my mind. "My pen exploded?"

She sighs. "Do you know how hard it is to get ink stains out?"

"Somewhat," I say under my breath. Replacing the milk

in the refrigerator, I begin to rummage through the contents, looking for something else to satisfy my perpetual hunger. I take a small container and pop off its lid, reaching in with my fingers to grab what's inside.

"No!" Jessamyn cries, and I look up, alarmed, the fruit halfway to my open mouth. "Don't you know what that is?"

"Pineapple?" I reply, wondering if this is yet another trick question.

"Which gives you *hives*," Jessamyn points out.

"Right," I say, dropping the spear back into the container. "Forgot."

"You forgot the week you spent in the hospital when your throat closed up and you couldn't breathe?"

I hesitate. "It's been a long day," I say, and I grab my satchel and sweatshirt, hoping to flee before I do anything else wrong.

★ ★ ★

I'm in my room absorbed in my studies, trying to understand why all of these chemicals have two-letter nicknames that make absolutely no sense, when I hear a chime on the computer.

Delilah's face fills the screen. I wonder if this is the way she saw me when I was inside the book—close enough to touch, but two-dimensional. "What are you up to?"

"Chemistry," I say. "Tell me: in what part of the word *Iron* do you find the *Fe*?"

"*Ferrous*. It *means* 'iron.'"

"Then why isn't it *called* that?"

"Because chemistry's a whole special circle of hell," Delilah says. "Why don't you come over here and we can figure it out together?"

"Something tells me we wouldn't get very much accomplished." I grin. "Which actually sounds rather perfect."

After Delilah's overreaction to Allie McAndrews's writing her phone number on my arm, I'm relieved to know that she still wishes to see me. But all the same, I scrub those numbers off my skin before I leave home. I don't want to remind her of why she grew angry. I tell Jessamyn that Delilah's mother has invited me for dinner and take Edgar's bike from the garage. Delilah's home is a short ride away, but it's all uphill. As I huff my way to her house, I think longingly of Socks, my stallion, who used to be the one doing all the work when we traveled.

When I ring the McPhee doorbell, a dog starts barking. Humphrey is a rescue, a gift from Mrs. McPhee's boyfriend, Dr. Ducharme. He looks enough like Frump to make me homesick every time I see him, and I can't help talking to him the way I would address my best friend—as if he might actually answer me back. "Good day, Humphrey," I say as Delilah's mother answers the door and pulls him away by the collar. I offer my most winning smile. Mrs. McPhee has softened toward me in the months since Delilah fled to Wellfleet, but I get the feeling she doesn't truly trust me. "Hello," I say. "So good to see you again. You're looking radiant."

She raises one eyebrow, dubious, but I am being honest. Delilah's mother cleans other people's houses, and she reminds me a bit of another story from Rapscullio's shelves, about a young scullery maid who possesses both glass footwear and inner beauty, which makes a prince fall head over heels for her.

"Aren't you the charmer," Mrs. McPhee replies, opening the door so I can step inside. "How was your first day of school, Edgar?"

"It's everything I'd hoped it would be," I say. "I can't wait for tomorrow."

"Maybe some of that joy will rub off on Delilah. I think the last time she enthused about school was when her second-grade class had Willy Wonka Day and they ate candy for eight straight hours."

Delilah's feet pound down the stairs, and she gives Humphrey an absent pat on the head. "Okay, thanks, Mom. If you're done totally humiliating me, Edgar and I have to study."

"Oh, is *that* what they're calling it these days?"

Delilah rolls her eyes and pulls me up to her room. She leaves the door open a crack—that's her mother's rule, and the only way I am even allowed upstairs. When I asked her why I couldn't be trusted, she said it's because chivalry really *is* dead.

I know every inch of her bedroom, because I had to draw it in excruciating detail during one of our failed attempts to get me out of the book. In the fairy tale, Rapscullio had a magic easel, on which he'd painted an exact replica of his lair. When he sketched a butterfly onto the background scene, it would pop off the canvas, suddenly alive. I tricked him into painting Delilah's chamber, in the hopes that I could then draw myself onto the easel and reappear, alive, in her world instead of mine. But sadly, even though I materialized in her three-dimensional bedroom, I remained in two dimensions, and we had to start back at square one.

Because my life literally depended on my knowing it so well,

Delilah's bedroom is more familiar to me than anywhere else. Every other object is pink, and she has so many stuffed animals piled on her bed I have no idea where she sleeps. The tops of her bureaus are cluttered with mismatched earrings and hair ties and spare change. Portraits of Delilah—some alone, some with Jules or her mother—are arranged in a mural on the wall behind her headboard.

I flop onto her bed, crushing a stuffed panda beneath me. Delilah stretches out beside me, propping her head on one hand. There are six inches of space between us, and it's excruciating.

I slip my arm into the curve of her waist and pull her closer, tracing a trail of kisses from her collarbone to her jaw. I bury my face in her hair; she smells of vanilla and cinnamon. "Aren't we supposed to be working on your chemistry?" Delilah whispers.

"We are," I say, rolling her on top of me. She flattens her hands on my chest and settles her mouth over mine. Her heart beats against mine, keeping time.

Once, Orville told me that when stars collide, universes are born; galaxies expand. That's how it feels when I kiss Delilah—like the whole world just doubled in size.

Inside the book, I could run and leap and fall without resistance, and it is still taking a bit of getting used to, to simply exist here with gravity. But in this moment, I'm thankful for it. I can feel her pressing against me from collarbone to toes, a weight that sinks into my bones and grounds me in this brand-new world.

It's not just a physical gravity I'm still adjusting to—it's the serious reality of having my dreams come true. Of being free to do what I wish. Of feeling as if I have everything—every*one*—that I need.

It's odd—love in the fairy tale always felt so fast, skipping over the details to get to the happy ending. With Delilah, I'm moving just as quickly, but I don't miss a single moment. I notice how she chews her pencil when she's nervous; how when I touch her hand, she jumps a little as if there's been an electric shock; how when she says my name, it's softer than any other word in the sentence.

Suddenly Delilah pushes herself away from me and leaps off the bed, her jaw dropping. I sit up quickly, expecting to see Mrs. McPhee in the doorway, but there's nobody there. "What's wrong?"

Delilah points behind me, and I turn around.

Hanging in midair are two words I hoped I'd never see:

COME HOME.

EDGAR

How come things are never as awesome as you want them to be?

The first day of kindergarten, my mom told me it would be amazing. I'd have so much fun riding the bus and making new friends, and I'd get to spend the whole day doing exciting things with other kids my age. This was the reality: on the bus, a kid threw up in the seat next to me. We spent two hours tracing the letter *A* over and over and over. And at recess, a girl tossed sand in my face, nearly blinding me. Oh yeah, those were *totally* going to be the best days of my life.

I figured that here, it would be different. After all, this was all my idea. This was kindergarten all over again, except *I* was teaching the class. I made all the decisions, and nothing could happen unless I wanted it to. And yet . . .

Well. I can't say I'm not disappointed.

Don't get me wrong. It's still cool to get to wield a laser gun and meet an actual live dragon. It's great to be the center of attention for once, instead of the kid whose name everyone forgets. And I genuinely like the people I'm with. Frump is always at my side, which rocks, considering that the only pet I've ever been allowed to have is a hermit crab that slowly lost all its limbs and was just depressing. Seraphima looks especially hot in a spandex intergalactic space-fighter suit. Captain Crabbe is nice, but he's kind of obsessed with teeth, and every time I try to strike up a conversation with him, I catch him checking out my overbite. As for Socks, I've never met someone with even less self-esteem than me, but he's always the first one to ask me how my day is going or to invite me to go for a trot on the beach.

The thing is, although I've rewritten the plot so that Oliver can live outside the book and I can take his place inside it, although every character in here with me knows the new story and has practiced it endlessly, we're the only ones who know anything has changed. Delilah has the only copy of *Between the Lines,* and she hasn't cracked it open once since the switch. Which I guess I understand, since she was reading it because Oliver was inside. And now it's just me in here.

But without a reader, a story is only half complete. It's like blueprints that never get built; like a swimming pool without water. The foundation's there, but it's useless. Without a reader, the words just sit on the page, waiting to come alive in someone's imagination.

This morning, just like every other morning I've been here, I am awakened by the sound of Pyro doing his seven a.m. flyby. Roosters have nothing on dragons, which sound like a cross between a howler monkey and a braying donkey; I have no idea how he doesn't wake up the entire kingdom as he streaks his way across all sixty pages. I blink at the stone ceiling of the castle, still kind of expecting my mom to walk in and tell me I'm going to be late for school. Then I sit up and let my gaze fall on the spacesuit draped over the golden chair in the corner of the room.

In the new story, I lead the citizens of the kingdom to battle the Galactoids from the planet Zugon, in order to bring down the mighty Zorg. It involves the kidnapping of space princess Seraphima, which starts an intergalactic war, and includes trolls swiping spaceships from the sky with their meaty paws, fairies listening in on top-secret meetings (giving new meaning to the term *fly on the wall*), mermaids running covert submarine operations into the core of the Earth, and Rapscullio being exposed as a double agent working as a henchman for Zorg. The skeleton of the story was part of a video game I used to play back in the other world; all I did was connect the dots. I used to spend six hours a day with a controller in my hands. Sometimes I'd even wake up thinking about ways to make it to the next level. It's every gamer's dream to actually live as your avatar—to swing the sword instead of pushing a button to make it happen, to kiss the princess instead of watching the action unfold on the screen while your score goes through the roof.

I'm totally psyched to be here. I *am.*

I just have to keep reminding myself.

After I get dressed and brush my teeth, I head down the spiral staircase, sniffing out the source of the heavenly aroma that has been wafting through the castle. I find Queen Maureen, wearing her silver supersuit, her platinum-braceleted wrists sunk in a bowl of dough. "Good morning, Edgar!" she says, smiling brightly. "How did you sleep?"

"Great, until that dragon flew by."

"He *is* an early riser," she muses. "You get used to it."

I grab a scone from a stack that's still warm from the oven and grunt in response.

Maureen hesitates, then offers me a half smile. "I was just wondering . . . do you mind if I finish baking before I come down to rehearsal? After all, it's been weeks since we were read . . . surely it won't be a problem if I miss an hour to finish this *pain au chocolat*?"

When I don't answer right away, she wipes her hands on a dish towel.

"That's fine, then. I can always finish later—"

"No, no," I reply. "Whatever. Stay if you want to. If we need you, you're only a shout away."

Her face brightens. "I'll let you have the first taste," she promises.

I strap on my laser pistol and my force field interrupter, planning to head down to Everafter Beach to rehearse. I have to admit, it took a little while to get used to living in two dimensions. When you first walk through this world, it feels like you're crossing through a pop-up picture book. Pluck a flat apple off a tree, and in your hand, it somehow morphs into something tangible, luscious, and real. I'm not sure if that's because it actually *becomes* a true apple or because I'm as flat as *it* is. And it's disconcerting to have to leap the fault line that the spine of the book creates to get from a left-hand page to a right-hand one. There's gravity here, but it's different—it's not like being in water, where you have to work to stay sunken, but it's not as strong as the pull in the real world either. I can easily do a backflip or climb a sheer rock wall without breaking a sweat—everything is somehow effortless. And there are no maps, and no roads to speak of. You don't count turns, you count pages. To get from the castle to Orville's cottage, for example, is seven jumps. And moving from page to page isn't just continuing down a path—you step off into a great, black, dizzying nothing, letters swinging overhead, and suddenly find yourself standing at your destination without any memory of how you got there.

Just when I pass the drawbridge on my way out of the castle, Pyro screams overhead, and I turn around. For just a moment, I'm not seeing the scene in front of me. The path leading to the castle winds and twists in the exact same pattern as my driveway at home—which I remember failing to back out of while practicing to get my driver's license. My whole body aches, and I realize there's a reason it's called being home*sick*. Suddenly I want nothing more than to be sitting in my kitchen with my mom giving me the same old cereal boxes to choose from. I want her to yell at me to pick up the clothes littering my bedroom floor. I want . . . well, my mom.

My mother created this book; her fingerprints are bound to be all over it. But the whole point of coming into the fairy tale was to have an adventure. And I'm not going to let a little bit of homesickness ruin that for me. I take a deep breath and turn away from the castle walkway, which might look familiar but is actually a whole world away from what I'm used to.

Everafter Beach is the last page of the book, so it takes the longest to reach from the castle. I hike through the Enchanted Forest, past the troll bridge and Orville's cottage. Grimacing, I dive off the cliff into the ocean, past the mermaid scene, and emerge dripping wet on the shores where Pyro lives. By the time I get to Captain Crabbe's ship, I know I'm late, because nobody's around. So I scale the rock wall extra fast and dive out the window, somersaulting onto Everafter Beach.

Frump stands on a stump, trying to get the attention of the others. The trolls Biggle and Snort are having a laser fight, which is good practice for the new plot, except I think they're getting more joy out of beheading palm trees and igniting sand into glass than out of rehearsing actual swordsmanship. Pyro is snoring, rings of smoke puffing from his nostrils. The mermaids are having snail races, betting with pearls. Trogg the troll is playing his flute. The fairies have braided daisy chains that they're weaving through Socks's mane; he's beaming so much he basically emits a glow. Orville and Captain Crabbe are playing five-card stud, using sand dollars and shells for chips.

"What's going on?" I ask, putting my hand on Frump's shoulder.

He jumps, scratching his ear, a reflex. Old habits die hard, I guess. Until a couple of months ago, Frump was a basset hound. "I think people just aren't feeling . . . inspired," Frump says.

"Well, how could we?" Seraphima announces, arriving on the page. "We haven't had a Reader for, like . . ." She rolls her eyes up, as if she's counting, and then her eyebrows knit together. "For, like, a long time."

Seeing her, Frump hops down from his perch. He takes her hand and kisses it. He is so whipped. "Princess," he says, "every time I think you can't look any more radiant, you prove me wrong."

"I don't think she looks radiant," I point out. "Where's your space gear?" She's wearing some silly dress from the Renaissance, with little slippers that look about as substantial as socks and are totally inappropriate for kicking alien butt.

"Oh, do shut up, Edgar," she says with a sigh. "As *if.* The aliens haven't come for us. This is all just a joke. I am a princess. I'm not doing your dirty work for you anymore."

Frump and I exchange a glance. On her good days, Seraphima is about as smart as a brick. Somehow, even performing a fairy tale over and over has not clued her in to the fact that she is not actually a princess but only a character in a book. I thought she would be the easiest to convince, when I came inside, that the story had a new twist, one in which Oliver was an imposter and this fairy tale was a decoy to keep the aliens from Zorg from annihilating our planet. But when she learned that she would no longer be wearing her royal gowns and getting married to a prince every day, she lost interest.

Rapscullio comes up to us. "Hate to interrupt," he says, "but I can't help noticing that everyone here is a little . . . shall I say . . . *on edge*? I've been taking a self-taught course on conflict resolution, and, well, I don't mean to belittle your contributions, Edgar, but the problem does seem to be stemming from the revisions to the story. Seraphima has a point—it's been a while since we had a Reader, and one can only assume that perhaps the changes aren't appealing to our audience. Maybe we should try returning to the original version. You can learn Oliver's lines, and as for the rest of the cast, we can go back to doing what we do best. We're pirates and princesses and fairies, not space warriors. The mermaids know how to scare the living daylights out of sailors. Socks is a grand master of dressage." His gaze cuts across the beach to where Snort is setting Biggle's hair on fire with an errant laser beam. "And the trolls really should stick to construction. Without power tools."

It's easier to change one character than to change thirty. I suppose I could have worked my way into the book by switching Oliver's name to mine, by deleting him from his own life and replacing him with me. But that isn't what I signed up for.

What if it turns out I'm stuck here, doing something I never asked to do? The whole reason I agreed to swap with Oliver was because I'd get a chance to experience adventures and thrills I'd only witnessed on a computer screen. But every time you play a video game, it's different. In this world, it's like I play a tape of the same game over and over again. I know what's around the corner. I know what creature is going to jump out at me. I know when the aliens are landing, and that I will ultimately kill Zorg. The element of surprise is gone, and that was the fun of it in the first place.

Now I get why Oliver wanted to leave. But if he knew this was a prison, why would he wish it on anyone else?

"You know," I say, "what we all need is a breather."

Seraphima stamps her tiny foot. "I absolutely refuse to put any more gear on."

"I just mean we need a break." I turn to Frump. "Do you want to do the honors?"

Frump climbs back onto his perch and barks. Even though in my revised story, he's been changed from a basset hound back to a human again, I guess you can't teach an old dog new tricks.

"Attention!" he cries. "All characters are dismissed for the day."

There is a moment of shocked silence on the beach, and then a bustle of excitement and activity as everyone realizes that they're being left to their own devices. The fairies zip by my face like fireworks.

"Milady," Frump says to Seraphima, "since we have a bit of a break, maybe you could walk me? Erm, I mean, maybe we could go for a walk?"

The princess's eyes flicker over him. "Rain check?" She picks up her skirts and floats across the sand, toward the edge of the page.

Frump looks disappointed for only a second, then turns to me. "Guess I'll head out too," he says. "Someone has to make Seraphima's bed before she realizes she doesn't actually have handmaidens."

Suddenly a blinding light slices the sky in half. I wince, raising my hand as a shield. The ground shifts under my feet, and I watch everyone instinctively grabbing the nearest solid object: a tree, a rock, a dangling participle. I go tumbling head over heels and smack into a troll's bottom, which feels like the side of a battleship. "Sorry," I mumble, and Trogg shrugs.

"No worries. We've all had a bit more practice."

The sand stops whirling and the ocean settles as the pages flatten, and I find myself looking up at a giant replica of my own face.

"Oliver!" Frump says, his butt wagging. Seraphima races

from the edge of the page to stand front and center, her hands clasped at her chest. Queen Maureen—who appeared on Everafter Beach with everyone else as soon as the book was opened—waves with delight. The characters, excited about being pulled into place for an actual reader, are even more pumped to see who it is.

Oliver, on the other hand, doesn't look so happy. "Is everything all right?" he asks. A second face appears beside his: Delilah's. She looks scared to death.

Frump tugs at the hem of his shirt. "We're fine!" he says, cheery. "You know how it goes. Business as usual. I mean, granted, we haven't had too many Readers lately. . . ."

Their faces relax. "Then who sent the note?" Oliver asks.

I frown. "What note?"

"Hold on tight," Oliver says, and the world spins again as he gently lifts the book, turning it away from him. It seems to be a girl's bedroom, blurry, the way things look underwater. I see a crapload of pink, and as things slowly start to come into focus, I can make out a collage of pictures over the bed. Most of them are of Delilah with a girl who looks like a pierced hedgehog. I mean, a really pretty pierced hedgehog, but still.

I don't understand why Oliver's showing us Delilah's wall, and then I notice the floating letters.

COME HOME.

"What is that?" I ask.

The book tilts and rights itself again, so that Oliver hovers above us. "I assumed you would be able to tell me."

"Well, I didn't write it," I say.

"Rapscullio?" Oliver asks. "It came from *your* easel."

"Sorry, Ollie. The only thing I've drawn lately is a *teinopalpus imperialis*. Gorgeous specimen, with iridescent wings . . . normally found in India and—"

"Perhaps someone else has been using your easel," Oliver interrupts. He peers at each of the characters in turn.

We all start glancing at each other nervously, wondering who is unhappy and unwilling to admit it.

Guess I'm not the only one.

Could it be Frump, missing his best friend? Maureen, missing her fictional son? Could Rapscullio's comments about the new version of the story not working out be only the tip of the iceberg? Could Seraphima—stuck with a guy like me—be dreaming of the prince she used to have?

It's hard to believe that I could be just as much of a disappointment in the world of this book as I was in reality.

Frump clears his throat, the way he does when he is commanding us to start rehearsal. "It appears that all of us are *just* fine." He tilts up his chin. "But enough about us. How are *you*?"

A slow grin stretches over Oliver's face. "This place," he says, "it's everything I dreamed of. There are so many people in this world I can't name them all. When I talk to them, I have absolutely no idea what they're going to say. Every day since I've been here has been different—there are so many scenes you could spend your life trying and never see them all." His eyes cut to Delilah. "And of course," he says, "the company is rather enchanting."

Oliver takes Delilah's hand and kisses the back of it. To my right, I hear Seraphima draw in her breath, and Frump moves slightly closer to her.

"How's my mom?" I blurt out. Until I've said that, I don't realize how much she has been on my mind. I wonder if she can tell that Oliver isn't me. It's really hard to think that I'm missing her but she has no idea she's supposed to be missing me.

"She's perfect. Except when she tells me to clean my room." My chest gets tight. "She does that. A lot."

A strange expression must cross my face, because Oliver's gaze narrows on mine. "Edgar," he asks, "are you all right?"

I open my mouth, about to tell him the truth: I miss my mom. I miss my home. Nobody likes me here; nobody likes my story; nothing is going the way I planned. But all that comes out is "Great!" My face tightens into what might pass for a smile.

"Well, if you're sure . . . ," Oliver replies. "Delilah's mother is about to serve supper." He hesitates. "I miss you all. I miss you . . . a lot. There are many people in this world, but none like you." Then he tosses us another smile. "All right, then. Hang on tight." As he starts to close the book, as we tumble through the pages, I hear his voice fading away: "I promise I'll read you later."

As the characters disperse, I listen to their chatter. Socks walks with Captain Crabbe. "He looks great, doesn't he? So handsome."

"He looks *happy*," Maureen adds. "What more could a mother ask for her son?"

The mermaids slip into the shallows of the water. "I guess you can eat, breathe, and sleep true love," Kyrie says, "but I'd go for the chocolate, the oxygen, and the featherbed instead."

Seraphima is the only one frowning. She walks off the page

slowly, her arms wrapped tightly around her body, as if she's hoping to hold herself together.

I sit down on the beach, tossing the remaining sand dollars from the poker game into the water. When Frump comes up behind me, I'm surprised. I thought I was alone.

"You did a good thing, Edgar," he says.

"What do you mean?"

"You're not the only one hiding something to make him happy." Frump turns around, lifting up the back of his shirt, to reveal a long brown-and-white tail. He faces me again, sober. "Rapscullio may be more right than he knows. It's not just the characters who want to return to the original story. It's the book."

Think about the last time you got a new shirt.

What made it new?

That the tag still itched? That it smelled like the store and not detergent? That you weren't used to seeing it hanging in your closet when you opened the door? That you wanted to wear it more than any of your other clothes, because it was unique?

At some point, that shirt stopped being so special.

At some point, it became just another shirt in your wardrobe.

When does something stop being new? When does it start just being . . . yours?

OLIVER

There's a treadmill in Jessamyn Jacob's spare bedroom, where she runs for an hour every day, going absolutely nowhere. This, Delilah has informed me, is *exercise.* To me, it seems pointless.

There's a little red wristband she wears while she's running in case she falls off the moving walkway or gets hurt. If this happens, a cord on the wristband makes the machine stop dead.

I imagined that is exactly what happened when I left the book. I pulled the cord, and everyone else stayed frozen in the moment, static, waiting for me to start them up again.

But I suppose I was just kidding myself.

They all seem to be going on with their lives and their stories, as if they never needed me in the first place.

I should be happy for them. I should feel good about the fact that they, like me, have moved on. But I'm fairly certain happiness doesn't feel like a stone in the pit of one's stomach.

When I opened the book and I saw that beach, I could still

picture myself looking up at the words hanging like balloons in the sky. I could feel the spray of the ocean, and the sun beating hot on the back of my tunic.

For the first time I can remember, seeing Seraphima was a delight, not a chore.

I couldn't even make eye contact with Queen Maureen because it hurt too much.

And Frump . . . well. Seeing him on Everafter Beach, so happy and human—I wanted to be excited for him. But all I noticed was him standing beside Edgar, and how easily Edgar seemed to have replaced me.

Once upon a time, Frump and I swapped out the salt for the sugar in Queen Maureen's pantry, causing her to make the world's most inedible cake for a birthday party for Ondine the mermaid. Then there was the time we painted Socks electric pink while he was fast asleep. I can't count the number of hours we spent playing chess on the beach, using the fairies as pieces. Sometimes I wouldn't even have to tell Frump what I was thinking. He just *knew*.

I can't imagine my life without Delilah in it. But to be honest, I always believed Frump would be there too.

I reach over Delilah's bed to the words COME HOME, which are still floating like lanterns, and crush them in the palm of my hand. They leave smudges on my skin. When I toss them in the trash, they look like a tangle of black ribbon.

Delilah puts her hand on my arm. "Are you okay?"

I nod. "I just . . . I thought they might *need* me a little more."

"*I* need you." She leans forward, and I tuck her against me. Her skin is soft as satin. This is what's real. This is why *I'm* real.

★ ★ ★

It's Delilah's idea to take a walk in the woods. We strike out behind her house, following an overgrown path littered with fallen leaves the color of fire. "I used to come here and make fairy houses out of acorns and pine needles and twigs," she says.

"That's ridiculous," I scoff. "Fairies would never live on the ground; they'd be stepped on. They make their homes in the notches of trees."

She laughs. "Well, not all of us have the benefit of firsthand experience."

"I had a spot in the Enchanted Forest where I used to play with Frump as a child. It looked just like this," I tell her. "We built a fort between two boulders and spent hours trying to hunt a squirrel for dinner."

"Queen Maureen would have let you eat a squirrel?"

"No," I admit. "Luckily we never caught one."

"Come here," she says. "I want to show you something." She takes my hand and leads me through a thicket of overgrown brush and tangled roots, which opens suddenly into a small clearing. A canopy of leaves filters the sunlight above us, dappling the ground. A willow tree arches like a dancer, its arms extended and its long hair cascading. Delilah parts the vines, revealing a mossy log. She sits down and pats the space beside her. "I used to come here when I wanted to run away from home."

I think about Delilah's cozy house, her attentive mother. "Why would you do that?"

"Because no one is always happy where they are. Every time

I got mad at my mom, or frustrated because she was working too hard to be around a lot, I wanted to escape. So I'd pack everything I thought I should take with me into my pillowcase and I'd come here. And then, by the time the sun went down, I couldn't remember what had made me want to leave in the first place. All I could think of was the dinner my mother was probably cooking, and the way my pillows sank down just the way I liked, and my favorite pair of pajamas. It was all those little things that reminded me of why I couldn't run away." She looks up at me. "I'm scared, Oliver. I'm scared the sun is going to go down and you're going to realize you want to go home."

I frame her face in my hands, looking into her eyes. "I *am* home," I tell her.

★ ★ ★

After supper, Delilah's mother pulls out a stack of photo albums. Delilah is mortified, her cheeks flaming, but I can't get enough of the pictures. I watch her morph from a tiny baby waving a pair of oversized sunglasses to a child on a swing to a young girl in a sunflower dress at her piano recital. Delilah's mother sits beside me, the dog curled at her feet. "Look, Lila," she says, turning the page to reveal a preteen, all angles and elbows, with a full mouth of metal. "Remember how we thought you were going to have your braces till you were thirty?"

At that, Delilah practically leaps over me, slamming the album closed. "Shut it down," she says.

"Kids grow up so fast," her mother says. "Edgar, I'm sure your mother would agree."

"Maybe not," I murmur under my breath. I've been a teen-ager my whole life.

Delilah's mom strokes the cover of the photo album as if she would rather give up her life than lose what's inside. It's exactly the way Delilah looked when she used to open the fairy tale. Her mother glances from Delilah to me. "One day you two will understand."

"Oh my *God*, Mom. *No.*" Delilah pulls her mother to her feet. "Don't you have a date to get ready for?"

The date in question is with Delilah's former psychiatrist, Dr. Ducharme. I would have expected Delilah to be less than pleased, but actually, she's overjoyed. Once they started dating, Delilah stopped having to go for appointments, because it was a conflict of interest.

Mrs. McPhee looks at her wristwatch. "You're right. Greg's going to be here in fifteen minutes. Delilah, help me with the dishes?"

Humphrey leaps to his stubby feet, waddling into the kitchen behind them in the hopes of catching a dropped scrap. Meanwhile, I carry the albums back to the shelf where Delilah's mother found them. As I return them to their spots, I notice one thin slice of an album labeled HALLOWEEN. Inside it, Delilah changes from a pumpkin to a gypsy queen, to a monkey, to a bunch of grapes.

On the next page, I pause.

Delilah is young—maybe six or seven. She is wearing a blue ball gown, long white gloves, and a jeweled tiara.

This is what she might have been like had we met as chil-dren in the middle of my world instead of hers.

With a grin, I slip the photograph out of its protective sleeve and into my pocket.

She would have made a lovely princess.

★ ★ ★

On Saturday, I run out of clothes.

Unlike in the fairy tale, where there's always a fresh tunic and hose whenever I need them, in this world one is left to one's own devices to ensure a clean wardrobe. For the first month or so, I didn't even notice the difference—Jessamyn would simply disappear with my hamper full of worn clothes and they would magically be returned, pressed and folded, to my bureau. But today, when I pull out the drawer, there's a single folded shirt. I check my closet and realize my dirty clothes are still in the hamper.

Perhaps Jessamyn has forgotten. I call out for my pseudo-mother, but there's no answer. Jessamyn told me she might go grocery shopping today—another extraordinary inconvenience in this world. In the book, our pantry is always full. But I'm not in the book. I'm not a prince. I have to learn to take care of myself. How hard could this possibly be?

Cheerfully I carry the hamper down the stairs into the laundry room, where I've watched Jessamyn go through the motions at least a dozen times. I know it involves pouring a liquid soap and pushing a series of buttons. I dump the tangle of laundry into the belly of the metal beast and pick up the bottle of detergent to read the directions.

FILL CUP.

What cup?

I wander into the kitchen and stare at the glasses we use at the dinner table. There are two sizes—a tiny one for juice, and a large one for water. *Well, the cleaner, the better,* I think, reaching for the larger glass. In the laundry room I fill it to the brim with blue detergent, then add an extra splash just to make sure I have enough. I close the lid and press the big green start button. The machine shakes to life, grumbling and gurgling as it fills with water.

I lean against it, awfully pleased with myself. Wait until I tell Delilah what I've done all on my own.

That's what I'm thinking, anyway, when the back of my shirt suddenly grows sopping wet. I spin around, my eyes widening at the washing machine, which is foaming at its mouth. It spews bubbles at an alarming rate, froth cascading to the floor. I try to scoop it up in my arms, hastily shoving as much as I can into the empty dryer, but I fail spectacularly to keep up. By now, my sneakers are hidden in a white sea, and the bubbles have leaked out of the small laundry room into the hallway.

I run to the phone, slipping and falling three times on the way. By the time I reach it, I am wearing a suit of bubbles, and I have trouble holding the receiver without it sliding from my palm. I wonder if perhaps I will be the first person to die by drowning in soap.

Delilah answers on the second ring. "Thank God," I say. "I'm having a crisis."

"What's wrong?" she asks.

"The washing machine has exploded."

"Wait," Delilah says. "What?"

"I tried to do my own laundry and—"

"I'll be right there," she interrupts.

The phone goes dead in my hand. I turn, looking toward the laundry room. A river of foam oozes from the doorway. I trudge through it, kicking at the bubbles, and climb on top of the machine, which bucks beneath me like a spirited stallion. Maybe if I can just keep the lid shut, the bubbles will diminish.

This is how Delilah finds me fifteen minutes later, huddled on top of the washing machine, clutching it for dear life.

"What the—" Before Delilah can finish, she slips in the bubbles and goes completely under. She surfaces with a white beard and hat. "Oliver," she says, laughing. "How much soap did you use?"

"It said a cup?"

"Was it the *Stanley* Cup?" she asks.

"I don't know Stanley, or his cup. It was a regular glass from the kitchen."

She puts a hand to her forehead, then reaches for the detergent, its blue bottle only dimly visible in the catastrophe of bubbles. She unscrews its tiny cap and holds it out to me. "*This is a cup, Oliver.*"

It holds roughly one-eighth the amount of soap I used.

Delilah breast-strokes forward, shoveling bubbles out of the way. She reaches past me for the illuminated panel and presses a button. The machine shudders to a stop. I let out a sigh of relief.

Delilah glares at me. "I cannot believe you did this."

I grin, scoop a dollop of bubbles onto my finger, and touch it to her nose.

She wipes it away, pretending to be annoyed, but then she lifts a handful of bubbles and palms my face with it. Laughing, we fight a war in a battlefield of soap, slipping out of each other's embrace as we tumble to the ground. Then I kiss her, or maybe she kisses me, until we're completely enveloped in a foam cocoon, and for a few moments, neither of us cares one bit about the mess.

Eventually, though, reality comes crowding in, when the taste of Delilah begins to morph into the bitter taste of detergent. I sit up, pulling her with me. "How do we get rid of all of . . . this?" I ask, gesturing at the foamy swamp that surrounds us.

Delilah rummages in the cleaning closet and returns with a blue bucket. She scoops an armful of bubbles inside and instructs me to go dump them in the bathtub upstairs. She does the same, using Jessamyn's spaghetti pot. We cart the evidence away one trip at a time, running cold water in the tub until the soap dissolves down the drain.

Finally we mop the floors and walls with a towel, leaving the house in an even tidier state than it was, ironically. Then we collapse onto the floor, exhausted. "I suppose I should be grateful you didn't start your independent streak by attempting to flambé baked Alaska," Delilah says.

Her hair is straggling out of her ponytail, and her shirt has started to dry stiffly against her skin. But despite the mess, she's still the most beautiful girl I've ever seen.

I cup my hand around the back of her neck, pulling her closer. "You know your pupils get bigger the closer you get to me. That means you love me."

"Or that you're blocking my light."

I laugh. "My girlfriend is such a romantic." Leaning forward, I start to kiss her, when suddenly the door clicks open and Jessamyn walks in holding two large grocery bags.

Delilah and I spring apart, putting a foot of space between us.

Jessamyn's brow furrows as she examines the two of us, still drenched and matted. "What on earth happened to you two?"

I offer my most brilliant smile. "We cleaned the house!"

★ ★ ★

A week of high school has taught me the following:

1. Packing one's own lunch is preferable to eating the questionable mass that is served in the cafeteria.
2. Nobody actually studies in study hall.
3. The same six boys in gym class play the game of the day as if their lives depend on it, no matter if the game is dodgeball or badminton.
4. Everyone has a phone, but no one ever seems to use it to make a phone call.
5. There is something called Facebook that is neither a face nor a book.

I've noticed that the school isn't divided by grades as much as it is by personality.

There are boys who insist on carrying their lacrosse sticks to each class as if it is a standard bearing the family crest. Some students take notes as though they are writing a novel, while others don't even pick up a pen but instead paint their nails and regard their features in the tiniest of mirrors while the teacher speaks. A roving gang of minstrels uses the school as a performing ground, riding wheeled boards down the staircase rails and hopping over concrete benches in the main entrance. There are some who look like creatures of the night, pale as the moon, with black hair and painted eyes and jewelry shaped like skulls. And then there are the girls I can't even look at without blushing—the ones who dress in so little clothing that I asked Delilah if they work at the local brothel.

Unlike the characters in the book, however, these different sorts of people don't seem to mix well. It is like the salad dressing Jessamyn makes: a little bit of olive oil, a squeeze of lemon, and some red wine vinegar. If whipped, they combine. But leave them to their own devices and they will sort themselves out again.

I don't really understand this. When you have so many people, each one inevitably fascinating, why would you limit yourself to only those like you? If I behaved as most of the students in this school do, I would never have talked to Charlie, who recruited me for the fencing team, or Darrell, who sells homemade sock puppets to raise money for children in Uganda, or Tina, who is having a baby this winter. I wouldn't have joined the drama club *and* the Ultimate Frisbee team *and* the Dungeons & Dragons society (though, truly, I was born for that). It doesn't matter to me if the person I'm speaking with is talking about comic books, or sales at Sephora, or how many touchdowns he made at the homecoming game. I just like listening.

I guess maybe because of that, it's easy for me to move between groups. Instead of feeling as if I'm being judged by someone different from me, I learn from them.

Today in pre-calc Mr. Elyk is explaining the standardized examination we will be taking on Saturday morning, a day we usually do not have to go to school, when I usually am with Delilah instead. The test has something to do with sitting and sounds relatively simple, since all we have to do is fully fill in the bubbles with a number two pencil. After the fifth time he repeats this, I begin to tune out, sketching mermaids and pirate ships in the margins of my notebook. Suddenly a pencil lands in front of me, and I look up. Raj, the skinny kid sitting to my left, holds up his calculator. Across the screen is a number:

58008

I lift a shoulder, shrugging.

Raj grins and spins his calculator so that the numbers are now upside down.

80085

"*Boobs,*" Raj mouths silently, and giggles.

I laugh out loud, and Mr. Elyk turns. "Edgar, is there something you'd like to share?"

I smile. "I'm super excited for this test, that's all."

He sighs. "I know, I know, everyone hates the SATs. But it's a necessary evil, like flossing and in-laws."

The bell rings, and I turn to Raj. "What else can you spell?"

"Tomorrow I'll show you how to draw a naked girl in Microsoft Word."

After math class, Delilah and I meet up at her locker. When she approaches, I've got my nose buried in my calculator. "You can take the guy out of the math classroom," she says, "but you can't take the math out of the guy."

I laugh and proudly present my calculator screen.

31770

"Let me guess. Your prison number?"

I put my hand over hers, twisting her wrist so that it's upside down.

OLLIE

"How cool is that?" I say proudly. "I can type my name in numbers."

Delilah smiles. "I see pre-calc is really paying off for you."

"Wait, I'm not done."

I take the calculator back and write BOOBS, then show it to her.

She rolls her eyes. "Ugh. You're acting like such a teenage boy."

"I am one," I say proudly. "Wasn't that exactly what you wanted?"

Delilah turns the calculator off and gives it back to me. "I should have listened to that genie," she replies. "Be careful what you wish for."

★ ★ ★

In the fairy tale, countless armies faced Pyro the dragon. Grown men shook in their armor, crying out for their mothers as the flames licked their shields. They pleaded with the heavens and sank to their knees, certain they had met their end of days.

The fear of these men was nothing compared to the faces of

the students surrounding me as Mr. Elyk begins to pass out the SAT Reasoning Test. A cheerleader sitting behind me is swallowing convulsively, as if her breakfast is about to come face to face with my back. Raj keeps checking the battery life on his calculator. Even Chris looks a little pale.

"I don't understand why everyone's panicking," I whisper to Chris. "All you have to do is color in the circles."

"It's not about how you color the circles. It's about finding the right answer to know which ones you color. Based on this test, I could wind up at Harvard or bagging groceries for the rest of my life."

"No more talking," Mr. Elyk says. "We're about to begin." He lifts up a piece of paper and begins to read from it, a litany of directions that has something to do with sections and time and point systems that sounds like gibberish to me. I stare at the grid of circles that will apparently decide my destiny.

"Now everyone break your seals," Mr. Elyk says, "and begin."

I do as he says, then look down at the first question in my booklet:

> For pumpkin carving, Mr. Smith will not use pumpkins that weigh less than 2 pounds or more than 10 pounds. If x represents the weight of a pumpkin, in pounds, he will not use, which of the following inequalities represents all possible values of x?
>
> a. $| x - 2 | > 10$
> b. $| x - 4 | > 6$

c. $|x - 5| > 5$
d. $|x - 6| > 4$
e. $|x - 10| > 4$

What the devil is wrong with a man who doesn't even know how to use a proper scale? If it keeps reading x, it's time to purchase a new one.

Clearly this is a trick question. So in response, I decide that the best use of my time is to fill in the circles in the way that will be most pleasing to the eye of the person who is grading it.

I must say, the picture I create is really a masterpiece. There's a silhouette of a fire-breathing dragon, and a swashbuckling prince holding his sword aloft.

"Put down your pencils," Mr. Elyk says. I glance at Raj. He seems to have forgotten how to blink.

"Now we will begin the next section," the teacher reads.

I pick up my pencil, delighted. I think this time, I'll draw a castle.

★ ★ ★

On Mondays during Activity Period, I drop Delilah off at the school library, where she works shelving books. We move through the halls holding hands, which seems rather tame when compared to couples like BrAngelo, who are basically mating as they navigate the building, blindly slamming into lockers and terrified freshmen.

The buzz that morning in school is still about the dreaded

SAT test. "It wasn't that bad," I tell Delilah. "I don't want to brag, but my dragon was rather creative."

"Is that a metaphor?"

"No. I drew a dragon. Literally."

She bursts out laughing. "The guidance counselors are going to have you committed." Delilah releases my hand and links her arm through mine instead, hugging me closer. "So I was thinking . . . you and I have never been on a real date."

"We've had supper with your mother."

"That does not even begin to count."

"Then what did you have in mind?" I ask.

"Well." Delilah looks up at me; it's like the sun coming out from behind a cloud. "I thought maybe—"

"Yo, Edgar," I hear, and I turn around to see the captain of the school hockey team passing by. He fist-bumps me over Delilah's head. "Hey, thanks for the help in English. I totally passed the test."

"Anytime!" I say, and turn back to Delilah. "You were saying?"

"I was thinking we could go out to a restaurant, like—"

Suddenly James appears in front of us. "You coming to Friday's meeting, Edgar?"

I nod. "Wouldn't miss it. I'm bringing the snack."

"Awesome," James says, and at the last minute, acknowledges Delilah. "Hey," he says, nodding before he walks past.

Delilah's grip tightens on my arm. "Anyway." She exhales. "I was thinking maybe you'd like to try Chinese food—"

"EDGAR!" A gaggle of girls surrounds me, pecking at me like chickens with their questions. *Did you do the history reading?*

Should I get a pixie cut? Can you show me how to throw a Frisbee sometime? Is it true that you went to camp with Harry Styles?

I can feel Delilah's nail dig into my skin. "Girls," I say. "I'll catch up with you later." Then I turn the full force of my charm on Delilah. "Where were we?"

"*I* was making dinner plans," she answers, her voice tight. "*You* were signing autographs."

I watch her turn into the library, completely confounded. The problem is that Delilah brought me into her world. But now it's mine too.

★ ★ ★

At Ms. Pingree's urging, I've joined the drama club. They meet during Activity Period as well, in the school auditorium. Every week, we act out scenes from different plays. Last Monday, it was Tennessee Williams. This time, it's Shakespeare.

I must admit, Shakespeare is a more comfortable fit for me.

"Now, *Romeo and Juliet* is something you all should be able to relate to: two teenagers who can't keep their hands off each other, even though circumstances are forcing them apart. Edgar," Ms. Pingree says, "would you like to take the reins as Romeo today?"

This is not a surprise. I'm the only male in the drama club. "It would be my greatest pleasure," I say, and Ms. Pingree's hand goes to her heart.

"Now. Who shall be our tragic Juliet?"

The hands of the fifteen girls in the room shoot up. "Claire, dear." Ms. Pingree points. "How about you?"

Claire has an upturned nose and a cloud of fuzzy red hair,

and she favors a sweatshirt with a sequined unicorn on the front. She rises, unable to make eye contact with me as she steps forward, giggling uncontrollably.

Before she can reach the stage, however, Allie McAndrews slaps her aside. "I'll take this one."

I reach toward Claire, trying to help her up, but I'm yanked away by Allie, who pulls me into the center of the stage with the brute force of an ogre. She tosses her shining hair and looks up at me from beneath her lashes. "You ready?"

I toss a sympathetic glance toward poor Claire, who is still attempting to get up from where Allie shoved her, and then clear my throat. "'If I profane with my unworthiest hand / This holy shrine,'" I say, "'the gentle fine is this: / My lips, two blushing pilgrims, ready stand / To smooth that rough touch with a tender kiss.'"

It figures. The most romantic scene in the most romantic play in all of literature, and my stage partner is Delilah's worst nightmare.

I draw in my breath. For years, I acted as if I truly were in love with Seraphima. This can't be any worse.

So I stare into Allie McAndrews's eyes, and I imagine Delilah's. I reach for Allie's hand, and I pretend I am holding on to the love of my life.

"'Good pilgrim, you do wrong your hand too much / . . . which manly—'"

"Mannerly!" Ms. Pingree interrupts.

"'Man . . . nerly,'" Allie repeats, "'devotion shows in this; / for saints have hands that pilgrims hands do touch . . .'"

I raise the flat of my hand and press hers against it.

"'And palm to palm,'" she says, transfixed, "'is holy palmers' kiss.'"

Stepping forward, I gently brush a strand of her hair away from her cheek. My voice drops to a whisper. "'Have not saints lips? And holy palmers too?'"

Allie stares at me. Gaping.

"Line!" I call out.

Ms. Pingree reads, "'Aye, Pilgrim . . .'"

"'Aye, Pilgrim,'" Allie parrots. "'Lips they must use in prayer.'"

I groan. "'O, then, dear saint, let lips do what hands do; / They pray, grant thou, lest faith turn to despair.'"

Her gaze is steady, luminous, hopeful. "'Saints do not move, though grant for prayers' sake.'"

I cup her face in my hands. "'Then move not,'" I murmur, "'while my prayer's effect I take.'"

I lean in, close my eyes, and kiss her.

As our lips meet, the seal of the auditorium door opens, admitting a slice of light that immediately draws my attention. Standing there is Delilah, looking as if I have crushed her.

She turns around while Allie is still in my arms, and starts to run.

"Delilah!" I cry, and I jump off the stage to race after her.

★ ★ ★

I chase Delilah past the gym, out the back doors of the school, and into the deserted student parking lot before I manage to grasp her arm. "Just let me explain," I say.

She rounds on me, furious. "No," Delilah says. "This isn't your book. You don't get to close it and start over."

"I was just reading lines. How is this any different from what I had to do every day with Seraphima, when I was part of the fairy tale?"

"Back then you had no choice. But this time, you could have said no." Her eyes well up. I realize, with a pang, that I've never made Delilah cry before. "How could you do this to me? And with *her*?"

"I didn't do anything to you. I was acting. She means nothing to me."

"That's not how it looked," Delilah argues. "It might as well have been real."

Frustration flares inside me, making heat rise in my cheeks. "That's the point of drama club."

She scoffs. "You know, I actually came to the auditorium because I felt bad about the way I treated you back at the library. But now I realize I have nothing to apologize for. Just go back to Allie. It's obviously where you want to be."

As much as I want to fix things with Delilah, I don't understand why I'm in the wrong. "For heaven's sake, Delilah, how many times do I have to say it? She's just a friend."

"She's a bitch. You just don't see it yet. She once told me that my new haircut made my face look less fat."

"That's a compliment!"

"I hadn't gotten a haircut!" Delilah says, her teeth clenched. "She spread a rumor about Jules being a hermaphrodite. When one of her own friends finished a treatment program for eating disorders, Allie told her she was pretty enough now to be a plus-size model."

"You're being just as judgmental as you claim Allie is," I point out. "Have you ever even tried to open up your friend circle beyond a single person, and get to know her? You might find she isn't the monster you make her out to be, if you'd just talk to her."

Delilah's eyes glitter with tears. "You weren't just talking," she whispers, and she walks away.

* * *

For the rest of the day, I keep replaying my fight with Delilah. I don't hear anything around me; I don't see anything in front of me. When I walk down the halls, even though they're crowded, they seem empty.

At home, when Jessamyn asks how my day went, I walk right past her and into my bedroom, shutting out the world.

This isn't the first time I've had troubles, but it is the first time I haven't had anyone to share them with. In the past, my confidants were Frump and Queen Maureen, but even if the fairy tale were in my possession and not Delilah's, I know I couldn't turn to them. They're happy, and my problems should no longer be theirs.

I fall asleep, tossing fitfully. My dreams are full of Delilah—the tears that made her eyes too bright, the way her voice shook. The expression on her face when I turned out not to be the person she'd hoped I would be.

In the book, it was so easy. I fell in love, I kissed the girl, she loved me back unconditionally. I've never had a script for an apology.

Suddenly I understand all the façades Frump put on, trying to win Seraphima's heart. I know what it feels like when being oneself isn't good enough.

I wish that someone would flip backward through the pages of the story of me and Delilah, bringing us back to the Once Upon a Time.

★ ★ ★

I wake with a start, the blankets tangled around my feet. My hair is damp with sweat, my fists curled in the sheets, and nothing has changed. Delilah is still farther away from me than she's ever been.

I have to make this right. I swing my legs over the edge of the bed, then sit down in front of the computer. There is a little green circle next to Delilah's name. I quickly click CALL, waiting for her face to fill the screen.

Instead, a box pops up. CALL ENDED.

Before I can try again, the little circle next to Delilah's name disappears.

I bury my face in my hands. What's the point of being in this world without her?

All right, I think. *Pull yourself together, Oliver.* It's perfectly normal to feel overwhelmed. This is a problem I've never encountered before—it has nothing to do with getting out of the pages of a book or seeing letters appear in midair or bleeding ink. For once it is a completely ordinary problem that could affect any teenage boy who quarreled with his girlfriend. Which means that maybe I'm not alone after all.

The house is dark, although it is only eight p.m. Jessamyn has left dinner for me on the kitchen counter, but I am not hungry. I pad upstairs again and pause outside her bedroom. Slowly I open the door, fearing she may already be asleep.

Jessamyn is perched on the edge of her bed. When she hears the door creak, she whips around, wiping her eyes.

It takes me aback. I've been so wrapped up in my own problems that I never stopped to consider I might not be the only one who is struggling.

"Are . . . are you all right?"

"I'm fine. I just have a bad headache, that's all." She fakes a smile. "Did you need something?"

"No, no. You're ill. I'll leave you be."

I don't know Jessamyn Jacobs very well. But in that moment, she looks very small, and very tired. "Good night, Edgar," she says.

"Good night . . . Mom." I start to pull the door closed behind me, and at the last moment duck back inside. "Try leeches," I suggest helpfully. "They work wonders for me."

★ ★ ★

"Dude . . . what's up with you?" Chris asks me. "You've been staring at that beaker for, like, fifteen minutes."

"Delilah and I had quite an argument yesterday," I say solemnly, measuring out hydrochloric acid. We have been left to our own devices to complete the day's chemistry lab. I'm trying to follow directions to the letter, because I'm so distracted I fear I may accidentally cause an explosion.

Delilah wasn't waiting for me today when I arrived at school. She wasn't at my locker.

Chris hands me an eyedropper. "Girls go crazy. It's just what they do. Give her a couple of days to chill, and she'll forgive you for whatever you did." He glances at me. "What was it, anyway?"

"I kissed Allie McAndrews."

Chris winces. "Bro, Delilah's not coming back to you."

"Thank you so much for the support," I mutter.

"Well, damn, what were you thinking?"

"We were role-playing," I explain.

"Call it whatever you want," Chris says, smirking.

"It was for the drama club. Delilah walked in at the worst possible moment."

He shakes his head. "I don't know what to tell you, man. From her point of view, it doesn't look good."

I pass him the evaporating dish so he can hold it over the Bunsen burner. "I'd do anything to take it back."

"Well, unless you have a time machine, that's not gonna happen," Chris says. "What you need is a grand gesture. Something that makes her completely forget what she saw."

"I don't understand."

"I'm talking going all out. Flowers. Get down on one knee. Confess your love. Haven't you ever seen *The Notebook*?"

I look at him, dubious. "That sort of thing really works?"

"Chicks eat it up," Chris assures me.

The evaporating dish cools, leaving behind pure white crystals, tiny diamonds. It is remarkable to think that something so beautiful was born from acid.

Maybe Chris is right.

Maybe there's still hope for me.

I just wish there were a recipe I could follow that would make it easier.

★ ★ ★

"What's wrong?" Jessamyn asks that evening, when we are sitting at dinner.

"Nothing," I say, using my fork to push around the peas on my plate.

"Well, you're not eating. Or at least, you're not eating as much as usual. . . ."

I put down my utensils. "Did you ever fight with . . . Dad?" I ask.

"No," Jessamyn answers, straight-faced. "We were Barbie and Ken." Before I can even ask who on earth *they* are, she continues. "Of *course* we fought, honey. All couples argue. If you're in a relationship and you're not fighting, you're probably doing something wrong."

"Delilah saw me kissing another girl," I blurt out.

She chokes on her sip of water. "Excuse me? Is one girl not enough?"

"It isn't what you think," I explain. "It was part of a play."

"I might have to take her side on this one. . . ."

I rest my head in my hands. "I'd apologize, but she won't even give me a chance to speak."

Jessamyn's gaze softens. "Once, I bought a brand-new pair of designer heels. I had them in a bag outside my closet door. When I came back that night before bedtime, the shoes had disappeared. I asked your father if he'd seen them and he said, 'Oh, you mean the stuff you put out for Goodwill?' He'd accidentally donated a pair of Jimmy Choos to charity." She shakes her head, lost in the memory. "I didn't speak to him for a week."

"Then what happened?"

She grins. "He bought me an even more expensive pair."

"I don't think shoes will work here," I say glumly.

"It's not about the shoes," Jessamyn replies. "It's about what the shoes represent. A simple *I'm sorry* can go a long way."

"If she ever listens to me again . . ."

"Give her time. She'll hear you out."

"But it hurts me to know I can't fix this."

"Well," Jessamyn says, "imagine how much it hurt *her* to see you with someone else."

I glance up. "I guess you're right."

"Of course I'm right; I'm your mother." She blots her mouth with her napkin. "I'm just glad you're speaking to me. I'm used to you grunting through dinner."

My mouth quirks upward. "Thanks, Mom."

"You're welcome, Joseph."

"Joseph?" I repeat.

It's Edgar's father's name. I've seen photos of him, with his name and a date scrawled on the back. He looks exactly like King Maurice.

Jessamyn presses her fingers against her temples. "Oh my

God. I'm getting so old." She smiles at me. "Give it a day. You two will be all over each other."

I wince. "God, Mom!"

She laughs. "Now, there's the Edgar I know and love."

At least *someone* does.

*   *   *

I have planned it to perfection.

With Ms. Pingree's permission, I have raided the drama club costume closet, picking out an ill-fitted yet passable prince's tunic, crown, and boots. A plastic sword is strapped to my side. I sneak into the biology class greenhouse with a pair of art room scissors and cut the stems of a dozen tulips, gathering them into a bouquet before a teacher can catch me in the act. Then I stride proudly into the cafeteria, my gaze narrowing like a beam on Delilah.

I can feel the entire room watching me, and their whispers are cobwebs I easily brush aside. I march to her table, fall to my knee, and present her with the flowers. "Milady," I say, "your eyes are but twin stars in my universe. Your voice is sweeter than a robin's song. You are the very beat of my heart; the rush of my blood."

I believe I'm doing quite well. The cafeteria has begun cheering me on, and two spots of color appear on Delilah's cheeks. Chris was correct; I am surely going to win back Delilah. After all, what girl doesn't want a knight in shining armor?

"ED-GAR! ED-GAR! ED-GAR!" My borrowed name echoes in the room.

Those two roses blooming on Delilah's cheeks have somehow spread, making her entire face as red as a lobster. She
doesn't meet my eye, and if I'm not mistaken, she seems to be
sinking farther and farther under the table.

She still hasn't taken the bouquet. I shake it a little, still on
bended knee, and clear my throat. "You're the breath in my
lungs. You're—"

"Done," says Jules, appearing out of nowhere to yank me
upright by my velvet collar. "Get your royal ass away from my
best friend."

She tugs at my tunic, spins me around, and shoves me toward
the cafeteria door. It's all I can do not to stumble. The voices
of other students follow me out: *Nice try, man. Better luck next
time. I would have said yes!*

I realize that I'm still holding the flowers. And that they've
already begun to die.

★ ★ ★

Slumped against my locker, I'm trying to understand how I've
managed to make things even worse than they were. "What
you need," Raj says, "is to wow her with your intellect. You
know what they say is the largest and most powerful sex organ
in the body, right?" He taps his skull. "The brain."

"I don't think Delilah wants me to say one more word, Raj."

"Listen. You walk up to her and you say: 'Are you made
of nickle, cerium, arsenic, and sulfur? Cuz you've got a NiCe
AsS.'" When I stare at him blankly, he says, "Get it? The chem-
ical symbols? They spell out . . . Oh, never mind."

I turn to him. "Have you ever had a girlfriend quarrel with you?"

Raj shrugs. "Well, I mean, like, obviously, there've been women. . . ."

"Have you ever had a *girlfriend*?"

"I'm not entirely sure," he says. "In sixth-grade gym, I *did* fall off the ropes course and land on top of Charlotte Tazinkski and technically my lips grazed her mouth." He looks at me. "Does that count?"

"No, Raj," I sigh. "Not even a little."

I drop my head into my hands, closing my eyes, which is why I don't see Allie approach. She crouches down and lifts my chin with one finger, giving my costume a full once-over before she speaks. "I see I'm not the only one who can't wait for drama club," she purrs.

I push her away. "No, Allie. In fact, I think I'm quitting. I'm going to join the football team or something, where I'm less likely to encounter the opposite sex."

She smiles at me. "You can't tell me that was all just for show, Edgar. I felt something. I know you felt it too."

"Honestly, I'm just a good actor," I say. "I'm with Delilah. I'm sorry if I did or said anything that made you think otherwise."

Her eyes flash, reminding me of the mermaids. "Really," she says, her voice cooling. "You'd choose *that* over *this*?" She stands up, skimming her hand over her waist. "I took pity on you, because you were the new kid," Allie continues. "But hey, if you want to socially exile yourself, be my guest."

She walks away, hips swinging, her heels staccato on the tile floor.

It takes me a moment to remember that Raj is still sitting beside me. His jaw is practically hitting the ground. "Did you just break up with Allie?" he manages. "Are you an idiot?"

★ ★ ★

James calls my name at the end of the LGBT Alliance meeting. "Your Oreos were a hit," he says. "There's only crumbs left."

"Thanks," I say, distracted. Ever since my run-in with Allie, I've been trying to figure out how and when I can get Delilah alone for a minute, so that I can make a full apology before Jules tosses me down a flight of stairs.

"So rumor has it you went full Romeo in the cafeteria today," James says. "What's up with that?"

"I was told that a grand gesture is the way to a woman's heart."

"There's such a thing as *too* grand," James says. "You might want to take it down a notch."

What was I thinking? Delilah's not one for a show. The happiest hours we spent together were just the two of us, talking through the book. "Well, I probably won't even get a chance," I mutter. "I'm pretty sure she doesn't want to speak to me."

"Aren't you the one who told me you believe nothing should stand in the way of two people in love? What's in your way?"

I look up at James as understanding dawns. "Me."

"Maybe instead of pretending to be someone you're not, you should just be yourself," James says. "After all, isn't that who she fell for in the first place?"

The fog in my head finally clears. I understand what I've

been doing wrong. James is correct—but it wasn't just the cafeteria scene that was an act. I've been playing a role the whole time I've been here.

I don't know how to apologize like a teenage boy who's gotten into a fight with his girlfriend. I don't know how to figure out who's friend and who's foe. I don't understand the social conventions of high school.

But I'm an expert at happily-ever-after.

DELILAH

I'd rather be in Siberia right now, losing all my extremities to frostbite. Or talking to my pet cockroach in a maximum-security prison. Or sweating buckets in hell. I'd rather be anywhere but in the school cafeteria with everyone laughing at me.

I feel my face catching fire. If only it were a real fire, so I could disappear into ash.

Jules, my volunteer personal bodyguard, stands with her hands on her hips, ready to body-check any soul who dares to come close to me. Not that anyone is trying. They're all applauding for Oliver as he and his ridiculous knight's getup slink away.

"All he's ever done is act," Jules points out. "Maybe he wasn't expressly trying to humiliate you."

"Aren't you my best friend?" I ask. "Whose side are you on?"

"Obviously yours. All I'm saying is maybe you should cut him a little slack. He's been in high school for what, a week? It takes freshmen two whole years before they know what the hell is going on."

I look at her. "He kissed the one girl in this school who would dance on my grave. No, actually, she would plan a schoolwide dance on my grave."

"Well, you've at least gotta give him points for creativity," Jules says.

Oliver used to be creative, back when he was in the book. He had a new idea every time I opened the fairy tale, some crazy scheme about how to get off the page to be with me. But things were different back then.

He was different back then.

I thought, when Oliver was in the fairy tale, that he understood me better than anyone else. I got used to him being pages away. But having him physically and wholly with me is something I was not prepared for. Sensing that he's come into a room before I even turned around to see him. The way his skin always smells like the inky freshness of a new book. The heat of his breath falling into my ear when he whispers my name. If Oliver in the book was captivating, then Oliver in 3-D is completely overwhelming.

Who would have thought that having your dreams come true would suck so much? I mean, I should be happier than I've ever been. For the first time in my life, the guy I like actually likes me back, and he isn't imaginary. Yet that perfect prince, who used to be all mine, now has to be shared with the entire world. And I guess it should be no surprise that everyone adores Oliver, just like I did. But that doesn't mean it doesn't hurt me to see it happen.

In the few weeks Oliver's been in school, I've actually noticed a couple of freshmen starting to imitate his style—classic jeans, solid T-shirt, leather satchel. In the hallways, kids hang on his every word. Girls go out of their way to "accidentally" bump into him. I know he didn't *mean* to be popular—to have everyone string along behind him like the tail of a kite. In fact, I thought that the quirks of being a fairy-tale character dumped into reality would kind of make him an automatic outsider, like me. But that would be okay, because we would have each other.

Instead, he's the Zac Efron of our school, and I'm still absolutely nobody.

Oliver doesn't understand, because he hasn't been in public school as long as I have. He thinks life is like Disney World, with magic around every corner. He doesn't realize that the longer he hangs out with the cool kids, the harder it's going to be to stay with me.

Not that I've really encouraged him to do that, lately.

I'd heard before that love can turn you into someone else . . . but I never imagined that *this* is who I'd be: a jealous monster. *I* don't like who I've become. So why should *he*?

It's hard enough watching other people want a piece of him—a smile, a conversation, a high five—when he used to be just mine. I can't shake the feeling that if he keeps giving away these pieces, eventually there will be nothing left for me. And then, when I walked into the auditorium and saw him kissing Allie McAndrews, terror flooded me in a way I've never experienced before. It was like being in a car, the moment you realized the crash is happening. Like being tossed off a boat into shark-infested water, only to discover you're paralyzed. No matter how much he assures me that the kiss meant nothing, that he was only acting, how can I trust him? How can I know that he wasn't also acting when he said that to me?

Oliver comes from a place where there is only one person he was meant to be with. Literally, there is only one human girl his age in the book—Seraphima. He has only loved one girl because there was never an alternative. But I can't help feeling that this kiss made him realize I'm not his only option.

Because if you hold me up against Allie McAndrews, I lose. Every time.

I am doing my best to only make eye contact with the condiments on the table, but from the corner of my eye, I see Allie walking toward me, her entourage in tow. They hang off her like ornaments, the decorations that turn a plain old spruce into a Christmas tree. I square my shoulders, trying to remind myself that without her followers, a mean girl is just a mean girl.

She sidles up to my table in a cloud of Chanel perfume and confidence. "Oh no, Allie," Jules says. "Did someone leave your cage open?"

She slices a look toward Jules that could cut steel, then turns to me. "Hey, Deborah," she says.

"It's Delilah." Really? She doesn't know my name, after I broke her knee *and* her nose? I honestly can't tell if Allie's being intentionally mean or if she's truly just that stupid.

She smiles, revealing a row of perfect teeth. She probably chews Crest Whitestrips like gum. "So I totally had a nightmare last night," Allie says. "I dreamed I was *you*." She laughs, and the sound echoes through her posse.

Jules looks at her with pity. "It's scary to think people like you are allowed to breed."

Allie ignores her. Her gaze is a laser on my face. "Your boyfriend's a great kisser," she says sweetly.

"That's it," Jules says, getting to her feet. "Piss off, Allie."

Allie glances around, looking at everything but Jules. "Do you hear that?" she replies. "It's the sound of no one caring."

She and her army strut out of the cafeteria as if their exit has been choreographed.

"Don't listen to her," Jules says, hunkering down beside me again. "She's irrelevant."

I nod and try to smile at her. But deep down, I'm afraid that Allie is right. No one cares.

Not even Oliver.

★ ★ ★

I will never forget the morning Oliver first got out of the book—when we realized that we were together but not two-dimensional or trapped in a fairy tale. We sat on Jessamyn Jacobs's porch steps in Wellfleet, and Oliver held on to my hand like a child grabs the string of a balloon, afraid that letting go meant I might just float away. We truly believed that we had been through the worst—that the struggle of getting Oliver out of the book was no match for any obstacle we would face in the future. It didn't matter that Jessamyn lived in Wellfleet and I lived two hundred miles away in New Hampshire. It didn't matter that Oliver had to pretend that he had been Edgar Jacobs for his entire life. It didn't matter that my mother was going to ground me for eternity, because I ran away. None of it mattered, as long as we could sit on that porch step and hold tight to each other.

He felt the same way, back then.

One of the first snafus we discovered when Oliver moved here was realizing that Edgar had his driver's license and Oliver didn't even know what a car *was*. We couldn't very well stick Oliver behind a wheel without it ending catastrophically—but we also couldn't have Jessamyn ask him to drive to the grocery store and wonder why he refused. So we decided he would tell Jessamyn that he was now a tree-hugger out to single-handedly save the planet, intent on reducing his own personal carbon emissions. It was left to me to teach him how to ride a bike.

First I lowered the seat so that Oliver's feet could brush the ground. "Sit," I told him. "Don't put your feet on the pedals. Just push around a little bit."

Oliver wouldn't take his eyes off the pavement. "You know, horses are easier," he muttered. "They balance themselves."

"I would have started with a tricycle, but unfortunately they don't make them in your size." I waited until he met my gaze. "Just trust me, okay?"

Eventually Oliver began to push off the ground a little harder, gliding for moments in between. I ran alongside him, but he wouldn't let me step away, and we couldn't go more than ten feet before he tipped off the bicycle, falling into my arms.

"I don't get it," I said, laughing, after this happened fifteen times in a row. "You climbed towers. You leaped through pages. Why can't you *do* this?"

He shook his head, his eyes sliding away from mine. "I don't know. . . ."

"Try again," I urged. "But this time, I'm going to let go."

He climbed on the bike, took a few wobbly pedals forward, and, seemingly defying gravity, tumbled off the bike. Oliver knocked me flat on the ground, landing heavily on top of me. His shoulders were shaking, his face buried in my neck.

I pushed him off me, trying to see if he was hurt. "Are you all right?"

But when Oliver rolled over, he was laughing so hard he couldn't catch his breath. "I'm sorry. I couldn't resist. I figured it out the first time. But you're so cute when you're frustrated."

Back then, it seemed like I could never be mad at him. When did we fall out of the honeymoon phase?

I lie on my bed, staring up at the ceiling, with Humphrey snuggled against my side. My mom says that even though the dog was a gift for her, he might as well belong to me. He stays on my bed most of the day when I'm at school, loving me unconditionally.

At least *someone* does.

Only days ago I was lying right here, wrapped in Oliver's arms, when a message appeared. When he took the book from my shelf and opened it, my blood froze in my veins. What if all it took to suck him out of this world was one reminder of who he used to be? What if just opening the pages meant saying goodbye?

But none of the characters admitted to writing that desperate plea.

The thing is, someone *did*.

Oliver knows that. But he chose to ignore the fact that there's someone in the book who really needs him.

Is it because he's afraid he might have to trade his freedom and go back to the story? And if he *is* afraid, is it because he doesn't want to leave me . . . or because he doesn't want to leave *here*?

It just seems strange that after we saw that message, he didn't dwell on it. After all, it wasn't all that long ago that he sent a similar, desperate message to me.

I can't shake the feeling that maybe he was just using me; that I was a hand to pull him up, a means to an end. What if he only acted like I was important to him because I was his way out of the book, and now that he's here, I'm expendable?

There's that word, *acted,* again.

My throat tightens. Am I really so desperate to be loved that I can be played that easily?

I wish I'd never met Oliver. Because then I wouldn't know how much I'm missing now.

There's a chime from the laptop on my desk, and the screen glows to life. A graphic of a ringing phone appears, and a name beneath it: PRINCE CHARMING.

I'm the one who gave him that Skype name.

Rolling onto my side, I reach for the keyboard and decline the call. I doubt there's anything Oliver can say that will make me feel better. And I don't know what I would say to him right now. It seems like the more miserable I get, the more I lash out at him, and that certainly isn't going to make him want to stay with me any longer.

In fact, knowing me, I've probably screwed this up so badly that it's already over.

I may be mad at Oliver, but I'm even angrier at myself.

I curl into a ball, hugging my knees close to my chest, sobbing. It's not a pretty cry; I'm practically triple-tearing, secreting from my eyes, nose, *and* mouth all at once. Not to be outdone, Humphrey howls too.

The door bursts open, and my mother rushes to my side, grasping my shoulders. "What's the matter?" Her voice feels like a rush of cold water. "Are you sick? Does something hurt?"

I curl into her arms, like I did when I was little and thought a thunderstorm was a monster running toward my bedroom, snapping trees with every step. My face is hot and swollen. "I think I messed up."

"Do you need help hiding the body?" my mother asks.

I pull away from her and look at her face. "What? No."

"Then it's nothing that can't be fixed." She smooths my hair. "Does this have something to do with a certain guy who's been hanging around here a lot?"

"We got in a huge fight. And then he tried to make things better and I basically blew him off because I'm the world's biggest idiot and now I'm going to be the world's biggest *single* idiot."

My mom's arms tighten around me. "Being single isn't a fatal disaster."

"That's easy for you to say. You have Greg."

"For a lot of years, I didn't. I just had you. And that was enough."

"That is so sad," I wail, throwing myself face-forward into a pillow. "I'm going to be that kid who takes her own mother to prom."

"Somehow I doubt that," my mother says. "There are going to be plenty of other guys in your life before you find The One."

"I don't want any other guys. I want Ol—" I catch myself. "I want Edgar."

My mother draws away from me, serious. "Delilah," she asks, "do you love him?"

Is love really this hard?

Is it needing to be with someone so much that you can't breathe when you're not? Is it wanting to kill someone for making you feel like dying when he looks at another girl? Is it wishing to be with him every minute, but knowing it's too much to ask?

Is it handing someone your heart to hold, knowing you're also giving him the power to crush it?

A fresh wash of tears flows over my cheeks. "What difference does it make? I'm probably never going to see him again."

"You know," my mother says, glancing past me, "I wouldn't be so sure of that."

She gets up from the bed, calling Humphrey to her side, and I roll over to see Oliver standing in the doorway. "I knocked, but no one answered . . . so I let myself in," Oliver says. "Is this a bad time?"

"It's the perfect time," my mother says, and she leaves my room. After a tiny hesitation, she grabs the doorknob and pulls the door shut.

I sit up and open my mouth, but Oliver raises his hand to stop me. "Don't speak," he says. He walks toward the bed, stopping a foot away. "You've been trying to turn me into a high school student, but when I act like one, everything falls apart. That's because I'm *not* a high school student. I'm a prince. It's what I've always been, and no matter what world I'm living in, it's what I'll always be. I understand things feel wrong between us right now. But you and I, we're not broken."

He takes one small step toward me. "I know what this is. This is where I slay the dragon so I can climb the tower, kill the villain, and risk my life to be with you. This is the tough spot. This is the bit that keeps you on the edge of your seat so you can get to the good part, where you can finally let go of the breath you didn't even realize you were holding." A muscle works in his throat as he swallows, but he doesn't move an inch. "This isn't the end for us. This isn't how fairy tales finish."

"If it's not the end," I ask, "then what is it?"

He reaches for my hands and tugs me to my feet. "This is the part where I look you in the eyes," Oliver says, his gaze locked on me, "take you in my arms . . ." He pulls me against his chest. ". . . and say: Delilah McPhee, I love you."

His mouth closes over mine, stealing my breath and all of my doubt. His hands tangle in my hair and anchor my lips against his. I sink into him, as if the heat from his body is melting mine.

This isn't just any kiss. This is the shooting-star, fireworks-finale, earth-shattering kiss that makes time stand still, so that we are spinning inside a universe made for two.

This is what love is: never wanting to give up.

I pull away just far enough for a promise to fit between us. "Oliver," I say, "I love you too."

How come love sounds so violent?

You fall head over heels.

You're struck by Cupid's arrow.

You take the risk of having your heart broken.

From an outside perspective, it sounds impossibly painful, not worth the trouble. And yet we do it every day. We keep coming back for more.

Why?

If it weren't so perilous, maybe we wouldn't crave it so much.

Maybe it has to be brutal, in order to work. People come in so many shapes and sizes that it takes a bit of force in order to fit together perfectly.

But you know what they say about a break that heals: it's always stronger than before.

EDGAR

I didn't notice the first time I saw it, but now I realize Orville's cottage is familiar.

It's almost an exact replica of a cabin my mom and I rented one summer in Maine. There was no electricity, and a spider the size of my fist lived in the shower with us the entire week we were there because neither one of us wanted to touch it. The splintered wood of Orville's door has a knot in the middle that kind of resembles Gandhi, just like the door in Maine. And like the roof of that cabin, Orville's roof sags a little on the left side, possibly about to fall right in.

I think of them as déjà vus, these hidden details of my mom's life that she's sprinkled through the fairy tale. I have to admit—I kind of like seeing them. It's like when she used to put notes in my lunch box, just to let me know she was still thinking of me when she wasn't there.

I'm just leaving the page with Orville's home and crossing

onto the beach, when suddenly Socks gallops into sight and comes to a halt in front of me.

"This is a disaster!" he wails. "This is catastrophic. The world might as well be ending."

Without even glancing at him, I say, "You look fine, Socks." I'm used to these dramatic displays of low self-esteem from the horse, when he is reduced to Jell-O by the appearance of a non-existent wrinkle or a dimple of cellulite.

"I'm not talking about *me*," Socks scoffs. "Jeez, do you really think I'd be *so* self-centered?" He pauses. "Wait—are people saying that about me?"

"I don't have time for this," I tell him. "Where's Frump? Everyone's here waiting for him."

Everyone is gathered on the beach once again for our morning run-down—except our ringleader is a no-show.

Socks rolls his eyes. "That's exactly what I've been trying to tell you. Frump won't leave his doghouse. I suppose I *may* know a thing or two about locking yourself in your barn stall because of an issue with your appearance . . ."

Captain Crabbe sidles closer to us. "Beg pardon for eavesdropping, but if it's fleas again, I'd ask the mermaids to whip up a lovely kelp salt scrub before you release him back into the public."

Socks sighs. "It's going to take more than a spa remedy to fix this."

I exhale heavily. "All right. Where is he?"

"Excuse me?" I turn when I feel a tap on my shoulder. Queen Maureen smiles apologetically. "Sorry to bother you, dear. But is there any chance my fellow characters and I might get a little update? It's awfully hot to sit in this galactic armor, and people are getting a wee bit antsy."

I hop up onto the stump that Frump uses to address the cast. "Ladies and gentlemen . . . and, uh, trolls. We're experiencing some technical difficulties. Please stand by." With that, I leap down and climb onto Socks's back. "Let's get this over with," I say.

Behind the castle are the royal stables and pens for the peacocks, as well as the dovecote used during the wedding on the final page of the fairy tale, where the birds rested up between readings. Tucked against the rear door of the kitchens is a tiny purple structure with white trim, a miniature Victorian house complete with shutters and flower boxes. The only element that hints at its original use as a doghouse is the swinging flap it has as a door.

When I first came into the book, Queen Maureen offered to give Frump his own bedroom in the castle. After all, he's human now. He stayed a couple of nights, moving from the mattress to the floor, and finally decided he got a better night's rest in his own home.

"Frump," I call, knocking on the wall of the doghouse. "What's wrong?"

"Don't come in, Edgar," he yells. "I just need to be alone right now."

"I can't help you with your problem if you don't tell me what it is."

Frump hesitates. "Things are getting a little hairy."

I glance at Socks, who shrugs. If a horse can really shrug,

that is. "It's okay. I'll help you delegate so you don't feel over-whelmed. Just come out here and let's talk."

There's a rustle of plastic as the dog door opens, and Frump crawls out and gets to his feet. His arms are furry; his face is covered with a beard and muttonchops.

"No, literally," he says, crestfallen. "Things are getting a lit-tle hairy."

Socks gasps. "Holy Abraham Lincoln."

"The tail . . . ?" I ask hopefully.

"Still there."

I digest this information. "This is fixable!" I pronounce. "We can handle this!"

Socks leans forward and drops his voice to a whisper. "Glint the fairy gives the smoothest Brazilian wax." He averts his eyes. "Not that I'm speaking from personal experience or anything."

"Look at the bright side," I suggest. "Your ears haven't grown in."

"Give it a day," Frump says, glum.

"Listen, you have nothing to be embarrassed about, and no one's going to say anything to you. You're among friends," I tell him.

Frump shakes his head. "I don't want her to see me like this."

Socks bursts into tears. "This is the most ill-fated love affair ever. It's like Cleopatra and Mark Antony. Pyramus and Thisbe. Beauty and the Beast."

I grit my teeth. "You're *not* helping, Socks. Pull yourself to-gether, and go tell Orville to meet us in his cottage."

Socks sniffles. "Okay." He trots off, his head still hanging.

I put my hand on Frump's shoulder. "You know, she's already seen you as a dog."

"But she never noticed me until I was human," Frump laments. "I can't go back to being invisible to her."

"You won't have to," I promise. "I'll make sure of it."

Frump scratches behind his ear. "I know Oliver left some pretty big boots to fill. But . . . you're a good friend, Edgar."

Before I came into the book, I was more likely to be found alone in my room with a video game controller than in the company of another human. The closest I've come to having friends is playing the avatars of strangers in online battles. Having someone who doesn't just want to hang out with me but seeks me out for help—and believes I can actually make a difference— well, that's something I've never experienced before. It makes me want to do everything I can not to disappoint him.

"You're a good friend too, Frump," I reply, and I wonder if he realizes that I need him as much as he needs me.

★ ★ ★

As it turns out, I never get to Orville's cabin. I'm halfway there when suddenly the book is vigorously ripped open, and I find myself somersaulting through the pages until I land in a heap on Everafter Beach with a mouth full of sand. All the characters are there, of course, because the book has been opened, but I notice that Frump is hiding behind a giant rock and is wrapped head to toe in one of Rapscullio's goth cloaks. Brushing myself off, I look up at the watery film at the top of the page to see Oliver and Delilah looming over us.

"I'm still getting used to this," I say with a scowl. "You could be a little bit gentler."

Oliver looks furious. "Well, you could perhaps stop interrupting us every time we start to—"

"Oliver!" Delilah cuts him off. She shakes her head just the tiniest bit, trying to shut him up. "We got another message."

She tips the book again, and the world spins. "For God's sake," I mutter. "Some of us are still getting over our whiplash. . . ."

Delilah's room comes into full view, panning past a dog sprawled on her quilt who looks like a distant relative of Frump. Suspended in the space above her bed is a string of bobbing letters: I NEED YOU.

The book is wrenched back around and Oliver glares down at us, gripping the pages so tightly the world bends in at the corners. "Which one of you is responsible?" he challenges, his voice ringing over the beach.

Everyone looks around awkwardly, waiting for someone to fess up. Curiosity spreads like a fever. Could it have been Frump, hoping his friend could save him from falling back to a four-legged existence? Or Seraphima, missing her (fake) true love? Could this be Captain Crabbe's reminder of an annual dental checkup? Queen Maureen, pining for her fictional son? Or Rapscullio himself, accidentally pouring out his secret wish on the wrong canvas?

If you want to get technical about it, everyone on this beach has a reason to want Oliver to return.

I round on the cast, stepping up. "Well? Who is it? Which one of you keeps sending these messages?"

I'm greeted by silence.

"Fine," Oliver snaps. "If no one's going to admit to this, I'm going to figure it out for myself. Edgar, Rapscullio? Meet me on page six."

This time I get a running start, breaking through the pages like a ghost walking through walls, as Oliver and Delilah flip backward through the book. Breathless, I land heavily in Rapscullio's lair, knocking over a stack of canvases. Every single one is painted with Queen Maureen's face. I look at Rapscullio. "Dude, that's creepy."

Rapscullio shrugs. "Don't blame me. I was written that way."

The lair is a dark, narrow cave lit by tallow candles. Spiders hide in the crevices of the walls, and rats scatter across the floor like moving shadows. Everything seems a little bit damp, and there's a faint, incessant dripping sound coming from the stalactites.

While we wait for Rapscullio to locate the easel, I look up at Oliver. "So how's my mom?" I ask.

"She's an excellent cook," Oliver says brightly.

"No," I repeat. "I mean . . . *how's my mom?*"

"She seems to get tired often."

I shrug. "She's always tired. If she doesn't have five cups of coffee a day, you're living with an imposter."

Suddenly Rapscullio interrupts, placing the magic easel front and center. It's painted with a background that matches Delilah's bedroom. The same message Oliver showed us is scrawled in its center.

Rapscullio lifts the canvas off its frame. He shakes it like it's an Etch A Sketch he's trying to clear, but nothing happens. "Hmm," he muses. "Something's not quite right."

He settles the canvas back on the easel, takes a paintbrush, dips it in turpentine, and traces over the letters. One at a time, each loop and line vanishes.

"Is it gone?" I ask, looking up at Oliver.

He looks away from the book, his chin raised. "Yes," he says, sighing with relief. "But that doesn't answer the question of who wrote it in the first place. Someone in the book needs help, and I can't be expected to live with one foot in each world. These are your people now, Edgar. You're supposed to be keeping track of them."

My face flushes with anger. When Frump asked for my help, I thought I was finally getting somewhere . . . that I was becoming a real part of this community. But the fact that Oliver has found another message means I may have taken one step forward but three steps back. I mean, he of all people should know how hard it is to be inside this book. I don't really need him giving me lectures on responsibility, after all I've done for him.

"Really? These are *my* people? Why don't you tell them that? Then maybe they'll stop writing to *you* for help."

Oliver leans into the book, shouting. "Don't blame me just because you don't have the skill it takes to be a main character—"

"Stop it, you two," Delilah scolds. "You can both stop measuring your egos."

"Erm." Rapscullio clears his throat. "I think you need to see this."

I follow his gaze to the easel. Without a paintbrush or a pen, or any visible artist, the letters are tracing themselves onto the canvas: I NEED YOU.

I turn to Rapscullio. "Are you doing that? Is it magic?"

"I'm not doing a thing," he vows.

As we all watch, the letters soak into the canvas, disappearing like invisible ink. A moment later, they rewrite themselves, sinking in again, the process repeating over and over.

"Oliver!" Delilah cries. "Help!"

Rapscullio and I tear our gazes away from the canvas to see Delilah's room flooding with the black loops and curls of letters. They may be disappearing in our world, but they keep rising in hers, swarming like bats. The dog in her bedroom is barking and trying to bite the duplicating words. They tangle in Delilah's hair, pecking at her. Oliver tries to wrestle them away, but they wrap around his wrists and pull his arms down to his sides, trapping him. And still the words keep coming, floating in the space between them, turning the air black and drowning them in language.

Beside me, Rapscullio grabs the canvas and smashes it against the rock wall of the cave, breaking the frame in half. He punches his boot through the center.

At that moment, all the letters in Delilah's bedroom fall to the ground, so that she and Oliver stand ankle-deep in ink.

"What *was* that?" Delilah says, breathing heavily.

"Nobody sent the message," I murmur. "That canvas was writing on itself."

"It's not the canvas." I turn at the sound of Frump's voice. He comes through the doorway on all fours, completely transitioned back into a hound. He sits back on his haunches and turns sad eyes up to the top edge of the book, meeting Oliver's gaze. "It's the book correcting itself."

Oliver's face is stricken. "Frump," he whispers. "Why didn't you tell me?"

Frump's ears droop. "Because if I didn't tell you, maybe it wasn't really true."

"I thought maybe Orville could do something," I say. "It's worth a try, right?"

Oliver tries to offer an encouraging smile, but Frump looks defeated. "Maybe we were all just kidding ourselves," he sighs. "Maybe we can't pretend to be something we're not."

Oliver slips his arm around Delilah's waist. "Well then," he says. "We're not giving up without a fight."

★ ★ ★

Orville's home is awfully crowded when you stuff two humans, a dog, and a horse inside. Since Oliver and Delilah insist on being here as we try to un-dogify Frump, we are bound by the conventions of the book: we had to pick a page that includes all the necessary characters, in the right place. On page 32 of the original fairy tale, Oliver, Frump, and Socks came to Orville's cabin so that the wizard could show Oliver his future. In my adaptation, the scene's pimped out a little bit. Orville's crusty old shack is now a state-of-the-art laboratory where he crafts antigravity potions and synthetic alien DNA.

Above me, I hear Oliver whistle softly. "I like what you've done with the place."

Frump is pacing underneath a table. "What if it doesn't work?" he asks.

"Then we'll try something else," Oliver insists. "Right, Orville?"

The old wizard, now decked out in a lab coat and goggles, nods. "Let's see what I've got."

He digs out the old grimoire that was part of the fairy tale before I arrived, blows dust off its cover, and begins to flip through the pages. "Invisibility . . . no, no . . . Poisoned apple—that's not it. . . . Pumpkin into carriage, definitely not . . ."

There's a clatter from the other side of the room, and we all look up to see Socks stepping delicately through a pile of broken glass. "Oops," he says. "My bad. You don't happen to have anything for adult acne, do you?"

Five pairs of eyes glare at him.

"Nope? Not the time? Right. Okay." Socks ducks his head.

"Ah, I think I've got something that will work," Orville says. He pushes his goggles on top of his head, revealing a pair of thick glasses underneath. "It's a wishing spell. It can only be used once per person."

Oliver's jaw drops. "Wait a moment, are you *kidding* me? You had this all along?"

Orville glances up at him. "I've only read about it being used once, when I was a young boy, and the side effects were catastrophic. Chap named Midas, who wished for riches beyond compare, and for everything he touched to turn to gold. Didn't work out so well when his whole family became a bunch of solid statues. You wanted to give Delilah your heart, boy—for all we know, she might have wound up with two beating in her chest, and you dead on the floor in front of me."

"Oh, *fabulous*," Frump mutters. "Make me the guinea pig."

"Technically," Socks says, "you're a dog." He glances up, wincing at Frump's expression. "Too soon?"

Orville begins to move around the laboratory, grabbing vials and emptying them into a titanium crucible. "Desperation," he murmurs, dumping the contents of one vial. "Desire. A pinch of stardust." He drops in a four-leaf clover. "A hint of luck." Finally he pours in a silver powder. "A scoop of hope," he pronounces, and as soon as the material hits the liquid in the container, it begins to bubble.

A thick blue mist rises over the crucible, forming a watery screen, and projected across it the tiniest print:

WARNING

Make sure your wizard knows before you take this
potion. Not for use by children under twelve. Tell
your wizard if you experience chest pain, dryness
of the mouth, or the growth of a third eye. This
is not a love potion; another's affection cannot
be granted. This medicine should not be used in
conjunction with a Revenge Tonic or serious side
effects may occur. Be careful what you wish for
and please wish responsibly.

~~ This product was not tested on animals. ~~

"If it wasn't tested on animals, how do we know what it's going to do to me?" Frump asks.

Orville looks at him gravely. "We don't."

"You don't have to do this," Delilah says softly. "You're perfect just the way you are."

"Well, not everyone feels that way."

Oliver reaches toward the book and stops when he realizes he can't offer a reassuring pat anymore. "Frump, there's more than one girl in the universe, you know."

Frump just stares at him. "Really, Ollie? Is there?"

Oliver reaches for Delilah's hand. "No," he admits. "There isn't."

"Then put that stuff into my dog bowl," Frump says, his voice growing stronger.

Orville ladles the potion into a dish and places it on the floor for Frump. He approaches it carefully as the liquid glows. He looks up at me. "If it doesn't work . . . you'll tell her? You'll let Seraphima know that I tried?"

I nod. The blue mist surrounds Frump's face. He closes his eyes, leaning in, and then stops. "Oliver?" he asks, his voice very small. "What do you do when you're scared?"

Oliver meets his gaze. "I remember that my best friend is always by my side. And suddenly it's not so terrifying."

Frump lowers his head and laps at the potion.

The floor beneath me begins to rattle, and the walls feel like they're closing in, although the book is wide open. There's a deafening roar that grows so loud it drowns out the sound of Delilah and Oliver screaming our names. The laboratory stretches and twists, as if it's being turned inside out, and the book slams shut with a definitive clap. Then, finally, there's a blinding flash of white light, and every glass item in Orville's lab shatters.

It takes a minute for my vision to clear. I look up at the top edge of the page, but Delilah and Oliver are gone. Orville lies on his back, the lenses of his glasses cracked. He sits up, hold-ing his hand to his head. Socks, against all odds and laws of gravity, has curled himself into a fetal position in the sink.

I turn to where Frump should be, but he's missing.

Holy crap. Did this actually *work*?

"Where is he?" Orville asks, looking around.

"Socks, get out of the damn sink before you break it. I need you to gallop through the pages and see if you can find—" But before I can finish, Orville's lab coat, which has been tossed aside during the explosion, begins to wiggle.

I crawl toward it and tug the fabric free.

The dog that was in Delilah's bedroom is happily wagging his tail in front of me. His tongue snakes out, awkwardly round-ing to form a word. "Hi, I'm Humphrey," he says. "Are you my new best friend?"

OLIVER

The book literally leaps out of my hands, tumbling into the sea of ink on the floor of Delilah's bedroom. I reach down, fishing through a mass of black letters that slip through my fingers like eels, trying to locate the fairy tale.

"Um, Oliver," Delilah whispers. "We have a little situation here."

I glance up, ripping off a *U* that has leeched itself onto my sleeve, to find Delilah staring down at the dog on her bed.

The dog that isn't Humphrey.

If you aren't looking too closely, you might not notice. But this dog is slightly larger and older, and his spots have been rearranged. His collar has a royal seal.

"Frump?" I gasp.

He opens his mouth to speak, but a small yelp comes out instead. His eyes widen in terror.

"Easy, boy," I coach. "Just take it slow and try again."

This time, he barks outright.

"Okay," Delilah says, drawing in her breath. "I'm seriously freaking out, here. How did he get out of the book? And what happened to Humphrey?"

Frump scratches at his throat and then leaps off the bed into the clutter of language on the floor, letters splashing up randomly as he disappears beneath the surface. He bobs up, dog-paddling toward Delilah's desk, and hops onto her chair. Then he bites a pencil and, gripping it between his teeth, begins to slowly scrawl letters across a scrap of paper.

SWITCHED

We both wade toward the desk to read his response. "How?" Delilah asks.

Frump starts scratching out a message again.

WISH

"I thought you wanted to be human again," I say. "What the devil did you wish for?"

Frump rocks back on his haunches, looking up at me with, well, puppy-dog eyes. He tilts up his snout, and distinctly howls, "YOOOOOOOOOUUUU."

"I don't understand," I say.

"It's the same principle as you and Edgar," Delilah explains. "The way you were able to leave the book was by substituting something similar enough to you for the book to tolerate the change. Otherwise, it would correct itself."

"So Frump is truly here? For good?" I wrap my arms around his neck. This is really too perfect. Now I have everything I want in one place.

Frump starts scratching at the desk again with the pencil.

VOICE?

Delilah and I exchange a glance. "Excuse us just a moment?" I say to Frump. Pulling Delilah aside, I lean closer so that Frump won't hear. "There must be something we can do for him."

"Oliver," she says, "he's like the Little Mermaid! He traded his voice to be with the prince."

"He's not a mermaid. What are you *talking* about?"

"I'm sorry, Oliver. In this world, dogs don't talk." She glances at the desk. "It's pretty much a miracle that he can *write*."

"I'll take him home with me," I say. "We'll figure something out."

"You can't. He's not your dog," Delilah replies. "With any luck my mother will still think he's Humphrey. It would be immensely helpful if you could convince him to be a little less human until we can figure out how to get him back into the book."

"Wait," I say. "Why does he have to go back?"

"He doesn't belong here."

I hesitate. "You could argue that neither do I."

She grabs my wrists, pulling them up between us. "Don't ever say that. You belong where I am."

I smooth her hair back from her face and press my lips to hers.

A ringing bark slices between us. Frump sits up on Delilah's desk chair, his paws balanced on the back, trying to get my attention. His tail wags vigorously.

"Right," I say, clearing my throat. "Listen, Frump, here's what we're going to do."

Before I can continue there is a knock on the door. Delilah

and I freeze. "Just a second!" Delilah calls, and then she turns to me, hissing, "We have to clean this up!"

I look down at the pool of letters flooding Delilah's bedroom floor. "How?"

Her eyes roam around wildly. "Closet," she mutters, and she begins scooping up the words. They drip over her arms like tentacles, leaving behind an oily residue.

"I heard Humphrey barking," Mrs. McPhee says, through the closed door. "Is everything all right?"

I rip the sheet off her bed and start shoveling the letters into a pile in the center. Frump leaps down from his perch, biting one corner and dragging it closer so that I can tie them in a knot.

"He saw a chipmunk," Delilah says to her mom.

Together we wrestle the gargantuan bulge into the closet and manage to shut the door by leaning all of our weight against it. By the time we're finished, we're panting and flushed.

Frump hops onto Delilah's bed and she walks to the door just as I notice an errant *N* lying on the floor. I snatch it up and stuff it beneath her pillowcase as she turns around to make sure we're ready. Then she yanks the door open and smiles at her mother, who looks Delilah up and down and then glances at me and raises an eyebrow.

"I see you two made up," her mother says, and I think my cheeks must be as red as brick.

She pats her leg. "Come on, Humphrey. It's time for dinner."

Frump doesn't budge.

I clear my throat. "Humphrey, come now. Be a good dog."

Frump shoots me a look that could slay a dragon and jumps off Delilah's bed, trotting to her mother's side. As they leave the room, Delilah's mother reaches for the doorknob and then—on second thought—leaves the door wide open.

"Where's the book?" Delilah asks once her mother has gone downstairs. "I didn't come across it when we were cleaning up."

"I didn't either." We both begin to tear the room apart, looking for the fairy tale, which has floated somewhere in the recent flood of letters. "There!" I cry, spotting it beneath the bureau and crawling on my hands and knees to retrieve it.

Delilah rips it out of my hands and immediately opens to the page we were on last. Rapscullio, Edgar, and Socks stare up at us from the center of the laboratory, looking quite the worse for wear.

"Have you seen Frump?" Edgar asks. "Socks rode the whole book and he's missing."

"We have him here," Delilah replies. "Have you come across my dog, Humphrey?"

At the sound of his name, Humphrey comes skidding out from behind a laboratory table, carrying a model atom in his mouth like a tennis ball. He drops it, covered with drool, and wags his tail. "Hello, Most Favorite Person in the World. I found a ball. It's the best ball. Also, you are a giant."

"Oh my God," Delilah whispers.

"Yeah," Edgar says sarcastically. "So, thanks for *this.*"

"Orville, how do we get them to trade places again?" Delilah asks.

The old wizard shakes his head. "I don't know," he admits. "Anything that springs to mind is rather complicated. I fear that any spell I cast to bring Frump back to the book might accidentally take you too, Oliver."

My heart sinks as I realize that all of this—this world, this life, this *girl*—could be ripped away from me, simply because of Frump's accidental wish. He came here because he wanted my help. Could I really be so selfish as to refuse to give it to him?

I may dream of reaching the stars, but I'll never get there if someone else's dream is anchoring me to the ground.

Orville glances up at us. "I need a little bit of time to think."

"I'm so glad we're all together. Look at my friends. So many friends," Humphrey says. He flops down at Edgar's feet and rolls onto his back. "Skinny boy, will you rub my belly?"

Edgar sighs and looks at Orville. "Don't take *too* long."

Gently I close the book and set it back on Delilah's shelf. "If Orville's right, I can't ask Frump to sacrifice so much for me."

"What do you mean?" she asks.

"If we both stay here, he'll never see Seraphima again. He'll never speak again. He'll always be a dog."

Delilah's face is so still it seems like porcelain, like something that might crack at any moment. "What about everything *you'd* have to give up?" she says.

But I can't even think about that, about losing her. If I do, I know I'll never leave.

★ ★ ★

By the time I get home from Delilah's house, it's dark, but a buttery glow shines from the kitchen windows. Usually at this time of the day, I can see Jessamyn making supper—chopping vegetables or seasoning meat in preparation for cooking. But she is nowhere to be seen. After I put Edgar's bike in the garage, I walk inside. "Mom?" I call, belatedly wondering if she's gone to bed early again, because of one of her recurring headaches.

That's when I smell the smoke.

I run into the kitchen to find the air thick and hazy. Smoke billows from the oven. Grabbing a dish towel, I open the oven door and cough as the smoke clears around my face, revealing a blackened lump that must have been supper. I throw the window sash up, letting cold, clear air stream in. I take a step backward and trip.

Lying on the tile, with a halo of blood around her head, is Jessamyn.

I fall to my knees, grasping her shoulders and shouting in her face. "Jessamyn!" I cry. "Jessamyn!?"

Her eyes flutter open, and she winces. "Edgar . . . call nine-one-one."

I jump to my feet, shaking all over. Her blood is on my hands, and unlike the blood I've encountered in the fairy tale, it doesn't disappear when I close my eyes. I look down at her still body. "NINE-ONE-ONE!" I yell, fists balled at my sides. "NINE-ONE-ONE!"

But nothing happens.

"Edgar," she whispers. "With the phone."

I grab the phone from its cradle and press the corresponding buttons. Almost immediately a voice fills my ear. "Nine-one-one, what's the emergency?"

"My mother," I say. "She's bleeding."

"Where are you?"

"At home. Thirty-Nine Oak Hill Road."

"Is your mother responsive?" the woman asks.

"She's lying on the floor. I don't know what happened. I didn't see."

"Is she conscious?"

I glance at Jessamyn, whose eyes are closed again. "I don't know. She was talking and now she isn't."

My heart is pounding so hard I can barely hear the woman's response. "Okay, listen, I'm going to put you on hold for one second. I'm going to get an ambulance on its way to you, and then I'm going to come back and stay on the line with you until they get there."

I kneel down, afraid to touch Jessamyn, equally afraid to leave her alone. I wish Delilah were here; she would know what to do. I wish Edgar were here.

I wish it were anyone but just me.

"Sir, are you still there?" the woman says. "The ambulance is on its way. What's your name?"

"Oliver," I answer, realizing too late that in my panic, I've given the wrong answer. "Edgar."

"Oliver Edgar, do you hear any sirens yet?"

As if she has willed them, there is a wailing outside the door, and a firm, pounding knock. "They're here."

"Go answer the door," the woman tells me. "They'll take care of your mom."

But isn't that my job? Isn't that what I promised Edgar I'd do?

Within seconds, two uniformed men have Jessamyn lifted onto a rolling bed and wheeled it into the back of a tremendous van. "Can you follow us to the hospital in your car?" one of them asks.

"I—I don't know how to drive," I stammer.

"You can ride up front," he says, and he hops into the rear with Jessamyn.

There are flashing red lights as the van zooms and whines down back roads to a building I've never seen before: ST. BRIGID MEMORIAL HOSPITAL.

The men rush Jessamyn, still strapped to the bed, into the building. I run behind them, but as they are about to go through a set of double doors, a woman dressed in blue pajamas pulls me aside. "Are you her son?"

"Yes." I try to see through the glass as Jessamyn grows farther and farther away.

"You can't go in there," she tells me. "The doctors will help your mom. I'm going to bring you to the waiting room, and someone will come get you as soon as we know more about her condition." She looks at me kindly. "Is there anyone you'd like me to call?"

"Yes," I say, without hesitation. "Delilah McPhee."

★ ★ ★

She holds on to me so tightly, our fingers twined together, that I can almost believe we're one person joined at the hands. "I've never felt like this before," I whisper. "Really, truly scared."

Delilah looks up at me. "She's going to be okay, Oliver."

"But you can't be *sure*," I point out. "I thought never knowing what's going to happen next was a good thing, but I guess that's not always true." I lean my head back against the wall and close my eyes. "I'm useless."

"Oliver—"

"I mean it. I didn't know what to do when I found her. I don't know anything about doctors or hospitals. If she hadn't woken up, what would have happened?"

"You would have called me."

I look at her. "You can't be there to clean up my messes every time," I say. "Let's be honest, Delilah, I'm not Edgar. It's not going to be long before everyone finds that out."

The woman in pajamas—no, rather, they're scrubs, or so Delilah informed me—comes back to the waiting room. "Your mom's asking for you," she says, smiling.

Delilah squeezes my arm. "I told you so. I'll be right here."

I follow the nurse down the bleached white hallway and enter a room on the right, hesitantly drawing back a pink curtain to reveal Jessamyn, looking small and pale, propped up against pillows. There is a bandage at her temple.

"Mom," I say, and she holds out her arms.

I fall into them with relief. This is not my mother, but in this moment, she feels like it. "What happened?" I ask, my voice muffled against the spotted nightgown she is wearing.

"I'm fine, Edgar. I fainted, that's all, and I happened to hit my head on the way down."

"You fainted?" I say, seizing on the most important words of the sentence. "Why? Are you ill?"

"I was so busy today I completely forgot to eat," Jessamyn says, dismissing my concern. "Honestly, it was silly and stupid of me. I'm fine."

"So we can go home now?" I ask. After this day—with the message from the book, and Frump's arrival, and Jessamyn's injury—all I want is normal back.

"Well, they have to keep me overnight," she admits. "It's protocol."

"I'll stay with you," I say. "I'll skip school tomorrow."

"You're not getting out of class that easily." Jessamyn smiles. "It's going to be incredibly boring. Doctors running tests and me watching endless Spanish soap operas. Although . . . how will you get home?"

"Delilah's in the waiting room," I say. "She can drive me."

Her face relaxes as she sinks back against the pillows. "Do you think her mother would let you stay at her house tonight? I'd feel better knowing I don't have to worry about you being alone."

"I guess."

Her eyes drift shut. "Good," she sighs. "I love you, Edgar."

I lean down to kiss her cheek, but she is already asleep. "I'm sorry I'm not who you needed me to be," I whisper, and I slip out of the room.

★ ★ ★

I stand beside Delilah awkwardly as her mother hands me a stack of towels. "Thanks, Mrs. McPhee," I say.

"It's not a problem, Edgar. You're welcome to stay as long as you need." She pauses. "And if there's anything I can do for your mother, just let me know."

I nod, but I can't imagine how Mrs. McPhee, who works all day long, would have any time to run errands.

She's set me up in the guest bedroom, which is three doors

down from Delilah's. I must admit, knowing that she's going to be so close to me will make it terribly hard to sleep.

"Good night," Mrs. McPhee says, and as she starts to leave, Frump dashes between her legs and hops up on the narrow bed. "Humphrey!" she scolds. "Down!"

"Oh, it's all right," I answer. "I wouldn't mind some company tonight."

"Better the dog than my daughter," Mrs. McPhee murmurs.

"Mom!" Delilah cries.

"Say good night, Delilah," her mother replies. She waits with her arms crossed, and it's perfectly clear that she's going nowhere without Delilah. I must admit, I'm a bit offended. But then again, she doesn't realize her daughter's boyfriend is a prince who would never compromise his true love's reputation.

Delilah leans up and pecks my cheek. "Sleep tight," she says, and she follows her mother out of the guest room.

I strip down to my boxers and crawl beneath the covers. Frump sits up and cocks his head, and I scratch between his ears. "Some pair we are," I sigh. "Lost in translation. Maybe instead of thinking of all the good that could come from escaping that fairy tale, we should have spent a bit of time considering the aftereffects. You can't talk, and I can barely get through the day without messing something up." My mind flashes back to an image of Jessamyn lying on the floor. "She was so still," I whisper. "And there was so much blood. It's different here. It's a world of permanence. Consequences stick. You can't just turn a page and have the sword wound heal. For heaven's sake, Rapscullio falls nine stories in the climax and walks away without a scratch as soon as the book is closed. Here, cuts bleed and bodies break and there are no second chances."

Frump opens his mouth as if he is about to respond, but all that emerges is a whimper.

"I promised Edgar I'd take care of Jessamyn for him. Clearly I'm doing a rotten job. Yet once I tell Edgar what happened to her, surely he'll want to switch back. And that would break Delilah's heart."

Frump puts his paw on my arm. For a moment, we just look at each other, and it doesn't really matter that he can't speak, because I know exactly what he would say if he could. *Oliver,* he'd tell me, *tomorrow's bound to be better.*

I flop back onto the pillows, crossing my arms behind my head. Frump curls into a donut against my side and harrumphs into the covers.

I imagined a perfect life. I thought that escaping the book meant every dream I'd ever had would come true. But dreams, it seems, have costs. For every person you make happy, there's another one you disappoint. Sometimes I wonder—if Queen Maureen or Captain Crabbe were to see me in school, with my new clothes and my friends, would they even recognize me? Would I *want* them to?

Outside, the moon is a silver sliver. Every night, the shadow eats a slice of it, until it's nothing but this hollow rind. I feel the same way; with each day, I lose a little more of myself.

Frump snores in his sleep, his legs twitching, as if he's chasing Seraphima. Carefully I draw back the covers and slip out of bed, padding down the hall until I am standing in the dark outside Delilah's bedroom door.

I turn the knob as silently as possible and slip inside.

She is lying on her back, her dark hair fanned across the sheets, like a mermaid's underwater. Her skin reflects the moonlight, and the covers are tangled at her feet. She's wearing a T-shirt that seems to have swallowed her whole.

When you see the sunrise every morning, you get used to it. You forget to gasp at the mixing of the colors, at the way the sun's rays spill over the mountains and light the ocean on fire.

Being with Delilah every day, I've forgotten how absolutely stunning she is.

Delilah's eyes open slowly and she jumps, nearly levitating on the bed. "Holy crap, Oliver," she says. "You scared the hell out of me!"

I take a step backward. "I'm sorry. I didn't mean to scare you. I just— Why are you staring at me like that?"

"You're not wearing any clothes. . . ."

I glance down, mortified to realize I forgot to dress before leaving my room. "I'm so sorry. I'll go—"

"No!" Delilah says, swallowing. "This is good. Very good."

I hide my smile and sit down on the bed. "I couldn't sleep."

Delilah scoots, making room for me to lie down beside her. I curl onto my side, facing her, so we are inches apart.

"Sometimes when people have insomnia, they count sheep," she tells me.

I frown. "Who keeps a herd in the house?"

"No, it's a metaphor. The point is to just count *something*. When I was little, my mom had me count my blessings."

I think about that for a moment. Then I roll over, pinning Delilah to the mattress. I can feel her heartbeat speed. I wind my fingers through hers and whisper in her ear. "Number one," I say, "your hands." Then I drop a kiss on each eyelid. "Number two," I say, "your beautiful eyes." I slide my hands down her arms and slip them beneath the hem of her oversized shirt, spreading my palms across the small of her back. "Number three . . . your soft skin."

I nibble my way from her collarbone to her jaw, and she sighs. "Number four," I say, "the sound of your voice."

I trace her lower lip with my thumb. "Number five . . . your mouth."

And then I kiss her.

Delilah's lips move under mine, as if we are speaking the same secret. I break away only when there's no more breath to share, and bury my face in the curve of her neck. "I love you so much."

Her hands play over my shoulders. "When you say that to me . . . I feel like I'm flying."

With a groan I roll onto my side, curling my body around hers. I slip my arm beneath her waist and pull her tight against me, her back to my front. "I'll never let you fall," I promise.

★ ★ ★

Two days after Jessamyn's return from the hospital, we celebrate with a meal she calls "takeout" that is a collection of delicious foods from a foreign land. Although she doesn't seem to have much of an appetite, I can't stop eating. "I have never tasted anything so delectable in my life," I say, mopping up sauce with flatbread and stuffing it in my mouth.

"Really," Jessamyn muses. "Most of the time when I want Indian, you fight me to the death for Chinese instead."

"Perhaps my taste buds are evolving."

"Hmm," she says, raising a brow. "Who are you, and what have you done with my son?"

My blood runs cold. Has she figured it out?

Then Jessamyn laughs. "Does this mean I can start cooking brussels sprouts too?"

What the devil is a brussels sprout? I force a smile. "Let's take it slowly," I suggest.

I watch Jessamyn pour herself another drink of water. I've been watching her carefully since she's come home, as if her bones are made of glass and the slightest bump might shatter her whole. But with the exception of a small bandage on her temple, she seems to be her usual self.

Not that I'm entirely sure what that *is*.

I know I need to tell Edgar what happened to his mother—that she was in the hospital overnight. And I'm not holding the truth back from him, honestly. It's just that I want to wait until I'm able to give him good news—to tell him his mother is fine.

I want to be 100 percent certain.

Jessamyn begins closing up the ingenious little boxes that hold the food. "How about we watch a movie after dinner? Do you want to pick?" she asks.

One shelf in the living room is devoted to small folders containing disks that—like Orville's potion for the future—project a moving image onto the television screen. I've watched a few with Delilah. I let my finger trail over pictures of robots and aliens, which all seem to have numbers in the title, and finally come across one that looks much more palatable.

I hand the movie to Jessamyn, who takes it and smirks. "Very funny."

"What? It looks rather interesting."

"*The Princess Bride*?" she says. "The last time I suggested watching this, you said you'd rather cut off your own leg with a rusty spoon."

"Well . . . I thought *you* might like it," I say, holding my breath.

She smiles up at me. "Oh, the sacrifices a son is willing to make."

We settle on the couch, shoulder to shoulder, queueing up the film. Jessamyn has scooped us each a bowl of ice cream (which, frankly, is one thing this world has going for it that puts the fairy tale to shame. And here I thought "melt in your mouth" was simply figurative language).

"It's hard to believe that in a year, you'll be going off to college," Jessamyn muses.

I turn to her, horrified. "What if I don't want to go anywhere?"

"Edgar, since you were ten, you've dreamed of going to the University of Southern California to major in video game design."

Thanks to social studies class, I know that California is about as far away from New Hampshire as one can go in this kingdom without falling into an ocean. If I thought Delilah and I were separated when she was here and I was merely on Cape Cod, how could I ever withstand this distance?

"I can't leave here."

Jessamyn puts her arm around me. "Edgar, we've been through this. You shouldn't be worrying about me. What would make me happiest is knowing that you're following your dreams."

But my dreams have changed, now that I'm not Edgar.

Because I don't know what to say, I grab my spoon and start shoveling chocolate ice cream into my mouth.

I am halfway finished with the contents of the bowl when I realize Jessamyn is staring at me as if she has never seen me before. "When," she asks, "did you become a lefty?"

★ ★ ★

"What am I going to do?" I ask Delilah, pacing in front of my locker. "She knows I'm not her son. She wants me to go to California, for God's sake. . . ." When Delilah doesn't offer even a word of encouragement or support, I turn to her. "What's wrong with you today, anyway?"

Delilah rubs her eyes. She looks like she's been locked in a pirate's brig all night, not that I'm going to tell her that. "I got, like, two hours of sleep," she says. "Frump is refusing to eat kibble, which means I had to prepare a gourmet meal after my mom went to bed. And he snores. Like, *super* loud. And every time I tried to take the sheets away from him, he actually *kicked* me."

"Wait, *what?*" I say, my head snapping around. "He slept with you? In the same bed?"

"Yes. Just like Humphrey did. Remember? You're not the only one with the hidden identity!"

"I've seen what you wear when you sleep."

"He's just an animal, Oliver!"

I grit my teeth. "Exactly."

A grin breaks over Delilah's face. "Someone's jealous." She leans closer to me. "And you know what else? I've seen him naked."

I frown. "Not funny," I say, slamming my locker. It's been two days since Frump arrived. "Have you heard anything from Orville?"

"No. Frump and I opened the book last night, and he's still working on a remedy."

I consider this, and Delilah tilts her head. "What are you thinking?"

"That maybe we should fashion a pair of pants for Frump in the meantime."

"I'm pretty sure my mom would notice," Delilah says. "Honestly, Oliver? He's really not my type."

Only slightly mollified, I look down. "Then maybe *you* could wear pants to bed," I suggest.

Delilah turns, about to lecture me, but she is interrupted by the arrival of Chris, who needs to get into his locker. "I'm so glad you guys are both here," he says. "I need your advice."

Chris looks at Delilah. "You know your friend Jules?"

"What about her?"

"I was kind of thinking of asking her out. . . ."

Delilah's eyes widen. "Really?"

"Yeah, except for one thing. She scares the hell out of me."

"Why?"

"Just yesterday," Chris says, "I watched her make Mrs. Jacon cry in homeroom, telling her that by taking her new husband's name she was a disappointment to the female sex."

"Jules may be tough, but trust me, she has a soft side. She cried twice watching *Titanic*."

"I cried *four* times," Chris murmurs.

"Perhaps we should all go courting together."

"Dude," Chris says, "not all black people are into basketball—"

"He means a date," Delilah explains, and I nod. A slow smile unfurls over her face. "So you finally want to take me out, huh?"

I shrug. "It seems fitting, since we've already gone to bed together."

Delilah's mouth drops, and Chris's eyebrows shoot up to his hairline. "That's my cue to leave," he says, and he walks off down the hall.

Shaking her head, Delilah sighs. "Oliver," she says, "you and I need to have a little talk about slang."

★ ★ ★

Delilah drives Jules home after school, so that she can pick up some things before the double date. Then we continue to Delilah's house, with Jules sitting in the backseat, fidgeting. "This is the stupidest idea you've ever had," she says. "I don't even know why I said yes."

"Because you don't want to die alone and surrounded by cats," Delilah replies.

"You know my track record," Jules mutters. "He'll probably be gone by dessert."

"Maybe Chris will be the exception," I suggest.

Jules snorts. "Easy for you to say. You're lucky. You already found your dream girl."

"Actually, *she* found *me*." Delilah catches my eye, and I grin at her.

"This is really helpful, you guys," Jules says. "Now all I have to do is stuff Chris inside a book and try to pry him out."

"Those are just details," Delilah tells her, pulling into the garage of her house. "The point is you never know who's going to be the one."

"She's right. If I'd given up, I never would have bothered looking when Delilah opened the book. I might never have known that she could hear me. Just be yourself," I suggest. "Or perhaps a slightly gentler version of yourself."

"What the hell is that supposed to mean?" Jules argues.

I turn in my seat and raise a brow.

"Ugh. Fine," she says. "I'll try to tone it down." Jules gets out of the car. "It's not my fault that my awesomeness intimidates people."

We both watch her carry her bag upstairs. Delilah slips her hand into mine. "She's right. We *did* get pretty lucky."

What if Delilah hadn't opened the book that day? What if I hadn't looked up?

What if this isn't permanent?

What if we *did* get so lucky that we're due for something terrible?

I drop a kiss on the crown of her head. "I know."

★ ★ ★

It seems silly to me, but Delilah insists that when it comes
to a double date, she and Jules are incapable of dressing themselves alone. Delilah says it's a girl thing; I wouldn't understand.
To that end, Jules has come to Delilah's house with a suitcase full
of enough clothes to last her for a month, although she is only
staying overnight. I've been exiled to the living room, where I
wait with Frump. Upstairs, there is a symphony of squeals and
shrieks. I'm not certain if they are doing each other's makeup,
as Delilah has said, or if they are murdering each other.

The doorbell rings, and Delilah calls down from her bathroom. "Can you get that?"

Chris is standing on the threshold, holding a bouquet of
flowers.

"Oh," I say, reaching for them. "Thank you. I'm so sorry. . . .
I didn't get you anything. . . ."

Chris rips them back out of my hand. "I didn't get *you* anything," he says. "These are for Jules."

I lead him into the living room. "Delilah says they're almost
ready," I tell him. "Of course, she said that about an hour ago."

Chris claps me on the back. "Thanks for doing this, man.
I didn't expect to have as good a friend as you once I moved
here." At that, Frump leaps off the couch, his teeth bared, and
is about to sink his fangs into Chris's calf. "What the—"

I grab his collar. "No!" I yell. "Bad *dog*!" Frump whimpers
as I drag him away from Chris, scoop him into my arms, and
put him on a chair as far away from us as possible. I lean down
on the pretense of patting him. "He's just an acquaintance," I
whisper. And then, more loudly, *"Stay."*

Frump snorts.

"Are you quite all right?" I ask Chris.

"This is why I have cats," he says.

Suddenly there is a flurry of noise as Delilah and Jules descend. Jules is still wearing her trademark combat boots, but she's sporting a simple black dress that is surprisingly devoid of studs, skeletons, and safety pins.

However, it's Delilah I can't stop staring at. She is wearing a filmy white dress that seems to breathe over her curves. The low neckline reveals a constellation of freckles on her collarbone. Her hair is twisted into an intricate braid, and a few tendrils escape at the nape of her neck. I can't help but think how perfectly a tiara would settle atop her head.

"You look great," Chris tells Jules.

"Tell me something I *don't* know," she says.

"I, um, brought you these. . . ." He hands her the bouquet.

"Ohhh . . . thanks for the corpses of murdered plants."

Delilah clears her throat. "Jules!"

She rolls her eyes. "I mean, wow, *they're so pretty.*" Then Jules looks at me. "Edgar. You're drooling."

I tear my gaze away from Delilah as the girls start walking toward the front door. Chris puts his hand on my arm. "She hates me."

I consider this. "No," I say. "That's just Jules."

★ ★ ★

Delilah has picked a restaurant for dinner that seems as if it has been ripped from the pages of a storybook. Tables nestle in a copse of trees, which are illuminated by strands of twinkling lights. Small stone fire pits dot the premises, and servants in starched white linen aprons stand at attention as we pass by.

When we reach our table, I pull out a chair for Delilah. "My lady," I murmur, and she beams up at me.

Chris, halfway into his seat, jumps up and tugs at Jules's seat when she is already half inside it. She glares at him. "You don't think I'm capable of getting into a chair by myself?"

"N-no," Chris stammers. "You look very capable." He buries his face behind his menu.

"What kind of place *is* this, Delilah?" Jules asks, reading the selections. "Candied celery and lemon-verbena foam and sorbet quennels. Is that actually a *word*?"

"Shut up," Delilah says. "This is the only fancy place with vegetarian options."

"You're a vegetarian?" Chris asks.

Jules straightens her spine. "I don't support the slaughter of helpless animals for man's desire for barbecued flesh . . . so yes, I am."

"Barbecued flesh?" I repeat.

"She means steak and hamburger," Delilah says. "She's just being dramatic."

"Dramatic?" Jules repeats. "Where do you think your meat comes from?"

I blink. "The refrigerator?" At the castle, our meals just . . . appeared. And here, Jessamyn goes to a special store and comes back with ingredients.

"Cows," Jules says. "Meat comes from cows."

My eyes widen. "What?" I gasp. I turn and speak in a whisper to Delilah. "I knew all of our cows by name in the kingdom. You let me eat our *pets*?"

"What kind of bubble *is* Cape Cod?" Chris says. He turns to Jules. "Well, you know what they say about vegetarians. They're just vegans who couldn't cut it." He smiles. "I've been one since I was twelve."

"Really?" Jules says, arching a brow. "*You're* a vegan?"

Chris leans back in his chair. "There's all kinds of things about me you would never expect."

"Well," Jules says, smiling for the first time since the date began. "Good thing we have the whole night."

★ ★ ★

To my surprise, Jules and Chris spend the entire meal with their heads bent together, talking about everything from the best science fiction film-to-book adaptation to the institutional oppression of cafeteria food. Now Chris is yammering on and on about constellations, which he studies with a telescope in his bedroom each night. "That one's Casseopeia," he tells Jules. He lifts her hand and guides her arm, to point. "And that's Canis Major. You can tell because Sirius, the Dog Star, is in it." Chris locks eyes with Jules. "It's the brightest star in the night sky."

"Looks like this has been a huge success," Delilah says quietly to me.

"I must admit, I'm surprised that Jules is his type," I whisper back. "I'm surprised that Jules is *anyone's* type."

Delilah laughs, and the waiter returns, placing a math worksheet on a small silver platter in front of me. "Thanks," I say politely, "but I'd much rather have an éclair."

"That's the check," Delilah explains.

Suddenly it all makes sense: Jessamyn pressing crisp bills into my palm before I left on my date, telling me a gentleman is always the one to pay.

Chris pulls out his wallet. "Let's split it," he suggests, scanning the paper.

I wait for Chris to put money on the small dish, and match the same amount. Then I stand, pulling out Delilah's chair and offering her my hand.

Chris is helping Jules put on her jacket. "I know the most amazing vegan cupcake place," he says. "We could go there for dessert."

I think about the éclair I didn't get. "That sounds wonderful!"

"No!" Delilah widens her eyes at me. "We're leaving."

"But I *like* cupcakes. . . ."

She loops her arm through mine. "Then I'll make you some at home," Delilah says, and she adds, under her breath, "We're giving them time alone." Turning to Chris, she asks, "I'm assuming you can drop Jules off at my house later?"

"You bet," Chris says.

We walk to the parking lot, and Delilah and I watch them drive off in Chris's car. "They grow up so fast," she jokes. Then she grabs my hand. "Come on. Maybe we can talk to Orville before she gets back."

I let her pull me toward her car. "But you promised me cupcakes. . . ."

When we return to Delilah's, we almost have the house to

ourselves—Mrs. McPhee, who was out when we left, is still out with Dr. Ducharme. Frump meets us at the door and, after an embarrassing show of charades, makes clear that he needs a moment on the privy of the front lawn. Afterward we all convene in the kitchen while Delilah rummages through the cabinets for a box of dessert. She pours powder into a bowl, then cracks two eggs and adds a dollop of oil and some water, insisting that this will materialize into something edible. While the mixture is baking in the oven, Delilah and I speculate on how Jules and Chris are getting along.

"I did not see that coming," Delilah muses. "The last guy Jules was interested in had tattoos running from neck to navel and owned a pet falcon. By comparison, Chris seems so . . . tame."

"There's no logic to the laws of attraction," I say, grinning at Frump. "I mean, this one's hung up on Seraphima."

Frump looks over his shoulder at me and growls.

A bell chimes on the oven, and Delilah takes her concoction from its belly. She cuts me a square and hands it to me as I lean against the counter. It may not be a cupcake but I must admit, it smells heavenly.

"Happy?" she asks.

I put the treat down and lift Delilah by her hips so that she is sitting on the counter and I am standing between her legs. Leaning forward, I kiss her until her arms come around me and Frump starts barking. "Very," I say, smiling.

By now, Frump has gotten the tail of my shirt between his teeth and is trying to drag me backward. Delilah holds up a hand. "Okay, okay. We'll get a room." Jumping down from the counter, she tosses Frump a square of cake. "Speaking of which, let's go get the book."

That's all it takes to remind me that I still need to tell Edgar about his mom.

Frump trots into Delilah's bedroom, jumps up on his hind legs, and tugs the book from its spot on the shelf. He brings it to Delilah, his tail wagging. "Thanks," she says, surreptitiously wiping the drool from the book's spine. "Now. Let's find Orville."

I crack open the book, but to my surprise, nothing is where it's supposed to be. Although we were always in place and ready for the Reader when one came, I seem to have caught the characters unaware. On page eleven, in the enchanted forest, the fairies are braiding each other's hair. On page thirty-one, the trolls haven't bothered to rebuild their bridge. The mermaids aren't even *on* page twenty-seven, having swum off to sun themselves on Everafter Beach.

I realize that when I was in the book, and everything ran like clockwork, it was because Frump was there barking orders. I glance at him, and he shakes his head and rolls his eyes, as if to say: *Amateurs.*

Flipping through the story, I try to find Edgar, but he is nowhere to be seen, which is particularly troubling since—as the main character—he's supposed to be present on practically every page. We locate Socks, lolling on his back in the unicorn meadow with Humphrey, as they look up at the clouds passing by. "Socks," I say, and he scrambles to his hooves.

"Hi, Ollie," he neighs. "Humphrey and I didn't hear you coming."

Humphrey sits up, his entire body wriggling with delight.

"This is my new best friend. He's the biggest dog I've ever seen." He turns to Socks. "I love you."

Socks beams at this attention. "And I love *you*."

"For heaven's sake," I sigh. "Where's Edgar?"

"Don't know, Ollie. I haven't seen him at all today."

"Then who's running the book?"

Socks whinnies. "I guess nobody," he says. "Since Frump disappeared, everyone's been left to his own devices."

Frump barks at the book, drawing Socks's attention. "Hey!" he cries. "You look really great. I guess it's not true what they say, how the outside world puts on ten pounds. . . ."

"Socks, where can I find Orville?" I ask.

"Oh, he's getting his teeth cleaned," Socks says.

"Thanks," I say. "Hold on to your horses." Humphrey wraps his paws around Socks's hindquarters as I flip through the book to page thirty-seven, where Captain Crabbe leans over Orville as he reclines in the commander seat of a space shuttle. "Hello, laddie," Captain Crabbe says from behind a paper surgical mask.

Orville tries to speak but has a mess of instruments in his mouth.

"One wee moment, now. All right. Spit," Captain Crabbe orders, holding up a cup for Orville, who then reveals a blinding white smile. "Ye're missing out, Oliver. These new space chairs are so much more comfortable than the old braw ones on the pirate ship."

"Orville," Delilah asks, "have you had any luck?"

Orville shakes his head. "This is the first free moment I've had since you last opened the book—and I've already rescheduled twice. There have been more pressing matters." He exchanges a look with Captain Crabbe. "The book's not reacting well to all these changes," he confesses. "It's in a stage of degradation."

Captain Crabbe interrupts. "He means to say it's fallin' apart at the seams."

"How?" I ask.

Orville sits up, ripping the paper bib from around his neck. "A sinkhole's opened on Everafter Beach that's pulling trees from the Enchanted Forest into its depths. It's already taken out five fairy huts."

"Part of Pyro's cave collapsed yesterday. Thank goodness he was out when it happened."

"Isn't the book fixing itself like it usually does?"

"That's the problem, laddie," Captain Crabbe says. "It hasna responded that way since Frump left."

"It's as if the book has lost so much," Orville muses, "that it's just given up."

"Who are you guys talking to?"

Delilah and I freeze at the sound of Jules's voice. She's come into the bedroom, wearing Chris's jacket. On the page, Orville and Captain Crabbe look at each other, panicked, unsure what to do. Usually when a new Reader arrives, there's a cue—the opening of the book, and Frump's orders—but in this case, no one is in their correct place to act out the story.

"It's okay," Delilah says to them, and she lifts the book to her chest. "Jules, remember when I told you that the characters in the fairy tale I read over and over were talking back to me?"

She narrows her eyes. "Yes."

"You said you believed me, back then."

"Yeah . . . but that's what you always say to your best friend," Jules points out. "If you told me you were going to vacation on the moon, I would have nodded along too."

"Well, the thing is," Delilah says, "I wasn't lying." She turns the book so that the pictures are facing Jules. Captain Crabbe and Orville awkwardly wave.

Jules grabs the book from Delilah's hands. "This is insane," she murmurs, turning it over and shaking it.

"Please stop!" Orville yelps.

"Where are the batteries?" Jules asks, peering at the end-papers. "Is this like the next-generation e-reader or something?"

She turns the book upright; Orville and Captain Crabbe are tangled in a heap at the bottom corner.

Suddenly the page lifts, although Jules hasn't touched it. It flips backward, and then the next sheet does the same, and so on, a cascade of paper like a curling wave.

"What's happening?" Delilah whispers.

But I have no idea. I've never seen this before.

The paper falls flat at the very beginning of the book—the copyright page. It's a territory we've never explored—mostly empty space with small clouds formed of letters that cast shadows on the ground. It's quite far away from all the other pages, and without mountains or trees or water or castles, there just isn't any reason to tread there, which is why we characters have pretty much forgotten it even exists.

Jules looks up at us, her eyes shining. "This night just keeps getting more awesome," she says, and in that instant, she disappears.

EDGAR

I'm going to kill him.

It's been two days since Frump disappeared, and ever since then, I've been trying to shake this stupid dog, which has basically become my shadow.

"I love biscuits," Humphrey sighs as he walks beside me, practically vibrating with joy. "Delilah gave me biscuits. They're my favorite food. Do you like biscuits? We should get some biscuits."

"Is there a mute button for you?" I ask.

I walk a little faster, trying to put some distance between us. "How about we play a game," I suggest.

"Games? I love games!"

"Shocker!" I say, sarcastic. "This one is called Count Every Room in the Castle."

"Oh, that sounds fun. Can we use a Frisbee? I really like Frisbees." He sits back on his haunches, his tongue wagging. "Once," he says, "I ate a shoe."

"And?"

"I threw up."

I nod slowly. "Okay, then. So that game . . . ? On the count of three, I want you to go find every room in the castle, and then you come back here and tell me how many there are. Ready? One . . . two . . . go!"

Humphrey doesn't move.

"What are you waiting for?"

"You didn't say *three*."

"For God's sake. Three," I sigh, and he takes off like a shot up the stone staircase, his toenails scabbering as he rounds the corner.

Immediately I head in the opposite direction and slip into a broom closet. In the dark, I try to figure out how long I'll have to stay here until Humphrey loses interest in trying to find me. His attention span, from what I can see, is less than a nanosecond—but I can't be too careful. I swear, that stupid animal has some kind of radar, because every time I think I've escaped, he turns up out of thin air, wagging his tail.

As my eyes adjust to the darkness, I see a shelf of folded sheets and towels. The sheets on the bottom are printed with small purple flowers. Just like the ones that are always on my mother's bed.

The door to the closet opens, and my heart sinks when I think Humphrey has found me. But it's only Queen Maureen, who blinks at me, and says, "Oh, hello, dear. Could you pass me that mop?"

I hand it to her, expecting her to ask me why I'm hiding in a broom closet in the middle of the day, but either she doesn't care or this is just something people do here. "Have a nice time," Maureen says. "Let me know if you get hungry. . . ."

"Shhh," I warn her. "I'm trying to hide from Humphrey."

"Ahh. I see," she answers. "Well. Carry on, then."

Before she can shut the door, however, there's a crash so loud that it shakes the timbers of the castle. I step out of the closet to find Humphrey sitting in the hallway with his tail between his legs. "Something happened in the kitchen," he whispers. "And I love you so much."

★ ★ ★

It's easier to come up with battle tactics to defeat Zorg than to distract Humphrey long enough for me to get a moment alone. "Humphrey," I say, waving a toy the fairies made out of sticks, acorns, and straw. "Fetch!"

I throw it as hard as I can, practically into the margins.

"Oh boy oh boy oh boy!" Humphrey cries, dashing after it. A moment later he returns, the toy clamped between his jaws. He shakes his head vigorously and then drops the toy between his paws. "I love this toy with all my life," he snuffles, biting at it. "I love it so much that I want to eat it." He pulls and chews. "I love it. . . . I love it. . . . I love it. . . . Oh no, it's dead." Humphrey steps back from the scrap heap that seconds ago was his toy and looks up at me in distress.

"Okay," I sigh. "That took thirty seconds." Maybe I can tire him out. "How about a run?"

"I'm the fastest runner ever," Humphrey says, and he bolts into the next chapter. I jog after him as he dashes ahead and then loops back just to make sure I'm still here. He tracks a scent, nose down, through the Enchanted Forest, weaving through the trees. He dog-paddles across the ocean and runs circles around Orville's lab. Finally, at the base of Timble Tower, he skids to a stop, panting. "That was so fun. Let's do it again. I can totally keep my eyes open. I'm not falling asleep at all." And then he conks to the side, snoring.

I sigh. *"Finally."* I probably have less than a minute till he wakes up again, and I will have to find yet another way to distract him. My gaze falls on the tower rising before me.

Dogs can't climb.

I grab on to the stone cliff that leads to the tower, fumbling for a hand- and foothold. Hoisting my weight, I start to inch upward, swallowing the nausea that hits me like a wave when I look down at the churning ocean.

Finally I reach the open window of the tower where Seraphima is imprisoned in the story and hurl myself inside head-first, landing unceremoniously in a heap on the floor.

Thank God, I think. *Peace and quiet.*

"What are *you* doing here?" A muffled voice comes from a pile of quilts across the room.

I squint. "Seraphima?"

I've never seen her like this. She's wearing a nightgown and mismatched socks. Her hair looks like there are small woodland creatures hiding inside it. And I'm pretty sure it's been days since her last shower. "Um," I say, "are you feeling all right?"

"No," she wails, bursting into tears. "I don't know *what* is happening to me. No one's left chocolates on my pillow at night. I can't find my slippers anywhere. There's been no breakfast waiting outside my door. And I can't even remember the last time someone told me I was pretty."

I suddenly remember Frump telling me once that he had to go make Seraphima's bed, as part of the continuing ruse that let her believe she was a true princess. I wonder if that's what love is: giving in to someone's delusions, just because you know it makes them happy.

"You know what you need?" I say. "A change of scenery. I'm trying to get rid of a dog—"

Seraphima wails even louder. *"I miss Frump!"*

"Believe me," I mutter. "You're not the only one. Listen, do you know any good hiding places in this book?"

She stops crying and blinks twice. Then she lifts the hem of her sheets and blows her nose into them. "Let me think," she says, sliding off the bed and behind a folding screen. I turn away, reddening, as she takes off her nightgown and I see her naked silhouette. A moment later she emerges, in a wrinkled, stained gown, sporting one blue shoe and one green one. Her hair has been yanked into a messy bun that sits off-center on her head and only contains half her hair. "Do I look all right?" she asks.

"Um. Sure."

Her shoulders sag. "It doesn't matter anyway. It's not like I have anyone to impress."

I glance out the window and see Humphrey starting to stir. "We have to hurry," I say. "Please tell me I don't have to climb back down?"

"I usually just jump."

"Are you *insane*?"

"Even Rapscullio can do it," she says, "and he's a big baby." She hikes her skirts up and hooks one leg over the windowsill. With a smile, she hurls herself out.

"Seraphima!" I yell. I hesitate for only a moment, glancing down at the waves breaking over the rocks below, and her body, which grows smaller and smaller as she falls. Then I dive after her.

This hero thing *sucks*.

The ground is rushing up at an alarming pace. I find myself thinking: *This is how I die.* Flashing before my eyes are all the things I will miss the most: my mother, the new Star Wars movie premiere, meatballs and spaghetti . . .

As if I'm attached to a bungee cord, I stop in midair an inch before my body is smashed on the rocks. But unlike on a bungee cord, I don't snap back up. Instead I hover, turning my head to see Seraphima suspended the same way. She delicately arches her foot and tiptoes a few steps down to the ground. "Well?" she asks, looking up at me. "Are you waiting for an invitation?"

I take a deep breath and jump, landing squarely on both feet, safe and sound. "Now what?"

"Follow me," Seraphima replies. She grabs my hand and starts to run, flying through the pages until we come to a stop on a tundra made of snow. Or that's what it looks like, anyway. It's nothing, as far as the eye can see, but it's not cold.

"Where *are* we?" I ask.

"Past the title page," Seraphima says. "I've only been once."

I take a step forward and my entire body leans to the right. The only way I can walk is on a slant. I look up, my head brushing against the low-hanging letters.

Of course. Italics.

Seraphima too is struggling to keep her balance. The silence is shattering, an utter vacuum.

"This is perfect. Humphrey will never find me here," I say, my voice echoing as if it's fallen to the bottom of a canyon. "How did you ever find it?"

"By accident. Once, I had a . . . a blemish," Seraphima confesses. "I couldn't bear for Oliver to see me that way. So I wandered as far from him as possible, and this is where I wound up. It's not easy being perfect all the time, you know." Her attention is distracted by a small pulsing circle some distance away. "What's that?"

It looks like a manhole cover. Seraphima walks closer on the diagonal, tripping as she slides at an angle. Her princess slippers don't offer any traction, and she skids down the slope of white toward this pinprick of ink. "Help!" she cries. "Edgar!" Her fingernails claw at the wide empty space.

I put one foot out gingerly, testing the ground before I inch closer, scared that at any moment I'll slip as well. It's like a world made of invisible slides. I manage to creep nearer and stretch out my hand. "Seraphima!" I shout. "Grab on!"

She reaches toward me, her fingers brushing mine, and that tiny movement sends me barreling head over heels. Seraphima, tumbling in front of me, is sucked through the whirlpool of black. I reach out my hand to brace myself and realize that the swirling vortex is the letter *C,* surrounded by a circle.

I fall right through the middle of the copyright symbol.

I land hard on my back, surrounded by piles and piles of random objects.

There are potion bottles and swords and armor. A statue of a golden leopard with jeweled emerald eyes. A baby carriage and a prisoner's chains and a stack of mattresses, a glass slipper and a genie's lamp and a red cloak. A spinning wheel and a beanstalk so high that I can't see its top. There are heaps of coins and treasure maps, abandoned bicycles, a half-inflated hot-air balloon, and a black witch's hat. Across one wall is a bookshelf that stretches for miles, stuffed with tiny bound manuscripts and labeled with a brass plaque that reads ALTERNATE ENDINGS. I pull one out and read the last page:

> And Rapscullio and Queen Maureen lived—and loved—happily ever after.

"Wow," I breathe, craning my neck to look around.

"Edgar?" Seraphima's voice emerges from a pile of plundered jewels. I haul a pirate's chest out of the way and untangle her from ropes of pearls. "What *is* this place?"

"It's an Easter egg," I say. "In video games, the creators sometimes leave behind inside jokes or messages for players to find. They can trigger a secret game level, or a hidden shortcut." I glance around in wonder. "I think this is the portal to my mom's imagination. These are all the stories she read that led her to create this one . . . and all the plots she decided *not* to write."

I know that if I try to sift through all this stuff, I will never find the end. This room, wherever it is in the book, is as limitless as my mother's dreams.

Seraphima reaches for a fur coat and slips it on. As soon as she does, the hood tightens around her neck and two yellow eyes glow on the top of her head. "Take it off!" I yell, struggling to yank it off as it holds on to her, tight. We tumble backward, landing in an awkward heap, Seraphima's knee firmly jabbed into my chest. "Don't touch anything," I grit out. "We don't know what these things are, or what they'll do to the story if we disturb them."

She frowns, disappointed, and gets off me in a tangle of silk and petticoats.

I get to my feet, and that's when I notice the painting.

The king wears a golden crown and an ermine-lined velvet robe. In one hand he carries a golden orb. In his other arm, he cradles a baby.

I know this picture. Except when I've seen it before, it's been on my mother's desk. The man is wearing not a crown but a baseball cap. His royal robes are a Boston Red Sox T-shirt and jeans. The golden orb in his hand is just a baseball, and the baby he holds is me.

I can't stop staring at my father's face, and maybe that's why I don't notice Seraphima moving toward another pile of knickknacks. "Oooh, pretty!" she cries, lifting a small, hinged enamel pillbox. Written in silver calligraphy on the lid are the words *Heart's Desire*.

She flips it open to reveal a tiny pot of pink gloss. "Seraphima," I call out. "Don't!" But it's too late. Dipping her finger into the dish, she touches the makeup to her lips.

Seraphima convulses and her lips part. Smoke snakes from her throat, spelling out five letters:

FRUMP

The smoke swirls, wrapping around her body from head to toe, consuming her whole. I scream her name and leap forward, trying to pull her free, and tackle her.

As the cloud around us dissipates, I climb off her. "Are you all right?" I ask, and then my jaw drops.

The girl staring up at me has blue hair, piercings, and combat boots. "Who the hell are you?" I say.

PART TWO

Reader, do you believe in Fate?

Do you believe that somewhere, there's a grand plan for each of us? That our lives are written in the stars? That our lives are written for us?

If so, then we might as well consider ourselves to be characters . . . and our lives a story.

Or maybe you believe that we fall into our future blindly, drifting from adventure to adventure, our journey zigzagging not according to plan but according to pure chance.

Or just maybe, as random and haphazard as our lives seem— maybe that's exactly what the author had in mind.

DELILAH

When Jules disappears, there's a bracing gust of wind that rattles my bureau, strips my sheets, and rips the posters from my walls. Something strikes me in the face and tumbles to the ground. I reach out to grab it: a jeweled tiara. And in the next breath, sprawled on the floor in a cloud of silk and tulle and long blond hair, is Seraphima.

I grab her shoulders and haul her upright. "What did you do with my friend?"

She stares back at me, wide-eyed. "I—I don't know. I was putting on some lip gloss. And then all of a sudden I was here." Her gaze travels past me to fall on Frump, and she bursts into tears. "It's been so awful! Without your command, everything's out of control. And the servants have left the castle. No one's taken care of me!" Her voice drops to an embarrassed whisper. "I had to brush my own hair."

Frump yelps in response and Seraphima nods. "That's so

very kind of you to say, but I know I don't look as flawless as I usually do."

"Wait," Oliver says, stepping forward. "You can understand him?"

Seraphima hurls herself into Oliver's embrace, and both Frump and I stiffen. "Ollie!" she cries. "You're here too? This is just the best surprise ever!" She clasps her hands and smiles. "I want to thank you all for being here. I had no idea you were planning this. It's not even my birthday for another month—" She beams. "I will be accepting presents now."

"This isn't a party for you," Oliver says.

Frump barks, and Seraphima blushes. "He said I don't look a day over sixteen," she translates.

"How can you talk to him?"

"Oh, Ollie, what did you *think* princesses do in finishing school? I live in a tower. My best friend for four years was a bird. I'm fluent in Animal. Except Fish. They always sound a little muddled to me." She glances at me. "Peasant? Might you draw me a bath? It's been a very trying travel day."

"No, Seraphima. This is *Delilah*."

"Oh. Sorry." She smiles at me. "Delilah? Might you draw me a bath? It's been a very trying travel day."

I fold my arms. "I am not her slave."

Frump trots out of the bedroom, and a moment later I hear running water in the bathroom. He returns, his tail wagging. "Thank you so much, Frump." She raises her brows at Oliver. "You really should train your servants better, Oliver."

She sweeps out of the room. "Delilah, come attend to me."

I glance at Oliver, furious.

"Please," he begs. "Just this once."

I follow Seraphima into the bathroom. She stands with her arms extended. I grit my teeth and unlace the back of her gown. "Are we good?"

Seraphima clears her throat. She is now wearing nothing but a thin cotton shift, which is apparently too heavy for her to remove by herself. I pull it up over her head, and she turns around, buck naked. "You're a peach," she simpers, and before I can step away, she throws her arms around me for a hug of gratitude.

Honestly, the last thing I need to know is that underneath all her clothes, my boyfriend's ex is just as perfect as her face looks on any given day.

I leave Seraphima to her own devices in the bath (knowing her, she'll probably drown) and head into my bedroom. Oliver has located the fairy tale, which exploded out of Jules's hands the moment before she vanished. The book is already open. "I don't understand," he says. "What do you mean they're missing?"

I peer over Oliver's shoulder to see Orville shaking his head. "We've got a search party out for them now. But the fairies and Socks have already canvassed every page and every margin of this book, and we can't locate them anywhere."

"The book isn't long," I chime in. "And seriously, how hard could it be to find a punk-rock chick in a fairy tale?"

"Rapscullio's painting LOST posters; the mermaids are doing a dive-and-rescue search. I promise you, as soon as we know anything, we'll send a message."

"How?" Oliver points out, exasperated. "The magic easel is broken."

"Good point," Orville muses.

"We'll keep checking in," I suggest.

Frump whimpers.

"What should you do with Seraphima?" Orville repeats.

Oliver frowns. "Am I the *only* one here who doesn't speak Dog?"

"I suppose I'd just try to keep her from getting into too much trouble," Orville continues, and he grins at Oliver. "I believe you have a bit of experience doing just that, Ollie, don't you?"

Oliver gently closes the book as Frump scratches at the door to get out, no doubt so that he can take up guard duty outside the bathroom. "Oliver," I say, "we can't do this. A strange girl—emphasis on the *strange*—can't just show up in my room without raising some suspicions. And what am I supposed to tell Jules's mom?"

Oliver reaches for Jules's iPhone, plugged in and charging. "Why can't Jules tell her?" he asks. "Do that thing you do, with this."

"You're brilliant." I grab the phone from his hands and text Jules's mom.

Can I stay over at Delilah's for the whole weekend?

I hold my breath, waiting for a response. A moment later, there's a ding.

Did you finish all your hw?

YUP, I type. ☺

DON'T STAY UP TOO LATE.

"There," Oliver says. "One problem solved."

"Only temporarily. I bought us two days. But what if Jules isn't back by then?"

"She will be," he says, reassuring me.

"And Seraphima? How am I supposed to explain to my mother why Jules and some delusional princess have exchanged places?"

Suddenly an idea dawns. It's a long shot, but maybe I can convince my mother—and everyone else—that Seraphima is a visiting exchange student. It would go a long way toward explaining her lack of knowledge about, well, everything in an American household.

I turn to Oliver. "We're going to tell everyone she's from another country."

"Which one?"

I think for a moment. What language would people be least likely to know? The last thing I want is someone attempting to communicate with Seraphima in her so-called mother tongue. "Iceland," I decide.

Oliver nods. "That almost sounds *real*."

"That's because it *is*."

From the hallway comes a bark, and then, "Yoo-hoo! Delilah! I'm ready to be toweled dry!"

I glance at Oliver. "I'm not doing it. I absolutely, categorically refuse."

He bites his lower lip. "Of course. Well, I suppose *I* could help her—"

I shove him so hard he staggers backward. "Not on your life," I answer. At the threshold, I turn around. "She'd better be gone by Monday."

★ ★ ★

When Oliver leaves for the night to go home, my mother is still out on her date with Dr. Ducharme, buying me a little more time to perfect my story before I have to introduce Seraphima to her. I've let Seraphima borrow my robe to wear over her thin shift, and I've had the dubious pleasure of brushing her hair one hundred strokes with what I insisted was definitely a 100 percent boar-bristle brush like the one she has in her tower, and not a one-dollar comb from a drugstore.

"All right," I announce. "It's time to go to bed." I lift the sleeping bag Jules brought over and hand it to her, but it falls right through her arms. With a sigh, I unroll the sleeping bag perpendicular to my bed. "There you go," I say, gesturing to the makeshift mattress.

Seraphima delicately lifts her cotton gown, stepping gingerly onto the purple sleeping bag as if it's a red carpet. She walks the length of it and then promptly crawls into my bed. "This is lovely," she says, pulling the covers to her chin.

"Lovely," I mutter. I slip into the sleeping bag just in time for Frump to use me as a springboard to jump onto the bed beside Seraphima.

"Try to get a good night's rest," I say.

"Oh, I always do," Seraphima replies earnestly. "Beauty sleep is critical. You sleep well too," she says, glancing at me. "It looks like you've missed a few hours."

Frump yowls, curling at her feet.

"You're so sweet," Seraphima says to him. "But I'm sure I could be more beautiful if I tried."

There's another yelp, and a soft bark. Seraphima giggles.

"Of course I remember. You had the fairies spell my name in

the sky. And you had Queen Maureen make my favorite apple tart, but you didn't tell her you'd stolen the apples from Rapscullio's orchard." She reaches down and absently starts patting Frump's head. "What about the time I made you that biscuit for your birthday but I overcooked it into a pile of ash, and you *still* ate the whole thing because you didn't want me to feel bad?"

He waddles up the mattress until he is closer to Seraphima's face and licks her cheek. She blushes fiercely.

"You've always been so good to me, Frump," Seraphima whispers. "How come I didn't see it until you were gone?"

Frump whimpers softly, and she shakes her head.

"The way you looked never mattered to me. I always knew, you know. That it was you who lined my slippers up at the edge of my bed, and who made me breakfast, and who tidied my closet and washed my linens. So you're a dog. So what. You make me feel like the princess I always wanted to be."

Although I probably shouldn't be eavesdropping, I can't help but smile. They sound the way Oliver and I did, when he was still trapped in the book, and I would talk to him for hours beneath my covers. To anyone else listening it might have sounded like a one-sided conversation, but we knew better.

I fall asleep to the thump of Frump's tail, the sound of pure happiness.

★ ★ ★

The sun has barely broken over the horizon when I'm awakened by the sound of someone singing in an earsplitting soprano.

"Welcome, welcome, big bright sun. . . . Oh, this day will be such fun. . . . Come to sing me their hellos . . . little birds with little toes!"

I crack open an eye to see Seraphima dancing—literally dancing—around my bedroom. "What are you doing? It's six-thirty freaking a.m. On a *Sunday.*"

"Oh, good morning, serf. I was just greeting the new day!" She flutters to the window and presses her palms to the glass. "It's the loveliest morning!"

I put a pillow over my head. "It's still night. Go back to bed, Seraphima. Let's do this all over again in four hours."

"You are wrong. A lady rises with the sun. . . ." Seraphima sits down at my desk, trilling her lips in rising and falling scales. It is quite possibly the most annoying sound on the face of the earth.

"What. Are. You. Doing," I grit out.

"If I don't warm up, how do you expect me to sing all day?"

"I don't expect you to sing all day!" I yell.

When I raise my voice, Frump growls, and Seraphima nods. "I know. She *is* being excessively loud."

"I'm being loud," I repeat.

She puts her hands under the curtain of her pale blond hair and fans it out over her shoulders. "So I'm thinking I'd like a bun, wrapped in a braid. Maybe accented with a few flowers."

I slip out of the sleeping bag and gather her hair in my hands. "Ponytail it is," I say.

"This is completely unacceptable," Seraphima says. "I'm telling Oliver you're poorly suited as a housemaid. You'd do much better in a stable."

That's it. I lunge for Seraphima, and for a second I think

I might get a slug in, but Frump grabs the back of my T-shirt with his teeth and hauls me back.

Seraphima throws the window sash up and leans halfway out. *"Welcome, welcome, big bright sun—"*

I slam the window shut. "No! You might have grown up in a tower, but us peasants? We have *neighbors*." I sigh. "Let's get you dressed."

Frump is suddenly alert. I exchange a look with Seraphima and then drag Frump by his collar out the bedroom door, leaving him in the hall. I open my dresser and pull out a bra and underwear. "Try these on," I suggest.

Seraphima looks at me and then reaches for the bra, draping it over her ponytail and latching it under her chin like a bonnet.

"Not quite." I wrestle it off her head, and hold it up to my T-shirt to show her how it's done. "Take off your gown, and put *these,*" I say, "over *those.*"

For once, she does as she's told. Then she turns around, smiling. She's absolutely busting out of my bra.

I sigh. "Of *course* your boobs are bigger than mine."

I reach into my closet for the biggest sweatshirt I can find, the one I wear on my fat days. "Take off the bra and put this on," I say. "And cross your arms when you walk."

Then I Skype Oliver, hoping the chimes on his computer will wake him up. He stumbles, bleary-eyed, hair askew, in front of his screen. "Why are you awake?" he asks.

"Because Little Miss Sunshine here is an early riser. If you come over, I'll cook you breakfast."

Suddenly Seraphima leans close to my laptop, pressing her hand against the screen. "Oliver!" she gasps. "You're so *flat!*"

"Hurry," I say. "Please?"

At first Seraphima refuses to leave my bedroom, because she doesn't believe leggings are actually acceptable clothing for women. I manage to entice her downstairs with promises of food. By seven a.m. I have cooked her an omelet, pancakes, bacon, and oatmeal, all of which she has devoured. I'm convinced she is hollow.

My mother comes into the kitchen wearing her Sunday clothes—a flannel shirt and pajama pants. "You're up early," she says, surprised to see me. Then her gaze falls on Seraphima. "I thought *Jules* was sleeping over."

"Um, no, remember? I told you about Seraphima," I lie. "She's the exchange student who's living with us for a couple of days. We talked about this last week when you were getting ready for your date with Greg. God, you don't even listen to me anymore!"

"Um—of course I remember," my mother says. "I just forgot it was *this* week." She smiles at Seraphima, speaking slow and loud. *"Where . . . are . . . you . . . from . . . dear?"*

"She's Icelandic, Mom, not deaf."

Seraphima turns to her. "Are you the innkeeper?"

"Innkeeper . . . head of household . . . The words are almost identical in Icelandic," I interject.

Seraphima holds out her hand. "You are pleased to make my acquaintance."

My mother laughs. "I am," she says. "Welcome to America." She sees Frump curled up at Seraphima's feet, with his snout resting on her thigh. "Humphrey, shoo!"

"It's quite all right. Frump and I are old friends," Seraphima says.

"It's crazy," I jump in. "Apparently in Iceland, all dogs are called the same name: Frump. Seems like it would be confusing, but hey. To each his own!"

"How long are you over here, Seraphima?" my mother asks.

"First we have to find a way back into the book—"

"—a ticket," I finish. "Book a ticket." I pull Seraphima up from her chair. "We're off to the mall today. Getting some souvenirs."

Once I say it, I realize this is a brilliant idea. Seraphima can't go around in my giant Nantucket sweatshirt forever, and we don't know how long she's going to be here. If I want to prevent as many questions as possible, the first step is to at least make her *look* like she fits in.

My mother pours herself a cup of coffee and sits down across from Seraphima. "I've always wanted to go to Iceland. I've heard it's beautiful. What's it like where you grew up?"

"Well, I lived alone in a tower overlooking the ocean," Seraphima says. "But I could see everything from there—the pirates, the dragons, the mermaids—"

We are saved from imminent disaster by the ringing of the doorbell. My mother answers the door, and Oliver comes inside, his cheeks red from the wind. "Hello, Mrs. McPhee," he says. "I daresay you look younger every time I see you."

My mother—my *mother*—blushes. "Lila, where'd you find this one?" she asks, shaking her head. Still carrying her coffee mug, she walks upstairs.

"Thanks," I say, kissing his cheek. "You saved me from having to explain to my mother why Iceland has apparently become a scene from *Game of Thrones*."

"Why have we not played this game? It seems like a missed opportunity. I'd surely trounce you."

"Never mind," I reply. "Let's go see if they've found Jules in the book."

★ ★ ★

To my great relief, the minute I open the book, Edgar is front and center on Everafter Beach. And standing beside him is Jules.

At least, I *think* it's Jules.

She doesn't look like my best friend ever looks. For one thing, she's wearing a ball gown. She's traded her signature Doc Martens for *ballet* slippers—Jules, who says ballet is just an excuse for an eating disorder. And her blue hair has a streak of silver running through it. "Jules?" I whisper.

"Okay," she says, pointing to Oliver. "Suddenly he makes a lot more sense."

Seraphima stamps her tiny foot. "That is *my* gown!"

"Cool it, sister," Jules says. "That's my *friend.*"

Orville steps forward. "Edgar's been telling us where he's been, Oliver. I think you'll find it quite interesting."

Edgar looks up at us. "Seraphima took me to the copyright page, to escape for a little while."

"I've never been to the copyright page," Oliver murmurs.

"Exactly. But that's beside the point. While we were there, something happened." He hesitates. "There's a portal. Seraphima and I fell into one of those in the book, and from what I can tell, it's like a secret place between the words that's like a giant warehouse of ideas. Thoughts and images and characters that never made it into this book but that were in my mom's head."

Your mom's head. Oliver and I exchange a glance, immediately thinking of Jessamyn.

Oliver clears his throat. "Edgar, there's something you need to know. Your mother . . . she fell down. She had to go to the hospital."

Edgar's jaw drops. "Is she okay? What happened?"

"She fainted. She said she forgot to eat that day," I say. "She's much better now, really."

But Edgar isn't convinced. He starts pacing on the page. "I've got to get out. I have to make sure she's all right."

For Edgar to come out, however, means that Oliver must go back. Somewhere deep down, I knew that Edgar would want to be with his mother again, once he heard the news. But I hadn't thought far enough ahead to realize what I'd lose in the process.

Oliver looks at me, and I know he's thinking the same thing. "Maybe there's another way," he whispers to me. He turns to Seraphima. "Edgar said you came through a portal?"

She shakes her head. "It was just makeup."

I raise my brows. "Edgar?"

"It really *was* makeup. But the container was labeled *Heart's Desire.* Seraphima must have been wishing for Oliver, and that's what brought her to you."

I look at Seraphima, who is staring right at Frump. Oliver wasn't who she was wishing for.

"That doesn't explain Jules," I say.

"Yes it does," Oliver points out. "Humphrey swapped with

Frump. I swapped with Edgar. The only way for the book to eject a character is to suck in something similar enough to replace it."

That's exactly why I'm going to lose him.

But even if Oliver and Edgar look alike, Seraphima and Jules couldn't be more different. I glance at the silver streak in Jules's hair. If the replacement isn't similar . . . will the book change it to fit the mold?

"Why don't you just go get the Heart's Desire," I ask, "and wish Seraphima back in?"

"Don't you think I tried that?" Edgar says. "I've been to the copyright page a whole bunch of times, but the whirlpool that sucked us in before isn't there anymore. I don't know what made it open when it did."

Oliver frowns. "So basically no one is going in or out."

"That's really not an option. I need to get home," Edgar says. "It stands to reason that if there's one portal in the book, there might be another one." He reaches for Jules's hand, and I watch her jaw drop. "We're going to find it."

★ ★ ★

Seraphima stands in the atrium of the mall, her hands clasped in front of her and her eyes wide. "I've never seen anything like this," she breathes. Before Oliver and I can stop her, she dashes down the main corridor, bouncing from shop window to shop window like a pinball in a machine. She waves at the mannequins as she passes, and at Bath & Body Works, when an employee offers a spritz of perfume, she happily accepts. Then she looks down at the woman. "You may fix my hair now," Seraphima orders.

"There's an Ultima salon on the second floor," the employee suggests, and I link my elbow with Seraphima's to drag her away.

"Come on, Princess," I say.

There are two types of little kids you see at the mall. The first kind shuts down from overstimulation, like when I brought Oliver to the mall and turned my back for a moment and found him crouching behind a bench where an elderly man had fallen asleep. The second kind of kid thinks she's landed in Disney World—she runs straight for the gumball machine and asks for a hundred quarters.

That's Seraphima.

"Where should we take her first?" Oliver asks.

"Victoria's Secret."

"You can trust me," he says earnestly. "I won't tell a soul."

"No, it's a store—" I glance around and realize Seraphima has wandered away. Through the milling crowd I catch a flash of silver-blond hair. "That way," I say, and we rush toward her.

We round the corner and find Seraphima on top of the miniature plastic castle that's part of the children's play zone. She stands atop a turret, shoving away toddlers. "Begone, trolls," she yells. "This is my kingdom!"

"Oh God," I groan.

I step forward, but Oliver puts his hand on my shoulders. "I've got this," he says. He falls to one knee, hand on his heart. "Princess, oh, Princess," he calls. "Come down from your tower!"

Seraphima's eyelashes flutter. "Oh yes, my noble knight. I've been waiting all my life for you."

The mothers surrounding the play zone, who have protectively curled their toddlers close after the arrival of Hurricane Seraphima, start to clap. Tentatively at first, and then louder. Seraphima steps down from the plastic play structure and takes Oliver's hand, curtsying to the audience. Then she spies something in the distance. "Oh, look!" Seraphima exclaims, and she's off and running again.

She darts toward the food court, zipping through the crowds. We attempt to chase her, but we're waylaid by lines of hungry shoppers and obstacle courses made of strollers and bags. "Delilah?" Oliver asks. "Why are we being followed?"

I glance over my shoulder and see a woman with a white apron and a visor running behind us. "I don't know," I say as we finally locate our prey, peering into the window of the Tiffany & Co. store. "Seraphima!"

She turns around, holding a full tray of kung pao chicken samples. The woman racing behind us skids to a stop, and I hand over the platter, apologizing. She shakes her head and walks away, muttering under her breath.

"I'll wear *that* one," Seraphima announces, pointing to a glittering diamond tiara.

At this, I laugh out loud. "Not even *you* can afford that, Your Highness."

Oliver and I anchor Seraphima between us—like a toddler or a psychiatric patient—and steer her toward the lingerie store. As soon as we walk into Victoria's Secret, however, Oliver drops Seraphima's arm to cover his eyes. "Good God, Delilah," he says, hoarse. "This isn't decent!"

I lead him to a bench just outside the store. It is populated with dads, boyfriends, and husbands, who are all stuck in the purgatory of their significant other's shopping.

"Please don't go anywhere," I beg. "I can't worry about both of you."

Seraphima and I head inside. I walk straight past the angel wings and lacy garter belts and sexy maid outfits to the more serviceable underwear in the back. As I sift through the sale section, trying to estimate Seraphima's bra size, she flits from table to table, burying her hands in the piles of rainbow satin. She dances around me, holding up a pink corset trimmed with white lace. "Isn't this perfect!" she cries.

I snatch it from her hands. "First off, this is a hundred dollars. Second, if we wanted a corset, we'd use the one you brought with you." I hold up a white cotton bra. "This is what you need."

Seraphima frowns. "I like this one," she says, pulling out the least functional bra I've ever seen. It is hot pink, with a tulle ruffle at the bottom, and it is bedazzled with gemstones that spell *V* on one boob and *S* on the other.

I rip it out of her hands. "No," I say. "Just . . . no." Dragging her into a dressing room, I shut the door behind her and toss the white bra over the door. "Put it on."

A moment later the door opens and there stands Seraphima wearing nothing on top but the white bra—and a gigantic smile. "It's so *free*!" she gasps. "Watch how much I can move!" She twists from side to side, bends over, and then swings back upright.

"I'm glad you like it. Now take it off so I can pay. . . ."

Instead, she shoves past me, running up to the other women

in the dressing room. She points to her chest. "Doesn't this look *splendid*?" she asks.

Some of the other customers nod, but most pretend to ignore her. I pull her hand to keep her from exiting the dressing room and showing off her cleavage to the entire store.

It is a struggle to convince Seraphima to put on the sweatshirt again, until I bribe her with the thought of buying new clothes too. Collecting Oliver, I start walking to the Gap, in search of a T-shirt. "Oh, this is perfect!" Seraphima exclaims, and she runs to the far corner of the store, yanking a baby onesie off a rack. Sewn around its waist is a tiny silver sparkling tutu.

"This is Baby Gap. That wouldn't even fit on your foot," I say. I walk to the adult area and find something I think will satisfy Seraphima's appetite for glitter—a pink shirt with a sequined star emblazoned on the front. "Look, Seraphima," I say. "Shiny!"

Fifteen minutes later, we leave the store, with Seraphima decked out in her new T-shirt, as well as a pair of jeans that don't end at her calf, and ballet flats. Every five steps, she squats or kicks or turns around to look at her butt. "Who is the ruler of this mall?" she asks. "I should like very much to meet him and congratulate him on his invention of these jeans."

"I don't know if we're gonna have time for that," I mumble. "But I'll pass along the message."

Oliver leans closer to me. "You *know* him?"

Suddenly Seraphima grabs the shopping bag I'm carrying with the clothes she wore into the mall, and runs up to one of the bare-chested models standing outside Abercrombie. "Dear sir," she says, placing her hand on the guy's chest. "I'm so sorry you've fallen into such misfortune that you cannot even afford to clothe yourself. Please accept this small donation from me— and I hope things turn around for you soon." She offers a brilliant smile and presses the sweatshirt into the model's hands.

In that moment, I miss Jules *so* badly.

★ ★ ★

Three hours later, I've explained to Seraphima that Free People is not a place to purchase servants, and that they do not sell princes at Express Men. Exhausted, I announce that we are going to get some coffee at the food court. Seraphima immediately blanches. "Then I must prepare myself first!"

Oliver glances at her. "You look lovely," he says, in a tone that lets me know he's had to say this very thing a thousand times before.

"But I can't meet the king and queen looking so unkempt!"

"It's not that kind of court," I explain.

When Seraphima looks disappointed, I tell her she can pick where we eat. Unfortunately she interprets this to mean that it's perfectly all right to order from every stall that sells food. I watch her navigate the tables with a tray piled high with chicken fingers, pizza, hot pretzels, fried rice and egg rolls, french fries, a Big Mac, and a chocolate shake. "For a princess," I say to Oliver, "she eats like a trucker."

Seraphima flounces down at a table and picks up a corn dog. She holds it like an ear of corn and nibbles around the edges like a hamster.

I bump Oliver's shoulder with mine and grin up at him. "So how does it feel to officially have survived the worst nightmare of most teenage guys: a shopping day with your girlfriend?"

He glances sidelong at Seraphima, cringing slightly as she puts an entire chicken finger in her mouth at once. "Technically," he says, "that's not my girlfriend." He reaches for my hand and squeezes it on the bench between us. "Besides, I don't know what those fellows would be complaining about. A whole day with you? That sounds absolutely perfect to me."

He leans toward me, and I tilt my chin up for a kiss.

"Eww. Please!" Seraphima interrupts. She is staring at us with revulsion and talking with her mouth full. "I'm trying to eat."

"I'm beginning to understand why you wanted to leave home," I murmur to Oliver.

Just when I think things can't get any worse, Allie McAndrews sashays into the food court, like the lead goose in a formation flying south for the winter. Her entourage fans out behind her, moving in unison, each holding a tray with a bottle of water on it and nothing else.

I told Seraphima there's no queen in this court, but she just arrived.

As if she has radar, Allie manages to home in directly on the table where we're sitting. Her eyes narrow at the sight of me with Oliver, and she makes a beeline for us. "Girls! This table seems to be free. Do you see anyone here? Because I don't." She slams her purse down between me and Seraphima.

"Allie," Oliver says, "perhaps you need spectacles—"

"Forget it," I interrupt. "Let's just go."

But Seraphima doesn't budge. She looks Allie over from head to toe, fascinated. "I would look *so* much better in that outfit."

Allie finally notices that someone is sitting with Oliver and me. "Who are you?"

Oh God. "Seraphima's an exchange student from Iceland. She's staying with me for a little while."

One of Allie's clones leans toward Seraphima. "You have the most beautiful hair!"

Immediately Allie's eyes flash and she turns around. "Chloe!" she hisses.

Seraphima smiles. "It's quite all right. My hair *is* beautiful."

My jaw drops. I'm actually enjoying this. It's like watching *Clash of the Titans.*

I can practically feel a force field of anger bristling around Allie. She purses her lips, considering Seraphima's corn dog. "You really should watch what you eat," she says sweetly. "You wouldn't want to lose your figure."

Seraphima blinks innocently. "It's the funniest thing! No matter how much I eat, it all goes to my breasts!" She peers at Allie and then turns to me. "Is it normal here for girls to have a mustache like boys?"

I practically spit out my drink.

Oliver stands up and grabs Seraphima's arm, hauling her upright. "We're going to go before someone loses an eye."

Seraphima frowns. "I'm not done eating."

"Delilah will bake you a cake when we get home."

Allie and her clique float into our places, like an heirloom linen being spread across the dining room table and settling all at once.

"Well," Seraphima says. "Looks like we must move along. It's been so lovely meeting you common folks." She leans closer to Allie. "And this really *is* a perfect location for you. The only other people are five tables away, and you look *so* much better from a distance!" She tosses her a perfect, genuine white smile, leaving Allie speechless.

I walk off beside Seraphima and Oliver, knowing that Allie is staring at us as we go.

Maybe having Oliver's ex around has its perks.

★ ★ ★

The minute we step through the door of my house, Frump starts barking. He circles Seraphima in her new outfit, sniffing her jeans and biting at the tail of her T-shirt. "Stop!" she cries. "Frump, you'll rip it!"

He barks and sits back on his haunches.

"Well, *I* think I look rather fetching," she argues, crossing her arms.

Oliver intervenes. "Frump, she can't flounce around here in a gown all day without drawing attention to herself."

"And," Seraphima adds, "look at what I can *do* in this outfit!" She lunges and stretches, as if she's about to run a marathon.

Frump shakes his head so hard his jowls flap. He lets out a pitiful yelp.

A tiny frown mars Seraphima's flawless face. "I don't care.

I love this place. I love what I'm wearing. And I'm staying *forever.*"

"You can't," Oliver says immediately. "You don't belong here."

"And we need to get Jules back," I chime in.

"You don't belong here either," Seraphima tells Oliver. Her eyes fill with tears. "I've never gotten to be myself. I've always been the princess everyone expected me to be. Even the prince in my story didn't love me. For once, don't I deserve to be happy?"

Frump starts barking so loud that I'm certain the neighbors can hear him. "What's he saying?" I whisper to Oliver, but neither Frump nor Seraphima is paying attention to us.

"What was wrong with being ourselves in the fairy tale? Everything!" Seraphima wails.

He bares his teeth, growling low in his throat.

"Maybe I'm not becoming someone different," Seraphima says to Frump. "Maybe this is who I always was."

He yips and turns in a circle, looking pleadingly at her.

"But we *are* talking," she answers. "We're talking right now."

Frump goes very still, and his head hangs low, the tips of his ears dragging on the ground. His tail is tucked between his legs.

The fight goes out of Seraphima. She sinks to the ground, lifting his snout in her hands. "No," she admits. "I guess you *can't* talk to me. But what would you say to me there that you can't say here?"

Frump raises his nose to the ceiling, his white throat bare. He howls, his long tongue looping awkwardly around the vowels, in a way that almost sounds like human speech. *"Iiiiirrrruv-vvvvvooooo!"* he howls.

Stricken, I watch this scene unfold before me. There was a time, briefly, when Frump was a boy again and Seraphima was the girl he loved, and he didn't muster the courage to tell her how he felt. And now it's too late. What would happen if the people we were meant to love were in the right place at the right time? What if we told each other before it was too late? How come love is never simple?

I watch emotions flicker over Seraphima's face: shock, pain, regret. And love. I know she loves him. And I know what it feels like to think that no matter what, you're never going to get the chance to be together the way you want to be.

I feel Oliver's hand reach for mine, and I know he's thinking the same thing.

Tears streak down Seraphima's face. Caught in a storm of feelings, she stumbles to her feet, opens the front door, and begins to run.

No matter how fast she goes, I know she won't be able to outdistance her own thoughts.

Frump leaps to his feet and dashes out the door, following Seraphima before Oliver or I have the presence of mind to grab his collar. He barks, and then he barks again, trying to get her attention.

Finally she stops and faces him. He pauses in the middle of the street, panting, just staring at her—and in that moment, it doesn't really matter that there are no words.

None of us sees the car coming.

OLIVER

I've never felt anything like this.

Like someone's hollowed me out, scraped me raw, left me as nothing but a shell. I feel a white-hot poker of pain every time I look down at him. I can feel his weight in my arms; I can still feel the heat of his body and his wiry fur prickling against my skin. He's here, but he's not.

I want to close the book. I want to start from the beginning. I want him to be standing by my side in front of Queen Maureen as I tell her I'm off to rescue a princess. I want us to walk through the story a million more times together.

I feel like I'm in a glass box. I can see Delilah's mouth twisting as she calls my name, and her fists pound on the transparent wall to get my attention, but I hear nothing but the blood rushing in my ears.

"Frump?" I whisper, shaking him gently. "Come on. Wake up."

Suddenly Delilah's hands close over my shoulders, shaking

me hard. At that second, the whole world comes crashing over me, like a rogue wave that sends you somersaulting and steals your breath and your bearings. I surface, and everything is too loud, too bright, too painful. Delilah's fingers press so hard into my skin that they leave marks in the shape of half-moons. Seraphima is crumpled into a ball, rocking back and forth, wailing. I have no recollection of how we got back into Delilah's house; there is just a trail made of drops of ink that lead from the street to the kitchen floor.

"You have to help him," I say to Delilah, the words catching in my throat.

"Oliver," she whispers. "There's nothing we can do. He's gone."

But she's wrong. He's right here. "We just have to get to the beginning. You have to close the book—"

"There is no book," she says softly. "We can't go back."

Something about her words breaks through my haze, and I look up at her face, stricken.

Death, to me, has always just been a word. A mention of a king I never knew, a villain whose demise led to a happy ending. Never have I seen it; never have I felt it; never have I held it in my hands.

Never has it been *forever.*

Seraphima kneels in front of me, stroking Frump's limp body. "No, no, no!" she sobs. "You can't leave me. I love you. Do you hear me? I *love* you!" She looks up at me, her blue eyes glittering with tears. "Why isn't he waking up, Oliver?"

Delilah puts her hand on Seraphima's arm. "That's not how it works here," she explains.

Seraphima's lip quivers. "I want to go back to the way it was." She throws herself against my shoulder, crying so hard that her entire body shakes. "Take me home, please," she begs. "Take me home."

Over Seraphima's bent head, I meet Delilah's gaze. It's like a mirror. I can see the same anguish reflected on her face that must be on mine.

She walks to a cabinet in the kitchen and pulls out a white cotton tablecloth. Gently, she comes closer to me and lifts Frump out of my arms, to wrap him in a cocoon.

When I let go of my best friend, it feels like a part of me is missing. I look down at my hands, stained with ink.

★ ★ ★

With every strike of the shovel, I clench my teeth. My hands are blistered, and my shoulders ache, but at least this kind of hurt I understand. The hole I am digging gets deeper; the pile of earth grows. I don't look behind me. I can't, because I know what I'll see.

Delilah sits on the back porch cradling her phone, trying not to cry as she explains to her mother what happened. I catch snippets of the one-sided conversation:

"... *car came out of nowhere* ... *driver offered to bring us to the vet* ... *too late* ..."

My hair falls into my eyes as I stab the shovel even harder into the ground.

Delilah was the one who made me realize that we couldn't wait for Mrs. McPhee to come home from work before we buried him. As far as she was concerned, Frump was and always had been Humphrey. It would be too hard to explain why her dog's shroud was spotted with ink, why I was so broken up with grief over a dog that didn't belong to me. After getting Seraphima a cup of tea and settling her in a chair with a blanket around her shoulders and a box of tissues in her lap, Delilah and I carried Frump into the yard to find him a final resting place.

I picked a spot beneath a willow tree, because we had willows back at home too and I think he would have liked that. Then, without saying another word to Delilah, I began to dig.

I feel a drop of water on my hand, and then another. It would be fitting for the sky to weep. But when I look up, I see sunshine, and I realize that I am the one who's crying.

Delilah approaches, her hands tucked in her back pockets. "That's perfect. Let me get Seraphima and—"

"Not yet," I interrupt. "I think maybe just a little deeper."

The hole, I know, is plenty big. It's just that I am not ready for what has to come next. I fear I may never be.

"Oliver," Delilah says. "We *have* to. My mom'll be home soon."

I nod and set the shovel down. I kneel in front of Frump while Delilah goes to fetch Seraphima.

I lean over and whisper. "Remember when we convinced Socks that if he kept eating carrots, he'd turn orange? And when you gave me fleas and Queen Maureen quarantined us both in the tower?" I am quiet for a moment, lost in the past. "All those times we walked through the forest and the unicorn meadow, you'd run ahead, and then you'd always circle back, just to make sure I was still there." I rest my hand on Frump's head. "Don't forget to circle back, my friend."

Delilah returns, her arm around Seraphima. I can tell that without Delilah's support, she would have collapsed by now. She stands stiffly in front of the open grave, her eyes swollen and her cheeks red, as I lift Frump into my arms and gently lower him.

Seraphima starts to cry again and presses a tissue to her nose. "Sometimes at a funeral," Delilah says, "people say a few words."

Seraphima nods. "A few words," she repeats solemnly.

"Frump," Delilah continues, "I didn't know you very well. But I've never seen someone love as hard, or as loyally, as you did."

She looks up at me, and I realize it is my turn to speak. I clear my throat. "I hope that wherever you are, you're finally who you want to be."

Seraphima falls to her knees, sobbing, and Delilah glances at me, communicating silently. I lift Seraphima into my arms and carry her back inside, settling her on the living room couch. By the time I come back out, Delilah has already filled the pit halfway with dirt.

For a moment, I am frozen with agony watching her. Then I grab the shovel from her hands and begin to viciously toss heaps of earth into the grave. My whole body trembles with the effort, and sweat pours down my back. It takes Delilah three tries to wrench the shovel from my hands.

"Stop!" she pleads. "That's enough!"

My face twists with sorrow. "This is my punishment," I say. "He wouldn't have been here if it weren't for me."

"Oh, Oliver," she murmurs, and I fall into her arms, giving in to the grief.

★ ★ ★

When you love someone, silence isn't awkward. Delilah sits next to me, her arms wrapped tightly around me, and neither of us speaks. I was born in a sea of words, I lived and breathed language, but right now, this quiet is the most comfortable place in the world.

★ ★ ★

When Delilah's mother comes home, she spends an hour outside at Frump's grave with Dr. Ducharme's arm around her. Seraphima retires just after supper, saying she has a headache, although I know it is just the day's events that have overwhelmed her. For the first time since I came to the house this morning, I find myself alone with Delilah in her room, with a Herculean task ahead of me.

"Are you ready?" Delilah asks as she pulls the fairy tale from her shelf.

I take a deep breath and open the book to the final page.

The entire cast of characters stands in position on Everafter Beach, in an odd mash-up of fairy tale and science fiction. The mermaids swim in the shallows; Captain Crabbe steers a spacecraft; the trolls are shooting lasers from behind a barricade. Edgar stands with his sword raised high in victory. Beside him, Jules is pulling at the chafing neck of her princess gown. As soon as she sees our faces, she relaxes. "I *told* you guys it would be Delilah and Oliver," she says. "*Now* can I get out of this corset?"

But I'm not focusing on her words. My eyes fall to the spot where Frump would have stood and where, instead, Humphrey now holds a laser gun in his jaw.

"Whoa, boy," Edgar says, grabbing the gun as the dog swings it wildly back and forth. "That's not a toy." He glances up at me. "And before you ask, no, we haven't found another portal yet. But maybe if you stopped interrupting us by opening the book, we could actually get some work—"

"That's not why I called you here." I swallow. "I don't know how to say this. . . ."

Delilah covers my hand with hers where it rests on the edge of the page. "It's Frump."

"He . . . he's dead," I manage to say.

Queen Maureen blinks up at me. "For goodness' sake, darling. That happens to Rapscullio every day. Just close the book."

"I don't live in a book anymore," I reply. "And neither did Frump, when he died. It's different here. There are no second chances. It's . . . permanent."

A cloud of shock settles over the cast. "What if we bring him back here?" Socks asks. "Maybe he just needs to be back in the book?"

"It doesn't work that way, my boy," Orville answers. "When

you're in a given world, you must play by its rules. Frump can't die out there and be resurrected here."

One of the mermaids starts to cry, and then another, and then the third, and the tide begins to rise. Pyro exhales a plume of white smoke. Socks sits down heavily on his rump. "But he was my *friend*," the horse wails. "How can he just be gone?"

"I know it hurts," Delilah says, "but every day, it will hurt a little less." She turns away from the book to wipe her eyes.

If I stay with them while they grieve, I'm going to be ripped apart all over again too, and I have barely managed to regain control since the funeral. "It's more important than ever that you find a way for Seraphima to return to the book," I tell Edgar. "She needs to be back there with all of you."

Rapscullio puts his arm around Queen Maureen's shoulders. One by one, the fairies emit a shower of sparks, becoming memorial candles for Frump.

"I'm sorry," I tell everyone, my voice husky with regret. "I never thought something like this could happen."

And then I can't hold myself together anymore. I step back before everyone sees me fall to pieces. Before I can, however, Delilah closes the book.

I sit down on the edge of her bed, burying my face in my hands. "How can anyone survive in this world?" I ask. "How can you keep letting go of people you care about?"

I don't really mean for Delilah to answer, but she sits beside me and threads her fingers through mine. "Because you know they're in a better place," she says quietly. "That's what everyone always tells you, but I didn't really think it was true, until now."

There is something in the tone of her voice, a catch to her words, that makes me look up at her. Her eyes shine with tears, and she's biting her lower lip. "Since Edgar told us he wanted to get out of the book, I've been trying to find a way to keep you here too. When you love someone, you want to keep him safe. It's why Frump wanted Seraphima to go back to the book with him." She takes a deep, rattling breath. "I am so scared of losing you forever. I don't think I could live, if you didn't. Which is why I realize Seraphima isn't the only one who needs to leave."

Slowly her words swim into focus in my mind, and I realize what she's saying. "But I love you."

"I love you too. So much that I'd rather have you a world away, safe, than not have you at all."

I want to argue, but I know I'll never win. The proof is in Delilah's backyard, under the willow tree. The proof is in the dirt still caked beneath my fingernails.

Delilah throws herself into my arms, and I clutch her, as if holding her tightly enough were all it would take to keep me from falling back into those pages. I hold her as if she could leave her impression on my skin, on my heart.

I try to commit all of this to memory: how it feels to touch her, the vanilla scent of her hair.

I wonder how many people I will lose in one day.

Death is the guest you didn't invite: arriving when you least expect it, when you least need it, and when you least want it.

It's a blow from behind.

A knife in the back.

The shadow that's following you.

It's why you always keep looking over your shoulder.

EDGAR

How do you explain the idea of *never* in a world where possibility is endless?

Socks turns to me, his eyes clouded with confusion. "So when Oliver said that Frump isn't coming back," he asks, "he just meant, like, this *week* . . . right?"

I look around to find everyone staring at me, waiting for answers.

The way people explained death to me, after my dad was gone, was a load of crap. *He's in a better place. He'll always be with you. As long as you remember him, he's still alive.* None of that's true. When someone you care about dies, no matter how hard you hang on, he starts to fade away. One day you can't remember the pitch of his voice anymore. Then you forget the way he smells. And before you know it, the only memories you have are the ones that come from photographs.

"Not this week," I tell Socks. "Not ever."

"Could we maybe talk to Frump about this?" Socks asks. "I'm pretty sure I can get him to reconsider dying."

"It's not his choice," I explain. "It's like getting erased. Like he's not part of the story anymore."

"Like Oliver?" asks Glint, the fairy.

"Yeah, kind of . . . if Oliver could never open this book. And if you were never able to speak to him again."

I glance around at the stunned faces on the beach, wondering if I'm only making this worse. If Oliver were here instead of me, he'd know exactly what to say. As usual, I'm just a poor substitute.

Socks's upper lip trembles. "But I didn't get to say goodbye."

"That's the thing about death," I hear as Jules steps forward. "You hardly ever do."

Until now, I almost forgot about her.

The streak of white in her hair has tripled in size. She still looks ridiculous in a princess's gown and combat boots, but the characters are hanging on her every word, as if each one is a precious gift.

"The fact that you don't get to say goodbye is what makes it feel so unreal," Jules continues. "That's why it's so hard to wrap your head around. You feel like if someone's going to leave forever, there should be a last hug or kiss, right? But death's a bitch." She sits down on a rock. "Maybe you'll see a cloud the shape of a dog bone and you'll call out Frump's name, so that he can see it too—but he isn't with you anymore. Or you might dream about him digging in the castle's strawberry patch as if he's still here, when he's not. But as much as you think it hurts now, I'm sorry to say it only gets worse. Once the shock wears off and the truth sets in . . . that's when you realize how much you're missing."

Queen Maureen frowns. "Then what do we do?"

Jules glances at her. "We keep on living."

As the group begins to disperse, Jules walks toward me. "Thanks, Dr. Phil," I mutter.

"Shut up, Edgar."

I flinch, remembering what high school was like. It was a hell of a lot easier to be silent and overlooked than to be constantly shut down.

A spark of anger flares in me. "What makes you the expert on death, anyway?"

"None of your business." She glances at me. "We'd better get moving if we're going to find that portal. Because I'm not planning on sticking around another day."

★ ★ ★

There must be a thousand trees in the Enchanted Forest, and we have to examine every one. Jules and I stuff our fists into the small hollows of the trunks where squirrels usually live, trying to see if there's a hidden passage out of this book. Glint, Ember, and Sparks crawl into crevices in the trees as well, lighting them up like display cases in a museum as they peek inside, trying to find something of value.

"I don't get it," Jules says, up to her elbow in a willow. "Haven't you guys *done* this before?"

"Oh yeah. I stick my hands into trees whenever I get a chance."

"No, I mean the whole escape-hatch thing. Isn't that how you and Oliver switched lives in the first place?" Jules cranes her neck around a trunk. "Can't we just *Freaky Friday* this and be done with it?"

"If it were that simple, don't you think I would have already done it?" I point out. "The way Oliver and I traded places was by rewriting the plot so that it was a sci-fi battle starring me instead of him, saying he was an imposter all along. And yeah, I guess we were able to fool the book long enough to make the switch. But the book wants to go back to its original form. It started leaving notes for Oliver in the real world. And it started to turn Frump back into a dog, before he left."

"So . . . if we wait long enough, won't we get spit out of this book anyway?"

"No, it's not like that. It seems to be able to tolerate swapping characters but not messing with the story. It wants a happily-ever-after."

Jules rolls her eyes. "That's so Disney."

"So was Miley Cyrus," I say, and Jules laughs.

"Can I ask a stupid question? What are we looking for? Is it an actual Easter egg?"

That makes me think about my mom, and what Oliver said happened to her. Delilah assured me she's totally fine now, but I want to see for myself. "It could be anything."

"Then I've definitely found it," Jules tells me, and she holds up a handful of squirrel poop. "*This* is totally going to get me back home."

"You're right. We're not going to find anything here." I knock against one of the tree trunks. "Hey, Glint," I say, and she pops her tiny bright head out from the knothole. "You guys are free to go."

The fairies zip away, leaving a trail of light behind them, like the phosphorescent glow of a Fourth of July sparkler.

"Now what?"

"The ocean," I suggest. "Warning: the mermaids are major hoarders. Who knows what we'll find in there."

"My aunt's a hoarder," Jules says. "I swear, when I was there this summer, I had to army-crawl to the bathroom. And I'm pretty sure Amelia Earhart's body is stuffed somewhere underneath piles of newspapers in the living room."

"Why were you at your aunt's?"

"My parents told me it was so that I could experience the joys of country living, like hauling slop buckets to the pigs and cleaning out the chicken coop. But in reality they were just trying to ditch me."

"Why?" I ask.

Something in Jules seems to shut down. "They thought it would be *good* for me or something."

I dig my hands into my pockets. "That's why my mother wrote this book," I tell her. "After my dad died, I was kind of terrified. Of everything."

"Your dad died?"

I shrug. "I guess neither of us lived up to our parents' expectations, huh?" I was never going to be the kid my mother hoped I'd turn out to be—namely, Oliver. I could only be myself, but that didn't seem to be good enough.

I turn the corner at the edge of the last paragraph and find myself at the page break. Jules, I realize, has stopped walking. "What's up?"

She shakes her head. "I'm still getting used to this."

I grin. "Someone's got a fear of gaps. . . ."

"Cut me some slack; I've only been here a day." She takes a deep breath, trying to look cool, but I can see how red her cheeks are and how she's working hard to calm herself down. It's kind of weird to see Jules—who could probably survive a tsunami or face down the entire Taliban—get so shaken by a page break.

Finally, something I can do better than she can.

I reach for her hand. "Try not to overthink it," I say, and I leap onto the next page.

We land in the unicorn meadow. I'm still holding on to Jules. I look down at our linked hands and feel a shiver run the length of my spine. Suddenly Jules pulls her hand away from me. "I could have done it myself," she snaps, and she walks off.

"That seems about right," I mutter to myself. It's not the first time a girl has looked at me like I'm pond scum.

I catch up to her halfway across the meadow. For a moment we just walk side by side, silent. "Hey," I say, trying to break through the awkwardness. "What's a hipster weigh?"

Jules doesn't respond.

"An Instagram." I pause. "Get it? Instag—"

I break off when Jules stops dead, staring at a unicorn that's munching on silver grass. "Am I in a drug dream?" she asks.

"Oh, wait. It gets better. This is the unicorn meadow . . . and they're eating *moon grass.*"

"How high was your mom when she wrote this book?" Jules asks.

At that, I laugh. My mom doesn't even like to take Tylenol. "There's an outhouse behind that tree, and I'm pretty sure it's where Elvis died. . . ."

Jules grins, and just like that, any weirdness between us is gone again. "So . . . if we're headed to the ocean," she asks, "how come we're landlocked with a bunch of mythical creatures?"

"Shortcut," I explain, pointing to the cliff in the distance. "The water's on the other side."

We hike across the field, Jules gently patting a unicorn as she passes by. A swarm of butterflies forms a cloud around us, a festival of color. She glances around with delight. "You know what it means when you see this many butterflies at once, right?"

I hesitate, expecting her to say what girls always say: that it's a guardian angel, or good luck, or just plain romantic.

"It means there's something dead nearby," Jules continues. "Butterflies feed on carrion."

I stare at her, impressed. "Zombie butterflies," I say. "*Very* cool."

We reach the base of the cliff and start to climb. Jules is faster than I am and reaches the top a few moments before I do. I haul myself over the lip and onto all fours, then stop dead, nearly swallowing my tongue. Jules is stripping off her gown. "What?" she asks. "Haven't you ever seen a girl in her underwear before?"

Well. Actually, no.

"You're not wearing clothes," I point out.

"Thank you, Captain Obvious. And technically, I'm wearing the equivalent of a bikini. Aren't we going swimming?"

"Yeah but . . ."

"Do *you* swim fully dressed?"

"N-no," I stutter.

"Last one in's a rotten egg," Jules says, and she does a perfect swan dive off the cliff into the ocean.

You can do this, I think. I hop on one foot, trying to pull off my spacesuit, and stare down with shock at a pair of dark gray tights that I did not put on this morning.

Great. So now this book is trying to turn me into a prince.

I try to wrestle the panty hose off my legs, wondering how on earth women do this.

"What's taking you so long?" Jules calls, and I glance over my shoulder to see her treading water, her hair slicked back.

I decide I'm going to impress her with my best backflip. I manage to peel one leg free of the tights. But when I'm trying to strip off the other side, I lose my balance, and instead of executing an Olympics-worthy flip, I wind up flailing in the air and smacking into the surf with a thundering belly flop.

Sputtering, I make my way to the surface. Jules is laughing. "That was so sexy," she says.

We are quickly surrounded by a whirlpool fashioned from the strong tails of Marina, Ondine, and Kyrie. "You have to kiss one of them," I tell Jules.

"What? This is *not* spin the bottle."

"No, it's so you can breathe underwater." Ondine pops through the surface. "She's all yours," I say.

"I don't think we've officially met. I'm Ondine," the mermaid says, and she kisses Jules, dragging her underwater.

A moment later, Kyrie puts her webbed hands on my shoulders. "Ready, handsome?" she asks.

"Shouldn't you at least buy me dinner first?" I joke, and she seals her lips over mine and pulls me below the surface.

It's the strangest sensation I've had while in this book: breathing water. At first you fight it, certain you're drowning, as your lungs fill. But then, just when you're sure you're a goner, your chest seems to burst, and the water rushes in and out of your nose like oxygen. I keep an eye on Jules, who is struggling in Ondine's grasp as she gives herself over to the feeling.

Her eyes open, and her hair snakes out around her face, tendrils of indigo with silver stripes. "This," she says, "is wicked awesome!"

"I know, right? Just wait." I turn to the mermaids. "Hey, guys, can we get a fin?"

They link their arms in ours and swim us to the very bottom of the ocean floor in a matter of seconds. Jules can't stop smiling like a kid on her first roller coaster. I watch her reach out toward a sea horse, which tickles its way up her arm. Finally the mermaids release us at the entrance to their underwater cave. Jules looks appreciatively at Ondine. "You would so totally kick butt on our school swim team."

"I'm pretty sure that having a tail counts as cheating," I point out. I glance around the cavern. Stalactites and stalagmites form the ceiling and the floor, like the jaws of a giant beast. Bright orange brain coral colors the walls, and in the center of the cave is a slab of granite—their dining room table.

"What are we looking for?" Marina asks.

"A way out," I explain.

Kyrie snorts. "You've come to the wrong place," she says, and she unlocks a small wooden door. Half a dozen skeletons drift toward us, still draped in bits of ribbon and velvet and clinging to their swords. "If these guys didn't find an escape hatch, I doubt you will either."

I expect Jules to be terrified by this, but instead she breast-strokes closer to one and shakes its hand. "Cool," she breathes.

Marina nods, impressed. "I *like* this girl."

I begin shucking oysters, hoping to find something other than an ordinary pearl. Marina swims into the depths of the skeleton closet, strip-searching the inhabitants. Ondine sifts through kelp and Kyrie flips over flounder and starfish on the ocean floor. Meanwhile, Jules sits cross-legged on the granite table, elbow-deep in a giant pink clam filled with keys. "What about one of these?" she asks. "These all have to open *something.*"

"At one time, yes. They were the keys to kingdoms, to shackles, to diaries. Most of them are long past their use," Kyrie says.

Jules starts examining them one by one and sorting them into piles. Some are rusted, some are shiny. Some have seaweed tangled around them, some are ornate, some are plain. Nothing stands out as extraordinary; nothing screams, *This is your escape.* "This one has writing on it," she says, holding the key up to the crackling light of an electric eel. "I can't make it out."

I take it out of her hand and read the Latin inscription out loud: " '*Carcere aqua,*' " I say.

"Water prison," Jules translates.

"You speak *Latin*?"

"SAT prep, man. I'm a vocabulary *beast*." She frowns. "Do you have any idea what it means?"

I glance at the skeleton closet. "That's the only water prison I can think of in this book." Taking the key, I close the door and try to lock it, but the bolt won't turn.

Marina purses her lips. "Isn't there a jail cell on Captain Crabbe's pirate ship? He locked me in there once when I didn't floss."

I stuff the key into my pocket and turn to Jules. "Time to surface," I say.

With the aid of the mermaids, we rise to the top of the ocean, breaking into the air about five miles from the shore of Everafter Beach. Looming nearby, like a great gray whale, is Captain Crabbe's ship. I start flailing my arms, shouting, to grab the attention of the hands on deck.

Suddenly I hear the pirate's gruff voice. "Edgar, laddie, is that you?" he cries. "Man overboard!"

★ ★ ★

Captain Crabbe's ship slices through the waves like a knife cutting through butter. The salty spray splashes over the gunwale, soaking the rough blanket the first mate gave me after hauling me up to safety. Sitting on an overturned crate is Jules, wrapped in her own blanket, holding a mug of hot grog. Her hair is starting to dry, and by now there's more silver in it than blue. I keep thinking it's like a ticking time bomb, that we'd better figure out how to get Jules back to the real world before she's fully blond and singing to birds and bugs on her windowsill.

Captain Crabbe stands in front of me, his feet planted wide to keep him steady as the deck rocks back and forth in the surf. "Tell me again, mate, why a landlubber like yerself was swimmin' in these parts? Is there a cavity botherin' you?"

"No, my teeth are fine." I unclench my fist to reveal the key. "We found this in the mermaids' cave, and we're looking for the lock that it fits," I say. "I think it could be on your ship."

"I didna misplace any keys," the captain says thoughtfully, "but ye're welcome to take a look around." He extends a hand to Jules, helping her to her feet, and she smiles. As soon as she does, he leans in a little closer. "Ye have a twisted eyetooth," he murmurs. "I could get ye a retainer that would fix that. . . ."

"Thanks," Jules says, "but I've done my time in braces."

Captain Crabbe sniffs. "Well. Whoever ye went to clearly wasna a perfectionist."

I wander around the top deck, trying the key in various padlocks, but nothing works. I glance around for Jules, but she seems to have gone AWOL. Then I hear her cry: "Look, Edgar: I'm king of the world!"

She straddles the bowsprit, her arms extended wide in a T, doing her best Leonardo DiCaprio impression. "Great. When you're done playing *Titanic*, can you get down here and help?"

"You're no fun," Jules says, but she scrambles down and walks over to Walleye, one of the hands, who's mopping on the starboard side of the ship. "Is there another floor?"

Walleye glances down at the wood beneath his mop. "This is the only one we got."

"She means a lower deck," I explain.

"Oh. Why didn't you say so?" Walleye grunts, leading us down a ladder to the two tiny cells in the belly of the ship.

"Okay, *this* is creepy," Jules says. "Why is there a prison in a fairy tale?"

Captain Crabbe shrugs. "It came with the boat."

I pull on the iron bars of one locked door. "Where are the keys?"

The captain looks at Walleye, who lets his gaze slide to the floor. "Dunno," he admits. "Scuttle was the last one who had 'em."

"Scuttle!" Captain Crabbe yells.

The second mate comes out of the galley, wiping his hands on a dish towel. "Ye called?"

"Where are the keys to the cells?"

"I keep 'em in the cookie jar," he says. "Just wait here a minute." Scuttle disappears into the kitchen again, and we hear banging and rattling and a gigantic crash. "I'm fine!" he yells, and a moment later he comes back with a small ceramic container. He empties the contents on a rough wooden table: a dozen stale hardtack crackers filled with mealworms that I can actually see moving, and a single brass key.

Scuttle presents the key to the captain, who hands it to me. I open the cell on the left and Jules and I crowd inside. It's barely big enough for one person, much less two, and we have to dance around each other as we pull loose boards and kick at the dirt on the floor. Jules turns to me, and I can feel her breath on my neck. I can't help but think of how close we are, even though that's the last thing I'm supposed to be focusing on.

"Looks like there's nothing here," Jules says. "Should we try the other one?"

I grab the key with the Latin inscription and wiggle it into the lock. When the tumblers turn, all the hair stands up on the back of my neck.

This is it.

For a moment, I hesitate. What if, the minute I open this door, Jules disappears just as suddenly as she arrived? What if the best thing that's happened to me since I've been here vanishes before I get a chance to really know her?

"What are you *waiting* for?" Jules asks, and she shoves past me and pushes open the barred iron door.

I draw in my breath, expecting the worst to happen.

Except, it doesn't.

Jules stands in the middle of the cell, rattling the bars. "Looks like this one's a dud too."

Captain Crabbe draws himself up. Just one glance and his two crewmates scatter above deck. We follow and stand at a distance below the sail, watching the fireworks between them ignite.

"Do either of ye two numbskulls care to tell me how our key wound up on the bottom of the ocean floor?" the captain yells.

Scuttle and Walleye exchange a glance—well, as best they can, since Walleye's gaze goes in two different directions. "Well, Cap'n, it's like this. . . ." Scuttle swallows hard. "We dropped it in the ocean."

Captain Crabbe sighs. "Do ye ken how hard it is to find decent help around here?" he mutters. "Now that we *have* the key, perhaps we should test it by lockin' the both of ye up for a few hours."

"We didn't mean to," Scuttle says.

"Aye," Walleye agrees. "We just wanted to see if it would float."

As they bicker, I spot Everafter Beach gleaming in the moonlight a few hundred yards away. I nudge Jules with my shoulder. "Feel like a swim?" I murmur, crawling onto the ship's gunwale and holding out my hand.

She grabs it so I can pull her up beside me. "I thought you'd never ask," Jules says, and together, we jump.

★ ★ ★

It is a longer swim than I thought. By the time we reach the beach, we're both out of breath. Jules rolls onto her back, letting the surf wash around her, too tired to inch her way to a drier spot. I lie with my cheek pressed into a scallop shell.

"Why didn't you just ask that pirate to drop us off?" Jules pants.

"*Mmmmpht thkkkng,*" I say, my mouth full of sand.

It takes me a few minutes to catch my breath, and when I do, I get to my feet and walk to higher ground, sinking down on the beach. I grab a chunk of coral curved like a candy cane. "A perfect *J.*"

"Huh?" Jules has come to sit beside me.

"My mom and I used to walk the beach on Cape Cod, looking for coral shaped like *E*s and *J*s." I toss it to her. "*J* for Jules."

She turns it over in her hands, like a small glowing bone.

"I'm worried about my mom." I look away. "I miss her. I mean, I see little bits of her everywhere. Queen Maureen uses her scone recipe. Her favorite flowers—daisies—are the only ones that grow in the unicorn meadow. And . . ." I point to the coral in Jules's hand. "Well. That. But it's not the same, you know?"

Jules hugs her knees to her chest. "It's kind of like that with my sister."

"You have a sister?"

"Had," Jules says. "Her name was Sofia. I'm an expert at death." She rolls the coral between her palms. "I was six when my mom got pregnant, and I was so excited about having a sister that I asked, like, a hundred times a day when she was going to get here. Finally my dream came true. Sofia came—four months early. She only lived a couple of hours. I know it wasn't my fault, but sometimes I still think . . . if I hadn't wanted her here so badly . . . if I hadn't wished quite so hard . . . would she be alive?" Jules dashes her hand across her eyes. "This is so stupid. I don't even know why I'm telling you."

"No . . . I'm glad you did," I say. "It's kind of nice to know I'm not the only one who's messed up."

Jules laughs. "You're more messed up than I am."

"You're right," I agree. "Because I'm actually kind of psyched that we didn't find a portal in the pirate ship."

"You are?"

"Yeah." I turn, meeting her gaze. Her eyes are as dark as the night. "All I could think, when the key turned in that lock, was that you were about to go . . . and I wasn't ready to give you up yet."

Gathering every shred of courage I have, I reach for Jules's hand.

Just like the last time I touched her, in the unicorn meadow, she instantly pulls away. "No!" she yelps. "Edgar—I'm sorry. . . . I just . . . can't."

I feel my cheeks burn. Jeez, how repulsive *am* I?

"I mean, you're really hot and everything . . . but it seems so weird and wrong. I mean, you look *identical* to my best friend's boyfriend."

My jaw drops. "You think I'm hot?"

Her mouth tips up in a half smile. "Don't be getting all cocky, now."

"So the problem here is that I look like Oliver?" She nods. "Then close your eyes."

Her lashes drift shut, and I lean forward.

I am pretty sure I am about to throw up. My heart is literally rattling my rib cage, it's beating so hard. What if I do this wrong? What if my nose winds up in the wrong place? What if I miss her mouth? Why didn't I think about Googling this, or steal my mom's *Cosmopolitan* magazine when I had the chance?

Enough, Edgar, I tell myself, an internal pep talk. *Don't think. Just do.*

And then wonderfully, miraculously, I'm kissing her.

Jules melts against me and my arms go around her. I'm afraid to move, because if I do, I'm going to wake up. So instead I just keep my lips on hers until I start to see stars in the corners of my eyes, because I'm running out of air.

She breaks away from me, gasping. "It's always the quiet ones," she murmurs.

I wonder if I ever would have met Jules if I'd stayed in the real world. If the magic between us has to do with fiction, or if it would have happened no matter where we were introduced.

I wonder if she's wondering the same thing.

I lie down on the sand, looking up at the stars, Jules's head pillowed on my arm, smiling so hard I think my skin is going to crack.

This has been a good day.

"I used to be able to find the Big Dipper," I say, "but I'm pretty sure my mom knew nothing about astronomy, since these stars look totally random. Do you know any constellations?"

Jules freezes. "I, um . . . someone recently tried to show me a few, but I can't remember them exactly."

I shrug. "Then let's make up our own." I point to the sky. "That one there? It's called the Rocker. See how it looks like a chair?"

She grins. "Oh yeah, I totally see it. And over to the left, with the two eyes and the jagged mouth? That's the Joker." Suddenly she sits up. "Edgar," Jules says. "Do you see what I see? There's something wrong with that star. It looks . . . flat."

I peer into the sky. Against the velvet of the night, one of the Joker's eyes is twinkling. The other, though, is not shining back at us. It's lifeless, dull.

It looks more like a hole punched through the sky than a star.

Or in other words: a portal.

★ ★ ★

The hammering is deafening. The trolls are nailing together the tallest ladder I've ever seen, but it starts in the middle of the ocean, because this particular star—of course—is not directly over the beach. As a result, this is an engineering marvel requiring the coordination of the trolls, who are designing the mechanism; Captain Crabbe, whose boat serves as the platform for the ladder; and the mermaids, who are frantically swimming against the current to control the wave patterns buffeting the ship.

Jules and I swung by the castle for a change of clothes before gathering our building committee. To my shock, in my bedroom wardrobe, there were no spacesuits anymore—just rows of tunics and tights. It took ten minutes for Jules to convince me to walk outside, and even now I can't believe I'm dressed like freaking Robin Hood.

"How much longer?" I ask Biggle as he moves past me with a claw hammer in hand. Dawn is practically clawing at the edge of the night. What if the stars fade before we have a chance to reach this portal? What if we wait till tonight and it's gone?

Biggle snorts at me. "We're on the last plank," he says. "We've used up all the wood that's available. Any more and we have to start cutting down the Enchanted Forest."

I can't even imagine how pissed off the book would get at us if we started to raze the trees.

Trogg calls down the all clear. Captain Crabbe gives the base of the ladder a hard jerk. "Looks sturdy," he says.

"Hope you're not afraid of heights," Jules says with a laugh, lifting up the edge of her gown. Her combat boots have vanished, and she's wearing these ridiculous little slippers that look like they have all the protection of a sock. "Because I'm not climbing in these."

"I'll be just fine," I lie.

I put my foot on the bottom rung, feeling my boot slip, and hoist myself up, starting to climb. The ship rocks beneath my feet, and the ladder lurches from side to side. I'm climbing in total darkness, which is actually a blessing, because if I could see below me, I'd never make it. The splashes of the mermaids' tails and the voices of the trolls fade as I get closer and closer to the top edge of the book. And yet it seems like no matter how far I climb, I never arrive.

Finally I reach the top of the trolls' ladder. I grab on for dear life as it swings from left to right, nearly pitching me off. I crane my neck, staring at the stars. One of them is definitely different from the others. It's five-pointed, white, outlined in yellow. While the other stars wink like diamonds, this one stays still and muted, as if it's been glued into place.

I go up on my toes and stretch as far as I can with my right hand, but I'm still several yards away from even brushing the edge of it. I briefly consider whether I could reach it with a sword and cut it loose or take one of the trolls' clubs and swat it from the sky. But even if I were able to reach it with a weapon of sorts, I couldn't be sure that I wouldn't damage it in the process. Reluctantly I begin to shimmy down the ladder, until I am again standing on the rolling deck of Captain Crabbe's ship.

"Let's see it, laddie," he says.

"I couldn't reach it," I admit.

"How about Rapscullio?" Jules suggests. "He's taller, isn't he?"

"He's not twelve *feet* taller," I point out, and I turn to the trolls. "There really isn't any more wood?"

Snort shakes his head. "As it is, we dismantled the castle outhouses."

"You might want to remedy that," I say. "Preferably before Queen Maureen wakes up."

"So we're out of luck?" Jules asks. "There's no one tall enough to grab a star?"

I think about this for a moment. "Maybe it's not height that we need." I cup my hands around my mouth, calling into the distance. *"Ember! Sparks! Glint!"*

Fairies have extraordinary hearing, a little-known fact. It's why they're so good at eavesdropping. But it also works in my favor, as they appear almost immediately, three little fireflies that come whizzing closer, so that I can see each of their tiny glowing bodies.

"What's all this?" Ember asks, any anger over missing her beauty sleep dissipating when she sees the teetering ladder.

That's another little-known fact about fairies: like all gossips, they hate being left out of anything.

"See that star?" I ask, pointing. "The one that looks like a button instead of a jewel?"

Glint and Sparks zip higher into the air to get a better view. "What about it?" Sparks asks.

"I need you guys to bring it down here."

"No problem," Ember says. "Girls?"

The three fairies shoot up like firecrackers. As they zoom into the night, I watch their lights grow smaller and smaller, blue and green and red, as tiny as the points of lasers.

For a moment, there's only silence. Then, suddenly, we hear a crash. A hail of jagged black letters rains down around us, slicing the rungs of the ladder and ripping the mainsail of Captain Crabbe's ship. Jules narrowly misses being impaled by a *K*, which pins the hem of her dress to the wooden deck.

"Watch out!" I cry, grabbing her and pushing her beneath the doorway of the hatch that leads belowdecks.

A moment later, a fireball rips out of the sky, smacking hard against the wood. Ember lies there, her arms and legs splayed, the light in her body flickering. One of her wings is torn, and black splinters jut from her shoulder, her leg, and her belly. Captain Crabbe immediately scoops her into his hand as Glint and Sparks zip close.

"It was the letters," Glint gasps. "We couldn't see them in the dark, and with the book closed, they form a barricade."

The captain takes a bandana from around his neck and fashions a tiny hammock. He gently places Ember on it and gives the corners to her sisters. "Get 'er to Orville straightaway," he instructs. "He'll ken what to do."

I turn to Jules, who is staring at the spot on the deck where Ember fell. "We almost killed a fairy," she says woodenly. "I'm pretty sure you go straight to hell for that."

"I think," Captain Crabbe says, "ye may be out of luck, laddie."

I glance up at the night sky, at the letters I can't see that are scrawled on the paper of this book. "What beats paper?" I ask Jules.

"Scissors?" she replies.

"No," I say, grim. "Fire."

★ ★ ★

As we sprint through the pages to Pyro's cave, I explain my plan to Jules. Fairies may be the strongest creatures in this story, but they couldn't break through the letters with brute force. That means there's no way we can break through with strength either. But letters are printed on paper, and paper burns. So all we need is a little bit of portable fire.

Jules looks impressed. "Wow. I guess you're more than just a pretty face."

"What can I say: I'm the whole package." We edge around the cliff toward Pyro's cave, Jules's hand firmly clasped in mine.

"Is that fairy going to be all right?" Jules asks.

I stop walking and look at her. "Don't worry. Ember can't die in here. At the very worst, the minute Oliver opens the book again, she'll pop right back to her old self."

"She just seemed so . . . hurt." Jules shudders. "What if that happens to us? Will we pop right back too?"

I remember what Orville said: you play by the rules of the world you're in. "Yes," I tell her. "In here, you and I are invincible."

A smile spreads across Jules's face. "Okay. Then after we do this thing, we're totally starting a fight club."

A few minutes later, we reach the entrance to Pyro's cave. The part that fell down—the book making its displeasure known—has been restored, probably with the same stubborn magic that's got me decked out in tights. The dragon is snoring on his back, puffing smoke rings.

Jules digs her feet into the dusty ground. "Are you sure this is safe?"

"You've met him. He's like a giant golden retriever."

"It just seems like an unspoken rule: never wake a sleeping dragon."

I glance at her. "You're thinking of babies." I walk up to Pyro's colossal head to whisper in his ear. "Pyro," I call. "Rise and shine!" My voice is drowned out by his vibrating snores. "PYRO!" I yell, louder, and he startles awake, his massive wings flying open like an umbrella. His red eye focuses on me slowly, and he bares his teeth in a terrifying grin.

"I need your help," I explain. "Can you fly us to the top of the last page in the story?"

The giant beast nods and lowers a wing so that I can climb on. To my surprise, Jules scrambles into place behind me. "Really?" I ask.

"Oh please. How many times in my life am I gonna get to ride a dragon?"

I feel her arms tighten around my waist. Through my thin hose, I feel Pyro's scales scratch and shift as he gets to his feet and crawls like a lizard from his cave onto the ledge.

"Hang on," I say over my shoulder as Pyro shoots a blast of fire from his jaws, illuminating the valley below for a moment before it falls into darkness again. He leans back on his haunches and springs forward, his wings catching the wind and luffing like a sail as we lurch into the sky.

Here I am—a guy who basically lived in his room and whose friends were avatars, who was afraid of everything from gym class to social interaction—riding a *dragon* with a hot girl holding on to me for dear life. Finally I'm the hero. *If only my mother could see me,* I think.

If only I could see *her*.

Jules screams with delight as Pyro weaves over the mountains, rising and falling like a roller coaster that's run off its track. She's clinging to me so hard her knuckles are white, and I can feel her face buried in my shoulder. I think, in this moment, I could soar around on Pyro forever.

When Pyro leaps across a page, there's an extra blast of wind, and he flies a little higher, until finally we reach the end of the story. "Slow down, boy," I say. Even though I can't see it, according to Ember, this is where she ran into the wall of letters.

I pull back on Pyro's leathery mane, a rein. He comes to a halting stop, his wings pumping in midair, his powerful muscles flexing under my thighs. "Pyro," I command, "light up the sky!"

Pyro opens his jaws and paints a wash of fire across the sky. The world, for a moment, is bright orange. Silhouetted against the flames is what looks like a junkyard of letters, a tangle of words smashed and tumbled together, pasted back to back, sealing the facing pages together.

"Get closer," I instruct, and the dragon inches forward. "On the count of three, I want you to torch it. One . . . ," I say, and Pyro sucks in a giant breath. "Two . . ." His cheeks puff out, illuminated by the fire inside. "THREE!" I scream, and Pyro blasts the letters with a burning blaze.

The letters begin to drip, turning into a black rain that falls from the sky, staining the ocean below. When there's a hole large enough for us to fit through, I pull at Pyro's mane again. "That's enough," I tell him, patting his neck, and he rumbles in response. I gently tap his side with my boot, the way you might spur on a horse. Pyro lurches forward, swimming in a sea of stars.

Behind me, Jules gasps. It's like someone has flung a handful of diamonds at us, and as we brush up against the stars, they tinkle like broken glass. Finally we reach the one that isn't glowing, isn't sparkling. "I'm going to hold him steady," I tell her. "Can you grab it?"

I hold tight to Pyro's mane, keeping his strength in check long enough for Jules to lean to the right, stretch her fingers out, and grasp the star. "Got it!" she says.

As she plucks the star loose, the others shimmy and realign in small clusters, leaving an empty space in the night sky.

The ride back to Pyro's cave is beautiful. By now the sun's come up, licking the sea with a pink tongue. Birds swoop and dive around us as we break through clouds. Pyro swings over the castle, braying the way he does every morning, except this time, I'm not there to be awakened. I haven't slept, but I can't remember ever feeling so alive.

When we land on the ledge of Pyro's cave, he yawns widely, belching smoke. "You're a champ," I tell him, and hop off his back, reaching to help Jules down.

The dragon slithers into the recesses of his cave and is already snoring by the time Jules and I sit on the ledge, dangling our feet over the edge. Jules pulls the night's treasure from the bodice of her dress. "For real?" I say.

"What?" she replies. "There are no pockets!" She presses the star into the palm of my hand.

I expect it to burn a little. To be warm to the touch, or prickly, and heavy as a meteorite. The star is none of these things. In fact, at close range, it looks exactly like a sugar cookie, five-pointed, edged in yellow frosting.

I turn it over in my hand and notice that the piping continues on the other side. WISH UPON A STAR, it reads.

"Jules," I breathe, "I think we found it."

What would you do if you only had one day left in this world?

Spend it with the people you love?

Travel to the far corners of the earth to see as many wonders as possible?

Eat nothing but chocolate?

Would you apologize for all your mistakes? Would you stand up to those you'd never had the courage to face? Would you tell your secret crush that you loved him or her?

Why is it that we wait till the last minute to do the things we should be doing all along?

OLIVER

The way my story is told, at the moment my father was battling with a dragon, my mother was giving birth to me, attended by three fairies who were there to bestow gifts on her baby. The first fairy gave me wisdom. The second gave me loyalty. But just before the third was going to give me courage, my mother had a vision of the king's impending death and cried out, *Save him!* The third fairy, mistaking her plea, did not give me bravery after all. Instead she breathed life into me, so that at the very moment my father died, I was born.

I've always thought maybe that's what made me so restless between the lines. I was the only character in the book who had literally been given life—it was only natural to want to experience it to its full potential, not inside the confines of someone else's story, but rather in a tale of my own making. I chafed at my boundaries; I dreamed of bigger things. What was the point of having a life if you never had the chance to live it?

When you are on the inside looking out, though, you picture that other world as perfect. You never peer at the dark corners where there are cobwebs; you never flip over the cloud with the silver lining to see the storm beneath; you never imagine what might go wrong.

Here is the truth about things that are real: they can be broken.

At first, when I open my eyes and swat the alarm clock on the nightstand, I am blissfully, completely unaware. I'm still lost in that foggy zone between sleep and consciousness. I don't remember yesterday. I don't remember what's to come.

But then, all at once, memory collapses on me, knocking the breath from my body.

Frump. The car. Digging a grave.

Leaving Delilah.

Each recollection feels like I'm being stabbed, but that last one, it's the twist of the knife.

I rub my hand over my face, wondering how I'm supposed to go through the motions today—put on my fake American accent and teenage persona, pretend to listen to my high school friends' problems as if they matter, act like a typical student. I can't even imagine facing Delilah and pretending that I'm not counting down the minutes we have left together.

I pull the covers up on my bed (something I won't have to do when I'm back in that blasted book—somehow my bed always manages to make itself). Then I stumble into the bathroom, brush my teeth, strip off my boxers, and step into the shower, letting the water cascade over me.

The moment I close my eyes, though, I see Frump. How

long will it be before that doesn't happen? And if it stops, does that mean I've forgotten him? Once Delilah and I are separated, will it be the same?

No, I tell myself, because she can always open the book and talk to me, just like she used to.

But what happens when she finds someone else—when she goes on a date and comes back with her cheeks flushed, thinking of a boy who isn't me? When she gets married, and has children, and grows old, while the whole time I stay sixteen, and a prince, forever?

It wouldn't matter to me if her hair went white and wrinkles lined her face. I know I'll love Delilah till the end of time, which, in my experience, is infinite. But that's not the case for her. I have nowhere to go, no way to move on, but Delilah's life will evolve. Her world will force her to forget me, even as mine forces me to remember her.

Turning the faucet so that the spray stops, I stand in the shower stall with my hands pressed against the tile for a moment, trying to prolong the inevitable. Then I wrap a towel around my waist and pad into my bedroom, pulling on clothes that I haven't worn long enough to find familiar. Packing up my satchel, stuffed with books and homework I didn't complete, I hurry downstairs for a quick bite of breakfast before the bus comes.

Jessamyn is in the kitchen. She has already set out a bowl of cereal that I assume Edgar likes but that rather tastes like earth to me. When she turns around, I realize that there are dark circles under her eyes and that her face is unnaturally pale. Has she been sick again? Have I once again been too wrapped up in my own drama to notice?

"Are you feeling all right?" I ask.

Jessamyn shrugs. "I didn't sleep well last night. It must be a full moon or something." She reaches into the refrigerator and pulls out a carton of orange juice. I expect her to reach for a glass and pour me some, but instead she leans over my bowl of cereal and fills it with the juice.

"Jess—Mom! What are you doing?" I grab her arm to stop her. "That's not milk."

"Of course it is, Edgar," she argues.

I point to the bowl. "It's *orange*."

She blinks, staring down at the bits of cereal floating in the liquid as if she is seeing it clearly for the first time. "Oh . . ." She forces a laugh. "I guess I'm more tired than I thought." She smiles faintly. "Maybe it's time to turn me in for a newer model."

I suddenly realize that this might be the last time I see Jessamyn Jacobs. That, if Edgar has done his job well, I could be gone by nightfall. This woman has taken care of me for nearly four months, giving me the benefit of the doubt when I said or did something out of character for Edgar. I may have known her in person for only a short time, but she created me, and because of that, she still feels like a parent.

"You've been a really great mom," I blurt out. "I just thought you ought to know."

Jessamyn blanches, and then, just as quickly, seems to recover. "Wow. And it's not even Mother's Day," she jests, pouring

me a fresh bowl of cereal—this time with milk. "So serious before eight a.m.? You make it sound like today's the end of the
world."

I dig my spoon into the bowl and force a smile.

It might as well be.

★ ★ ★

Delilah is waiting for me when I arrive at school. I stare at
her face for a moment—her golden eyes, her chestnut hair, the
freckles that dot her nose and cheeks. Her lips, pink as ribbon
candy and just as sweet. I commit every feature to memory,
locking each one into my mind so that I can keep it forever.

This may be the last time I step off the bus, the last time I
walk through the halls holding Delilah's hand, the last time I
get to hear the music of her voice.

Today is full of lasts.

"How are you doing?" she asks quietly.

"I've had better days," I confess. "Where's Seraphima?"

"She wouldn't stop crying, so I locked her in my bedroom
with a box of tissues and enough Twinkies to fill a Hostess
truck."

I take her hands. "It's not too late to reconsider this," I say.
"To come up with another plan."

Her eyes fill with tears. "I can't lose you."

And yet that's exactly what's going to happen.

"So what do we do?" I ask.

"Well," Delilah says softly. "I suppose we have to talk to
Edgar." She unzips her backpack, revealing the fairy tale.

It feels as if I swallowed lead for breakfast. I don't have the energy to move, or the resolve. Stiffly I follow Delilah through the halls, trying to smile as other students pass and mumbling responses when my friends and acquaintances say hello. Can they tell that I'm already a ghost?

Raj grabs my shoulder and shakes me. "Man, any day now! I'm freaking out!"

I stare at him, wondering how the devil he knows that I may not be here for long.

"I mean, all I dream about is my SAT score," Raj continues. "It's going to totally determine the rest of my life. I heard a guidance counselor talking to Mr. Elyk, and he said we should be getting the results this week."

"Yeah," I say, trying to fake enthusiasm. "It's going to be crazy. Look, I have to go. . . . I'm late for . . ." I let my voice trail off, unable to even think of a good lie.

"I wonder how you would have fared at college," Delilah murmurs.

Suddenly Chris walks up to us, his face troubled. "Hey, guys. Look, this is kind of awkward, but has Jules said anything to you about me?" he asks Delilah. "I mean, I thought we had a pretty awesome night, but she hasn't responded to any of my texts."

Delilah exchanges a glance with me. "She's really sick. . . ."

"Oh man. That sucks. But I'm kind of glad it isn't just me," Chris confesses. "Maybe I'll stop by her house with some soup later."

"Um, don't," Delilah blurts out. "There's no way she wants you seeing her like that. Especially after just one date."

Chris nods. "Okay, then can you at least tell her I was asking about her?"

"Absolutely," Delilah says, and as soon as Chris is out of sight, she lets out the breath she's been holding. "How do you feel about cutting first period?"

"I doubt it will make a difference, given that I'm leaving."

She takes my hand, hers small and cool around my own, and leads me out the door by the gymnasium to the football field behind the school. There she ducks beneath the bleachers, where we will not be seen.

Delilah unzips her backpack and reaches for the book, but I still her with a hand on her wrist. "Promise me one thing?" I ask. "I get to say goodbye to you."

I am thinking of Frump. I am thinking of how hard forever is, when you don't see it approaching.

Delilah meets my gaze, her eyes steady. "I promise," she says.

Together, we flip open the book, landing on the final page. The cast is assembled haphazardly on Everafter Beach. "We did it," Edgar crows, holding up something tiny I can't quite make out.

I frown at him. "Why are you wearing my hose?"

"Why do you even *have* hose?" Edgar replies. "Believe me, it's not by choice. The book apparently doesn't like my writing quite as much as my mom's. I figure we only have a matter of hours before I start talking in a British accent and Jules here starts spinning straw into gold."

"Wrong fairy tale," I mutter.

"What did you find?" Delilah interrupts.

"Another passage," Edgar explains. He whistles to the fairies, who flutter to his side, each taking a corner of the small item. "Good to see you're feeling better," he says to Ember, who flickers in response. The fairies fly the tiny disk closer to the surface of the book so that we can see it better.

"Is that . . . a biscuit?" I ask.

"Well. We're not sure," Jules admits. "We haven't done a taste test."

I read the piped inscription: WISH UPON A STAR. "Have you tried wishing?" I ask.

"Of course," Edgar says. "It didn't work. I even said the whole *star light, star bright* thing."

"You're not supposed to wish on the cookie," Delilah interjects. "You have to eat it."

"Why on earth would anyone eat a star?" I ask.

"Haven't you ever read *Alice in Wonderland*?" she asks, and glances at both Edgar and Jules, who shrug. "Jeez. You two really need to pay more attention in English class. This is just like the treats Alice eats that make her grow and shrink."

"Treats?" says Humphrey, nudging Edgar's tunic. "Can I have one?"

"For heaven's sake, don't let him eat that biscuit," I say. "It will start raining tennis balls."

Orville takes a step forward. "Oliver has a point," he muses. "Whoever eats the biscuit should have the purest wish. That's the only way to be certain that everyone winds up where they need to be." He glances between Edgar and Jules. "For example, Edgar, you appear to have a newfound conflict of interest."

Delilah's eyes widen. "No way. *You two?*"

"You of all people should understand that he's hot!" Jules says.

"What about Chris?" Delilah asks.

"Yeah," Edgar asks pointedly. "What *about* Chris?"

"Can we please talk about this later?" I interrupt. "Orville, you were saying?"

"Whoever is chosen to consume that biscuit must be focused on nothing but getting you and Seraphima back home."

Queen Maureen clears her throat delicately. "I'll do it," she volunteers, breaking through the crowd. "I miss you terribly, Oliver. There's nothing I'd like more than to have you here again, as selfish as that may be. And to be frank, I've never understood the whole Zorg plot anyway." She glances at Edgar. "No offense, dear."

"None taken," he murmurs.

"Shall I do it now?" she asks, reaching for the biscuit.

"No!" I yell, and everyone on the beach freezes. "Erm, I mean, Seraphima isn't with us. She's at Delilah's home. We'll come back in a few hours and make the switch then."

Trogg waves to me. "Wait'll you hear the nocturne I've written for the flute, Oliver!"

"You'll have to see what I've done with my cave," Rapscullio adds. "I've completely redecorated."

"I'll make your favorite meal," Queen Maureen promises.

I paste a smile on my face. "I can't wait," I tell them, when in reality, I'd rather postpone this forever.

Delilah shuts the book and zips it into her backpack. I hold out my arms, and she settles into them. "We have seven hours," she says quietly. "I can't believe we have to spend them in school."

I look at her. "Who says we have to?"

★ ★ ★

We can't go to Delilah's house, because Seraphima is there, still sobbing. We can't stay on the grounds of the school, because we will be caught. So instead we get into Delilah's car and drive until the road ends. She parks in front of a low wall, over which I can just see the ocean.

This time of year, there is no one on the beach. It's cold, and we only have each other to keep warm. As we sit on the sand, I hold Delilah's hand, rubbing my thumb over her knuckles. "How much trouble will you get into for skipping school?"

"It doesn't matter," she says, leaning her head against my shoulder. The wind whips her hair around us.

"Do you remember when I told you that you were the biggest adventure of my life?" I ask.

She nods. "Before you left the book."

"Until you came along, I didn't think I had a purpose. Why was I written? Why was my existence even necessary? But when you read me, you made me real. And when you fell for me, you made me understand why I'm here." I tuck a strand of hair behind her ear. "It's to love you, unconditionally."

Delilah turns, her eyes damp. "I don't know who to be, without you."

"You'll be who you always were. The girl who brought me to life . . . and took my breath away."

"More like the resident pariah," Delilah replies.

I lift her palm and brush a 'kiss over it. "I'm rather fond of pariahs," I say.

When she looks at me, as if even the sweetest compliment has shattered her, I fall to pieces. "I don't want to go," I whisper, my voice shaking.

"Oliver—"

"No." I put a finger against her lips. "Right now, I'm not leaving. Right now, I'm not gone forever. Right now, it's just you and me, like it was the first time we met . . . when this was all I dreamed of." I pull Delilah into my arms and kiss her, softly at first, and then more insistently. We lie back on the cool sand, and her arms close around me, a vise. I run my hands from her shoulders down her spine, tracing every inch, locking her hips against mine. I try to press into her skin a memory of what it feels like to be held by me.

How can one feel this much passion, pain, sorrow— *emotion*—without breaking apart? How do ordinary people fall in love every day?

The rest of my existence will consist of me rescuing a princess I care little about, kissing her, wishing for a life with her. But every time, I will be saving Delilah. I will be kissing Delilah. I will be dreaming of forever with Delilah.

★ ★ ★

By the time we return to Delilah's house that afternoon, I can't let go of her. I hold her free hand while she drives; I slip my arm around her waist as we walk inside and climb the stairs. I feel like a condemned prisoner, marching to his death.

Luckily Delilah's mother is still at work, so she won't ask what's wrong when she sees us, red-eyed and grim. Delilah reaches for the knob of her bedroom door, hesitating. "Are you ready?" she asks.

"I'll never be ready," I tell her.

She wraps her arms around me, burying her face against my neck. "I heard it's going to rain tomorrow," Delilah whispers.

Puzzled, I draw back. "I beg your pardon?"

"I just want the last words I say to you here to be totally ordinary. Something I might say to you if I were going to see you tomorrow and the next day and the day after that."

I nod gravely. "Perhaps it will be sunny on Wednesday," I say, playing along.

She takes a deep breath and opens the door.

Sitting cross-legged on the bed is Seraphima. Her eyes are swollen; she is surrounded by a heap of plastic food wrappers. She takes a tissue from the box and blows her nose, loudly, in its center. "When can I go home?" she asks, sniffling.

I sit down beside her as Delilah takes the fairy tale from her backpack. "Now," I tell her. "Edgar's found a way. And you're not alone." I look up at Delilah, holding her gaze. "I'm going with you."

Seraphima throws her arms around my neck, crying again. "I'm so glad," she sobs. "I was afraid to go back by myself. What if something awful happens?"

Something awful already has, I think.

Delilah sets the book on the bed and threads her fingers through mine. "Here goes," she says, and she opens to the last page.

Delight immediately breaks over Seraphima's face as she sees the family she has missed. Edgar and Jules scramble to their feet. "Ready?" he asks.

I nod. "Are you?"

He takes a deep breath, reaching for Jules. "Yes," he says, and he turns to Queen Maureen, who gives me an encouraging smile.

Edgar reaches into the pocket of his tunic—*my* tunic—and his face freezes. "Where did it go?"

"What do you mean?" I ask, my heart starting to race. If he can't find the biscuit, I can't go back into the book.

"It was right here a minute ago." He turns to Queen Maureen. "Did you take it?"

"Why would I take it, dear? You were guarding it like it was the crown jewel."

He begins to turn in a circle, staring at the ground. "Nobody move," he cautions. "I don't want to crush it, if it fell. . . ."

Humphrey begins to sniff around, drooling a trail. "I can smell it. . . . I can smell it. . . . I can smell it. . . . No, wait, it's a horse."

He smacks into Socks's considerable bottom. The pony turns around, half of a star biscuit dangling from his lips. He looks absolutely chagrined to be caught in the act. "I couldn't help it," he says, his teeth still clenched on the treat. "It was literally calling my name. *So-o-ocks . . . I'm only a hundred calllllllories. . . .*"

"I can't believe this!" Edgar shouts. "Don't take another bite."

"I swear," Socks promises. "The diet starts tomorrow."

Edgar rips the remainder of the biscuit from Socks's mouth and hands it to Queen Maureen, who wipes the horse slobber on her velvet robes.

"Half a cookie won't do," Orville says. "It's too risky. The magic might be diluted. Socks will have to be the one to wish you back home."

Socks looks anxious and holds a hoof up to his chest. "Me?" he asks. "I don't know. I mean, I didn't prepare for this. I haven't practiced a speech. And I'm not wearing the right color saddle or *anything*. . . ."

"Socks," I say firmly. "You can do this. I believe in you."

He looks up at me. "Thanks, Ollie. But what if I mess up?"

"You want me to return, don't you? You want to be able to take a breathless ride through the unicorn meadow with me on your back. And you want Seraphima there too, so that she can braid daisies into your mane just the way you like."

Socks thinks about this. "I *do* look good in daisies. . . ."

"You see? It's simple. All you have to do is eat that biscuit, close your eyes, and imagine your dreams coming true."

He hesitates. "I was going to wrap up the other half and save it for later. . . ."

"Are you kidding?" Delilah says. "Socks, I was actually going to say something to you. You look way too thin. I can even see your ribs. I'm worried you haven't been eating enough."

Not only can we not see Socks's ribs, we can't even see anything behind him. But Delilah's tactic works. "Well," Socks simpers. "In *that* case . . ."

He leans toward Edgar's outstretched hand and gobbles the rest of the biscuit in a single bite.

"Now," Orville coaches, "make a wish."

Delilah immediately grabs my hand so tightly I can feel her fingernails cutting into my skin. Socks's eyelids drift shut, and I hold my breath.

Slowly, meticulously, Socks's bottom begins to shrink inch by cellulite-dimpled inch.

"Socks," I yell. *"Focus!"*

The horse's eyes snap open, and he shakes his head with regret. "Sorry, sorry . . ." He closes his eyes once more, and I start to feel a tingling in my fingers and my toes. I look down at my hand, still in Delilah's, as it begins to fade.

In that last, horrible second, I realize what Delilah has been trying to explain to me: if you love someone, you have to let them go.

I grab her shoulders while I still can. She is staring at me in terror, her mouth trembling. "Listen to me, Delilah: Live your life. Fall in love again." I take a deep breath. "Don't you dare wait for me."

She is sobbing, wrapped tight in my embrace, and I am kissing her, and then suddenly . . . I'm not.

★ ★ ★

Becoming two-dimensional again feels like being crushed from head to toe, having the breath forced from one's lungs, and being rolled out and flattened like a piecrust. I find myself face-down on the beach, the wind knocked out of me. When I try to push myself upright, I fail at first: the muscles I used to move in Delilah's world do not work as well here; action is executed through thought and intent, not brute physical force.

It's like learning to ride a stallion again. By the time I manage to flop onto my back and Rapscullio offers me a hand up, Socks is prancing in a circle. "I did it, I did it!" he sings. "Do I get a medal for this? I'm thinking gold goes best with my eyes. . . ."

I am surrounded by well-wishers—the trolls, who clap me hard on the back; the mermaids, who blow me kisses; the fairies, whose excitement shows in small bursts of sparks. Queen Maureen folds me into her arms. "How grand it is to see you again, Oliver," she says.

Over her shoulder I look around to find others helping Seraphima to her feet. She looks dazed and rattled. Then she catches sight of something behind a boulder and rushes toward it, her eyes wide with wonder and joy. "Oh, Frump! You *are* here," she cries, and she kneels in front of Humphrey, reaching out to pat him.

The hound wags his tail, happy with the attention. He cocks his head. "Hello, beautiful woman. I am Humphrey, and I would like to sleep at your feet tonight." Seraphima's face falls, yet she lets Humphrey lick her face. She looks completely out of place in her jeans and T-shirt, but then again, so do I. I glance down; Delilah's tears still stain my shirt.

I stumble away from the crowd and crane my neck toward the top of the page. Delilah's face looms over me, pale and pained. She lets out a small sob and very slowly closes the book.

"All clear!" calls Orville, the same words Frump used to say when the book was closed by a Reader.

The characters begin to wander off the margins. "Does this mean we don't have to have laser practice anymore?" Biggle asks Snort.

Queen Maureen pats my arm as she passes. "I'll get supper started, dear."

Orville is the last to leave. "I know this may not be what you wanted, Oliver," he says, "but we're glad to have you home."

But home, to me, is Delilah. Without her here beside me, the world is just the place where I take up space.

I sit on the beach by myself long enough for Queen Maureen to finish cooking dinner and the air to grow cold. I sit long enough for the sky to turn black and the moonlight to dance on the ocean. The stars overhead look ragged, knocked out of position by the removal of the wishing biscuit. There's a giant dark space in the heavens where something seems to be missing.

As I watch, a new star is born. It flickers twice and then burns more steadily, bright and effervescent, outshining all the others around it. The smaller stars are tugged into order by its gravitational pull, forming a constellation I've seen before.

Chris called it Canis Major, and he pointed to the brightest beacon in the night sky: Sirius. The Dog Star.

I smile, having underestimated Frump's loyalty to me. "Welcome back, old friend."

I am fairly certain he winks at me.

From my pocket I pull the photograph of Delilah that I stole weeks ago: that Halloween picture, where she is young, dressed in a princess's gown, with a crooked tiara balanced on her head. "We all made it back here," I say to her. "Me, Seraphima, and even Frump. You're the only one who's missing."

I wait for her response, but of course, it's no longer that easy. With a sigh, I get to my feet and go to slip the photograph back into my pocket, only to find that my sweatshirt and jeans have already become a green velvet tunic and hose, that my sneakers have given way to black leather boots.

In the distance, I can make out the buttery lights of the castle.

And just like that, I'm merely a prince again.

DELILAH

I've made a terrible mistake.

It hits me when it's too late, when Oliver grabs my shoulders and tells me to forget him: I just pushed away the best thing that has ever happened to me.

Before Oliver, I was just the strange kid with her nose stuck in a book, and a life so small it could fit in a thimble. But then we met, and he made the impossible happen. I experienced the world, instead of simply reading about it. I was no longer alone. I was loved.

And now I've pretty much done everything I could to ruin that.

I grab his shoulders tightly, but the fabric of his sweatshirt slips through my fingers. "Wait!" I cry. "Don't leave me!"

But he's already gone.

Behind me, I hear a crash and a muffled swear, but I don't even turn around. I can't tear my eyes away from the book,

where Seraphima and Oliver have landed. They're surrounded by the other characters, being embraced and welcomed back into the fold. Oliver, I realize, looks just as lost as I feel. He staggers forward, pushing away from the pack, and stares up at me, his hands balled into fists at his sides.

He swallows, but he doesn't speak. He doesn't have to. I don't think there's a word in the English language big enough to describe what it feels like to lose your other half.

"Holy crap," Jules says. "That *actually* worked?"

I lift the edge of the fairy tale's cover as gently as if it's made of glass, and close the book.

At that moment, I'm tackled from behind as Jules throws herself at me. "I never thought I'd say this," she admits with a sigh, "but I am so glad to be back in this hellhole of a town."

Edgar gets to his feet, brushing himself off. "What town *is* this, anyway?"

I realize that when Edgar left, we were in Wellfleet, not here in New Hampshire. I'm about to answer, but when I turn to look at him, his face makes me stop short. I know it's not Oliver. But his eyes are the same green as Oliver's; his black hair is disheveled; the curve of his jaw is one I know by touch. It's not Oliver, but it might as well be.

I haven't said a word, but Jules watches me carefully, then sidles closer to Edgar, slipping her hand into his. "So how's *this* gonna work?" she asks pointedly.

It is enough to snap me out of my trance. Horrified, I realize that everyone at school thinks Edgar is my boyfriend . . . and it's not going to look good if my best friend is hitting on him.

I groan. "I don't know. I didn't exactly think this through."

"I need to get home to my mom," Edgar says, then hesitates. "I don't even know where I *live*."

There's a knock on the door, and the three of us freeze. My mother pokes her head inside. "Oh, Jules!" she says. "You must be feeling better."

"Um. So much!" Jules replies.

"Where's Seraphima?" my mother asks.

"She left early. All the Icelandic exchange students decided to spend their last week in Canada," I say.

My mother's eyes move from Jules to Edgar. "Nice tights," she says, trying not to laugh.

"Halloween!" I blurt out. "We were trying on costumes. We're going full-on Shakespeare this year."

Edgar and Jules smile so wide I think their faces are going to crack. "So!" Jules says, breaking the awkward silence. "I'm going to go. . . . Edgar, I'll walk you home!" She grabs her duffel bag from the floor of my bedroom and takes Edgar's hand. She starts pulling him toward the door.

"Great idea," I reply. "Jules, I'll text you after dinner so we can talk about, you know, what you missed at school." I turn to Edgar. "I guess I'll . . . Skype you later?"

He looks at me, baffled. "Whatever."

"Edgar . . . ?" I say pointedly. I turn so that my mother can't see my face and, through clenched teeth, hiss: *"Kiss me."*

Edgar's eyes dart to Jules. I raise my eyebrows and give him a tight smile. The more we can convince everyone that things are normal, the better this will go.

He rolls his eyes, leans forward, and pecks me on the cheek as if I've asked him to kiss a toad.

My mother laughs. "Honestly, Edgar. No need to act like a prince just because I'm here. You can give her a real kiss good-bye."

"Awesome," Edgar sighs. He puts his hands on my shoulders, leans forward, and presses his lips against mine.

All I can think is: *He's not Oliver.*

After a moment I pull away from him. Jules is glaring daggers at me. "Shall we?" she bites out. She grabs Edgar's arm and yanks him roughly out the door.

We hear the front door close behind them when they leave the house. My mother turns to me. "Got a lot of homework?"

"Not really," I say. *When you don't go to class, you don't get homework.*

"Well . . . it's just the two of us for dinner. What do you say to a main course of popcorn, and one of our favorite films?"

I swallow back tears. "That sounds perfect," I tell her. At this moment, all I want is to get under a pile of blankets and watch a classic Disney movie with my mom. All I want is to know that there's at least one person left here for me.

* * *

So I'm missing my Doc Martens, the text from Jules reads. Do u think there's a lost & found for fairy tales?

I pick up my phone from my nightstand and reply:

Ask Cinderella.

☺, Jules writes back. And a moment later, there's another buzz:

I can't believe that really happened.

I told u so, I write. Welcome 2 my life.

There's a pause.

Do u miss him? Jules asks.

Like u wouldn't believe.

The first time Oliver saw me text someone, he grabbed the phone from my hand, trying to figure out how the small person inside was writing back.

It's weird being back. I was getting used 2 it.

My thumbs fly over the keys. U + Edgar???

. . .

+ Chris? I type.

Can I have them both?

I grin. Only if ur a Mormon fundamentalist.

K, Jules writes. Good to know.

I hesitate, knowing I have to start a conversation with her I don't really want to have. U no I have to pretend Edgar's still my bf.

Just don't 4get I'm ur BEST friend.

Never, I reply. How did things get so messed up?

U fell 4 a guy in a book, Jules types.

I sigh. Nobody's perfect.

C u 2morrow? Jules writes.

Yup. Get ready 4 a Tony-winning performance from me.

LOL, Jules says. Oh—1 last thing . . .

??? I ask.

Don't use tongue.

★ ★ ★

I'm lost in a nightmare, but I'm still awake.

It's three a.m. and all I can think about is the fact that Oliver told me to move on. As if everything we've shared up till this moment meant nothing, as if he's so easily replaceable. Or did he tell me not to open the book because he knows, like I do, how hard it will be, now that we have lived the alternative?

I take the fairy tale from my shelf and pull it into bed with me. I run my hand over the gilded cover. I'm just going to do it: open the book. Whatever Oliver said was probably his way of being chivalrous—trying to keep me from slipping back into my sad little life as a loner, obsessed with a fictional story.

I fan through the pages, about to skim directly to page 43, the illustration where Oliver is alone on the cliff. It's where we had most of our conversations, before he escaped the fairy tale. But at the last minute, I hesitate: while Oliver is safe in the book—protected from runaway cars and illness and death—I'm not. Inside the pages, he gets to live in a bubble, forever sixteen. And maybe that's all right, for now. But what about when, one day, I open the book and my hair is gray? When I have wrinkles? When I'm not the girl he fell in love with anymore?

What will happen to him when I die?

To open this book is to give him hope: that I will be with him forever, that I am willing to put my real life on hold for a character in a book. But that's not fair to Oliver, is it?

I take the fairy tale and put it back on the shelf.

But.

I'm 100 percent sure that no matter who I meet in the future, no one will be like him.

I reach for the book again.

What is a relationship if you can't go on a date? If you can't hold hands? If you can't ever kiss him again? How long is it going to be before I can't remember what he tastes like, what he smells like, what it feels like to be in the circle of his arms?

I toss the book onto the floor.

The thing is, without Oliver, I can't even remember who I am anymore.

I grab the fairy tale and let it fall open to page 43.

Oliver springs to the rock wall, holding on the way he would if anyone ordinary were to open the book. When he sees that I am the Reader, however, his eyes widen.

"I'm sorry," I say immediately. "I tried not to open the book, I really did. I know you think I shouldn't come here anymore. It's just . . . I can't not talk to you."

I realize that Oliver has hopped down and is smiling from ear to ear. "I'm glad you didn't listen to me," he says. "I can't stop thinking about you."

"What are we going to do?" I whisper.

"Well," he says bravely, "it's not all bad. It's sort of the way we started, isn't it?"

"I don't mean now. I mean in ten years. Twenty. I'm going to be ancient and you'll still be . . . perfect."

He grins. "You think I'm perfect?"

"I'm not kidding, Oliver." I shake my head. "It just doesn't work, if you're in there and I'm out here."

He thinks about this for a moment. "But you *are* in here. No matter what I look at, I see you."

"Can you really tell me that's enough for you? Won't you get sick of pining away for someone you're never truly going to be with?"

Oliver looks up at me. "You're a part of me," he says. "To get rid of you would literally tear me to pieces."

For the first time since Oliver has left, I smile. "I bet you say that to all the girls who were your ticket to freedom."

I expect Oliver to laugh, but instead he sobers. "Delilah," he says, "even if I'd been born in your world, I would have found *you*. I would have chosen *you*."

"How am I supposed to go to school, and be normal, and pretend that you never happened?"

"It's what I do every day," Oliver replies. "It's called acting. It's not all that difficult to be the person people expect you to be. It's harder to remember who you really are."

"Who I really am?" I repeat. "I guess I'm just a girl looking for a prince."

"Any prince?" he jokes.

"Just the fictional kind. I have a thing for two dimensions; I like my guys flat."

He sinks down against the rock wall, drawing his knees to his chest. "Wouldn't it be lovely if we could write our own fairy tale?" Oliver muses.

I curl onto my side, propping the book against the pillow. "How would it start?"

" 'Once upon a time,' of course," he says. "We meet at . . . the market."

"I ask you to reach the spaghetti on the top shelf," I continue.

"And it's love at first sight," Oliver adds.

"What would we do?"

"Well," Oliver says, "we'd live in a little cottage. With window boxes, where you'd plant violets. And every morning you'd cook me your amazing chocolate chip pancakes."

"And what would you be doing for me while I'm slaving away in your sexist kitchen?" I ask.

"*Someone* has to take care of the baby," Oliver replies.

"We have a kid?"

"Three. Two strapping lads and a little princess."

I pull the covers close. "Do we have pets?"

"Only a dozen dogs," Oliver says. "All basset hounds, of course."

"Every day," I add, "you go to work."

"I do?" Oliver asks, truly surprised.

"Our country's not a monarchy," I point out. "The peasants aren't going to pay for the college educations of your three kids."

"What on earth do I do?"

I think for a moment. "You teach . . . fencing!"

"And you own the corner bookshop," Oliver pronounces. "Filled to the rafters with fairy tales."

"After every dinner, we tuck the children into bed, and drink a cup of tea and watch the news."

"And the best part is at night, I get to hold you," Oliver says. "And I know that I never, ever have to let go."

"And we are absolutely, positively, blissfully ordinary." I sigh.

He looks up at me, and I stare down at him, and even though we're both smiling, there's a whole world of sadness between us. "Oliver? Will you stay with me while I fall asleep?"

"Always," he swears.

I put the book down on the pillow beside me, still wide open. One minute I'm awake and the next I'm not. It happens that fast, that effortlessly—like the moment night turns into morning, or summer shivers into fall. Like love.

You've seen those pictures of couples kissing in front of a Christmas tree, or clasping hands on their wedding day, or holding a newborn baby between them—a snapshot of joy. But what do you really know about them? Just that at the second the shutter clicked, they loved each other. You have no idea what trials and tribulations came before, or after. You don't know if one of them cheated, if they grew apart, if a divorce loomed on the horizon. You simply see that in one static moment, they were happy.

A fairy tale is a snapshot too. You never know what goes on post-happily-ever-after. It's simply a frozen minute, and the only one we seem to remember.

The difference is, in a fairy tale, the story can't be altered. The prince and princess will never have a fight. You'll never hear the queen raise her voice. No one ever gets sick; no one ever gets hurt.

Maybe love is only safe in places where it can't change.

EDGAR

We're standing at the end of my driveway—or at least, what Jules promises me is actually my new driveway. "So," I say. "Now what?"

She takes a step backward. "I guess I'll see you in school tomorrow."

She sounds less than enthused about this. In fact, she sounds like she's just announced that she needs a root canal, or that she's found a rat underneath her bed.

I go to jam my hands in my pockets and remember I'm wearing freaking tights. "Are we . . . good?" I ask.

Jules nods, but she doesn't look at me.

I reach for her hand and pull her closer to kiss her goodnight, but she stops me. "It's different here, Edgar."

"It's still you, and it's still me," I say.

"No. Here, you're my best friend's boyfriend." She gestures between us. "*This* can't be a thing."

"So you're just going to pretend it didn't happen?" I argue. "Us?" I think about how, in the book, she *got* me the way no one in my life ever has.

"It *didn't* happen. Not for real, anyway," Jules says. "Edgar, it was a fairy tale. You can't believe everything you read in books."

She turns away quickly, and I start to call after her—but I stop short. What if she's right? What if the guy I was in the book—someone confident and brave, a leader, not a follower— was just make-believe? It might as well have been a dream; I might as well have never left.

She walks down the street until I can't see her anymore. Looks like nothing's changed: World 1, Edgar 0.

Taking a deep breath, I walk up the driveway to the front door. I almost ring the bell before I remember I live here. Instead I turn the knob and follow the trail of light into the kitchen, where my mother stands with her back to me, cooking dinner.

Looking absolutely, incredibly normal.

In my whole life, I've never been so psyched to see her.

"Mom?" I cry out, and I envelop her in a hug, squeezing so tight she yelps.

"What is going on with you?" she laughs, turning around and holding me at arm's length. Now that I can see her face, I notice that there are dark circles under her eyes, and there's a Band-Aid on her forehead.

"First the dramatic goodbye this morning," my mother says, "and now this?"

I scrutinize her, trying to figure out if Oliver's right—if she *is* okay. "I just really missed you . . . today."

My mother's eyes travel from my face down my velvet tunic to my knee-high boots. "Care to explain?"

"Drama club," I blurt out. "I joined at school."

She seems delighted by this. "Really? That's incredible, Edgar. I swear, since we've moved here, you've been an entirely different person."

"Go figure," I murmur.

"Dinner's almost ready. Can you set the table?"

She takes a casserole out of the oven and sets it on the stovetop to cool. I open a cabinet that looks like it might contain plates but find cereals and crackers. I open a different door and find bowls.

"Seriously, Edgar?" my mother says, pushing past me to open a drawer that has plates in it. "You still haven't figured out this house yet?"

"Who keeps their plates in a drawer?" I say under my breath.

"Just get the glasses." My mother sighs and walks out of the kitchen, into the vast yonder that must contain a dining room.

I fling open all the cabinets, trying to memorize everything. Then, armed with two glasses, I follow my mother into the interior of my new home. *Not bad,* I muse, glancing around. I kind of miss the charm of our little place on Cape Cod, but this house is not too shabby. There are hardwood floors and giant windows, and all the furniture I remember from our old place is distributed in new combinations, making everything feel familiar and different all at once.

It reminds me of being inside that fairy tale, and seeing bits and pieces of my mother's life scattered through the pages.

We sit down and my mother serves me a heaping scoop of

lasagna. I breathe in deeply, thinking that even though Queen Maureen was a good cook, she couldn't live up to my mom's skill in the kitchen. I've wolfed down half of what's on my plate before I realize she's staring at me like I have six heads.

"Hungry?" she asks politely.

"Starving." I make an effort to stop eating like an animal. "So, um, did you have a good day?"

"Not as productive as I wanted it to be," my mom replies. "I think I napped more than I worked."

Oliver mentioned to me that she was tired, and I dismissed it. But what if it's something more? "Well, don't you work for yourself? Can't you just give yourself a vacation . . . or a raise?"

My mother used to be a pretty famous mystery writer. When my dad died and I was a mess, she wrote the fairy tale to give me hope for a happy ending. Oliver was the boy I was supposed to grow up to be. Except I didn't. In fact, now I'm a year older than Oliver in this fairy tale, so she's probably come to terms with the sad truth: I'm just me.

She stopped writing after she finished *Between the Lines*. After that, she did freelance editing projects to put food on the table. I suppose she can work anywhere her computer can be plugged in, which is why Oliver was able to convince her to move closer to Delilah.

"So what are you editing right now?" I ask.

"It's a debut novel about time travel."

"Does it suck?"

My mother laughs. "The author wouldn't know a comma if it hit him between the eyes, but it's a great premise. I mean, imagine how freeing it would be to wake up in a different world and get to start over."

I hesitate. "It's probably not as awesome as you'd think."

She stabs at her lasagna. "This coming from the boy who plays video games 24/7?"

Instinctively I say, "I do not."

"Actually, you're right," my mother replies. "You don't. Not since you've started dating Delilah."

This conversation has suddenly taken a turn for the worse.

"You two seem glued at the hip," she prompts.

"She's all right," I say.

"All right?" my mother repeats. "Spoken with such intense passion."

"She's amazing," I correct myself, but then I realize I can't really go on and on about Delilah, a girl I don't really know. In fact, there's only one girl in my life I'd describe as amazing. "She's fierce—she won't back down from anything. And she's totally her own person. She won't take no for an answer, and she doesn't care what other people think about her." Just saying these things makes me wish Jules were here.

I find my mother staring at me. "I'm glad you have someone like that. Someone who'll take care of you."

"Why?" I joke. "Are you planning to be abducted by aliens anytime soon?"

My mother tosses me a smile. "My starship leaves tomorrow at noon," she says.

★ ★ ★

It starts the moment I get on the bus.

Immediately I duck my head and move toward a seat in the back, where nobody will notice me. But before I can make it there, a half-dozen people are calling my name or high-fiving me as I walk down the aisle.

"Hey, Edgar," calls a kid in a polka-dotted bow tie. He points to the seat beside him.

"Uh, thanks." I slide in, realizing two things at once: I'm super popular here, and these people expect me to know who they are.

"I had the craziest dream last night," the boy says. "I was in a production of *Peter Pan* that was being performed in my grandmother's driveway, and I felt the urge to run, so I raced into the woods, but after a few minutes, I was starving because of all the exercise, and I looked down and realized my hands were made of cake. So I ate them. And I said to myself, 'James, *now* what are you gonna do? You don't have any hands.'"

James, I note.

"That's messed up," I say. And then I add, "Were they chocolate or vanilla?"

"Devil's food all the way," James says, grinning.

The bus screeches to a halt in front of the high school. This, at least, looks like every other public school on the planet. Pacing in front of a massive oak tree with gnarled arms is Jules, decked out again in head-to-toe black.

Maybe being in the real world isn't so bad after all.

I say goodbye to James and walk toward her immediately. "You're the sexiest ninja I've ever seen," I say.

"First, ninjas are naturally sexy. Second, I'm not sexy. Not to you. You know who's sexy? *Delilah.*"

Another kid walks up, snaking an arm around Jules—*my* Jules. "Feeling better?" he asks.

Jules goes beet-red. "Chris," she says, stepping away. "We're in public."

"So? It's been like a week since I've seen you."

She smiles. "Try three days."

I'm going to punch him. I've never punched anyone before in my life, but this feels like the time to do it.

I feel a tap on my back just as my fist curls at my side. Delilah stares at me and then at Chris and Jules. "Hey," she says, then belatedly adds, "honey."

Jules's lips tighten into a thin line. I wind my fingers through Delilah's and raise my brows at Jules. "Want me to walk you to class, babe?" I ask Delilah.

As we head into school, I can feel Jules's eyes burning a hole in my back. I wait till we're all the way inside the doors, far enough away from them not to be heard. Then I turn to Delilah. "Who the hell is he?"

"Your best friend," she says.

"You've got to be kidding me," I reply.

She pats my shoulder. "It's going to be a fun day." Then Delilah pulls a piece of paper from her backpack. "I've written out all your classes," she says. "And there's a map, marked up, so you know where to go. My phone number's on there too; text me if you get lost. Oh, and just so you know, today we have activity block in between third and fourth period. You start with chess and then go to drama club. By the way, you're starring in *Romeo and Juliet.*"

"Wait, *what?*"

"I'll save you a spot in the cafeteria at lunch," she says.

I don't want to live in this world, so close to Jules but unable to be with her. "We should break up." The words burst out of me, so forceful I didn't realize how hard I'd been working to hold them inside. "That way Jules and I could be together."

Delilah narrows her eyes, and her voice drops. "Do you really think I want to be with you?"

I remember the way she looked at Oliver when I was still in the book and able to watch them together. Slowly I shake my head.

"You made your mother move here for me," Delilah says. "And people are going to ask questions if you ditch me and the next day you're dating my best friend. This isn't forever. But it's for now."

I nod grimly. Then I slip my arm around her waist as if I actually like her, and we move down the hall in solidarity, if not in love.

★ ★ ★

Chess club is cancelled so we can be in homeroom for our guidance counselors to give us our SAT scores. There goes my college career; my standardized test was taken by a guy whose knowledge consists of how to tame a dragon. Once we are dismissed, I stand in front of my locker. I take a deep sigh and prepare to open the envelope.

Before I can even peek at the score, however, another stranger comes running up to me. "Dude," he says. "I got a 2280. I can totally work with that. I think if I have decent teacher recs, Harvard's still an option."

I frantically glance at him, looking for a clue to his name. Then I see it: on his backpack is a label reading RETURN TO RAJ PATEL.

"Raj," I murmur.

"Yeah? Come on. Tell me your score already."

"I haven't even looked . . . but I was really out of it that day. It was almost like I wasn't here. . . ."

Raj grabs the envelope from my hand and pulls out the paper inside. "Edgar," he breathes. "You are a god among men."

"What?" I grab the printout and turn it toward me: *2400.*

"You got a perfect score, man."

My jaw drops. Oliver's totally done me a solid.

Raj throws his arms around me. "Harvard 2020, dude! We could be *roommates!*"

He runs down the hall, sniffing out other students to compare scores with. I shake my head, still smiling a little. I wonder how on earth Oliver managed to pull that one off.

"Hey, Edgar," a voice says—a voice I recognize, unfortunately. "I'm really glad I caught you."

I turn to find Chris opening the locker beside mine. Of *course* we're locker buddies. Who else would I want to see every morning but the guy who's trying to make out with the girl I like?

"I want to talk to you about Jules."

Can this get *any* better?

"What about her?" I ask tightly.

"She's been really weird today. I mean, I thought everything went so well on Friday night—but now she kind of seems like she's not interested."

"Really?" I say, brightening. "Hey. You tried your best."

"That's the thing—I *haven't*. I really think I can still turn this around. I just need another chance. She won't turn me down if we go on another double date."

"You want to go out with Delilah and me?"

"Yeah," Chris says. "You guys are the perfect couple. Maybe it'll rub off on her."

The perfect couple, I think. *Ha.*

"So whaddya say?" Chris asks. "Minigolf? Today? After school?"

The last thing I want to do is watch this guy put his hands all over Jules again. But the first thing I want to do is spend more time with her.

"Can't wait," I tell him.

★ ★ ★

If it were the only activity left in the universe, I still wouldn't join the drama club. I lurk near the door, hoping I won't be noticed, but Ms. Pingree sees me and waves me forward with a beaming smile. "Ah, it's our Romeo," she trills. "Don't be shy, Edgar!"

There is a gaggle of girls sitting in a semicircle on the stage; when I step into the light, they twitter like a brood of chicks. One girl sits off to the side, staring at her iPhone. When she glances at me, I smile, and I'm pretty sure she bares her teeth in response.

"As I was saying," Ms. Pingree continues, "this is the most iconic scene in the play. What I'd like you all to channel is that moment you looked at a significant other and truly believed in love at first sight. The minute you felt that the universe had been working all this time to bring you two together . . ."

Uncomfortably I realize that every girl on that stage is staring at me as if I am food and she is starving. Suddenly I remember James's dream.

If this is what it's like to be a heartthrob, I think I preferred being anonymous.

"All right, let's get to it." Ms. Pingree hands out our scripts. "Romeo? Juliet? Center stage."

Awkwardly I move into position, waiting alone in a circle of light. "Allie?" Ms. Pingree says. "There's no Facebook in fair Verona."

The mean girl gets to her feet. She comes closer, so close that I can see the sparkles flecked in her lip gloss. As soon as the teacher turns away, she stomps on my foot.

"Ouch!" I yelp.

"Sorry. I was aiming . . . higher."

What did Oliver do to piss her off so badly?

"Any time you're ready," Ms. Pingree says.

I look at Allie and offer her a half smile as a truce. "I should warn you, I kind of suck at this."

She narrows her eyes. "What *don't* you suck at?"

Ms. Pingree clears her throat. "Now, remember, you two— you are in *loooove*. You lay eyes on each other and the stars collide! You complete each other!"

I pick up my script and stumble through Romeo's lines.

"Uh . . . 'Lady. By yonder blessed moon I swear / That tips with silver all these fruit-tree trops' . . . I mean, tops . . ." I glance up. "Who wrote this crap, anyway?"

Ms. Pingree's face falls. "The *Bard*," she whispers.

Allie snaps her gum. " 'O, swear not by the moon,' " she says flatly, " 'the unconstant moon . . .' "

"*In*constant," Ms. Pingree corrects her. "As in something that's changeable. What Juliet is worried about is that Romeo's love might be fickle."

"*Reeeealllly,*" Allie says, raising a brow. "Probably Juliet thought that he was going to kiss her and then humiliate her in the cafeteria in front of half the school."

Ms. Pingree frowns. "That might be a stretch, but if it helps you get into character . . ."

Allie shoves me with both hands: I stumble backward as she shouts her next lines into my face. " '. . . that monthly changes in her circled orb, / Lest that thy love prove likewise variable.' "

"You know," Ms. Pingree says, "Juliet's a little gentler in this scene. . . ."

Allie rounds on her. "I think you're wrong. I think Juliet is pretty pissed that Romeo just blew her off. Besides, she didn't really like Romeo all that much. It was just that he was new and more interesting than the hundreds of other lame guys fawning over her. But what she's really thinking is that Mercutio is way hotter than Romeo and he's in college and drives a vintage Mustang!"

I stare at her, speechless. I don't know if I'm supposed to bow in submission or call the local asylum and have her committed.

"You know what?" Allie shouts. "I can't work with idiots. I

quit." She hurls her script at a mousy girl wearing a sweatshirt with a glittery cat on it. "Break a leg, losers." Her high heels click the entire way out of the auditorium as she leaves in a fit of perfume and fury.

Ms. Pingree looks like she's about to throw up. Her hands flutter at her sides.

"Um, does that mean we can leave?" I ask.

"No, no," she says after a moment. "The show must go on. . . . Claire, you'll be our new Juliet."

The girl with the cat sweatshirt scrambles to her feet, standing too close to me and breathing heavily. Her braces catch the stage lights when she smiles. "Let's start at the kiss," she suggests, and she throws her arms around me and plants a wet, slobbery one on my lips.

He just *had* to join the drama club, didn't he.

★ ★ ★

Last year in school I took a Greek mythology course. There's a story about Tantalus, a guy who pissed the gods off so much that he was cursed to the deepest level of hell, stuck in a pool of water with a fruit tree hanging overhead. But every time he reached for the fruit, the branch would move out of his grasp. And every time he tried to take a drink, the water receded. So basically, he was surrounded by everything he wanted and needed but couldn't have.

That's exactly the hell I'm in on this double date.

I've never really been a fan of miniature golf. For some reason the courses always seem to be cracked or sloped weirdly or are full of kids throwing tantrums. Not even Tiger Woods could get a hole in one.

I'm the only person here, though, who even seems to care about the inaccuracies on the course or the fact that the water in the windmill pond at hole number 5 is a frightening, toxic green. Delilah hasn't smiled once, and is dragging her club around like it's a ball and chain. Jules, who considers sports to be one of the great downfalls of modern society, is doodling on the scorecard. Chris, on the other hand, seems able to golf below par when he's not even looking. Which is entirely the case, since his eyes are glued to Jules's butt.

"I can't believe we have nine more holes," Delilah says.

"Your enthusiasm, *sweetheart,* overwhelms me." I grab her arm and lower my voice. "You're the one who said we're supposed to act like a couple."

She sighs and holds my hand with about as much romantic intent as a nurse taking a patient's pulse.

"I think it's your turn," Chris says to Jules.

She steps up to the tee, wiggling her hips as she tries to line up her ball. "Ugh," she says. "I know I'm never going to get it in."

"Here . . . let me help." Chris puts down his club and walks over, fitting himself tightly behind her and sliding his hands down to her wrists.

"Ouch," Delilah says, and I realize I've got her hand in a death grip.

"It's all in the swing," Chris continues, swaying back and forth with Jules in his arms.

Dammit—she giggles.

I can't stand here and watch this. It feels like my head is going to explode. And it doesn't really help matters to know that Jules is doing nothing in her power to stop this.

How come she was all over me when we were inside the book, but here, I'm not good enough? Was I different in there than I am out here?

I used to be, that's for sure. The old Edgar would have looked at competition like Chris and given up, assuming that he had no chance with Jules.

But I'm not the old Edgar.

I pull Delilah into my arms. "Have I told you how beautiful you are today?"

Delilah looks at me, puzzled. *Are you on crack?* she mouths.

Chris laughs. "Get a room, you two."

I can feel the heat of Jules's gaze as if she could set me on fire through sheer force of will. She turns, faking a stumble so that Chris will catch her. "Wow," she says, feeling his biceps. "How many push-ups can you do, again?"

"How many do you want me to do?" Chris replies, grinning.

"Are you going to take your turn?" I snap at Jules.

"I don't know," she says testily. "Chris, I need your help. . . ."

As soon as she bends over, taking her stance, Chris spoons himself around her. "Ready? One . . . two . . ."

As he counts down, I pull Delilah close. On three, I start to kiss her. Deeply. Passionately. Wishing every second that she were Jules—who swings at the ball and sends it flying over the fence into traffic.

Delilah stumbles backward. "What the hell—" She breaks off, realizing that Jules and Chris are staring at us. "—did you stop for?" she finishes feebly.

Chris grins at Jules. "Maybe for your next turn you don't have to go full Hulk," he says.

After Delilah smashes the ball—almost as angrily as Jules did—we move on to the next hole.

"You know what I never asked?" Chris muses. "How did you two meet?"

Delilah and I look at each other, briefly panicked. She opens her mouth to explain, but I cut her off. "Babe, let me." I meet Jules's gaze. "She was helping me find something I'd lost," I begin. "We were searching everywhere. Through a field, in the ocean, on a boat. Finally we gave up and just lay on the beach, stargazing."

Jules's cheeks turn pink.

"So did you find it?" Chris asks.

"Find what?"

"The thing you lost?"

"Oh, yeah. My, um, car keys. They were in my pocket the whole time."

"Sounds like fate kicking in," Chris says.

"Doesn't it?" I ask pointedly.

For a long moment, Jules glares at me. Then she announces, "I'm going to go to the bathroom," and stalks off.

"And I'll help you find it," I say, hot on her heels.

I follow Jules into the ladies' room and lock the door behind me.

"What are you doing?" she cries. "You're screwing every-thing up."

"*I'm* screwing everything up? 'How many push-ups can you do, Chris? Your biceps are so big I can barely wrap my hands around them!'"

"I'm surprised you noticed, since you were so busy making out with my best friend!" Jules yells. "You can't just walk into my life and assume I'm going to drop everything that came before you."

"You think it's easy watching the girl I'm crazy about flirting with another guy?"

Jules shoves me. "You're the one who agreed to this date."

I shove her back, pinning her against the wall. "Yeah—so I could spend time with you."

"Then you're a moron!" Jules shouts.

"So are you!" I shout back.

There is one breathless, furious beat of silence between us, and then suddenly her hands are all over me and mine are tangled in her hair, and I'm kissing her in a frenzy of lips and teeth and heat, like I could devour her.

When we come up for air, my arms are still on either side of Jules, as if I've caged her. She smooths her hair into place and straightens her shirt. "We'd better be getting back," she says, and she pushes me aside, opening the bathroom door.

Maybe this day *isn't* a total wash.

I give her a few moments before I walk out of the bathroom too. I've only just turned the corner when I see Chris at the counter, picking up a replacement ball for the one Jules sent into the stratosphere. "Hey," he says, smiling. "This date is totally working."

"I couldn't agree more," I reply.

* * *

Delilah drives me home after minigolf. For five whole minutes she doesn't speak. Then, at a red light, she turns to me. "Do not ever, *ever* do that again."

"You're giving me really mixed signals here," I point out. "Am I or am I not supposed to act like your boyfriend?"

"Oh please. You and I both know that act wasn't for me."

My face falls. "It's really hard to finally find someone who totally gets me and then have her ripped away from me."

Delilah sighs. "You're preaching to the choir, Edgar."

"If sending them back into the book was the right thing, how come we're all so miserable?"

"I guess doing the right thing sometimes means not getting what you want," Delilah says. "At least you're in the same world. You get to see her, face to face. You and Jules, you're still *possible*."

I think about this for a moment. "Have you talked to him?"

She takes a deep breath and nods, looking pained. "I can't *not* talk to him. But when I do, it feels like I'm tearing out my heart."

I glance at Delilah. I haven't really considered how much worse this must be for her.

She pulls up to the curb near my driveway.

"Sorry I kissed you," I say.

"Sorry I'm not Jules."

I open the passenger door and step outside but then lean back down. "Hey, Delilah?" I say. "I know you're not really my girlfriend. But I'm awfully glad you're my friend."

She smiles a little. "See you tomorrow, Edgar."

My mother's car is in the driveway, but the house is empty. She's not in the kitchen getting dinner ready. She's not in the living room watching the five o'clock news. "Mom?" I call, heading upstairs to her bedroom, and I knock on the door, but there's no answer. Gently I turn the knob to find her bed impeccably made.

She's not in the bathroom or in my room either. Walking down the hall, I peek inside her office.

Papers are strewn across my mother's desk, some highlighted, some with red circles, and some with sticky notes along their sides. Since she's not there, I'm about to close the door behind me, when I notice the spines on a stack of books:

> *Brain Tumors in Adults*
> *The Last Walk: A Practical Approach to Preparing for*
>   *the End of Life*
> *Hope Is Where the Heart Is: A Guide to Beating Cancer*

Tucked into the top one, like a bookmark, is a brochure: ST. BRIGID MEMORIAL HOSPITAL, NEW ENGLAND'S LEADER IN CANCER RESEARCH & NEUROLOGY.

I break into a sweat, and my knees start to shake. My mom said she's editing a time-travel novel; why would she need any of these?

I walk toward the desk as if a live grenade might be inside it. Scattered across the top are printouts of the kind of articles only doctors can read, filled with jargon. I pick up the one on top.

CAPGRAS SYNDROME WITH RIGHT FRONTAL MENINGIOMA, I read.

> Abstract: A forty-seven-year-old woman with a right frontal parasagittal meningioma who developed the delusion that her husband had been replaced by a look-alike pretending to be her spouse. This type of delusion involves a compromise of the fusiform gyrus, the mechanism in the brain that allows facial recognition. Although historically patients with such delusions have been diagnosed with schizophrenia, we suggest that the cause may be biological and part of the tumor's pathology, as evidenced by the fact that postsurgery, the patient experienced a termination of the delusion.

I squint, as if that might make me understand the jumble of words better. Imagine what would happen if you woke up one morning and the son you knew better than anyone else looked exactly the same—but acted like a British prince. You'd look for an explanation, and the thought that your son switched places with a character in a fairy tale would clearly not be the first one to pop into your head. So maybe you'd start blaming yourself, thinking you were crazy. Or sick.

Maybe you'd even pack up your house and move to the town that had the best cancer treatment hospital in New England.

I'll tell her. I'll describe everything that's happened. If she stops thinking *she's* crazy and thinks *I* am instead, at least that's a start.

But here's the important thing: She's not dying. She doesn't have cancer.

She can't, because she's my mom, and she's all I have left.

Distantly I hear the door opening downstairs, and my mother's voice calling my name. I try to walk out of her office, but I find myself rooted to the spot.

She appears in the doorway, her cheeks flushed. She's wearing the black leggings and oversized sweatshirt she always wears when she goes for a long walk.

People who are really, really sick can't go for walks, I tell myself.

"Edgar," she whispers, looking from me to the desk with all of those horrible, awful papers. "I didn't know how to tell you."

"Tell me what?" I mutter through clenched teeth. I have to hear the words out loud. I have to hear her say it.

She opens her mouth. But before she can speak, her eyes roll up so that the whites are showing. Her whole body begins to convulse.

I catch her just before she hits the floor.

OLIVER

In here, everything is too bright. The trees seem neon; the moors glow. And there's a flatness to the landscape that is disorienting, something I never noticed before. I keep bumping into corners and edges, misjudging the space around me.

The worst, though, is the claustrophobia. I feel like I'm boarded up, boxed in. Like the walls are closing in on me. Or, at the very least, the pages.

This morning I walked the entire length of the book— twice—and I still feel restless. Socks trots behind me, the bells on his saddle giving me a massive headache.

"Must you make all that racket?" I snap, looking over my shoulder.

"Someone got up on the wrong side of the stable," Socks murmurs.

"Someone's going to wind up in the glue factory," I counter.

"C'mon, Ollie. Look on the bright side."

"Oh, *do* tell me the bright side. . . ."

Socks thinks for a moment. "Orville made me a hair mask."

"What the devil is a hair mask?"

"I don't know," he confides, "but it's supposed to help with my split ends." Socks hesitates. "I'm sure he'd make you one too if you asked nicely."

"I don't need a hair mask." I need Delilah.

"Can I ask you a question?" Socks says. "You haven't seen me in a while. Do I look . . . different?" He blinks at me when I don't respond. "Bigger? Smaller . . . ?" His voice trails off. "I hear that sometimes, when you're not with someone every day, you notice the changes more . . . and I've been eating only baby carrots for the past month."

"You look great, Socks," I say, without even bothering to glance in his direction.

He prances around me in a circle. "I knew it. I absolutely knew this would work better than the cleanse. You know, I actually *feel* like I have more energy."

Instinctively I leap over the edge of a page, onto the next.

"Are we going somewhere in particular?" Socks asks.

"No," I say.

"Okay, then." He moves amiably beside me, swatting at butterflies with his tail. And then, a moment later: "Do you want to play a game? I Spy, maybe?"

"Socks, I don't mind you accompanying me. But right now, I don't feel like talking."

He stops and looks at me. "I know. It feels wrong, doesn't it? To be just the two of us?"

Thinking of Frump hurts just as much now as it did two days

ago. "Yes," I say, my voice breaking. "I suppose this will never feel right again."

Will anything?

Socks shakes his head, so that his mane streams like silk. "What you need, Ollie, is a distraction. Something to lift your spirits. Like your surprise party!" His eyes bug out, and he grimaces. "Can you pretend you didn't hear that?"

I smile a little. "*You* were the first choice to distract me?"

"Everyone else had something important to do," Socks says miserably. "I tried to hang the banners, but I managed to get tangled in them instead, and Captain Crabbe had to cut me free with his sword."

"I promise to act surprised," I say.

"That would be really great. Especially when they show you your present, the—"

"Stop," I interrupt. "Just . . . stop."

Socks snorts. "Whew. That was a close one."

"So where is this shindig?"

"At the castle," he says. "In an hour."

We are at the far edge of the book; it will take nearly that long to reach the castle. "I suppose we'd best get on our way." I start off on foot, but Socks nudges me with his nose.

"Ollie?" he says. "For old time's sake?"

I want to walk, really. The only way I have been able to even exist here these past couple of days is by wearing myself down to such a level of exhaustion that I've simply passed out at night, instead of pining away for what I've lost. But he looks so hopeful that I put my foot into a stirrup and swing into the saddle. Socks breaks into a gallop, and the world begins to fly by. The wind catches my hair, and it almost feels like the first time I rode in a car in Delilah's world, with the windows rolled down. If I close my eyes, if I don't pay attention to the letters hanging overhead, it's almost as if I'm still there.

We reach the castle, and the drawbridge lowers so Socks can canter into the courtyard. He draws to a halt, his nostrils flaring.

Strung across the entryway are nearly two dozen of Rapscullio's canvases, each painted with an individual letter, spelling out WELCOME HOME OLIVER. The stone arches are decorated with bright banners in all the colors of the rainbow—except orange. Socks follows my gaze. "That was the one I got tangled in," he confesses.

A cake taller than I am has been wheeled into the center of the courtyard. It's decorated with violets—Delilah's favorite. And packed into every available corner is a character from the story. Everyone is here—even the mermaids, who are floating in Socks's water trough.

"Surprise!" they all shout.

I glance surreptitiously at Socks, then put my palm on my chest. "Oh my goodness!" I cry. "I never in a million years expected this! How on earth did you manage to keep it a secret!"

It is possibly the worst acting job I've ever done, and since acting is my life's work, this is saying quite a lot.

Queen Maureen embraces me. "Are you pleased? Is it too much?"

"It's perfect." I kiss her cheek. "You needn't have made such a fuss."

"Why, Oliver, it's not a fuss," she says, truly taken aback. "You're the closest thing I have to a son."

I realize in that instant how much I missed her. Missed all of them, really.

"Speech!" calls one of the trolls, and his brothers take up the call, smashing their clubs against the iron hitching posts.

I step onto a mounting block, not because I'm eager to deliver a monologue, but because I'd rather they not damage castle property, and I clear my throat. "Friends, I want to thank you all so much. These past few days have been hard, I know, for all of us, and it may feel as though we have little to celebrate. But instead of focusing on what we've lost . . . I suggest we focus on what we have." I glance around the crowd. "Each other," I say.

A cheer swells from the throng, and Scuttle and Walleye begin a chant to cut the cake. The fairies hover near my shoulders, plucking at the velvet of my tunic to draw me forward, toward the delicacy. Captain Crabbe unsheathes his sword. "Would ye care to do the honors, Oliver?"

I lift the blade and slice the cake. Chivalrously I carry the first three plates to the mermaids, who cannot serve themselves.

The mood is buzzy. People enjoy each other's company, laughing and waltzing to the music of Trogg's flute. Rapscullio and Queen Maureen take a turn on the dance floor. Seraphima has a third piece of cake.

I find Captain Crabbe beside the punch bowl, trying to hold a crystal cup in his meaty fist. He takes a swig of the juice. "How is it?" I ask.

"Could use a bit o' rum."

I grin, pouring myself a glass, and I'm about to take a sip when he reaches out and pulls my lower lip down. "Have ye been neglecting your gums?" he asks. "Oliver, we've been through this before. Gums are to teeth as soil is to a plant. If ye don't take care of the soil, nothin's gonna thrive, aye?"

Gently I place my crystal cup upon the table. "How do you do it? How do you just snuff out your dreams?"

"Pardon?"

"You clearly want to be a dentist. And instead you're stuck here, the captain of a pirate ship." I meet his gaze, intense. "How do you get up in the morning, knowing you'll never have what you want?"

Captain Crabbe seems taken aback by this turn of the conversation. "Och, boy, I canna understand why you think I've given up my dreams. I simply make do with what I have." He glances around, waving one hand to encompass this castle, this party, these people. "What could you possibly want out there that you can't find here?"

True love, I think, and I move among the crowd, feeling completely alone.

★ ★ ★

There's a story Queen Maureen once shared with me, about a blind man who was given a wish by a witch. When he wished for sight, she cast a spell, and miraculously he could see. The world became a circus of color, a whirlwind of movement, a bottomless well of discovery.

But one day the witch returned. "You've misunderstood," she said. "I never promised forever." Without warning, without time for preparation, the man found himself in the dark once again.

After living in Delilah's world, free and able to make my own choices, returning here feels like being in prison. Not only is there a finite number of people to see and conversations to have, but my confidant—Frump—isn't even here anymore to share my restlessness.

I am sitting in the great hall of the castle, my back against the stone, pitching a ball to strike the far wall and bounce back to me. I do this over and over, and the ball makes a satisfying thwack each time it hits.

Queen Maureen comes into the hallway wearing an apron, her hands dusted with flour. "Good Lord, Oliver, I thought we were under attack. Is that really necessary?"

"Sorry," I mumble. "I'm having a bit of trouble occupying myself."

"Well, I could use an extra set of hands. Come into the kitchen."

I let the ball drop, and out of nowhere, Humphrey comes flying to catch it in his jaws.

Maureen is in the middle of making a cake. "Why don't you frost this for me," she suggests, "while I start rolling out croissants?"

I look at the three rounds of cake and the bowl of pink frosting. I dip my finger into it and take a taste. As usual, it is delicious. Maureen is a master baker. "May I ask you a question?" I say. "Who exactly *eats* all the stuff you bake?"

"I know it seems excessive," she admits. "But it's always gone at the end of the day. About half of it winds up in Seraphima's tower."

Having watched that girl devour everything that was not nailed down at the mall, I hardly find this surprising.

I watch Maureen roll out a square of dough and begin to slice through it with a sharp knife, cutting it into triangles. "Now it's my turn to ask you something," she says. "What was it like?"

I glance at her. "You mean out there? Imagine no boundaries. No walls."

She holds her hand up to her throat. "It seems terrifying."

"It is. But in the best way," I say. "There are books with so many recipes you couldn't count them all." I glance around the kitchen. "There are ingredients and spices from countries whose names you can barely pronounce. Pans in every shape and size. And so many people . . . so many people that you could bake all day and all night and still not feed everyone."

Queen Maureen's eyes widen in awe. "I can see why you might be struggling to be back here."

I pick up the spatula and slop a layer of frosting onto the top of the first round of cake.

"It might not be ideal, in your situation, but we all must keep a stiff upper lip, you know. Make the best of things. It's the lot we've been given."

"But by whom?" I ask, jamming the second layer of cake onto the first. "Why should I have to be locked in here just because a woman decided to tell a story?"

"Why is the sky blue? Why does the sun rise?" Maureen says. "Can you honestly tell me that this girl of yours in the other world doesn't have to play by rules as well?"

I think of school, of chores, of Allie McAndrews. Of all the walls that box Delilah in.

I suppose the difference isn't that there is a box. It's that I'm not inside it with her.

"What you need to do, dear, is find an avocation. Something to occupy yourself. Perhaps you could take up whittling. Or I hear Sparks has started a knitting circle." She smiles. "Maybe you'll even find that you have a knack for baking."

We both look down at the creation between my hands. The confection lists to the left, frosting pooling on one side, with a large crack running down the center where I accidentally speared the cake with the spatula.

"Or maybe not," Queen Maureen says kindly.

★ ★ ★

Rapscullio and I sit side by side in the unicorn meadow, in front of our respective easels. On each is a bare canvas. We both pick up a palette of paints, and I mimic his actions. One of the beasts munches moongrass just a few feet away from us, completely oblivious to the fact that he is a model.

"When we think about foreshortening," Rapscullio instructs, "we really want to use our eyes. The horn facing us is going to be ten times larger than the back left hoof, simply because of perspective."

He looks at me with so much hope for my understanding that I give him a toothy grin, even though he might as well be speaking ancient Greek.

"Now," Rapscullio says, "pick up your brush, and *feel* the

energy. Let the art flow from your mind through your fingertips. No sharp edges, just gentle movements of the hand." He
sketches with his paintbrush, and a reasonable facsimile of the
unicorn appears on his canvas.

I take a deep breath and draw my first line.

"You know," he muses, "of all the people in this book, I'm
probably the only one who truly understands what you're feeling right now."

I frown. "What do you mean?"

"Well, after all, I know what it's like to *not* end up with the
girl."

I hesitate, my brush hovering over the canvas. "But that's
not *you*. That's your *character*."

"What is a man, if not his character?"

I shake my head. "It's different. You didn't choose to fall in
love with Maureen. It was written to happen that way."

"Did you really *choose* to love your Delilah? Do you remember the exact moment you made that decision? Or did
it just . . . happen?" Rapscullio cocks his head. "Perhaps your
romance was written too. By fate, by the stars. We all have authors, Oliver."

Suddenly Pyro, flying overhead, dips low and startles the
unicorn, which goes bolting into the Enchanted Forest. Rapscullio sighs. "I suppose we've lost our model. Let's see how
you've done."

On my canvas, I haven't drawn a unicorn. Just two stick figures, holding hands.

Rapscullio clears his throat. "Well," he says politely, "I think
you've really captured its essence."

★ ★ ★

When I burst into Orville's cottage, he is on a ladder, stirring a cauldron three times his size. "What are you—" I shake my head. "Never mind. I don't even want to know."

It is the first time since I've been back that I feel like I have a purpose. I may not be able to live in Delilah's world, but I know how to get a glimpse of it again. If I can just see her, that might be enough to get me through the day. After all, it's unreasonable to expect me to give her up wholly and completely, instead of weaning myself from her bit by bit.

"Ollie, my boy! I'm so glad you dropped by! I can use some help with this—Pyro is suffering from heartburn, and it's a challenge to stir a kilo of sodium bicarbonate into twenty gallons of yogurt, but that's the only way to keep it from tasting like tar."

"Orville," I begin, "do you remember when you showed me my future?" Before I escaped the book, the wizard created a plume of smoke that illustrated what was yet to come. A seed, for example, morphed into a vision of a flower. And a strand of my hair allowed me to witness a scene that now makes perfect sense: me, in an unfamiliar home, with an unfamiliar woman— Jessamyn Jacobs.

"Of course," Orville says.

"Do you have something that can show me the present?"

Orville looks at me, confused. "You mean . . . your own eyes?"

"No," I say. "I want to see the present somewhere else. I want to see someone else's life."

"Ah! Perhaps a telescope."

"I don't think that's going to reach quite far enough."

"This is an enchanted one," Orville explains. He climbs down from the ladder and rummages through a satchel that I've seen him wear numerous times around the book. "Sometimes, when I'm being called by another character, I use this," he confesses. "If my knees are stiff or if I'm just feeling a tad lazy, I check to see if it's an emergency before I expend the effort to hike all the way across the pages." He hands me the brass tube, and I extend it to its full length.

"How does it work?" I ask, peering into one end.

Orville snatches it away from me. "Not like that, naturally." He chuckles. He sets the scope on the ground and, with a flick of his fingers, sets it spinning like a bottle. "Round and round and round it goes. . . . Where it will stop, nobody knows!"

"Well, that's rubbish!" I exclaim. "What good is that going to do me?"

"No, that's the spell, Oliver. Say it, and it will show you what you wish to see."

"Oh." Feeling silly, I give the telescope a good spin and repeat the incantation. It stops spinning, and the end glows like the beam of a lantern.

I lift it to my eye and squint.

I'm staring at a place I've never seen before, but I know it's Delilah's world. There are cars and streetlights and billboards. Delilah is there, and Jules, and Chris, and Edgar. They are playing what seems to be a miniature form of croquet.

Jules starts to swing her mallet, and Chris ambles behind her, wrapping her arms with his own. He starts to count, and she releases the mallet.

All the breath leaves my body.

Edgar holds Delilah, kissing her the way I ought to be.

I drop the telescope as if it is burning my palm and run as fast as I can to page 43.

★ ★ ★

First I pace.

Who does she think she is?

She's already found my replacement.

I take out my dagger and begin to hack away at the rock wall.

Every time I think of her, I picture Edgar's mouth on hers, and I strike the rock until sparks shower.

By the time she finally gets around to opening the book, it is hours after I viewed that catastrophe through Orville's telescope. She smiles down at me as if she hasn't been snogging another fellow all afternoon.

I stand up, my fists balled at my sides. "You have quite some nerve!" I yell. "Tell me, will you take anyone, or is it just guys who look like me?"

Her jaw drops. "What are you talking about?"

"I *saw* you. Orville gave me an enchanted telescope, and I watched you kissing him."

Her eyes narrow. "You've been *spying* on me?"

"You've been *cheating* on me!"

"I have not. I didn't kiss Edgar; *he* kissed *me*. And it's not like either of us wanted it, trust me." She tilts her head. "How many times did I watch *you* kiss Seraphima?"

"You knew Seraphima meant nothing to me. It was a part I was playing."

"That's exactly what I'm doing!"

"FINE!" I yell.

"FINE!" she shouts back.

We stare at each other for a long moment, furious. Then Delilah lifts her chin. "Is that all you have to say to me?"

My eyes flash. "Well. I imagine you're tired from your . . . exertions this afternoon."

A muscle tics in her jaw. "If all you're going to do is insult me, I'm going to go." She curls her hand around the edge of the book and starts to close it. It feels like the world closing in on me.

"Wait," I say softly.

The book opens again, and she smooths the page flat.

"You have no idea how hard it was to see you doing that," I confess.

"It's just for a little while. Until we can come up with an excuse to stage a breakup."

There is a voice at the door—Mrs. McPhee. "Delilah?" she calls. "Who are you talking to?"

Immediately the world goes dark as Delilah shoves the open book beneath the covers of her bed. "No one," she says. "Jules."

"Which is it? No one, or Jules?"

"Jules," Delilah answers, flustered.

"Are you guys having a fight? I heard yelling."

"We were arguing about something stupid. What movie to see this weekend. No big deal."

There is a hesitation. "It sounded like a lot of shouting for just a movie."

"We're both PMSing," Delilah says. "I'm totally exhausted, Mom. Can't you see I want to sleep?"

There is a sound of the door closing, and suddenly Delilah's face comes into view again.

"That was rather harsh," I murmur. "What's this 'PMSing'?"

"You don't want to know," Delilah answers. She glances away from the book. "I wonder if my mom realized that my phone's plugged into the wall at my desk."

"So?"

"It makes it considerably harder to be having a conversation with Jules." She sighs. "How long until my mother thinks there's something wrong with me again, because I'm obsessing over this book?"

"I'm sorry," I say. "I'll try to be quieter next time I yell at you."

This, at last, makes her smile.

"When he touches you," I ask softly, "do you think of me?"

Delilah's eyes are like molten gold. "I think of how he's *not* you," she replies. "Of how no one ever could be."

I stare up at her. She's my sky, my whole universe. "Tell me about your day," I say.

★ ★ ★

The next morning, I decide to turn over a new leaf. Baking clearly isn't my forte, art isn't quite in my wheelhouse, and apparently stalking doesn't qualify as a hobby. So, borrowing some equipment from Scuttle and Walleye, I head to the beach to try my hand at fishing.

No sooner have I cast my line than Marina surfaces, her tail slicing through the ocean. "You know, fish have feelings," she says reproachfully.

"So do plants," I point out. "How was your kelp salad this morning?"

In a huff, she dives beneath the surface. For a few moments, I enjoy the sun beating down on the crown of my head, and the lull of the waves, and the distant cries of seagulls circling overhead. It feels good to stretch my muscles as I reel in and cast again. This . . . this is something I could get used to.

My solitude is shattered by the wet, messy, barking arrival of a tornado of fur, which knocks me to my knees and proceeds to slobber all over my face. "Humphrey!" I hear. "Heel!"

Immediately the dog sits, his tail still quivering, so that he is moving closer inch by infinitesimal inch. His tongue hangs so far out of his mouth it nearly brushes the sand.

Seraphima clips a leash onto Humphrey's collar. "Sorry," she says. "We're still working on basic training."

The dog looks up at her. "You're so pretty. Your hair looks like the sun."

She blushes and pats his head. "Thanks, Humphrey."

I put down my rod and get to my feet. "So," I say. "How have you been?"

Seraphima looks out over the ocean. "I keep thinking it was a dream. The crazy carriage without horses . . . and the indoor marketplace . . . and how Frump . . . well, you know. But it wasn't a dream, Ollie, was it?"

I shake my head. "It was real."

Her eyes light up. "*I* was real," she whispers. "I never thought about making my own choices before, I guess. I mean, when you're a princess, why would you want to be anything other than that?" She leans toward me, conspiratorial. "Can I show you a secret?"

"Erm . . . yes?" I say.

Delicately she lifts the hem of her gown, hiking it to her waist to reveal a pair of blue breeches stitched to look like a pair of jeans. "They're incredible," she enthuses. "You can run and climb and dance in these—you can do *anything*—and you don't have to worry about getting tangled up in your petticoats."

I grin. "Oh, I know. I'm always tripping over my petticoats. . . ."

"Right?" she agrees. "I traded Scuttle a needlepoint trivet for his spare pair of breeches. And then it really only took a few hours of sewing to alter them to fit."

"They look splendid on you," I say.

Her eyes grow wide. "You won't tell anyone, will you, Ollie? It'll be our secret?"

Of all the characters here with me, Seraphima alone truly understands what it was to live in a world other than this book. Ironically, the one person with whom I had nothing in common is now the only one I can really relate to.

I suppose that means we're friends.

"Have you ever been fishing?" I ask.

Seraphima blinks at me. "It's not ordinary princess practice."

"Good thing you're no ordinary princess."

A smile unfurls across Seraphima's face. She glances down the beach in both directions, then drops Humphrey's leash. He begins to run in circles, barking at the seagulls, while Seraphima unfastens the skirt of her gown and places it carefully on the sand. Dressed now in her bodice and her makeshift jeans, she crouches beside me as I pick up a worm.

"Ooh!" she cries. "Let me!"

I watch with no small amount of appreciation as she threads the hook through the worm. Who would have guessed that Seraphima is so bloodthirsty?

She stands, the rod in her hand and the worm wriggling. "Now what?" she asks.

Before I can answer, however, a breeze whips across the beach, whisking her skirt into the air like a kite. As I watch, it catches at her waist and wraps neatly around, fastening itself.

"That's odd," I say, the only words I manage to get out before being yanked off the beach and tumbled through pages and phrases and dangling participles that strike me in the face until I land, heavily, on the parquet floor of the throne room in the royal court.

It's been so long since I performed the story that at first, I don't realize what's happening.

Why the devil is Delilah starting from the beginning? Why not just meet me on page 43, as is our custom?

I do not appear on the first page of the story. That is a flashback to my birth, and so while I wait for my scene—the one where Rapscullio, our villain, convinces me that I must find his daughter, who has been kidnapped and locked in a tower—I am usually alone with Frump.

But that's not possible anymore.

Humphrey whimpers and moves from edge to edge of the page. "What's going on? What's going on? It's the end of the world. We're gonna die. Wait! I know. I'll chew through this wall. That'll help."

"Relax," I tell him. "It's not a thunderstorm. It's just a Reader. All you have to do is sit next to me and look like a dog."

"I . . . I don't know. I've never done that before. . . ."

"Trust me. You'll be a natural."

I can hear the lines being recited on the previous page, and I know my entrance is coming. Rapscullio slides effortlessly from the previous scene into this one, and I open my mouth, intending to ask Delilah what on earth she's doing. But Rapscullio gives me a nearly imperceptible shake of his head, and when I look up at the Reader, it's not Delilah at all.

It's her mother.

We are rusty. But we are professionals. I feel the words pulled from my throat, as if they are a ribbon. *Save who?* I say, scowling.

Surreptitiously I glance at Mrs. McPhee and I see her eyes widen as she squints at my face. Oh God. She's going to recognize me as Delilah's boyfriend.

It takes all the effort I can muster to angle my head against the illustration's will so that she can only make out my profile instead of my full features.

"What is inside this book that you can't live without, Delilah?" Mrs. McPhee murmurs absently. She finishes the page and turns to the next. Suddenly I stand with Queen Maureen, trying to explain to her why I am about to embark on a mission to save this princess. Maureen's lips tremble as I speak; I can register the fear on her face as she channels what it must be like as a mother to say goodbye to her son. She is doing an

acting job better than I've ever seen, but then, so is everyone ·
else. They are all bristling with energy, delighted to be read for
the first time in months.

All but me, that is.

I am reliving a nightmare.

I gallop through the Enchanted Forest and outwit the fairies, I nearly drown in the ocean, I cheat the trolls to ensure a
safe passage, and all this I do while managing to keep my face
turned away from the Reader. By the time I am on page 43,
scaling the cliff wall, my body is shaking from exertion.

When Rapscullio locks me in the dungeon, it's almost a relief, because my face is drawn in shadow.

Finally I am pulled to the white sand of Everafter Beach.
Humphrey is trying to eat the wedding rings attached to his
collar. The mermaids wave from the breakers; the trolls hold
the poles of the bridal canopy; the fairies have twined ribbons
around them. And Seraphima, as always, is in my embrace,
wearing her silver wedding gown.

And a pair of jeans underneath.

As Mrs. McPhee's eyes skim the last words of the fairy tale,
I am drawn inexorably toward Seraphima.

I think of Delilah, kissing Edgar.

And just as Delilah said about *that* kiss, all I can think about
is how Seraphima is the wrong size, the wrong shape, the wrong
everything. How she isn't Delilah.

But my lips stay pressed to hers, glued by a happily-ever-
after, until the back cover is closed.

Around me, the other characters start to cheer.

Well done! Bravo!

That was excellent.

Did you see the part where I—

Oh, how I've missed performing. . . .

I fall to my knees as if I've been punched, gasping for breath. Rapscullio claps me on the shoulder. "Just like old times, right, Oliver?" he says, smiling widely.

His words are the match that ignites the fire within me. Staggering to my feet, I start to run as fast as I can. I move across the pages so quickly that the scenes blur behind me; I don't stop to see where I am. I run until I pass my first scene, and the one before it, through the dedications, skittering past the copyright, until I skid into the great white morass of the title page. There, I hesitate, momentarily dizzied by the empty expanse.

There's nowhere else to go.

But that isn't going to stop me.

I hurl myself headlong into the margin, bouncing back. I beat myself against the cardboard cover, over and over, until my hands come away bruised. And still I force myself upright again, launching my body against the boundaries of this book.

Finally, battered, I fall backward on the frontispiece.

My fists leave smudges of blood on the vast white surface.

I stare up at the sky, at nothing.

After a moment I come up on my elbows, still panting. I flex my aching fingers. I watch the bruises fade. I watch my blood vanish, as if it never existed.

As if *I* never existed.

All the world's a stage, but actors aren't the only ones who play roles.

Even when you're not following a script, you might as well be. You don't behave the same way in front of everyone. You know what makes your friends laugh, and what makes your parents proud, and what makes your teachers respect you—and you have a different persona for each of them.

Given all these performances . . . how do you ever know who you really are?

Well, you have to find that rare someone for whom you're not putting on a show. Someone who shines a spotlight in your direction—not because you're who they need you to be, or who they want you to be . . . just because you're you.

DELILAH

The really crappy thing about being a teenager is that even if you have a legitimate, monumental problem—the sky is falling or the zombie apocalypse has begun or you've contracted the plague—you still have to do your geometry homework. So in spite of the fact that I am having possibly the worst Tuesday of my life, and my boyfriend is trapped in a fairy tale, and my best friend is hooking up with his clone, I have to prove that two triangles are congruent.

The way I am selling this to myself is a promise: if I finish this proof, I will let myself take an hour to talk to Oliver before I have to drag myself away to write an essay about the fall of Troy.

Suddenly the door of my bedroom slams open. I turn, scowling, ready to lace into my mom again about privacy—but it's Jules. "I can't find him," she says, completely on edge. "He's not at home; he's not answering his phone or his texts; it's like he's totally vanished."

"Who?"

She blinks at me. "Edgar? Oh my God. Did you not even notice he wasn't in school today? Seriously? You're supposed to be his fake girlfriend."

"Maybe he's just sick. He's literally been in a bubble for the past three months."

"Or," Jules says, her eyes flicking to the fairy tale on my dresser, "maybe he's back in the bubble."

"What? No he's not."

"Did you check?"

"I don't have to. Oliver's in there, which means Edgar's out here."

"When was the last time you talked to Oliver?" Jules asks.

A cold panic settles over me. If Oliver had sprung from the book again, he'd come straight to me. I know he would.

Wouldn't he?

Jules and I both scramble for the book at the same time. I fling it open to a random page—one where Oliver is riding Socks to Orville's cottage, with his trusty dog trotting along beside them. But I do it so fast that the saddle is facing backward with Oliver in it, and Humphrey has a turkey leg clamped in his jaws that Socks is hissing at him to hide. As soon as they all see my face, however, they relax.

"Thank goodness it's you," Oliver says.

"Who else would it be?"

"You'd be sur—"

"Is Edgar in there?" Jules interrupts.

"Unfortunately not," Oliver mutters. "Why?"

"Ughhh," Jules groans. "You're useless."

"I beg your pardon. . . ."

"Sorry," I murmur. "I'll talk to you later, okay?" I lower my voice to a whisper. "She's having boy problems."

I gently close the book, hugging it to my chest. "You seem awfully obsessed with Edgar, given the fact that less than twenty-four hours ago you were on a date with a different guy."

"That's kind of why I need to find him." Jules flops down on my bed. "I broke things off with Chris today."

My eyes widen. "Really?"

"Chris is great. He's smart, and funny, and cute. But Edgar told me that if you soak a body in pineapple juice for a week, all the skin will fall off it."

"Wow, he sounds *dreamy,*" I say.

"He *gets* me. And he's wicked hot. Well. *You* know." She glances up. "How long till you can break up with him?"

"How long till the gossip spreads that we're sister wives?"

I'm smiling, but I'm also thinking about how it's going to feel when I watch Jules and Edgar walking down the hallways at school, holding hands. Whispering to each other. Existing in their own little world. As happy as I am for Jules, I have to admit that it's going to be hard to see her get everything she's wanted while I lose everything I had.

All of a sudden Jules's phone buzzes. "It's him," she breathes. "Finally." But as she reads the text, her face goes white. She passes me the phone.

I know we don't really know WHAT we are, but you're the closest thing I have to a friend here, and I need you.

My mom's in the hospital . . . and I just don't know what to do.

Jules leaps off the bed. "Come on," she says. "We have to go."

I don't know if I've ever seen Jules so rattled before; very little shakes her. But her eyes are dark with worry, and she has a death grip on my arm. I want to be there for my best friend, but I don't know if it's my place to show up uninvited in a hospital room. "I . . . don't know if Edgar would want me there. . . ."

"You're his fake girlfriend. You have to be."

It's not until I get in the car that I realize I'm still holding the book.

★ ★ ★

Hospitals creep me out. They smell like cleaning fluid and bleach, which you eerily know is just to cover the smell of puke and blood. The lights always flicker. People walk through the halls crying sometimes, and it's like a scene straight out of a horror movie. I think the reason sick people recover is just so they can get the hell out of there.

Edgar texted Jules the floor where we're supposed to meet him. When we get off the elevator, there's a nurses' station straight ahead. Jules gets us visitors' passes, and we walk in silence down the hallway. Just before we reach Jessamyn's room, Jules turns to me. "I don't know what I'm supposed to say to him."

"Then don't say anything," I tell her. "Just *be* here so he has someone to talk to."

We peer through the open doorway, and both of us abruptly stop.

Jessamyn is lying in the bed, asleep. She looks tiny, ethereal, like the fairies in Oliver's book. Like she's already halfway disappeared.

The thing about a mom is that she's always there. She's the one who rubs your back when you have the flu, who manages to notice you have no clean underwear and does your wash for you, who stocks the refrigerator with all the foods you love without you even having to ask. The thing about a mom is that you never imagine taking care of her, instead of the other way around.

My mom has worked two jobs most of my life, just to keep us afloat. When she's not cleaning her clients' houses, she's . . . well . . . doing the same thing in *our* house. I can't picture her taking a sick day, much less being in a hospital. To be sitting at her bedside, the way Edgar is at his mother's now, would be like waking up one morning to find that the sky was green and the grass was blue.

I try to remember the last time I thanked my mom for everything she does for me, and I can't. With a pang, I resolve to do it as soon as I get home. I guess we all assume that tomorrow we'll say those words, or hug her just because. I bet Edgar thought that too.

His arms are folded on the mattress, and his head is pillowed against them. "Edgar," Jules says, and he looks up.

He glances at his mom, making sure she's still sleeping. Then, holding a finger to his lips, he steps into the hall and closes the door gently behind him, leading us into an empty lounge. On the television, *SpongeBob* is playing, muted, with subtitles.

Jules throws herself into his arms. "You came," he says, re-lieved.

"What happened?" I ask.

"She fainted," Edgar says. "Again. And I know you thought she was all better now, and that it was probably nothing." To my shock, his eyes fill with tears. "But the thing is . . . it *wasn't* nothing."

The explanation tumbles out in a rush of syllables and grief: *Glioblastoma. Neural subtype. Fatal.*

I stare at him. I don't think there are any words in the English language to express how I feel right now. Edgar's mother was *dying* of a brain tumor, and Oliver and I were too selfish to bring him back here to spend time with her.

"I'm sorry," I manage to say. "I'm so sorry."

"How long?" Jules whispers.

"Months." Edgar wipes his eyes with the back of his hand. "It could be a little longer if she got chemo and radiation, but it's only like a stay of execution—it means she gets fifteen months of puking and baldness, and wishing she were dead, before she really *is*. When my dad died, it took years. It was a living hell. My mom doesn't want to go through that. She doesn't want *me* to go through that." He buries his face in his hands. "I can't lose her too," he whispers. "I'll be completely alone."

What happens to you, if you don't have parents? Are there even orphanages anymore? Oliver never mentioned any grand-parents or uncles or cousins visiting. I think of Edgar rattling around in his house, all by himself, suddenly having to be the grown-up.

Edgar sinks into a chair. "I can't stop thinking of all those stupid video games I used to play. My mom would say, 'Hey, let's take a walk,' or, 'Want to run errands with me?' I blew her off, every single time. And instead I'd pick up that stupid controller." He looks up at me. "In a video game, when you die, you get a reboot. You start over. How come real life isn't like that?"

I watch Jules fumble for something in her pocket. She takes out a small piece of coral, curved like a *J,* and rubs her thumb over the edge. Then she looks at me.

When you're best friends with someone, you don't have to speak to know what she's thinking. You don't have to hear her cry to know that she's breaking into a thousand pieces inside. Jules presses the coral into the palm of Edgar's hand. "Life *can* be like that," she says. "Go to the place where you're invincible."

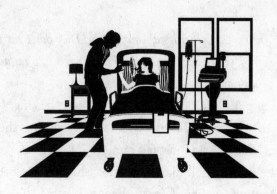

EDGAR

The conversation about her death was the worst conversation of my life.

Sit next to me, she said, patting the hospital bed beside her. *I'm not going to break.*

It started with a headache that wouldn't go away. And then, one day, I couldn't make sense of things. I thought I was hallucinating. I saw a boy who looked like my son . . . but who I just knew wasn't. The doctors call it Capgras syndrome—when you believe that a close family member has been replaced by an imposter. I went to a psychiatrist first, but he referred me to a neurologist. Someone who could take a look at my brain.

The MRI found the brain tumor. It's in the glial cells—they're sort of the glue of the nervous system. They hold neurons in place, and they supply nutrients and oxygen to the brain. They insulate one neuron from another. And they destroy toxins. Finding out that you have a glioblastoma is kind of like finding out that you have

termites eating the structure of your house. They don't eat the alu-
minum siding, your plumbing, or your appliances . . . but good luck
living in that house.

As she spoke, I felt like I should have been kicking. I should
have been screaming. Turning over tables. Yelling at the top of
my lungs. But instead I just felt numb.

As she spoke, I felt like my mother should have been sobbing, shouting, cursing. Instead she was relating the details in
an even voice, as if she had practiced.

It was like we were having a discussion about something
horrific that was happening to two people who were not us.

The reason we moved from Wellfleet was because the best neu-
rologist in New England happens to be here, at St. Brigid's. When
you were at school, I was at appointments. And I was trying very
hard to get the courage to tell you what was happening to me.

I don't get it. Why can't you have surgery? I asked. What
about chemo?

This type of tumor is so similar to normal brain cells that it's im-
possible to treat without destroying a lot of healthy cells too. So any
medicine or operation is only going to prolong the inevitable. I'm
going to die, Edgar. The question is whether I want to spend fifteen
months suffering through a treatment that isn't going to cure me,
or if I'd rather have four perfect months with you.

I swallowed hard.

Does it hurt? I asked.

Only when I think about what I'm missing, my mother said.
Cheering for you on your graduation day. Dancing with you at
your wedding. Holding my first grandchild. Watching you grow up
into a magnificent man.

But I couldn't imagine growing up without her there to witness it. I took a deep breath and tried and could only see a great, big blank. I felt like I was going to be sick.

What happens to me? What am I supposed to do without you?

Your birthday's in a week. You'll be eighteen—which means legally, you're an adult. You have cousins in California you can live with. You can go to college—your father and I set enough money aside to make sure of it. You'll go on, and you'll live a spectacular life.

What I wanted, in the middle of that conversation, was a do-over. Like when I used to go to the town pool with my mom and practice my somersaults off the diving board and wound up doing belly flops instead. *That one doesn't count!* I would yell from the edge of the pool, and she would nod, and I'd start again. I wanted this—this hospital room, this conversation, this reality—to not count. I wanted to go back in time, to before we were in this hospital. Before I went into her office at home. Before I found out her secret.

I tried to tell her this, but what came out instead was *I should have said I love you more.*

I'm your mom, she said. *Don't you think I know?*

I started to cry then. After my dad died, I thought I was safe—that the world could never get that bad again. I figured the worst had already happened and things could only get better from there. But I'd managed to win the suckiest lottery *twice*: two parents with terminal illnesses. I thought of how I willingly left my mother to go into a stupid book, giving up months I could have spent with her. I thought of how she would tell me to clean my room or take my dirty dishes to the sink and I would tune out, when now I wanted her to keep speaking so I would never forget her voice.

It's not fair, I whispered.

Oh, Edgar. She squeezed my hand. *Life's not fair.*

When I was in the fairy tale and miserable and Oliver came to check on us, I instinctively told him things were great, even though they weren't. It was Frump who said, afterward, that we all hide things to make the people we love happy.

So I forced a smile onto my face, a square peg in a round hole, a shoe two sizes too small.

I told her we'd better start working on her bucket list.

★ ★ ★

When I was five, my mother and I went apple picking on Cape Cod. It was September, and the farm had a corn maze. The air smelled like cider and fresh-baked donuts, and families were dotted throughout the orchard, collecting apples in canvas sacks. It was sunny and cold all at once, and the sky was so blue it looked like a movie backdrop. A shaggy horse pulled a wagon to the parts of the orchard where the trees hadn't been picked over yet. My mom and I walked as far as we could, to the edge of the field, where a bored teenager took our money to let us into the maze.

The stalks were taller than me. I ran down the straight edge of the corridor, high-fiving the fronds like they were my adoring fans. My mom chased after me, careful to make sure I didn't get too far ahead.

It was dusty and dry, and after about fifteen minutes my eyes and my throat began to itch. My mother scooped me up and put me on her shoulders so I could be her periscope, but even with that vantage point we weren't tall enough. I was pretty sure we were going in circles.

After a while the sun lit the tips of the cornstalks, as if they were candles. I was hungry and tired, deadweight in my mother's arms. *Edgar,* she said, *desperate times call for desperate measures.*

Instead of turning at the next fork in the maze, my mother kicked at the stalks with her boots, creating a small passage. Like ghosts, we began to walk through the walls. Finally we got spit out on the far edge of the farmland, in a field we had never seen before. It was like someone had pulled the rip cord, and night floated down over us.

"Where are we?" I asked. Everything looked unfamiliar, and I was starting to get that weird feeling in my stomach that came when I was scared.

My mother took my hand. *Let's find out,* she said, and just like that, I wasn't afraid. I was on an adventure.

★ ★ ★

Jules is right.

My mother is going to die if she stays here.

But what if she didn't have to?

Given the number of times characters have traded places with ordinary people, there's got to be a way. And no one would know that way better than the author of the fairy tale. But that means coming clean with my mother and explaining everything that's happened.

When my mother's eyes open, they are foggy for a moment, and then they fix on me.

"How are you feeling?" I ask.

She doesn't answer; she just nods.

"Mom, there's something I have to talk to you about. And it's going to be hard for you to believe, so I have witnesses." I motion for Delilah and Jules to come inside. Delilah is cradling the book in her arms. "You know Delilah already, and this is her best friend, Jules."

They step into the room gently, as if the floor is made of lava. "Jules, hello. And, Delilah," my mother says. "It's good to see you."

"I'm really, um, sorry . . . to hear that you're sick," Delilah says. "If there's anything I can do—"

"You already have. You've made my son very happy." She smiles at me.

"That's kind of what I need to talk to you about," I tell her. "Delilah isn't really my girlfriend." I pull up a chair beside the bed and sit down so I can take my mother's hand. "And when you thought I was an imposter, living in your house? You weren't really all that far off."

My mother frowns and tries to sit up in the bed. "I don't understand."

Delilah takes a step forward. "It all started with me," she says, gesturing to the book. "I found your story in my school library. And I fell in love with it. I read that fairy tale ten times a day. I knew every word, forward and backward. Then one of the characters spoke to me."

"It's always nice to hear when a reader feels a connection to a character," my mother says.

"No," Delilah explains. "This character? *Actually* spoke to me."

"It was Oliver," I jump in. "The prince you wrote."

"Except he didn't want to be a prince," Delilah says. "He wanted to be real. And he wanted my help escaping the book. So I did everything I could think of to help him—including coming to your house and asking you to rewrite the ending."

"But I wouldn't," my mother says, remembering.

"No," I agree. "And to be honest, I thought she was nuts. Until I opened the book, and Oliver spoke to me too."

"But that's impossible," my mother says, and then she relaxes against her pillow, as if it suddenly all makes sense. "This conversation isn't happening. It's the medication."

"We figured out a way to get Oliver out of the book," I tell my mother. "But it meant that someone else had to take his place: me."

"Edgar, honey, I know this has been a really difficult day for you. There are people here you can talk to who can help—"

"He's not crazy," Jules interrupts. "I was inside the book with him. And Delilah's been there too. I *know* it sounds insane. And I know every fiber of your being is telling you not to believe this. But you have to, because it's *true.*"

My mother turns to me. "All right," she says, in the tone you'd use to placate someone who's nuts.

"I know it doesn't make sense. Somehow we edited the story so that the book would think it needed me instead. Would think that *I* was the main character, and not Oliver. And it worked, for a little while. But the book has a mind of its own. When something's not right, it corrects itself."

"Well, of course," my mother says, as if I have finally begun to speak English. "What you're describing . . . that's what writing *is*. Characters get up and walk away with a plot all the time."

She's not getting it. "For a few months, Oliver was pretending to be me," I tell her, remembering what she had said earlier: *I saw a boy who looked like my son . . . but who I just knew* wasn't. That was what made her go to the doctor in the first place, and even if she hadn't been delusional—just really observant—it was also what made the doctors do the tests that found the tumor.

What if they hadn't? Would she not even know she was sick? Would that be better?

I push aside the thought. "Oliver is Delilah's boyfriend," I continue. "Me . . . I was hidden inside your story."

My mother looks from me to Delilah to Jules, as if she can't understand our strange conspiracy. "Edgar," she says quietly, sadly, "there's no such thing as fairy tales."

A long time ago, when my mother first wrote that book, she thought otherwise. I guess life can take you to a place where you are completely different from the person you used to be.

Before I know what's happening, Jules yanks the book out of Delilah's arms. She flips it open to the page where Oliver is climbing the tower wall. He looks up, sees a familiar face, and smiles. "Oliver," she says, "there's someone who wants to say hello."

She turns the book so it's facing my mother. Oliver's eyes dart up, and when he sees my mother's face, he looks shocked but recovers quickly. He grimaces and hangs on more tightly to the rock wall, doing his job, assuming that he isn't supposed to speak.

I lean closer to my mother so that he can see my face too. "Oliver," I tell him, "it's okay to talk to her."

Very slowly, his face turns toward us. "Hello," he says shyly. "It's quite a pleasure to officially meet you."

My mother's face goes white. "This is not happening."

"I'm sorry, should I perhaps go back to hanging on the wall?" Oliver asks. "But before I do that—might I just say, I loved playing your son, for a little while. You are an excellent mother."

After a long silence, my mother begins to speak. "When I was still a writer, I felt like the characters were speaking to me. I could hear them so clearly in my head."

"Maybe they were," Delilah says. "Maybe you just never answered."

★ ★ ★

Once, when I was little, I came home from kindergarten and my mother wasn't waiting for the bus at the end of the driveway. Hunching over, wearing my backpack like a turtle shell, I called her name. I wanted to show her the finger painting I'd done that day and give her the macaroni necklace I'd made. But she wasn't in the kitchen making me lunch either. I began to walk through the house, opening doors, getting more and more panicked. What if something bad had happened to her? What if something bad was about to happen to me?

The last door I opened was the door to her office. On the walls were sketches of a pirate ship, of princesses, of castles. There was a painting on her easel of a fire-breathing dragon, and a prince staring him down, all reds and oranges that looked like the coils on the stove I wasn't supposed to touch. My mother was sitting in her chair. Her eyes were closed, and her head was tilted back so that her face was lifted to the ceiling.

"Mom," I said, and when she didn't answer, I repeated it a little louder.

"Shhhh," she whispered. "They're talking to me."

I looked around the room, but we were completely alone. "Who?"

At that, her eyes popped open. "The characters," she said, and she smiled.

★ ★ ★

My mother looks at me blankly when I try to explain the concept of Easter eggs in games and videos. "It's like when you're watching *The Phantom Menace* and you realize that E.T. is in the Senate with the Palpatine supporters—"

Jules interrupts. "It's like when you put your winter coat on for the first time in months and you find twenty bucks in your pocket."

"So, something unexpected?" my mother says.

"Yeah," I add, "but in video games, when you find one, you can sometimes skip a whole level of play. Or wind up at the end of the game. Or even just automatically win."

"A shortcut," Delilah says, simplifying. "We found the ones you put into the book: the lip-gloss compact on the copyright page, and the star cookie."

I meet my mother's gaze. "Every time someone reads your fairy tale, Rapscullio falls out a tower window and dies. But not really, because the next time the book is opened, there he is again, conning Oliver into helping him." I take a deep breath. "There is no death. There's no sickness. The book won't allow it. If you can tell us where you've hidden just one more of those gateways, we can go inside. And once we're there, we get to live forever."

She is silent for a long moment.

"Edgar," she says finally, "you have some imagination."

"So did you. Which is why I think this might work." I reach for her hand. "You just had a conversation with Oliver, right? So you know that it's possible to exist—no, not exist, *live*—inside the book . . . and in spite of what you want to tell yourself, it has nothing to do with the meds you're on. If Oliver and Maureen are willing to trade places, and if you and I follow the plot instead of messing with it, there's no reason the book *wouldn't* take us. Sure, I'll have to wear tights for the rest of my life, but that's okay, if it means you're with me. And there are worse things than having the day job of being a queen, right?" I hesitate. "Mom, really, what have you got to lose?"

My mother's been awake for an hour now, and I can see she's exhausted. "Even if this were true, which it can't possibly be, I couldn't tell you where to find a portal." She sighs. "I didn't create them."

I look at Delilah and Jules. "If you didn't, who *did*?"

"I don't know. Students write papers about themes and symbolism in books . . . and half the time, the author never planned any of it. It just *happens*."

"You mean, like, subconsciously?" Jules asks.

"Maybe," my mother admits.

"Then who's to say there's not another subconscious secret passage somewhere? We just have to find it," I say.

"But they're not what you think they are. They're not bonuses, or extra points. They were wishes. The only reason they worked when they did was because the person who stumbled across them believed wholeheartedly. A wish is just words. Belief is the catalyst. It's what sets that wish into motion. When two people want the same exact thing and that wish is caught between them, there's nothing more powerful."

"Then why don't wishes come true every day?" I ask her. "If we both want you to get better, how come it's not that simple?"

She looks at me, her eyes wide and sad. "This world isn't filled with magic," my mother says. "Why do you think so many people escape through fiction?" She sinks into the pillow, her voice fading. "Edgar, I think I need to close my eyes for a little while."

I slip out of the room, followed by Delilah and Jules. "Do you think she's right?" Jules asks. "That they weren't portals or escape hatches—they were just two people believing in something at once?"

"Then why did you get sucked into Seraphima's wish?" Delilah asks her. "You clearly didn't want to go into the book, but you wound up there anyway. And for the record, Oliver and I did plenty of simultaneous wishing for him to get out of the book, and it did nothing."

"I don't know," I say, my mind buzzing. I don't have the answers. I just know I have to find them, quickly.

And I think I know who might be able to help.

OLIVER

I know something is wrong. I knew it the moment Edgar told me to say hello to Jessamyn and I saw the wires and tubes hooked up behind her, as if she were one of Orville's experiments. I knew from the look on Delilah's face before she closed the book, telling me she would explain everything as soon as she got a chance.

I have been pacing the bottom of page 43, waiting for her, but she hasn't opened the book.

Love isn't what you expect it to be. You imagine being drunk on happiness, but the truth is, you worry all the time. Is she ill? Hurt? Might she meet someone else? There's a moment when you realize that you've gotten everything you wished for. And right on its heels is the understanding that this means you have so much more to lose.

By the time I feel the ground shift under my feet and the

book beginning to open, I've worked myself into a frenzy, imagining all manner of horrors.

To my surprise, however, Delilah doesn't open the book to our usual page. I find myself springing through the story, until I am flung hard into Orville's copper cauldron. He winces in empathy. I sit up gingerly, only to have Humphrey smack into my face and send me sprawling on my back.

Socks trots onto the page, panting. "Mmm. Feeling that cardio," he says.

The scene swims before settling into place, and I glance up surreptitiously to find Delilah—in the company of Jules and Edgar.

"Are you all right?" I ask Delilah. "What's going on? And don't bloody close the book on me this time."

"I'm fine," Delilah assures me. "But Jessamyn—she's not. She's very sick, Oliver. She's not going to live much longer."

I watch Socks and Orville process this information. "Like Frump?" Socks asks after a minute.

"Not exactly," Delilah says. "Because this time we know it's coming."

I look up at her. "And you think you can stop it?"

Edgar is the one who answers. "I think *we* can," he replies.

I know what he is going to say before he even says it. And I am holding my breath, hoping that if Edgar plans to bring his mother into the book permanently, he also means to join her.

Because then I get to leave.

We listen as Edgar outlines his plan: if Jessamyn enters the book, she will automatically heal. Just like it made Jules's hair begin to turn blond and Frump become a dog again, the story will do what it has to do to make her fit the role of Queen Maureen—who is blissfully, absolutely healthy.

"But you scoured the pages," Orville points out, "and you only found that single star biscuit when you were looking for an escape."

"We may not need another portal," Edgar explains. "My mother swears she didn't write that intentionally into the book. She said it was just a wish that happened to be in the right place at the right time, basically."

"It's a puzzle," Delilah says. "We only have to figure out what all the swaps had in common."

"The first was Edgar and I. We didn't have any special short-cut, unless one counts the revised plot." I glance at Delilah. "And since you and I were never able to get me free using Rap-scullio's easel or ripping the pages or writing me out of the plot, we know there must have been some key point that made the difference."

"An equal trade," Orville says. "A body for a body. Oliver, you couldn't leave the story no matter how badly Delilah wanted you to—because there was no one to take your place."

"Right. But both Edgar and Oliver were willing to make the switch. When Seraphima came out of the book," Delilah points out, "Jules got dragged in unwillingly."

"Maybe the wishing doesn't have to be two-sided," Orville suggests.

"Then why wouldn't I have been able to get out on my own?" I ask. "Why didn't a stranger get sucked in?"

"I was the only one reading the book," Delilah points out. "And I did it in secret, because I was so embarrassed to be reading a kids' story."

"Which meant that there wasn't any male near you who could be pulled into the story in my place," I finish.

Socks whinnies faintly. "I don't mean to be a bother," he asks, "but why did Humphrey wind up here?"

"He was with us when the book was open," I say. "We were all watching Orville cast the wishing spell on Frump."

Orville nods. "What this tells us is that for permanence's sake, the story wants a replacement similar enough to the original character to be able to mold them in the same image."

"Then how come when I wished to be with Oliver all those times, I didn't accidentally switch places with Seraphima?" Delilah asks.

Before any of us can respond, Humphrey wanders to the far corner of the page and begins to lift his leg. "No!" I shout. "For heaven's sake, Humphrey, we don't do that here! There are rules in this world."

Humphrey's ears droop. "I'm so sorry. I'll pack my things and go. Actually, I don't have any things. I'll just go. . . ."

"Wait," Orville says, his eyes gleaming. "You're on to something there, my boy. There *are* rules in this world. And we must play by them, as I've said before. Yet in a story, anything is possible. So the wish must originate *here*."

I try to make a mental list of everything we've covered so far: If two people switch and only one of them has consented, there has to be an aid involved—a cookie, a portal, a spell, a magic lip gloss. If, on the other hand, two people want to switch, having given mutual consent, that can happen without any physical shortcut. All it takes is the power of the wish.

I look up at Edgar. "Your mother talked to me. But did she believe you when you told her you lived inside this book for four months?"

"I don't think so," Edgar admits. "She thought I was making it all up. She thought *you* were a hallucination."

"If she could be convinced, then from what Orville's saying, all it would take for us to swap places would be for you, me, your mother, and Queen Maureen to want it desperately."

Edgar shakes his head. "That's not going to happen. She already thinks her mind is playing tricks on her."

"Then you must find another one of your special tricks," Orville says.

We all fall silent, because we know how much harder that is than it seems. I glance up at Edgar and see the defeat written across his features. I think of Frump and how many times each day I wish he were still here: to laugh with me when Socks gets stuck in a mud bog, to marvel as the sunset paints the beach, to help me finish off one of Queen Maureen's lemon tarts. Edgar has already given up, I realize. He has already started to say goodbye.

"Right," I say briskly, stiffening my spine. "We'd best get moving, then. We have a lot of pages to cover if we're going to find something that will work to save Jessamyn."

Edgar shakes his head. "It's useless."

"No it's not. Even if she's doubtful, as long as three of us are wishing for the trade, and we have a boost of magic like Seraphima and Frump and Socks had before, when *they* made a wish, it might work."

"But we don't have time to find that boost of magic," Edgar says. "Believe me. Jules and I scoured every inch of this narrative."

Suddenly it hits me: what if we're looking not for a *what* . . . but rather a *when*?

"Delilah," I begin. "When does magic happen in your world?"

"When you use Photoshop?" she answers.

"No. I mean, you make wishes all the time. You wished on stars, and on eyelashes, and even once on that strangely shaped bone in the chicken your mother cooked. Does one of those feel a little more lucky than the others?"

Jules and Delilah glance at each other. "Birthday," they say simultaneously.

"When you blow out your candle," Delilah tells me, "that's the one wish people believe will come true. There's this huge buildup, because everyone's watching you make your wish, and you keep it hidden inside and never say it out loud. Eyelashes and shooting stars are for the little things—the wishes that don't really matter. Like when you yell out, 'Wish me good luck!' You know it won't make a difference, but you say it anyway. Your birthday wish, though—that's the one you think actually might happen."

"What did you wish for on your last birthday?" I ask.

Delilah blushes. "A prince, to sweep me off my feet."

"Wow," Socks breathes, impressed. "That's pretty close."

"It's my birthday next week," I announce.

"It was *my* birthday first," Edgar mutters.

"I may be eternally sixteen, chronologically younger than

Edgar, but I still celebrate the occasion. We all do, in here. We just never grow older.

"Don't you see?" I tell him. "It's perfect. If we both ask at the same time, on the same birthday, for the same thing, surely that will be a big enough wish to bring both you and Jessamyn here."

I'm quite chuffed to have figured this out—in the presence of a wizard, no less—but Edgar doesn't seem enthusiastic.

"And if it isn't," he says quietly, "it will be the last birthday I have with my mom."

I straighten, looking Edgar in the eye. "Then we'd best make sure it works," I tell him.

* * *

Queen Maureen is pruning the roses in the royal garden when I find her. I snap a rose from its stem and hand it to her gallantly. "A beauty for a beauty," I say, turning on the full force of my charm.

If I'm going to convince this woman to give up everything she's ever known, I'd better be at the top of my game.

"Let me guess," Maureen says. "You broke another dish?"

"Do you truly think that's the only reason I might come to see your lovely face today? It might be a surprise for you to hear, but I actually enjoy being in your company."

She smirks. "I'm betting on the broken plate."

I sink down on a marble bench. "Then you'll lose your wager," I say. "Although I do want to talk to you about something."

"Ah, you see," she replies, snipping a dead branch. "I knew it. Mother's intuition."

"About that . . ." I take a deep breath. "You've said you consider me to be a son. And I've always thought of you as my mother. I don't think family has to be related by blood, do you? Don't you think family is the people who love you the most?"

"Of course," Maureen says.

"And . . . well . . . if your son was going to move away, you'd want to go with him, wouldn't you?"

Maureen rolls her eyes. "I've told you before, you can't live above the cobbler's shop on page three. It's not seemly for a prince, and it doesn't make sense to haul a bed out there when you have a perfectly grand one in the castle."

"I don't want to move to page three. I want to live in the real world." I pause. "With you."

"Me? In the real world?" Queen Maureen chokes on a laugh. "I wouldn't know the first thing about how to live there."

"That's why you'll have me."

Her eyes find mine. "Is this about your Delilah?"

"Not this time," I confess. "It's about a boy who's going to lose his mother. And if we switch with them, well, I believe he won't have to."

"That's tragic," Maureen says. She sinks down beside me on the marble bench. "But why would you think that some ordinary woman and her son might be able to come inside here? You've seen how the other strangers were forced out."

"This isn't an ordinary woman," I explain. "This is Jessamyn Jacobs. She wrote this story."

Queen Maureen is silent for a moment. She plucks the petals

from the rose in her hand, one by one, letting them float to the ground. She stops before she picks the final petal, and places the stem between us. "She gave me life," Maureen says softly. "It's the least I can do for her."

★ ★ ★

So much has happened today that I'm not sure I will get a chance to speak to Delilah alone tonight. But then, shortly after the last star appears in the sky, there is a seam of light along the spine of the book and I feel myself being drawn toward our usual page.

"Hi," she says softly.

"Hello." I can't stop smiling at her. It's as if all the awful truth I've learned today has only served to remind me of how lucky I am to have found her. "So, you'd best have a spectacular birthday gift for me."

"You don't *know* it's going to work," Delilah says.

"You don't know it's *not*," I point out. "I'm thinking . . . we go out to supper first, and *then* you give me my present. And to be perfectly honest, I *am* expecting a cake. Preferably choco- late, but I won't quibble."

"I can't let myself hope this is going to happen," Delilah says, "because the stakes are so high if it doesn't. Not just for us this time either. For Edgar."

I look at her, sobering. "I know."

"I came home from the hospital today and I hugged my mother so tight she probably thought I was insane. I couldn't tell her about Jessamyn dying—because what if Queen Maureen winds up here, perfectly healthy? So instead I just said I had a really bad day and I needed my mother. But I can't stop thinking, thank God it's not *my* mom. And that's awful, right?"

"It's human nature, I suppose," I reply.

"Is this our fault?" Delilah whispers. "When Jessamyn fainted the first time, shouldn't we have tried to get Edgar back here immediately?"

"She swore to me that she wasn't ill," I say.

"She *lied* to you because she didn't want to worry you, the way we didn't want to worry Edgar." Delilah shakes her head. "We lost *weeks* he could have had with her."

Her eyes are full of storms. "We can't turn back time," I say. "The only thing we can do is try to ensure that Edgar and Jessamyn have more of it."

Delilah bites her lower lip. "I know you look like Edgar . . . but do you really think Maureen can pass for Jessamyn?"

"Close enough. From what I saw of family photographs when I was in her house, Maureen looks much like Jessamyn did when she got married—although, oddly, her hair color seems to have changed from brown to red. For that matter, King Maurice is the spitting image of Edgar's late father." I tilt my head, considering. "We should only hope we're lucky enough to have to disguise Queen Maureen to make her look exactly like Jessamyn."

"What will happen to Edgar if . . . the book doesn't let Jessamyn in? I mean, things out here aren't like they are in there. Food doesn't magically appear. You have to make money to buy it. You have to be able to pay your own mortgage. Edgar's only seventeen. He shouldn't have to grow up that fast."

"He won't have to. In fact, he'll never grow up," I say.

Delilah raises a brow, still dubious.

"If this has any chance of working," I tell her, "I must believe one hundred percent—and to do that, I need you to believe too."

She lowers her lashes so that they cast shadows on her cheeks. For a moment I think perhaps I've made her cry. When she looks at me again, I realize that desperation and hope are twins, merely altered versions of each other. "What kind of frosting?" she asks.

"Buttercream," I say softly.

Hope is what makes you look outside the window to see if it's stopped raining.

Hope is what makes you believe he'll text you back.

Hope is why you buy your jeans a little tight.

Hope is why you put a spoon under your pillow and wear your pajamas inside out when you hear there could be a snow day.

Hope is why you get out of bed in the morning, and why you dream at night.

Hope is what makes us believe that things can only get better.

Hope is what keeps us going.

DELILAH

Just when I think things couldn't possibly get more complicated, Harvey happens.

On the day I'm hosting a schoolwide Halloween/birthday
party—something I never thought I'd do in my lifetime—a hurricane that's supposed to blow out to sea in the Carolinas takes
an abrupt and unexpected turn and makes its way up the East-
ern Seaboard. Hurricane Harvey goes from a trickle of rain to a
hammering on the roof, and the lights flicker as Jules and I sit
in my bedroom, crossing off details on a checklist.

"I've got a bunch of six-packs of Coke and twelve bags of
potato chips," I say. "And I talked my mom out of bobbing
for apples, but she's still insisting on making vegetables in the
shape of a skeleton with dip."

"This is going to be the worst party in the history of parties,"
Jules mutters.

"Well, what am I supposed to do?" I argue. "My mother and

Edgar's mother are going to be there. I didn't think beer pong would be a viable option."

It's totally lame to throw a party at my house for Edgar's birthday with his own mother there as a guest—but this is the only way our plan is going to succeed. Besides, it doesn't matter if my reputation tanks because of this, since if it works, Oliver will be here, and he's the only one whose opinion matters to me.

It's been a week since Jessamyn was released from the hospital, a week that we've spent plotting with Oliver and the characters in the book, to make sure that this swap is flawless. Edgar has been mostly out of the loop, consumed with taking care of his mom. He says the hardest part is how normal Jessamyn seems. With the exception of the antiseizure medication she has to take every day, and a headache that won't go away, she might as well just be fighting the common cold.

"Has Edgar told Jessamyn why we're really throwing this party?" I ask. "Does she even know that we're trying to get her inside the book?"

"No. She still doesn't believe any of this is real. Edgar thought it would be better if she didn't know what we're planning. That way she's more likely to agree to be here."

It makes sense. Jessamyn totally didn't buy Edgar's secret-portal theory; even seeing Oliver alive and talking was something she managed to dismiss as a hallucination caused by medication. Since this all hinges on a wish, it won't do any good for Jessamyn to actively doubt the process. For all we know, that could be the one thing that makes this go wrong.

Hanging on the back of my closet door is the costume I

borrowed from Ms. Pingree and the drama department. Jules is going as Sally from *The Nightmare Before Christmas*. She was the one who made the astute observation that if this switch actually did pan out, we were going to end up with a guy in a prince costume in the middle of a high school party. Since it is only a week away from Halloween, it made perfect sense to dress everyone up—so that if Oliver and Maureen do arrive in the present day, nobody will blink an eye.

"So," Jules asks, her gaze sliding away from me. "Did you hear from Chris? Is he coming?"

I look up at her. "I had to invite him. He's Edgar's best friend. Well, Oliver's. You know what I mean."

"It's going to be so awkward," Jules says. "I haven't talked to him . . . since I ended things. And I didn't exactly give him a reason."

I put my hand on her shoulder. "Are you okay with all this? With Edgar leaving?"

"I kind of have to be, right?" She meets my gaze. "Let's be real. He wouldn't stay out here with me if the cost is losing his mom."

"For what it's worth," I tell her, "he really did like you. He's just got much bigger problems to think about right now."

She forces a smile. "Don't worry about me. I'm tougher than I look."

I laugh, glancing at Jules's ripped black tights, the studded leather cuffs on her wrists, the safety pin she's wearing as an earring, the thick black eyeliner. "That's terrifying," I say. "Remind me to never get in a fight with you."

Suddenly there's a crash of thunder, and the lights dim and

then buzz back to life. "I cannot believe this," I mutter. "What if no one shows up?"

"Does it even matter? The only people who *have* to show up, will. Besides, there's nothing like a little natural disaster to spice up a party." Jules glances at her phone. "I have to go home and change. I told Edgar I'd pick him and his mom up at seven, and my face paint alone takes half an hour." We both stand up, and impulsively she hugs me. "It's gonna work."

"It has to," I say.

As soon as I hear Jules's car pull away, I realize I've done all the checks for *this* party, but I haven't thought about the preparations on the other side. And if Oliver needs my help, or if something's going wrong, there's no way he can even tell me until I open the book.

It's not on my nightstand, where it usually rests.

Getting on my knees, I scan underneath the bed. I pull back the covers and sheets, searching. I dump the contents of my backpack. I tear my whole room apart, rummaging through every drawer and yanking every book off my shelves, but I can't find it.

Did I leave it at school? At Edgar's? Where was I the last time I talked to Oliver?

Last night. Under the covers. Before I went to sleep. And this morning I left the book on my nightstand.

I *know* I did. But then why isn't it there?

How could I possibly lose my own boyfriend?

And how could I possibly misplace the book on the one day I need it most?

I fling open the door to my room and run downstairs.

"Mom!" I yell, teetering on the edge between shouting and sobbing. "Have you seen my book?"

She turns, in the middle of wiping down the counter. "What book?"

"You know what book. *Between the Lines* . . ." I pull open random kitchen drawers, rummaging. "I need it. Right now."

"Delilah, calm down," my mother says. "I put it on the bookshelf with the photo albums."

"Why?" I ask, running into the living room and tracing the spines of the books until I find the one with the gold lettering. I grab it and clutch it to my chest, feeling my heart pound against the cover.

My mother walks up to me, surprised at my outburst. She reaches out to pull the fairy tale from my arms, but I twist away from her, shielding it with my body.

"Delilah," she asks gently, "what *is* it about this book? Why are you so attached to it?"

"You wouldn't get it."

"Try me. *Talk* to me. I thought it was just a phase—one that you grew out of when you started dating and making more friends. But now, all of a sudden, you're right back where you used to be—obsessed with a children's fairy tale. What happened?"

My throat is jammed with a hundred responses, none of which she would understand. "Stay out of my stuff!" I yell, and I run back upstairs.

When I reach my room, I slam the door and open to page 43. Oliver is still shimmying into position on the rock wall, clutching at his chest. When he sees me, he lets go of his tunic, and several rolls of bright-colored streamers fall from the folds of velvet, unrolling to the edges of the page. "Why are you interrupting me?" he asks. "I'm in the middle of planning my own birthday party."

"I know," I tell him. "I just wanted to make sure everything was going all right."

"Well, it rather was. Until you interrupted me." He smiles as he's saying this, though, so I know he's not really upset to see me. "And your preparations?"

"They were going fine until I temporarily lost you," I say. "My mother moved the book."

"Ah, right. I forgot to tell you, with all that's been happening and Jessamyn's illness—but your mother, she read us the other day."

"She *what?*"

"It was when you were at school, presumably. I thought it was you, opening the book as usual—except it wasn't."

"Are you serious? What is she doing in my room? Snooping?"

"Maybe she just wanted a good story to read." Oliver looks up. "We *are* a book, you know. Believe it or not, we do have day jobs. It's been so long since we were able to act the fairy tale out; everyone was quite delighted. Everyone except me," he confesses.

"But what if something went wrong? What if she *recognized* you?"

"I did the best I could to keep her from seeing my face," Oliver admits. "She didn't seem to think anything was amiss."

"*This* time," I point out.

"Well," Oliver says, "if it all goes well tonight . . . perhaps there won't *be* a next time." He grins up at me broadly. "I truly

do adore talking to you, Delilah, but I can't leave this page unless you're gone." He holds up two rolls of streamers. "And I
have an entire kingdom to decorate."

I hide a smile. "I love you too," I say, and very gently, I close
the book.

★ ★ ★

It takes a considerable amount of planning and effort to get
dressed in my costume. The first layer is a hoop skirt and a
corset, followed by a petticoat that gets tied—and knotted—
around my waist. After that comes the gown, draped with satin
and lace. The cherry on top is a tiara, a little comb that gets
wired into my hair and twinkles with fake gems.

I keep my Converse sneakers on underneath, because no one
will see them.

Then I step up to the dreaded full-length mirror inside my
closet door, where I usually take one last glance at myself before
I leave for school, always finding something to criticize—my
hair, my hips, my freckles.

But this time, I just stop and stare.

I look . . . pretty.

The pink gown makes my cheeks look rosy, and the way
the waist nips in makes me seem like I actually have a figure.
My hair, for once, doesn't look like a bird's nest. It's twisted up
partway to hold the little crown, and the rest cascades in curls,
thanks to the humidity of Hurricane Harvey.

I wonder what Oliver will think when he sees me.

If he sees me.

Shaking my head clear, I force myself to think positively. "When," I say firmly out loud.

If Jessamyn is right—if wishes are all it takes for a dream to come true—then it's at least worth trying. So although I feel silly, although I am not in the habit of talking to myself, I close my eyes, clasp my hands, and hope.

"Please," I whisper. "Bring him back to me."

At that moment, there is a crack of thunder so loud it rattles the house, and a flash of lightning fills the room. The next moment, the power goes out, and everything goes dark.

It just doesn't seem like a great omen.

★ ★ ★

If any party were suited to a lack of electricity, it would be a Halloween bash. My mother and I have set candles all over the house, on every available saucer we own—so many that I suggested inviting the fire department, just so they wouldn't have to make an extra trip. The flames flicker and cast shadows on the walls, making everything look ten times creepier. The raindrops that race down the glass panes of the windows are illuminated by the candlelight, and maybe because there's nothing else to do—no TV or computer—the turnout is huge.

There are kids dressed as pirates and cowboys and cops. James and his boyfriend are salt-and-pepper shakers. Raj is wearing a milk carton on his head with the face cut out of it, and the word MISSING across the top.

"Really?" I ask, when he first comes inside.

"It's clever," he tells me. "Chicks dig clever."

"But . . . really?"

"Brains over body," Raj insists. "So, where are the hot girls?"

I watch him scan the crowd, his eyes lighting on Claire, who is trying to channel "sexy nerd" with her costume but seems to simply be wearing what she had on yesterday, with a pair of hipster glasses. "Score," Raj says, and he moves off in her direction.

Everyone seems to be having a decent time—except Chris, who's moping by himself in a corner. I sidle up to him, as best as someone can sidle wearing a giant petticoat. "Hey," I say.

He glances down at me from beneath the brim of his red Super Mario hat. His lips twist beneath his fake mustache. "I'm guessing you heard."

I reach up and pat his shoulder. "I'm really sorry it didn't work out. But seriously, you're not going to have any trouble finding someone else."

He tries to smile but doesn't quite manage. "Did she tell you why?" Chris asks. "Was it something I did?"

"Trust me, it's not you. It's just . . . really bad timing right now."

He looks down at me, his expression pained. "I don't want things to get weird now, you know? I mean, you being Jules's best friend and all . . . ?"

"It's only weird if you make it that way," I promise.

Just then a car drives up, its headlights cutting across the room as it pulls up to the curb. I'm expecting Jules with the guest of honor and his mom—but to my absolute shock, when I open the door, there stands Allie McAndrews and her entourage.

Her minions are all dressed like sexy cats.

And Allie? She's wearing a gown that looks *identical* to mine.

"I didn't expect you to come," I say.

Allie raises a brow. "Please. I'm the one who's going to *make* this party. You should be honored."

I am *not* going to let Allie spoil this night. "Well, clearly you have good taste in costumes," I say amiably, gesturing at our matching dresses and trying to make a lame joke. "Two princesses in a pod . . ."

Allie looks horrified. "I am not just some stupid Disney princess," she says. "I'm—"

"Princess Peach!" Chris finishes, grabbing her hand and bowing over it, in his blue overalls.

Allie beams. "Thank you for rescuing me, Mario!" she twitters.

Chris laughs. "I didn't peg you as a Super Mario fan."

"Are you kidding me?" Allie says, animated, in a way I've never seen her before. "It's the best game ever. What else would I do while waiting for my toes to dry?"

I stifle a laugh, wishing Jules were here to see this. The cats standing behind Allie look at each other, completely confused. I guess that makes sense. It's not every day you learn that your Queen Bee is a gamer.

Allie turns on them. "Oh, please. Brittany, we all know you still watch *My Little Pony*. And, Chloe, your hairdresser's not the only one who knows you're not a natural blonde."

She sounds like Allie—mean, that is—but there's something different about it. She seems annoyed, as if she's sick of having to live up to an audience 24/7.

It's almost as if she's . . . well, human.

"Thank God *Super Mario 3D World* upgraded Peach," Allie adds. "I mean, how lame was it that when *New Super Mario Brothers* came out for the Wii, Nintendo couldn't afford the extra programming for her dress, so she wasn't a playable character?"

Chris's jaw drops. "Marry me," he jokes.

She slips her arm through his. "How about we start with a Diet Coke?"

As they walk into the crowd, the door opens again. Jules is holding an umbrella over herself and Jessamyn, who is dressed in scrubs, with a surgical cap covering her hair and a mask obscuring half her face.

Jessamyn catches me staring at her costume. "I used to be a writer," she explains, her eyes dancing above the mask. "I like irony."

"And I like dry clothes," Edgar mutters, standing in the rain behind them. "Any chance we could move inside?"

For a moment, when he first steps in wearing a full prince costume that matches Oliver's, I can't breathe. They look *that* much alike.

Which is why, I remind myself, *this is going to work.*

"Happy birthday," I say.

"Not until nine-fifteen," Edgar replies. "Remember?"

Not wanting to leave anything to chance, we have arranged with Oliver to blow out the candles on his own birthday cake at the exact moment of Edgar's birth.

My mother, wearing her witch costume, approaches when she sees Edgar enter. "You must be Jessamyn," she says. "I'm Grace. It's so nice to finally meet you."

"Thanks for taking care of Edgar a few weeks ago," Jessamyn replies. "I've had some health issues lately, and it's really nice to know that he has people looking out for him."

I follow her gaze as it lights on my mother, me, the crowd of Edgar's friends. These are the people in whose hands she thinks she will be leaving her son, once she's gone.

Gradually everyone notices that Edgar's finally here. His name is chanted, echoing around the house, birthday wishes falling like confetti.

My mother turns to Jessamyn. "I'm just going to get the cake ready, if you want to come into the kitchen. Unless, of course, raging is your thing."

She grins. "The kitchen sounds *great.*"

As they walk off, Jules, Edgar, and I huddle together. "Is Oliver ready?" Edgar asks.

"I guess so," I tell him. "Are *you?*"

"Yeah. Jules has an extra set of scrubs in her bag for Maureen to dress in when she gets here. People might notice if my mom's costume suddenly changes in the middle of the party." His eyes flicker to the kitchen. "I'm just going to make sure she doesn't need anything."

As he heads through the crowd, I'm the only one who sees the pain written on Jules's face. She turns away, and her eyes widen. "*Allie* is here? Who invited her?"

"Herself," I say mildly. "But, Jules, there's something you need to know—"

Just then Chris walks up to Allie, holding a can of Diet Coke. Their heads bend together, laughing, as they talk.

"And . . . *now* this night can't get any worse," Jules moans.

"I'm sorry."

"It's okay. He deserves to be happy," Jules says, but she isn't looking at Chris. She's staring at Edgar as he weaves away from her.

★ ★ ★

The party plays out before me like a scene from a movie, like something I'm watching but not part of. Laughter and talking and dancing and movement; conversations full of gestures that look, at a distance, like charades. Edgar comes up behind me, close enough to whisper in my ear. "Who knew a hurricane could be so much fun?" he says.

I turn, and when I see other people watching us I thread my fingers through his, putting on a show. "I was just thinking," I say, "about how it doesn't rain in the book."

He frowns, then nods. "You're right. I guess I never really noticed."

"When Oliver first came here and it rained, he asked who was crying. I think that's the only precipitation he'd ever seen—a reader's tears." I look up at Edgar. "You know how nobody likes the rain here? How we duck out of it, or complain when our shoes get wet, or get pissed off if we forget to bring an umbrella? Well, Oliver loved it. He thought it was the most miraculous thing, that the sky could leak and fix itself again. That first storm, he ran outside, flung his arms wide, and just turned in circles, laughing as he got drenched."

I glance out the window again. "The last week Oliver was here, it rained. I noticed when he came to school, he was carrying an umbrella. And I thought, *Did I do that to him? Did I make him stop believing in magic?*"

"Maybe we just adapt to where we need to be," Edgar says. "Maybe that *is* the magic."

I take a deep breath and nod as Jules approaches. She's fixed her makeup, but I can tell she's been crying—her eyes are red-rimmed.

"It's past nine," she says. "Should we get ready?"

I look from Edgar to Jules; they're staring so intently at each other that I expect the space between them to spontaneously combust. "Can I have a minute with Jules?" he asks.

"Of course," I say, but I'm pretty sure they don't hear me.

In the kitchen, I find my mother and Jessamyn sticking eighteen candles in the cake. "One for good luck," I tell her desperately. "You can't forget that. It's the most important."

My mother looks at me oddly but heads into the pantry to find an extra candle.

Jessamyn puts her hand on my arm. "Thank you, Delilah," she says. "For doing this for Edgar. And for me."

I open my mouth to tell her that she'll be celebrating many more birthdays with her son, but then catch myself. "Edgar loves you," I tell her. "More than anything. He'd give up everything for you, you know."

"I'm a very lucky woman," Jessamyn says, and over her surgical mask, her eyes are too bright.

She blinks away her tears as my mother returns, holding not just the candle but also a box of matches.

I glance at my phone. It's 9:10.

"Let's do this," I say, exhaling.

While my mother lights the candles, I go into the living room and turn off the laptop that's playing music. Conversation trickles, drying to silence, as everyone turns to me. "Where's the birthday boy?" I ask.

"Here," Jules announces. She walks into the room, pulling Edgar behind her. I have no idea what transpired between them, but they both look like they've been through a war. Jules lets go of Edgar when he reaches the dining room table, and comes to stand beside me, across from him.

It's 9:12.

"Happy birthday to you," my mother starts singing, and everyone joins her.

Happy birthday to you . . .

Happy birthday, dear Edgar . . .

Happy birthday to you!

I look at my phone. It's 9:13. Crap. Why is that song so short? Edgar stares at me, panicking. "Are you . . . one?" I call out. "Are you . . . two? Are you . . . three?" I clap at each number, and eventually the crowd chimes in.

By the time we reach eighteen, it's 9:14. I watch the seconds tick.

"Okay," I vamp, "I hope you've got a great wish!"

Ten more seconds. That's our cue. I nod at Edgar, who leans down toward the cake. It casts a glow over his features as his brow furrows and he concentrates. I see his lips moving silently as he says the words that have been prearranged.

Right now, inside the book that is safely waiting in my bedroom, Oliver is saying the exact same sentence.

I wish for a life with the person I love the most.

The alarm I've set on my phone dings—9:15.

At the last moment, Jules rushes forward so that she's close enough to Edgar to touch him. Suddenly there's a crash as a burst of wind blows open one of the old, uninsulated windows in our house. The gust swirls through the room, stealing the breath of every candle. For a heartbeat, the room goes pitch-black.

And then, with a whir of machinery and electronic beeping, the power comes back on.

"Awesome wish, dude," Raj calls out.

I blink, unaccustomed to the bright light. And immediately I feel sick—nothing happened. Nothing changed. Edgar is still bent over his cake, his eyes closed. Jules has her hand on his back.

"Edgar?" Jules whispers.

His eyes open at the sound of her voice.

He turns toward Jules.

And walks right past her.

Staring straight at me, as if I am the only person in the room, he smiles crookedly. A smile I know; a smile I fell in love with. And then Oliver swings me into his arms and kisses me.

EDGAR

I wish for a life with the person I love the most.

All of a sudden my hair is blown back from my face by a powerful wind, and everything goes black. There's a pounding in my head, and then so much brightness enveloping me that I squint, unable to see.

I feel a hand on my back. "Edgar?"

I turn, focusing on the doctor's face. Then she pulls down her mask, and I see my mother.

I look up to find us on the sand at Everafter Beach. In a horseshoe surrounding us are all the characters from the book. I crane my neck and see the tangled tails of letters overhead.

My mother takes a step backward, gasping. "Am I . . . am I dead?"

"No," I cry, throwing my arms around her. "No. You're very much alive." Over her shoulder, I grin wildly at the others. "It worked!" I cry, the words bursting from me like fireworks. "It really worked!"

A chorus of cheers rises from the beach. My mother, though, is panicked. She turns in circles, as if she is trapped, her eyes wide at the flat, two-dimensional oddness of the interior of the book, her body jumping slightly every time one of the characters speaks. She has a punishing grip on my arm. "Where are we?" she whispers.

I grasp her shoulder. "It's okay, Mom. I've been here before. And so have you. You're the one who wrote this."

She shakes her head. "This isn't . . . This can't be . . ."

Rapscullio hesitantly steps toward us. He reaches for my mother's hand, falls to one knee, and bows his head. "Your Majesty. It is an honor, and a privilege, to finally meet you."

Captain Crabbe approaches next and kisses her hand. "I swear my allegiance to you, always," he vows.

Humphrey runs a circle around my mother, licking the back of her knees. "You taste delicious," he says, and she gasps.

"You . . . you can speak?"

"Yes, I can," Humphrey replies. "I know lots of words. *Potato. Thermos. Pencil. Communism.*"

"That's . . . great," my mother says as Socks shyly drops a daisy at her feet. She pats his mane, a smile washing over her face. "You were always my favorite."

"I knew it," Socks replies, prancing away.

Orville is the first to fold my mother into a hug. "Welcome home, my dear," he says.

One by one, the other characters step forward to introduce themselves. The fairies zip around her face; the mermaids flip and splash their tails; the trolls reveal a sand castle built in her honor. Even Pyro soars through the clouds like a skywriter, spelling out her name.

"I hate to say I told you so," I murmur. "But I told you so."

My mother looks at me and shakes her head. "I'm dreaming this. I must be dreaming this."

"Kind of," I say. "You'll get used to the weird stuff. Like the way you can jump extra high and run extra fast and eat anything and never gain an ounce. Or the way you move from page to page. It feels like it must be a dream . . . but this is our new *real.*"

She created this adventure for me, years ago, when I was afraid of death. This time, I'm going to do the same for her.

"Come on," I say, taking my mom's hand. "There's a lot to see."

I can tell she still thinks she's going to wake up at any moment. I can tell she doesn't trust what's in front of her eyes. Maybe it's just going to take time.

At that thought, I can't help but grin. Because here, that's exactly what we have.

★ ★ ★

The castle is just the way I remember it: dazzling, grand, ornate. I watch my mother walk into the great hall, staring at the vaulted ceilings and intricate tapestries, occasionally reaching out to touch a marble statue or sword mounted on the wall. I take her into one of the towers, to Queen Maureen's chamber, and open the double doors, revealing a round room with a high carved canopy bed, a massive fireplace, and a gigantic armoire containing the finest silk and satin gowns, embroidered with golden thread.

"So?" I ask shyly. "Do you like it?"

"It's lovely," my mother says. "I can't wait to tell you all about it when I wake up."

I sigh. "You're not dreaming, Mom. You're here. *We're* here. For good."

The clock on the mantel chimes. It is made of bone china and gold, covered in rubies and emeralds and sapphires. My mother's eyes fly to its face, and she begins to reach into the pocket of the scrubs she is still wearing. "I have to take my medication," she says, but of course, the pills aren't there. They've already disappeared in the transition.

My mother pats down all the pockets. "They must have fallen out on that beach," she says. "We have to go back."

"No we don't. You don't need those pills here. You don't need them anymore at all."

"Edgar, you have to accept the fact that I'm sick. It's not what you want, and it's not what I want, but it's what we have to deal with. And it's going to be a lot easier to handle if I don't keep having seizures."

Frustrated, desperate to prove to her that she's going to be healed here, I grab the clock from the mantel and smash it as hard as I can against the stone wall. It shatters into hundreds of pieces: gears and springs and gems scatter across the parquet floor.

"What have you *done*?" my mother cries. She immediately falls to her knees, trying to gather the pieces, but they begin to tremble in her hands. They pop out of her palm, quivering, gears finding each other and notching into place, golden joints fusing together, until the clock—whole and restored—rests on the floor in front of her.

I pick it up and set it gently on the mantel. "This is what I'm trying to tell you," I say. "You can't be broken here. The book will fix you."

My mother stands and, with a shaking hand, reaches toward the clock to touch it. "Of course," she murmurs. "I understand."

"You . . . you do?"

"You never die in your dreams."

I close my eyes. No matter what I do to convince my mother of the book's magic—whether that's cutting myself with a sword and letting the wound heal, or jumping off a cliff and landing safely on my feet—she's going to think this is a dream, and it might as well be. After all, this entire story came from her imagination.

Suddenly I realize exactly where I have to take her.

★ ★ ★

The copyright page is a sea of white ice, as far as the eye can see. My shoes slip as I pull my mother behind me, teetering, trying to balance in the slant of the italics. The copyright symbol is a tiny divot that grows as we get closer—the only marker to let me know we're getting anywhere at all as we walk. Overhead, text hangs so low that I keep smacking my forehead against the tails of the *y*'s and *g*'s and *p*'s.

The closer we get to the copyright symbol, the more the

ground seems to slope. I've been to this page since Seraphima was sucked out of the book—but the vortex was sealed shut. I still don't really know what made it open that first time. I only know I'm going to do my best to make it happen again.

It's an optical illusion, but the whole page is shaped like a cone, with the copyright circle at the very bottom. Because of this, by the time we reach the bottom, my mother is struggling to keep from falling forward on top of me. "Grab hold," I tell her, reaching down to grasp one edge of the letter *c*. She follows my lead, and immediately the circle shifts to the left.

"I think we have to turn it," I say, and I put all my weight into pulling clockwise. Inch by inch, with a screech, the wheel unlocks and finally pops open like the hatch of a submarine. I look at my mother. "Jump," I tell her, and I disappear through the hole.

She lands lightly in a crouch beside me and slowly stands, in awe of what she sees. There are shelves of bound papers and thrones draped with cobwebs, a giant man-sized birdcage. There are baskets full of broken glass hearts and corked bottles stuffed with rolled-up notes. There's a dragon's tooth the size of my head propped against the wall, and a wagon wheel. In the corner, a cello is playing itself.

"Welcome to your imagination," I say.

I don't think my mother hears me. She is walking through the obstacle course of assorted objects, lightly touching them as she passes. Her hand stills on the statue of a leopard cast in gold. "It was a jealous leopard," she murmurs, "who begged a witch to make him the most prized animal in the kingdom. Because of his selfishness, she turned him into precisely that:

a golden statue." She walks up to the birdcage. "Mad science experiment gone wrong: the bird became the master." Then she runs her hands through the basket of bottles. "A man goes off to war. He marches upriver with the army and sends a love letter in a bottle every day to his wife, who lives at the mouth of the stream." She touches the cello that still plays. "A human boy falls for a muse, but the only way he can impress her is with a magic cello created by the gods that never ceases to play. The muse adores his music . . . and eventually the musician himself . . . but he can never let go of the cello's bow in order to hold her, because she will realize he is a fake." Finally she reaches for the portrait I saw the last time I was here: King Maurice, holding a baby. It might as well be a photo of my dad and me, dressed up in costume. My mother turns, her face filled with wonder. "These were all my stories," she murmurs. "The ones I never wrote down."

"You used to believe in the impossible," I say. "Couldn't you do it again?"

I shove aside a feather boa and a bearskin rug to reveal a pristine ivory desk with a quill pen and an endless curl of parchment. I pull one of the empty thrones closer to the desk, holding it out so my mother can sit.

Gingerly she picks up the quill and, for the first time in years, begins to write again.

★ ★ ★

Leaving my mother behind on the copyright page, I begin to wander through the book. It's like I'm seeing the scenery with new eyes. Suddenly the borders of the book don't feel confining; my tights don't even chafe. Everything's possible, just because I've managed to get my mom inside here.

I don't realize how far I've walked until my feet sink into the sand of Everafter Beach. For a moment, I just stand at the shore, watching the sun paint the clouds pink and splatter the sky with orange and red.

"Pretty, isn't it?"

Turning around, I realize I'm not alone. Seraphima sits a distance away, her knees hugged to her chest.

"Yeah," I reply.

"It's my favorite time of the day," Seraphima says.

"Sunset?"

"No," she answers. "Night."

Darkness settles, and the stars come out, as if the sun has shattered into thousands of pieces. Seraphima's face tilts toward the sky. "Before Ollie left, he showed me something," she confesses. She points to a bright, twinkling star. "That one's Frump."

I open my mouth to tell her that Frump hasn't turned into a ball of gas but then think otherwise. I mean, if it makes her happy . . .

"I miss him," Seraphima whispers. "I really, really miss him."

In the moonlight, I can see that she's been crying.

I don't really know what to do with a crying girl. I pat her back awkwardly, trying to make her feel better. The distance between Seraphima and Frump is pretty insurmountable, just like the distance between me and Jules.

Jules.

"I have an idea," I tell Seraphima, holding out my hand to help her up. "Do you trust me?"

She hesitates, but only for a second. I lead her off the beach, past Timble Tower and the Enchanted Forest and Orville's cottage, around the outskirts of the castle, and over a rocky ledge to Pyro's cave. "Stay here," I tell her, and I lean into the gaping entrance and whistle. There is a puff of smoke and my eyes tear. The ground shakes as Pyro wriggles his way onto the ledge of the cavern.

His red eyes glow in the night; his scaled skin ripples with every breath. When he sees me, his lips draw back, baring razor-sharp teeth. "Who's a good boy?" I say, patting his neck. I grab onto his mane and swing myself over the bridge of his neck. Then I lean down so I can help pull Seraphima up behind me.

"Are you sure this is a good idea?" she asks. "He isn't trained."

"Worse comes to worst, you fall off . . . and gently land on the ground." I grin at her. "Aren't you the one who taught me how to jump out a window?"

She smiles and wraps her arms around my waist, screaming with delight as I kick a heel into Pyro's side and he shoots into the sky.

We climb at a crazy speed, wind rushing past my ears. Squinting, I search for the words at the top edge of the page. ONCE UPON A TIME. I lean down over Pyro's neck, guiding him like an arrow through the o.

The o catches around Pyro's middle, like an inner tube, and then shatters, dusting us with black powder. Suddenly we are among the stars. They hang in front of us, brush our shoulders, tangle in our hair as Pyro swoops and dives in figure eights. Delighted, Seraphima giggles behind me.

I steer Pyro toward the constellation Seraphima pointed out from the beach. Holding the dragon steady, we pull up beside the brightest star. Seraphima reaches out, brushing it with her hand. The star tinkles, making a chime that sounds just like the tags on Frump's collar.

She lets the weight of the star rest in her palm, where it glows so brightly it's hard to look at. Then she snatches her hand away, wincing. She examines her palm. The outline of a heart is burned onto her skin.

Seraphima closes her fingers around it, like it's something she could hold on to forever. "Thank you, Edgar," she says. She's crying again, but this time it's different. This time, she's happy.

Pyro gently rides a downdraft back to Timble Tower so we can drop Seraphima off at her window. She climbs gingerly onto the ledge. "Maybe we can go again sometime," she suggests.

"That would be great," I say, smiling. I wave goodbye, about to turn Pyro toward the castle, but Seraphima calls me back.

She's silhouetted in the window, her silver hair as bright as the moon. "Edgar," she says. "It's good to have a friend in here."

★ ★ ★

It isn't until the middle of the night, after Pyro's back in his cave and my mother's been settled in her chambers, her hands still dotted with ink, that I let myself think of Jules.

In the minutes before I left, I pulled her into the tiny mud-room in Delilah's house. It was pitch-black, because no candles had been set there, but I didn't need to see Jules's face to know what she was thinking, what she was feeling.

"Jules," I started, but she cut me off, putting her fingers against my mouth. It was everything I could do not to kiss them.

"Don't talk," she interrupted. "I have to tell you something. Remember when I said it wasn't real? Everything that happened between us in the book? I was lying to you. I *had* to, because I was lying to myself too. It just seemed so *Disney* to finally find a guy who didn't go running for the hills when I said that a human head stays conscious for fifteen seconds after it's cut off."

"Yeah, I'm pretty sure our relationship is the plot of the next Pixar short," I told her.

Jules had laughed. "Jeez. Just my luck. What's that saying? All the good guys are either taken, gay, or stuck in a children's fairy tale."

I knew she'd told me not to, but I framed her face with my hands and kissed her. Like, *really* kissed her. In *this* world, at a high school party, I made out with the hottest girl. It was a good note to leave on.

Jules leaned her forehead against mine. "You just *had* to make me love you, didn't you?"

"You crash-landed in my story. What else was I supposed to do?"

In the dark, I saw the shine of her eyes. I thought she might have been crying, but she never would have admitted it. "Don't forget me."

"Jules, you're pretty unforgettable."

"Well," she said, "forever's damn long."

There was so much I wanted to say to her. There was so much more about her I wanted to know. But then, from the other room, we heard Delilah's voice: *Where's the birthday boy?*

And just like that, I ran out of time.

★ ★ ★

I toss and turn for so long that night I'm pretty sure I never fall asleep, but that can't be true, because I wake up to find Queen Maureen sitting on the edge of my bed.

I bolt upright, panicked.

But then my vision focuses and I realize that it's my mother, her red hair twisted in a tight bun beneath a jeweled crown. She's wearing one of Maureen's gowns. Tears stream down her face.

"Mom, are you all right?" I ask.

"I'm all right," she sobs. "I'm *better* than all right." Her eyes meet mine. "Edgar," my mother marvels, "my headache is gone."

DELILAH

This must be what it feels like to be superhuman.

Every sense is firing at once. Even with my eyes closed, I can see each color in the rainbow. I feel the change in heat in my body as Oliver's arms close around me. I run my fingertips along the velvet of his tunic, marking every stitch.

I am soaring through the universe, rootless, groundless, spinning.

I'm glowing, like I've swallowed a star.

And when I finally fall back to Earth, it's a safe landing, because I know he'll catch me.

"So," Oliver whispers, brushing my hair back. "I heard it's going to rain tomorrow."

I expected a profession of love, or at least a hello. Not a weather report. "What?"

He grins. "I just want the first words I say to you, here, to be totally ordinary. Something I might say to you if I were going to see you tomorrow and the next day and the day after that."

Suddenly I'm smiling. It's what I told him when we said goodbye, but with one critical change: I *am* going to see him tomorrow, and the next day, and the day after that.

Joy bubbles inside me; it feels like champagne in my veins. "Perhaps," I reply, parroting what Oliver once said to me, "it will be sunny on Wednesday." And I kiss him again.

Gradually I become aware of the rest of the world: the sound of conversation picking up, the clatter of plates and forks as cake is passed around, the smell of burned wax from the birthday candles.

Oliver won't let go of me. He glances from my tiara to the hem of my gown and smiles broadly. "Brilliant dress."

"I thought you might like it. . . ."

Suddenly Jules grabs my shoulder. "Um, if you lovebirds can spare a minute, there's a queen we have to hide."

Breaking away, I glance at my mother to make sure she's occupied—and see her serving cake. I grab Oliver's hand and drag him behind me as I follow Jules to the bathroom. She knocks softly, and the door opens.

Queen Maureen has turned on the faucet in the sink and is flushing the toilet. "Have you *seen* this, Oliver?" she asks, delighted. "Where does the water come from?"

"It worked," I breathe. "They're both gone."

Jules looks away. "Yeah."

"We must get you dressed," Oliver says. "Remember?"

Queen Maureen nods. She too has been informed of the

plan. She will dress in the spare set of scrubs Jules brought for her and then Jules will drive her home.

"My dear," she says to me, "would you mind unlacing my stays?"

I take the scrubs from Jules and disappear into the bathroom with Queen Maureen. She turns around and I pull at the bows on her gown, loosening it. She steps out of the dress, and I help her pull the scrubs top on. "Now that Oliver's not here," she whispers, hiking up the baggy pants and tying them at her waist, "might I ask you something?"

"Of course," I say.

"Seraphima told me of this magical place you took her. Might we go to this . . . mall?"

I laugh, twisting her braids into the surgical cap so that the color—darker than Jessamyn's—is hidden. I make a mental note to buy her some hair dye. "Absolutely," I promise. "We have all the time in the world."

When we step outside (after a few flicks of the light switch so Maureen can experience the miracle of electricity), I find Jules sitting on the floor, her back against the wall, and Oliver missing. I tamp down the immediate panic that swells in me. I have to be able to let him out of my sight without freaking out every single time and assuming he's been sucked into the story again.

Jules looks up at me. "Relax. I sent him back downstairs to say goodbye to the people who are leaving. It's weird if the birthday boy isn't even at his own party." Then she turns to Maureen, surveying her critically. "I think you'll pass. But we'd better get out of here quickly so we're not tempting fate."

I turn to Maureen. "Can you give us a minute?" Rummaging in the folds of my princess gown, I pull out my phone and thrust it toward her. "Here," I say. "Knock yourself out."

I leave Maureen pushing buttons and gasping in surprise as music begins to pour out of the tiny speakers. Taking Jules's arm, I drag her toward my room and close the door behind us.

"You shouldn't have done that," Jules jokes. "She'll probably hack your Facebook."

I sit down on the bed. "You can talk to me, you know."

Jules, in classic Jules mode, snorts. "Thanks, Dr. Phil."

"You can be as snarky as you want," I tell her. "I know how crappy you feel right now. I've been there. *Twice.*"

Jules jerks her chin up. "I'm fine. You just worry about Prince Charming. You don't have to worry about me."

"I *know* I don't have to worry about you. But I do. And I know you can talk to me . . . but you'd *rather* talk to someone else." Reaching past her, I take the fairy tale from the nightstand and place it in her hands. "I believe this is yours now."

I stand up. "I'm going to take Maureen downstairs and have her say goodbye to my mom. Preferably without ever speaking in her British accent. How about I meet you at the car?"

Jules looks at me and then traces her fingers over the lettering on the book's cover. Then, unexpectedly, she throws her arms around me in a tight hug. "Thank you," she whispers.

As I walk out of the room, she is just cracking open the story.

★ ★ ★

I find Oliver standing guard at the front door, thanking people as they leave. Raj fist-bumps him. "Great party, bro," Raj says, and Oliver grins.

"Glad you liked it."

Allie and Chris are the last to go. "See you Monday, dude," Chris says, putting his hand on the small of her back. Oliver looks up at me, shocked.

"I'll fill you in later," I murmur.

When it's finally quiet, my mother walks out of the kitchen holding a dish towel. "That went well!" she says brightly. "I'm thinking we should have Thanksgiving during a full-on tornado!"

I laugh. "Thanks for your help, Mom."

"I'd better be getting my mother back home," Oliver says. "Thank you so much for letting us use your house, Mrs. McPhee."

"Anytime." My mother gives Oliver a hug first, then Queen Maureen. "I hope you feel better soon."

"Thank you," Maureen replies, sounding only faintly British.

Just then, Jules comes running down the stairs, her cheeks pink. "Sorry," she calls. "I'm here." Her car keys jingle in her hand. "Ready to go, you two?"

She escorts Maureen out the door. Oliver lingers behind, his hand on my waist. "See you . . . tomorrow," he says.

Just hearing that word makes me smile.

He leans down and brushes his lips over mine, the way you say goodbye to someone you know you're going to have many more goodbyes with.

When the door closes, I turn around to find my mother shaking out a giant black trash bag. "No, Mom, I'll take care of it. You did so much already. Just go to bed and let me clean up."

"I'm not going to say no to that." My mother yawns. "You think Edgar liked his party?"

"I'm pretty sure this was his best birthday ever."

Her footsteps fade as she climbs the stairs, and I begin to sweep the debris of the party into the trash bag. I dump paper plates and cups and gather crumbs and frosting off the table with a sponge.

"Well, Delilah," I say out loud, pretty proud of myself for pulling this off. "What *can't* you do?"

"I was thinking the same thing."

I nearly jump out of my skin at the sound of a voice behind me. Oliver stands in the doorway, watching me clean up. "You scared me to death!" I say, but I'm smiling. I can't *not* smile. "Why did you come back?"

He walks toward me. "I told Jules to take Maureen home alone. It occurred to me that I had forgotten something." He plucks the trash bag out of my hand and sets it aside.

"What?" I ask.

"You never gave me my present." Oliver's hands settle on my hips. "So? What did you get me?"

I wrap my arms around his neck and slowly lean toward him. "Forever," I whisper.

Oliver dips his head, just a breath away from me. "Well, look at that," he says, dropping a kiss onto my lips. "It fits perfectly."

There's a difference between a house and a home.

Why don't you walk into your neighbor's apartment or your best friend's mudroom and think it's where you live? Obviously the surroundings are different. There will be odd bits of furniture, and walls that are the wrong color, and pets that don't belong to you.

But even if every house looked identical—if all the furnishings were the same—it still wouldn't feel like yours.

That's because home isn't where you are. It's who you're with.

OLIVER

TWO MONTHS LATER

Every day, I wake up to the smell of vanilla.

Maureen is up before dawn, frosting the cupcakes that have become the most sought-after sweets in New England. Her home-based business, the Queen of Tarts, has been featured in newspapers, in magazines, and even on television. Once she figured out the concept of basic economics—namely, the fact that one could sell cupcakes for a profit rather than just giving them away for free—and once she realized that the refrigerator would not restock itself every night, her career as a master pastry chef really took flight. People who taste her pies and cakes beg to know the secret ingredient, and she always answers, "A little dash of magic."

I take a quick shower, towel my hair, and throw on a pair of jeans and a sweater. Then, proudly, I grab my car keys from my desk. After several weeks of Delilah's Driving Boot Camp, she has deemed me worthy of Edgar's driver's license. Given that neither Maureen nor I knew how to drive when we first arrived, this was quite a necessity. Jessamyn's van is now officially my valiant steed.

From what Jules tells us, Jessamyn's career is blossoming too. She's writing again, for the first time since she penned *Between the Lines,* and at a rapid rate. The kingdom has been captivated by her books, which have a special sort of twist: she somehow is able to create a story that is exactly what the reader needs at the moment he or she is reading. What one person takes away from a book might be very different from what the next person takes away—almost as if the story is altered depending on who's reading, where, and when. But then, maybe all books are like that—a little different each time they are opened. The real question is who's doing the changing: the story, or the reader.

The best news of all is that Jessamyn is healthy once again, and is being courted by Captain Crabbe, who took her on a moonlight sail and learned how to use a knife and fork while eating, just for her.

And Edgar? Unbelievably, he's gotten to do some space travel after all, inside the book. It may not be the plot, but it makes a great hobby. His rocket ship is Pyro, and he navigates galaxies from the dragon's back. Even more unbelievably, he's not the only budding astronaut. Seraphima, who formerly couldn't hold a single thought in her pretty little head, now talks nonstop about black holes and pulsars and quasars.

When he's not flying missions, though, I hear Edgar spends a lot of time on page 43, talking to Jules.

I glance at the clock and hurry downstairs. I want to get to Delilah's house as early as possible. I have something I can't wait to show her.

Maureen glances up over a tiered cake. The fondant is already setting; she's piped pink petals along the edge, decorated with silver sugar pearls. Right now she's inscribing a message across the top. "Good morning, dear," she says. "How did you sleep?"

"Quite well, thanks," I answer, automatically reaching a finger into the bowl of frosting for a taste.

She swats me with a spatula. "I *need* that," she scolds. With her piping bag, she loops the word HAPPY across the cake.

I watch her work for a few moments, until she notices me staring. "What?" she asks.

"Are you?" I ask. "Happy?"

She smiles. "I don't think I really knew what happy was until I came here. I didn't know how much bigger the world could be, how much more there was to offer."

I exhale a breath I didn't even realize I was holding. It's good to know that for once, we all seem to be satisfied with where we are.

"If you wait two minutes," Maureen says, "you can have a fresh muffin before you go."

"Can't." I give her a peck on the cheek and head out of the kitchen. "Don't work too hard."

"It's only work if you don't like it," she calls back.

In the van, I turn on the radio and drive the ten minutes to Delilah's house. When I get there, her mother is just coming outside, holding a travel mug of coffee, on her way to work. "You're here early," Mrs. McPhee says. "Delilah's still asleep."

"That's all right. I just had some good news I wanted to share."

"Be my guest. I'm sure she'll be happier waking up to see you, instead of me." She waves as she ducks into her car, and pulls out of the driveway.

By now, Delilah's house is as comfortable to me as my own. I climb the stairs and gently creak open her bedroom door.

She's lying on her back, covers at her feet, arms splayed, her hair knotted across the pillow. She's wearing a giant T-shirt that reads BUBBA'S BBQ: YOU DON'T NEED NO TEEF TO EAT OUR BEEF! and a lone striped sock. I don't think I've ever seen anything quite so beautiful.

I kneel beside the bed, lean down, and kiss her until she wakes up. "Good morning, princess," I say.

"Mmmphrrm," she answers, eyelids at half-mast. "How," she mutters.

"How what?"

"How do you look like *that* this early in the morning?"

"It's a gift." I laugh and sit down beside her on the bed. "I have something to show you. I couldn't wait."

She rises to her elbows, yawning. "This better be good."

I take the letter I printed off the computer last night and place it in her hands. She unfolds it, and her eyes skim the first line:

CONGRATULATIONS. YOU'VE BEEN
ACCEPTED TO THE DARTMOUTH COLLEGE
CLASS OF 2019.

Delilah's eyes widen, and she throws her arms around me. "Oliver, that's amazing! I'm so happy for you."

"The best part is I'm only two towns away from you."

She grins. "I can't believe I'm dating a college guy." Then, just as suddenly, her face falls. "I can't believe you're going to be around college *girls*."

I sigh. "Delilah—"

"Don't tell me I'm being stupid. You don't know what it's going to be like until you get there. You might meet the girl of your dreams the minute you step on campus."

"I already met the girl of my dreams," I point out. "Might I remind you, I didn't fall in love with you because you were pretty or smart or popular. . . ."

"Aw, thanks." Delilah smirks.

"I fell in love with you because you had your nose stuck in a book. If you hadn't been, well . . . *you* . . . we never would have met," I say. "You have a lot more to worry about than some random girl I don't even know yet. You and I, we're going to argue, and make up, and go to prom, and suffer through exams, and give each other the flu, and exchange valentines, and every single day I'm going to make you remember why we fell in love."

Delilah looks down. "But, you know, in this world . . . it's not always a perfect happily-ever-after."

I lift her chin so that our eyes meet. "I would give up a thousand happily-ever-afters for right here, right now, with you."

She kisses me, pulling me back down with her so that we're curled together on top of her covers. Then, suddenly, she sits up. "I just remembered. I have a congratulations present for you."

"But you couldn't have known I'd be accepted—"

"I'm an optimist," Delilah says, smiling. She reaches into the drawer of her nightstand. "It's not wrapped, but still. . . ."

She hands me a leather-bound book. I open it, but the first page is empty. So is the one after that, and the next. In fact, there's nothing at all written on the pages. Confused, I look at her.

"It's called a diary," Delilah explains. "It's for you to fill out. I thought it was about time you wrote your *own* story."

I take her into my arms and think: *This is exactly where I'll start.*

Everyone has a story.

You might think it's not worth telling, but then again, it's a story no one has ever heard. What you do, what you say, how you carry the plot, just might leave a mark on someone.

Because that's what stories do. They help you escape, and they give you the chance to do things you never imagined you would or could. They let you feel heartbreak you've never had and experience adventures from the safety of your own room. They are dreams for those who are still awake. They can be as comfortable as an old pair of slippers and as unnerving as the blade of a knife. They possess the power to change you, to inspire you, to open your mind.

Stories are all around us, caught in the throats of the strangers you walk past and scrawled on the pages of locked diaries. They're in love letters that were never sent and between the lines of every conversation ever spoken. Just because your story's not written down doesn't mean it doesn't exist.

Perhaps someone's reading your story right now, in fact—imagining your eyes skimming over this page, your hands clutching the binding as you hurry to get to the last line.

You'd best get going. Your Reader is eagerly awaiting the next chapter.

Sincerely,

Jessamyn

ACKNOWLEDGMENTS

We'd like to thank Peter Antelyes, associate professor of English at Vassar College, for his insight and encouragement while writing this novel. We are also indebted to Abigail Baird, associate professor of psychology at Vassar College, for inspiring various characters and for researching brain tumors for us. Thanks too to Ryan Eykholt for coining the term "triple-tearing," and to Kevin Ferreira, who let us borrow his Instagram joke. Thanks to Kathy Reichs and Lisa Genova—fantastic authors in their own right—whose expertise helped us fill in factual gaps in our story. To Will Henderson—we appreciate your coming up with this title long before we even began to think about a sequel. Thanks to Barbara Marcus, Beverly Horowitz, Dominique Cimina, John Adamo, Kim Lauber, Stephanie O'Cain, and the entire Delacorte Press family at Random House Children's Books, who prove that fairy tales do come true. Finally, thanks to Tim/Dad for making us laugh and occasionally scaring us to death by creeping up the office stairs, and to Dudley, Alvin, Oliver, and Harvey, who provided much-needed moral support and puppy breaks.

ABOUT THE AUTHORS

JODI PICOULT is the author of twenty-three novels, including the #1 *New York Times* bestsellers *Leaving Time, The Story-teller, Lone Wolf, Sing You Home, House Rules, Handle with Care, Change of Heart, Nineteen Minutes,* and *My Sister's Keeper.* She also cowrote the #1 *New York Times* bestseller *Between the Lines,* the companion to *Off the Page,* with her daughter, Samantha van Leer. Jodi lives in New Hampshire with her husband and three children. Visit her online at jodipicoult.com.

SAMANTHA VAN LEER is a student at Vassar College. She cowrote the #1 *New York Times* bestseller *Between the Lines,* the companion to *Off the Page,* with her mother, Jodi Picoult.